BROKEN COLLAR

A NOVEL

BY RON MITCHELL

WORKING LIVES SERIES
BOTTOM DOG PRESS
HURON, OHIO

This book is a work of fiction. Names, characters, businesses, organizations, places, events and incidents either are the product of the author's imagination or are used fictitiously here.

CREDITS:
General Editor: Larry Smith
Cover and Layout Design: Susanna Sharp-Schwacke
Cover Photo of Town: James Jeffrey Higgins

ACKNOWLEDGMENTS:
I am grateful to many for help with the writing of this book. I thank Father John Galea, who gave me the ability to see priests as human beings and who allowed access into his priest psyche, to Monsignor Lewis Gaetano for his insightful interview, and to Rick DiCarlo and Norm Helber for perspectives from friends who have left the vocation with fondness, and to the many priests and nuns who serve for the sake of love, affecting those of us who have had contact.

Thanks to Lori DeBoer for coaching me through the first draft, and those gracious first readers who loaned real life perspective and continual encouragement: Patricia Morron (my sister-in-law), Mary Alice and Ron Mitchell (my parents), and Marilynn Windust, my angel wife who rode the ups and downs with unwavering support. Thanks to Mary Helber for her insights on marrying a priest, Richard Krawiec's edits, and the honest/conflicting feedback from my old writing group: Steve Jansen, Mary Purvis, Kay Halverson and Andy Erlich. I express gratitude to Sumner Brown, Sue and Mark Stodola for providing a peaceful place to write and to take a break from my characters when necessary. Special thanks to Gene Spencer for his endless inspiration and Fernando Blaze Pacheco for teaching me the bond of boxing.

I am indebted to Larry Smith whose patience and editing skills resurrected this novel and helped me polish the story, along with the dedicated family of Bottom Dog Press who manifest dreams into reality.

To Emily,

Jam our

B Mitchell

This book is dedicated
to Marilynn Windust.

Chapter 1

Hometown Parish

A distant shrill from the steel mill permeated through the stained glass windows and into St. Anne's Roman Catholic Church. Father Bob walked down from the altar and stood in the middle aisle, where his spiritual aura rose the more he handed out communion to friends from his past. This reassignment by the Bishop to his hometown parish provided his last chance at remaining a priest. He took slow, deep breaths to calm his anxiety. *God called me to the priesthood, not the Bishop.* He summoned the Holy Spirit. A warm radiance sparkled from his eyes once again, with that angelic gleam that could mesmerize. He looked up from the chalice, holding the body of Christ in his hand, and readied himself to focus on the soul behind the eyes of the faithful. A new set of glowing green eyes now locked onto his, sending him a sense of euphoria. He saw nothing else. That rapture quickly transformed into panic.

Maria.

His chest tightened. The lights of St. Anne's Church flashed a brief ray of pain through his left eye. Maria held his gaze. Her shiny red lips flickered into a grin. She did not hold out her hands to receive the Eucharist. Instead, she leaned forward, licked the corner of her mouth, and cocked her head back slipping out her tongue to receive communion. Hardly any Catholics held onto that tradition. Even the nuns received communion with their hands, cupping them together and lifting them in front, as if holding water. In the "old days" only a priest's hands could touch the consecrated Host.

Father Bob's heart fluttered. His hand quivered as he moved the Eucharist closer to Maria's tongue. "The Body of Christ," he said. When he placed the wafer inside of her mouth, a warm moisture brushed the side of his finger. A light breeze cooled the sweat on his forehead, yet he yearned to let his finger linger at her lips. He ran his eyes down through her cleavage, her tight black skirt, all the way to her black knee boots. Quickly he brought his gaze back up to hers. She looked as delightful now as she did back in 1970. How could he still want her, after fourteen years? Now, she'd stolen the Holy Spirit from him, sucked the glow clean out of his eyes with a simple glance.

He watched her turn and walk away. She chewed the host and glanced back at him while following the line of people back to their pews. The next person standing in line cleared his throat. Only a few folks were left standing, people whose souls he no longer saw.

Father Bob forced himself to concentrate on finishing Mass. He walked back to the altar, placed the remaining Hosts into the tabernacle, and sat on the bench to reflect in silence with the congregation. The clanging of railroad cars from the mill sent a vibration through the half-opened stained glass windows, fueling the working-class pride of the congregation, who stirred in their pews, waiting for Mass to conclude. Anthony, the altar boy, crunched his brow into a quizzical look, giving Father Bob a clue that his sitting was lasting far too long.

The tightness in Father Bob's chest progressed into a pressing pain. He feared that he might collapse onto the floor in front of everybody, yet he forced himself to stand. "Go in peace, to love and serve the Lord." He poured the sign of the cross over the congregation and then rushed past Anthony, through the side door of the sacristy that led to the rectory. No way could he face the crowd of folks waiting to greet him on the Church's front steps. He closed the rectory door behind him, stood out of breath against it, and held his hand over his heart. *Am I dying, Lord?* He rushed to the sink, stumbling over his dog, Jack, who yelped. Bending over, he splashed a handful of cold water onto his face.

"Is that you, Father?" Monsignor Murphy called from the living room.

Father Bob didn't respond. He straightened up, and the pain in his chest gently subsided. The sweat under his vestments cooled his body. *What is Maria doing back in Irontown?* All the countless encounters with women in his past life meant nothing, and yet there was Maria. *Help me, Lord.*

"Are you okay, Bob?" Monsignor Murphy's voice came closer to him.

"I'll be fine." He grabbed a hanging dishrag and wiped his face. "I think that coming back to Irontown and seeing so many old friends threw me off guard for a minute, that's all." He saw his reflection in the kitchen window and straightened a curl of black hair that covered the top half of his ear. The chubby reflection of Monsignor Murphy appeared next to his.

"I've forgotten how much easier it is to serve strangers." Monsignor Murphy cleared his throat. "Reminds me of the first time I heard the confession of my best friend's mother and I almost threw up right there in the confessional."

He wished that Murphy would just leave him alone, but had to turn around and face him. He looked down into his shiny eyeglasses. Murphy held up his hands and prayed. "Heavenly Father, shower Your Grace onto Father Bob, Your humble servant." His breath reeked of alcohol while he made the sign of the cross.

"Thank you, but I'm okay now. I have to go greet the parishioners before they've all gone."

"You sure? I'll do it for you if you want."

"No, I need to do this." Father Bob walked out of the kitchen and headed back into the church. He entered through the side door, so he could relax one final time while walking down the aisle along a row of stained glass windows with their portrait of holy saints. He stood on the opposite side of the front doors for a moment and paused, before stepping through. Then he scanned the handful of people as quickly as he could. Most folks had already left. *Where's Maria? Surely she'd hang around to say hello.*

"Well, there he is! We thought you ran out on us. Good morning, Father Bob. Welcome home." Mrs. Milovick called.

"Good morning, Mr. and Mrs. Milovick."

"Ronny. Call us Ronny and Bea," Ronny Milovick said as they shook hands.

"It's wonderful to see you two. Thanks for coming to Mass today."

"I just can't believe my eyes," Bea said. "You looked so handsome up there." She laughed. "You better stop by the park today and bless the Barrone family reunion. Billy couldn't make it back to town, but said to tell you hello. Remember all the trouble yunz used to get into? We're so grateful about how yunz turned out." She finally took a breath.

Father Bob remembered how they had nicknamed Billy, "Heat" because of his constant complaint of being cold.

Before Father Bob could respond, he was startled by a full-body hug. "Father Bear!" Barker grabbed him into a squeeze and kissed his cheek. Some of the small crowd laughed. He asked, "Do any of the priests call you Father Sugar Bear?" Father Bob had earned that street name from being hairy and sweet with the ladies.

He smiled. "No, Bark. Only a few from the past know that one." He looked Barker up and down, his arms sleeved with tattoos. "You're a full-fledged biker now?"

Barker adjusted his braided ponytail. "I heard you were back in town. I almost stopped by the rectory the other day, but, you know..." He was stoned. His red eyes and jittery movements gave him away.

"Come by the rectory anytime, really, and we could talk over a cold one."

Barker nodded. "Maybe I will. You goin' up the park today?"

"I think so. After I drop Monsignor Murphy off at the Knights of Columbus Hall, I can use his car."

"Let me know if you need a ride, if you don't mind ridin' bitch on my bike." He smirked. "There'll be lots of food and booze up there."

Father Bob bit his lower lip for a second, relieved that Barker didn't mention their doing just about every drug imaginable together in their youth. "Thanks for the invitation, Mrs. Milovick..., Bea. Hopefully I'll see you later."

Confident again, he walked back to the rectory. He dipped his right shoulder, stuck his arm out in front of him, and glided it around his body to where his fist rested on the small of his lower back. In the seminary, each time he "dipped," fellow seminarians urged him to leave his street strut back with his former life. They called it "un-priestly," especially when he pranced around the table like a chicken after beating them at chess or poker. Once he made them laugh, when he strutted around the classroom after a Theologian had warned the prospective priests, "Women will chase a broomstick if you put a collar on it."

He was glad that he had risen from the kitchen sink and come out to face the parishioners. "That went pretty well," he said as he entered the rectory again and spotted Monsignor Murphy sitting at the table. "Thanks for...Uh, hello, Maria." He was shocked to see her sitting at the table with Monsignor Murphy. Both wore expressions of expectation, as if waiting for him to say something. He just stood there, not knowing whether to hug her, shake her hand, or sit down.

Maria made the first move. She stood up and smiled. "It's good to see you, *Father*." She shrugged her shoulders and snickered. "How weird seeing you dressed like a priest. You look great."

He checked her out with as nonchalant a glance as he could muster. "You look good too." He opened his arms and she slid right into them. They hugged for several moments. His lips and nose pressed against the top of her head, which smelled like cotton candy. The softness of her breasts upon his chest was rewinding his lust, and so he let her go. He placed his hands on the front of her shoulders and gently moved her back so he could look at her face.

"Are you crying?"

"Oh, I'm sorry." She stepped back and quickly wiped her nose with the back of her hand. "I'm having some problems, no big deal. I gotta go now 'cause Grandma Amelia's waiting for me. We'll talk later, okay?" She touched his sleeve.

"Okay, sure."

She started to open the door when she turned around. "Thank you so much, Monsignor Murphy. I appreciate you listening to me and your advice and all." After she walked out, Father Bob shot a questioning look toward Monsignor Murphy, who raised his gray eyebrows above his glasses.

"She's going through a divorce and wants to come back to the Church. We will welcome her and her fourteen-year-old son back into the flock." He read Father's Bobs face and asked, "Are you ready for this?"

"What? You think I can't handle it?" Father Bob raised his voice.

"You'd better handle it. She told me she took communion from you. Is that why you got sick?"

He sat down. "Yes, I got shaky when I saw her at Mass today, along with so many old friends. Things all hit me at once. You know the story. It won't happen again."

"Yes, and remember, that whole episode with you and Maria was a long time ago." He gave Father Bob a stern look. His flushed, saggy cheeks shook as he spoke. "I need you to be a priest, and to view her as a priest would. Tell me you can do this, son. I stuck my neck out for you."

"Yes, yes I know. You've told me that ten times." He grew sick of hearing the "sticking out the neck" line, but wished that he hadn't snapped at Murphy. "With God's guidance, and your advice, I'll certainly maintain my vocation. I would never let you down, never."

Suddenly the peppered-hairdo of the housekeeper, Mrs. Hellinski, appeared around the side of the kitchen doorway. She'd been eavesdropping.

"I need to rid things up in the kitchen right now," she said. "So I can get up to the park and help set up food for the reunion. Yunz should come up and eat, 'cause I won't be cooking dinner today."

"Okay, the boss has spoken," Father Bob said. Mrs. Hellinski acted so reverent around Monsignor Murphy. Yet she didn't treat him with that kind of respect though, except when Murphy was around. Father Bob hoped to win her over. "We'll get out of your way."

"You may as well drive me to the Knights of Columbus," Murphy said. "That way, you keep the car and make an appearance at the reunion. I'm sure Stabo or somebody else will drive me home."

"Oh, I get it. I'm the one who has to represent us at the reunion. My penance for being the new kid on the block?"

Monsignor Murphy smiled. "Seniority has its benefits, son. Just make sure to bless all the families, not just the Barrones. People get real touchy about that around here."

*　　　*　　　*

He sat behind the wheel of Monsignor Murphy's black Lincoln Continental, dressed in black garb rimmed with a white collar. Monsignor Murphy rode shotgun, dressed in black, topped-off with a biretta that reminded him of a character in Mario Puzo's new book, *The Sicilian*. The priests said nothing during the short drive up the twisted, sylvan hills of Irontown, where wooden houses clung to the hillside with porch views of either the steel mill or a hollow below. Some of the roads had been newly asphalted since Father Bob had seen them. Near the Knights of Columbus hall, he was pleased to see that three baseball fields had been meticulously manicured. *They love their sports here.* He parked the Lincoln near the front door of the huge pole building, where they both got out and stretched in unison. At the bottom of a hill near the city park, human figures scurried around a large shelter house.

"Stop in and say hello," Murphy said as he opened the door to the K of C hall. He motioned for him to follow, and headed straight for the bar, where a few Knights sat. Most wore short-sleeved, plaid shirts and sported baseball caps.

"Look at this. It's the Godfather and his son," Stabo joked. His belly bounced. He was a "third-degree" knight. "Come

12

on over, Padres. We have miles of spaghetti and a slag ladle full of meatballs."

They shimmied up against the bar, where Stabo poured a double shot of scotch for Monsignor Murphy. "What's your poison, Father Bob? We don't have any Mad Dog 20/20." Sabo laughed along with three other Knights.

Father Bob remained cool. "Awe shucks, Stabo." He looked around at the others. "I guess I'll have to work on my beer belly then."

"Ooooh!" the other Knights egged on Stabo. Father Bob recognized one of them as Frankie, a man who once let him go after catching him as a kid stealing a package of sliced baloney from DiCino's hilltop market. Stabo looked at Monsignor Murphy.

"Hey, don't look at me. The boy can take care of himself." Murphy pushed his glass forward for another pour.

Father Bob locked eyes with Stabo's, who sized him up. "I'll pull you an Iron City." He rubbed his beer belly. "It takes a lot of good living to grow one of these, son."

His whole childhood in Irontown, Father Bob took a ribbing from Stabo. The fighter inside wanted to challenge Stabo, but the priest in there wouldn't allow it. Besides, Stabo was Murphy's best lay friend, a millwright in the steel mill, and about the same age. "Iron City sounds great. Thanks, Stabo."

Stabo laughed a baritone grunt. "Looks like the Pirates are going to stay in the basement this year." The conversation turned to baseball, while the Knights filled their plates. Father Bob quickly downed his draft. He waited for an opening, a chance to escape yet to another place where he did not want to go.

"Thanks for the beer, guys, but I'd better save myself for the reunion. I need to head down there."

Murphy waved. "Keep the car. Stabo can drive me home."

Father Bob drove the big Lincoln down a gravel road towards the park. The car bounced over a pothole, which flung the door of the glove box open. A silver flask lay on top of the operator's manual. He parked in the dirt lot, unscrewed the cap and took a healthy swig. The liquid burned down his throat and into his stomach. While sliding the flask back into the glove box, he noticed Anthony, the altar boy, standing nearby snuffing out a cigarette with a look of sneakiness. *Small towns have no secrets.* Crowds of people gathered under a shelter house in the distance. He stepped out of the car.

"Hey, Father Bob!" Anthony yelled while walking towards him with another boy, a slender kid with a black Afro. He wore a worn Aerosmith T-shirt. "This is my new friend, Boss. He's from Vegas."

"Hello, Boss, I'm Father Bob. Hey, nice to meet you." He extended his hand for a shake. A faint scent of marijuana lingered in the humidity.

"Hey, what's happening?" Boss squeezed his hand hard. "I think you know my mom, Maria Constantini." Boss flicked his cigarette into an arch where the red ash exploded on the dirt.

Father Bob stood frozen, looking for some resemblance of Maria in Boss's face. "Yes, of course, so you're Maria's son." He continued to stare at Boss, could see the faint reflection of his white collar through slits in the boy's eyes and felt a bit unsettled at how the boy was sizing him up.

Father Bob broke the long handshake, not knowing quite what to say. "Will you be attending Irontown High this fall?"

"Huh? I sure as hell hope not." He lifted his arm towards the woods. "We're supposed to move out West pretty soon. There's nothing happening in this old town."

"Father Bob!" Bea yelled, walking towards him from the shelter house. "Come on over." He rolled his eyes at the two boys. "Is your mother here, Boss?"

The boy did not answer.

Bea grabbed Father Bob by the arm and pulled him along and under the shelter house. Browned meatballs bubbled in vats of simmering tomato sauce, filling the airy inside with the aroma of an Italian house. On the other end, Grandma Amelia filled plates with homemade spaghetti, ravioli, and meatballs, to pass down along picnic tables covered with red and white-checkered tablecloths. Women filled wine glasses for everybody, including the older children. People handed dishes to each other haphazardly, while from a black cassette player, perched atop two cement blocks, Dean Martin blared "That's Amore," serenading this convivial production line.

Family members and friends of all ages sat elbow-to-elbow working their plates. "Hey everybody," Bea banged a pot lid with a metal spoon. "Listen up. This is Father Bob Santoro, Santo and Restituta's son. God rest their souls." Bea made the sign of the cross. Father Bob faked a smile. Hearing "Santo and Restituta's son" struck him awkward. He'd never been introduced that way before. His mother had died giving him birth and his father was killed in a steel mill accident three years

14

later. His Aunt Sophia had raised him, until she, too, passed away when he was a teen. "He's our hometown boy who came back to help out Monsignor Murphy."

"Coming back to Irontown is like a dream come true. It's a blessing to see all of you again," He declared, raising his hands up in the air about to say a prayer just as Grandma Amelia yelled, "Father Bob Santoro!" She dropped her serving spoon and hobbled over to him. She reached up with both hands to pull his face down to hers, kissing him first on one cheek, then the other. Her eyes beamed with excitement. "Please bless us and eat with my family."

Conversations stopped. Somebody turned down the volume of the song. He raised his hands again. "May God bless our food and protect all of us." He poured the outward sign of the cross over the crowd. They bowed their heads and stirred into a single line in front of him, as if he were handing out communion. One by one, about twenty of the Italian family members and friends greeted him with a hug, handshake or kiss, before returning to their filled plates and glasses of wine. He kept an eye out for Maria.

Next to the shelter house, a small group of elderly men played Bocce ball on a strip of smoothed, finely crushed slag, something he had not seen since his youth. Grandma Amelia filled a plate and set it down for him. Ravioli and meatballs piled on top of spaghetti with strands dangling over the side. Without a word, Father Bob sat down to do his duty. Somebody placed a glass of dark homemade wine in front of his plate, along with a shot of lemon liqueur.

"I think about Restituta and Santo every day," sighed Grandma Amelia standing over him and making the sign of the cross. "I wish they were here to see you. They'd be so proud. So would your Aunt Sophia, God rest their souls."

"I know, Grandma. God took them back, just like He did your Caesar, and son, Alphonso. They're all with us in spirit." He bowed his head for a moment of respect and then lifted it. "But we're still here, so let's honor them by celebrating life!" He lifted his glass of wine. "Salute!"

"Salute!" he heard in response. A slew of wine glasses rose from folks he didn't even know were listening.

Not to be outdone by the others, Ronny Milovick placed a giant plastic glass of draft beer in front of Father Bob. "Nostrovia," (Na zdrowie) they toasted before taking a healthy gulp.

Grandma Amelia hovered over the top of Father Bob. He would never be able to finish that plate, but knew all about the sinful act of not eating a served meal. She kissed the top of his head before whispering into his ear, "Maria and her son, Boss, came back home to live with me for a while, until the divorce is over. Please pray for them. I'm so worried about Boss." She made the sign of the cross again. "Please, I'll send him to the rectory tomorrow with some fresh baked bread for you and Monsignor Murphy."

"Thank you, Grandma. And don't worry yourself too much. God will take care of them. I'll keep them in my prayers."

Suddenly Barker appeared. He placed two shots of whiskey on the table and plopped down across from him. Grandma Amelia turned away and walked towards the serving vats.

"Don't you love these family reunions? I crash all of 'em. Shoot, it's the only time I get a homemade meal since the old lady left me." Barker laughed like a mad man, then aside asked, "You seen Maria yet? She's back and damn, she's hot."

He continued to down the macaroni yet frowned at Barker's lack of discretion. "Yes, I saw her in church this morning and she has a...maintained herself well. Is she here?"

"She left a few minutes ago. I saw her and that kid arguing with some nun out in the parking lot. Then they all disappeared." Barker picked up both shots, careful not to spill them, and handed one to Father Bob. "C'mon old buddy, we gotta shoot one for old times' sake."

Father Bob scanned the crowd. "No thanks, Bark. Maybe we could get together another time, away from the crowd. We could reminisce about the old days."

Barker downed one shot, followed immediately by the other. "What? You still a lightweight?" He slapped Father Bob on the back. "Damn, you're soaking wet."

"To tell you the truth, I've had too many already. I've got to get out of here before it's too late."

He made his way to the Lincoln, a little woozy, sneaking away without saying all those goodbyes. Halfway home, Father Bob stopped the car, opened the door, bent forward and vomited.

Chapter 2

Bless Me Father For I Have Sinned

Jack barked at the bedroom door. His yap woke Father Bob, who knew the dog needed to go outside. The old "Big Ben" wind-up showed six o'clock. They had slept for twelve straight hours. Father Bob had to go to the bathroom as well, so he threw on his gym shorts, opened his bedroom door, and let Jack fly downstairs. He followed Jack and let him out the front door, then rushed back up the stairs, where he almost doubled over from the pain of a full bladder. The bathroom gave him natural relief following a long day of drinking. As his urine filled the tank, he chuckled at the thought of a congregation watching a priest piss. *They forget that we're human.*

After brushing his teeth and saying his morning prayer, he plucked a few rogue hairs from his moustache. He dressed in workout clothes, despite the slight hangover. After all, he had vowed to never let alcohol stop him from activity.

Downstairs again, he let Jack into the house and followed him into the kitchen. The scent of frying bacon surrounded Monsignor Murphy, sitting at his usual spot reading the morning newspaper. He had sat in that same chair for years, as evidenced by worn half-circle grooves dug into the linoleum floor. Mrs. Hellinski hummed a hymn while scrambling eggs. The metal spatula scraping the cast iron skillet sounded a familiar ring, like that of a real family having breakfast together. Father Bob enjoyed this family-like activity while in the seminary. As a child, he had only seen such a thing on such television shows as "Father Knows Best." He was used to eating toast or pop tarts for breakfast on a TV tray at his aunt's, while watching black and white reruns of "The Three Stooges" before school each morning.

He walked to the counter and poured himself a cup of coffee. "Good morning, Mrs. Hellinski."

She turned her head around, looked him up and down, clearly inspecting his jogging regalia. "Good morning, Father Santoro. I hope you want some bacon and eggs this morning. I cooked enough for an army."

"*Bob*..., you can call me Father Bob."

"I have too much respect for the clergy to call you *Bob*. And do you want breakfast or not?"

"Thank you, but I'm going for a jog and wouldn't want to lose those eggs along the way." She cocked her head in confusion, so he explained. "You could get sick if you eat too much before running."

"Humph." She dumped a pile of scrambled eggs into a serving dish and topped it with bacon strips. She also scooped some onto a small plate and placed it on the floor for Jack, who whined with delight and devoured the treat within seconds. Father Bob wanted to tell Mrs. Hellinski not to give his dog "people" food, but also needed to win her over. He sipped coffee, silently laughing at Jack, who perked his ears above his big body watching Hellinski scurry about muttering, cleaning up and clearly avoiding eye contact. At last, she picked up her black-beaded purse and looked at Monsignor Murphy, still hiding behind his paper. "You both know I won't be back to cook and clean until Monday. There are snacks in the fridge."

Monsignor Murphy placed his newspaper down on the table. "Thank you very much. Have a nice day off tomorrow."

She waved her hand. "You know how to get a hold of me if yunz need something." She smiled thinly at Father Bob before walking out the door.

"I swear, I don't know what that woman has against me," Father Bob sighed.

"She has nothing against you. You're from different generations. That's all." He smiled. "I'll say this morning's Mass so that you can focus on confessions. Fathers Swinski and Brown are coming down. I also got one of your old seminary cohorts to help out, Father Callo. You'll be set up in four corners of the church." He picked up the newspaper again. "People come from all over the valley for this community confession, but with the four of you it shouldn't take more than two hours to finish. The servers will set up confessional screens after morning Mass. Anthony knows how to do it. All you have to do is show up by nine o'clock."

"It'll be good to see Callo," Father Bob said to the back of a fanned out newspaper. "I heard how much he loves teaching high school theology. Sorry but I hated teaching, just like I hated high school. At least I don't have to teach anymore." He took a sip of coffee and laid his cup on the countertop. *My "cohort" all right, the guy who never got caught committing pranks in the seminary, first to snitch, first to volunteer.*

"President Reagan and Vice President Bush are deferring opinion to the Supreme Court about public teachers in parochial schools," Murphy read aloud. "You'd think this wouldn't be such a complex issue this day and age. They have to litigate everything to death."

He didn't want to get into a long political discussion with Murphy. He cared little about the decision, as long as they left him alone and didn't make him teach. "Okay, I'll see you later." He grabbed a strip of bacon and flung it into his mouth while heading out the door, shutting it quickly and leaving poor Jack stuck in the kitchen to listen to Murphy's politics. He hated hearing Jack scratch at the door while he stretched on the porch, so he cut his stretch short and took off down the "Hill of Churches" towards the steel mill, where the scent of sulfur lingered in the fog.

Above the bank of the Irontown River, fields of mustard flowers on small flats intertwined with waist-high weeds, whose tops bent with the weight of white flowers. Moving along and finally alone, his headache diminished. He took a turn up Battle Ridge, a partly paved road through a wooded hollow, where rippling chimes echoed from a muddy creek. An occasional shine from the creek shot through some brush in the bottom. Deeper along the wooded road, he smelled oil and heard metal banging as he approached Rocco's junkyard, a Massive field of wasted cars. Several junkyard workers, in soiled T-shirts and greasy jeans, assembled around the car crusher machine. *Jesus came to earth to reach these people, not the righteous.*

A black-faced German shepherd barked and charged, baring his teeth. Father Bob bent down and pretended to pick up a stone, lifting his arm into throwing position, while his hand shook with adrenaline. "Get back!" he yelled at the beast.

The shepherd stood his ground, barked and snapped but didn't cross the road, as if an invisible fence penned him inside. He growled from atop a dirt island surrounded by mud puddles.

"He won't bite 'cha." A gaunt, filthy man nearly toothless smiled from behind a rusted Chevy pickup. "He might bite if you came on the property when we wasn't here. That dog ain't

19

used to seeing folks run out this way." The old man's laugh turned into a long cough.

"Thanks! I'll be gone soon." His sweat dripped into dots on the dirty road.

The old man held up a can of Pabst Blue Ribbon beer as a toast. Father Bob waved and almost stopped to join him for a beer and talk him into coming to Mass next Sunday. Instead, he resumed his run, avoiding drink.

The sun generated steam from moist locust trees. Milkweeds scented the air with sweet caramel. The month of June yielded buckeyes which crunched under his running shoes. Father Bob ran through a path that led to a remote, cool shaded area of the woods. A small creek trickled into a larger one, and he replayed skinny-dipping in the shallows and sliding over the slippery rocks of the "Falls" as a kid. He laughed at a vivid memory of Larry Hodgekirk, a hillbilly with a big nose and a long, bent, uncircumcised erection, who chased him and Barker around the shallows. They ran over the rocks naked, fearing what Larry would do if he had caught them.

Past a smaller junkyard, he turned uphill, towards the crest of Battle Ridge Road. Some people, likely Logan family members, were down in the depression of the hollow. One held a huge monkey wrench in his hand, and another lifted a greasy come-a-long chain, both studying an engine under the hood of a decrepit car. They looked alike, wobbling like pregnant penguins in dirty T-shirts which exposed the lower ball of their bloated bellies. *My church needs to reach the people who struggle just to survive.*

A flip-flop filled his stomach when a vision of Maria popped into his head. What was he to do about her? *She's definitely vulnerable, and oh, so hot.* His thoughts turned to how much he drank yesterday. He vowed to quit drinking in public, quit acting like everyone's buddy. *I'm no "Sugar Bear" carrying on like a street kid.* "Lord, give me the strength to serve You, and still have a good time," he prayed aloud, smiling.

Sodden with sweat, he reached the dump he used to set on fire as a kid. Here he began to shadowbox under the shade of a canopy of trees alive with squawking birds. He hadn't often thrown punches at an imaginary opponent during his fourteen-year tenure as a priest. Something about coming back home stirred the fighter inside of him. Monsignor Murphy had trained him into a decent amateur when he was sixteen. Still, the loss at the Junior Golden Gloves Tournament haunted him.

He conquered the crest of Battle Ridge Hill and sprinted down the final stretch of his five-mile run. Thick trees gave way to small houses down the slope. Finally, nearing the rectory he smelled the fresh scent of baked bread by Grandma Amelia's house. Along the small street past her sidewalk, he slowed his pace and caught his breath, scanning the windows. *Is Maria in there? Love to see her. But no, better not.* His stomach flittered again when he saw the trellis he used to climb to reach the roof of the front porch, where Maria used to sneak him in through her bedroom window. Her grandfather, Caesar, never allowed him into the house, called him a "street urchin," a term he never really understood. He also recalled how Grandma Amelia used to sneak baloney sandwiches to him in the alley, probably as some gesture of Catholic charity.

The house looked empty. Probably nobody home, since the window air conditioner wasn't running. He walked the final hundred yards or so to the rectory, cooling his body. Near St. Anne's Parochial School, Boss sat on a curb with his head in his hands and still wearing that same grubby Aerosmith T-shirt.

"Hello, Boss. Hey, are you bored?"

Boss flinched. "Ah…yeah, no, I'm cool." He scrambled up to his feet. "I was resting after delivering Grandma's bread. I dropped off some for you too."

"Thanks. I could smell it a mile away." Boss's cheeks were red. "There's a lot to do around here on such a beautiful day."

"Oh yeah, like what?" Boss made jerky movements.

Father Bob couldn't tell him the things that he used to do at his age, like set the dump on fire, or blow-up catfish with cherry bombs, or shoot 9-ball for money, or hop a train out to the creek, or try getting into the pants of some girl. "How about shooting some hoops?"

"I don't feel like it." He wiped his nose on his shoulder.

"Son, is everything all right?"

"Why? What's wrong?"

"Oh, nothing. I was just wondering that's all. You seem a little down in the dumps or something."

"There ain't nothing wrong," Boss said, irritated.

Father Bob shrugged his shoulders. "I'm sorry to upset you. Was just checking, that's all."

"Well, just check out yourself!" Boss turned and bolted for Grandma's house, sprinting down the sloped street like he was running from the cops. Father Bob watched him. *Strange kid.* He had only seen Boss twice now, but both times he got the vibe that something was awry, simply by the way he stood, how guarded he acted, and how he avoided any sort of friendliness. It must be the divorce situation. He decided to check-up on him; after all, Boss had no father around anymore and it could provide a perfect excuse to see Maria.

Father Bob took a long shower and then dressed into full priest garb. Down in the kitchen he wolfed down cold scrambled eggs straight from the serving bowl. As soon as he looked at the telephone on the wall, it rang.

"Hello?"

"Is this Father Bob?"

"Yes. Who's this?" he asked, even though his voice cracked when he recognized Maria's voice.

"Maria. Listen, I have a problem with Boss. Is Monsignor Murphy there?"

"No, but can I help you with something?" He heard mumbled conversation on the other end of the line, like Maria had placed her hand over the phone.

"Do you have time right now?"

He only had fifteen minutes before the large community confession…the one Saturday reserved each month for the forgiveness of sins. "Of course, I always have time for you."

"I'll send Boss over to talk with you. I don't know what else to do. Is that okay?"

He couldn't say no to Maria. He would be her knight. "Sure, send him over right now."

A few minutes later, Jack barked at the rectory's kitchen door. Father Bob saw Boss through the window. His head hung down as he shuffled from foot to foot on the porch. "Come on in, Boss. I'm glad you changed your mind about talking to me."

"I didn't change my mind. My mom made me." The boy stepped into the kitchen, still with his head down. Father Bob approached him with open arms and tried to hug him. Boss flinched backwards and raised his hands with a wild look in his eyes. "Don't touch me, man."

"Okay," he said. He had no clue how to approach this kid. He walked into his office and waved Boss into the modest room with a messy desk. "Have a seat." Boss sat on a chair next to another on the same side of the desk. Father Bob counseled this way. A chair sitting across from the desk put up too much of a barrier. He sat down and swiveled to face Boss. "What would you like to talk about?"

22

"I'm going straight to hell, Father." Boss looked towards the floor and shook his head. "My mom said so and told me to talk to you, but I don't think you can do anything about it."

"Tell me about it, son. Nobody but God will ever know."

"Well, Grandma made bread today, see, like always." He swallowed hard and glanced at Father Bob for a second, with moist eyes. "She asked me to deliver loaves to Mrs. Hellinski, you priests, and the nuns. When I walked through the alley between the rectory and the convent...I don't know, man."

"You're safe here. You delivered bread and you were in the alley."

"I heard water running and saw a window open." He stretched out his long, thin arms in front of his body. Veins popped out of his forearms when he twisted his palms towards the ceiling, revealing random patterns of tiny, white scars. "I looked down into the window and there she was, naked, stepping into the tub."

"Who was naked?"

"That nun—Sister Roxanne. I mean I saw all of her, even her hairy triangle." He covered his face with his hands and spoke through them. "Hey, I seen naked women before, but never a nun." His voice rose to a higher pitch. "That's when I ran into the church john and jacked off." Father Bob shifted in his chair, and Boss quickly covered his head with his arm, as if protecting himself from getting hit.

Father Bob looked away and saw Boss's reflection in a wall mirror. *This kid doesn't know how lucky he is.* He turned his glance back to Boss, almost patted his knee, but knew better.

"Son, listen to me. You're not going to hell." Boss rolled his chair a little closer to him. Father Bob had wanted to peep through that window. He met Sister Roxanne only once so far and she was young, well proportioned, and very innocent, yet she glowed with a seductive nature. "What time did you see this?"

"I don't know, a little while ago this morning when I was delivering bread. You know, right before you saw me sitting on the curb. Why? What?"

"No reason, it just explains why you looked upset, that's all. The good thing is that you recognize that this was wrong. You must never look into peoples' windows anymore. Masturbation is a human impulse, one that you must keep behind closed doors. Think about Jesus, and what He would do in a situation like this." He poured the sign of the cross over him.

"God forgives you, but never discuss this with anybody. It would be a sin to tell your friends. We musn't dishonor Sister Roxanne. You understand? Keep this to yourself."

Boss frowned. "I already told my mom. I mean, we tell each other everything. Her and I have to hang tight. She needs me, you know, I protect her."

"That's good, son. You need to stick together."

Boss squirmed in his chair. "She got pissed at me right away. Told me I was a pervert and going to go to hell and started freaking out, man. She's the one who wanted me to talk to that Monsignor guy, but you answered. You gonna call the cops?"

Why didn't Maria call for me first? Why Murphy? He concentrated back on Boss.

"Nobody's calling the police. You did a very brave thing coming to me and owning up to this." He had Boss hanging on his every word. He wanted to help the boy get in touch with his humanity, help him find a balance. "You're a teenager. We just need to ask Jesus to help you control your sexual urges. You are forgiven for this and all your sins, by the power and mercy of God. But what matters most, son, is how you act from this day forward." Boss finally maintained eye contact with Father Bob.

Boss shifted around uncomfortably. "What about Sister Roxanne? She visits Grandma and my mom." He twirled a silver skull ring around his middle finger, revealing a tiny, home-made tattoo of a zigzag. "She even teases me, saying how cute I am and all. She has no idea I'm a pervert." The boy grinned up at him. "Should I tell her?"

Father Bob read how Boss tried to act streetwise, the tattoo, scars, and cautious way he kept his distance, a little like he used to do when he was Boss's age. On the other hand, he sensed a naivety that suggested Boss didn't know how to handle women the way he did, even at that young age.

"Boss, first off, you're not a pervert. Please don't think of yourself that way. Hey, there was no real harm done here. Why make Sister Roxanne have to live with this? You have an opportunity to recover fully from this. Your sins are forgiven."

Boss finally relaxed. He hunched into his chair. "I guess you're not as bad a priest as my mom thinks. I swear I'll never do anything like this again."

Father Bob nodded. *Maria thinks I'm a bad priest just because we were lovers in high school?* "I want you to feel free to talk to me anytime you want. Jesus loves us no matter what."

Boss stood up. "When do I go to confession?"

"You just did," Father Bob smiled. "We don't have to use those wooden closets all the time. We rap like real people, face to face."

"Right on," Boss nodded. "Do I still have to say penance?"

Father Bob liked how quickly this kid recovered and figured that he had done a pretty good job of counseling. "For your penance, just sit in the church in silence. Think about all the good things God has given you in your life, like the love you get from your beautiful mother and grandma. Thank God for the delights in your life."

"Wow, man. Is that all?"

"Yes...As a matter of fact, you could walk over to the church with me right now. I'll be hearing confessions, and you could sit in a quiet spot to start your reflection. There'll be a powerful spirit of forgiveness in the church during this sacrament."

They walked in silence through the windowed hallway connected to the church, not knowing what more to say. Boss disappeared into the dark rows of pews. Small groups had gathered near the four corners of St. Anne's. Father Bob situated himself in his chair, already set up behind a portable "privacy" screen outside of the Sacristy.

Father Callo sat in the dim light by the opposite wall. Fathers Swinski and Brown must have been nested inside the wooden confessionals near the front of the church, in each dark corner.

He wanted to run over and wrestle Callo to the ground, the way they used to back in the seminary, but Callo had his head down as he listened to the confession of a man talking too loudly from the other side of the privacy screen. The man might as well have been making a public confession. Father Bob stared over at Callo, trying to get his attention. Finally, Callo looked up. His eyes lit and he waved at Father Bob. He tapped his wristwatch and shrugged his shoulders. Father Bob pretended to yank on an imaginary beard in an attempt to poke fun at Callo's long chin whiskers. He shook his head up and down, as a gesture of approval. Callo forgave the man's sins with the sign of the cross, then met Father Bob at mid altar. They hugged each other. Father Bob whispered, "Great to see you, old friend." He had forgotten just how short and stout Callo stood. He had grown a long Rip Van Winkle beard, like a band member of ZZ Top. He tugged Callo's whiskers. "You look like a monk."

Callo stood back and gave Father Bob a quick inspection. "You haven't changed a bit. And you're still late as usual. Don't worry, though, we've been clearing out the church while you were hanging out with your young friend."

Father Bob laughed sarcastically. "Let's get together after confessions for a glass of wine. Maybe we could snack on some of that food stuck in your beard."

Callo combed his beard with his fingernails. "I'd love too."

"Perfect, I'll meet you in the rectory when we're finished."

Father Bob sat in place..."Bless me Father for I have sinned," said a thin, elderly woman with a black veil covering her face. She sat in the chair behind the full-bodied privacy screen, rather than sit face-to-face with the priest, but her figure could still be seen. "My last confession was one month ago, and here are my sins: I listened to and spread gossip thirty-six times. I cursed about twenty times, and thought impure thoughts around six times."

Father Bob's intentional two-minute period of silence seemed like an eternity. Hearing confessions marked his least favorite part about being a priest, but fully rehearsed sins truly grinded at his patience. *What does she do, press a hand clicker each time she sins?* "Is there anything else you'd like to say or talk about?"

"Well, I wish I could stop gossiping. I confess this, and God forgives me, but I still keep doing it. I can't help it, I mean, everybody tells me everything."

He pegged this woman for one of Irontown's main sources of information and wondered what people were saying about him. "God is forgiving and gives all of us unconditional love. For your penance, think about the gossip you may hear, and before you spread it, imagine that you're talking about Jesus. See if that makes a difference."

"Uh, okay, I guess I can try that, Father. Should I say ten Hail Mary's too?"

"Yes, of course you can." He made the sign of the cross over the screen separating them, while she whispered the prayer for forgiveness, the act of contrition. She left, and a large man took her seat.

"Bless me Father, 'cause I'm a sinner." An odor of alcohol penetrated the portable screen, where the silhouette of a beer-bellied man fidgeted. "I ain't been to confession in years, but need to get my act together before it's too late."

"Welcome back to God's house. Where would you like to start?"

"I don't go to Church no more, can't stop drinkin' and the old lady says she's gonna leave me if I don't quit. Some nun in town's been fillin' her head up with all kinds of bullshit. How's that for starters?" He stretched his neck for a look around the screen. "Ain't chu Bobby Santoro?"

Father Bob returned the man's stare. He wore a blue flannel shirt like one of the Knights of Columbus guys he met the other day.

"Yes, but I'm *Father* Bob now. Would you care to come back another time after you de-tox a little?"

"De-tox? You kiddin'? Man, I'm gonna re-tox! I just got to get some things off my chest, that's all." His voice escalated as he walked around the screen, standing in front of Father Bob. He snarled, "You should know about how a man has to blow off a little steam once in a while. Shit, I remember seeing you passed out under the highway bridge with those Calhoon brothers, empty wine bottles all over the place. Didn't you used to live under there?"

Father Bob staggered one leg behind the other and twisted onto the balls of his feet, ready to jump from the chair and defend himself if necessary. He was weary of hearing stories of his wine drinking as a kid. "God forgives and loves you." He poured the sign of the cross up at the man. "For your penance, how about coming back to confession tomorrow morning before Mass? I'll come to the church early, just to meet you if you want." He couldn't place a name with the face, even though the guy clearly knew him.

The man waved his hand from his shoulder towards the ground. "Yunz guys don't understand the *real* world." He stomped away, passing a nun, whom Father Bob recognized as Sister Roxanne. She tried to speak to the man, then walked towards Father Bob's station. He also saw Boss watch Roxanne approach the altar. He looked over at Callo, who smirked at him.

"Hello, Father Santoro, I'm Sister Roxanne. We met a few days ago, remember?"

He nodded. "Bob, call me Father Bob." He wanted to ask her the name of the drunken man, but knew that would be inappropriate.

She pulled the chair around the screen and sat directly in front of him. Looked him in the eyes. "My last confession was two weeks ago, and here are my sins." She bowed her head. "I get so frustrated with Mother Superior. I know I vowed to obedience, but I think bad thoughts about her and praying isn't taking them away. She can be so insensitive."

He had heard this before, about how cruel and unresponsive some Mother Superiors could be. He waited a few moments, then spoke.

"You're human, Sister. In spite of your vows, you, or none of us are immune to the dark sides of humanity." He admired Roxanne's juicy lips at the bottom of her white, triangular frame of innocence. He tried hard to not picture her in the nude, the way Boss had described a short while ago. "We need to acknowledge our darker sides for what they are, and shed light upon them. Shower those thoughts with a golden flow of love, not only for Mother Superior, but also for yourself. Sometimes we serve others so much that we forget to love ourselves."

She smiled. "That was beautiful. Thanks for reminding me of that, Father." She adjusted her chair and whispered. "Well, speaking of loving yourself...I must confess something that makes me very uncomfortable." She hesitated. "There's no other way to say it." She cleared her throat. "I masturbate occasionally, Father. I'm so ashamed. I never confess this, except when I go to a different church to a priest I don't know." She placed her petite hand over those moist lips and spoke through them. "I mean, I lie in bed at night, so lonely I cannot sleep. Before I know it, I touch myself. Sometimes I relax in a warm bubble bath, and it happens again."

Father Bob willed himself to feel Christ's compassion. He struggled with the privilege of hearing Sister Roxanne's honesty, against his human reaction of arousal. He was glad to be wearing his long vestment overtop his pants.

"Sister, you're an attractive woman who devoted herself to God, at a time when other women your age are having babies and making families. Are you a sexual being?"

"What do you mean?"

"I mean, are you a human, with genitals?"

"Of course I am." She tilted her head sideways. "What are you saying?"

The way she looked at him, the light tone of her voice, made him want to embrace her. Her loneliness penetrated his soul. His own acts of carnal desires had gone too far as recently as six months ago. To see that same pain in such an innocent and devoted woman broke his heart. He knew exactly what she was feeling, so spiritual and vulnerable. *Why does God do this mean thing to us?* Roxanne and he could fill that void of loneliness together, if only their vows would allow it. For a moment of distraction, he looked over at Callo who seemed to maintain the appearance of a meaningful conversation, talking now to an elderly lady, who nodded her head from the other side of the screen. He looked back at Sister Roxanne.

"We can't deny the sexual being of our existence. The guilt surrounding masturbation does nothing but prevent us from getting closer to God." He swallowed. "I mean, masturbation in itself is natural and delightful. Celibacy and chastity can be so cruel that we end up shaming ourselves. I know your loneliness. We're all depraved, I mean, deprived, of the gift of intimate touch by the nature of our chosen vocation." He shifted in his chair. "For your penance, Sister, sit and thank God for all the delights in your life...anything that delights you. Let God guide you. Recognize that you're a being born of love, and He has called you to serve Him."

Tears welled in Sister Roxanne's eyes, yet her expression told him that there was something more she wanted to talk about. "Thank you, Father Bob. How I needed to hear something forgiving like that. Your words give me comfort. I'll work on trying to love myself."

She stood up and smoothed her black habit before walking down the middle aisle between rows of pews. There she turned into a row and bent down to drop the padded kneeler, in the pew directly in front of Boss. She gave Boss a quick wave, and the boy hustled out of the church. Father Bob smiled. *Boss must think she was coming for him. He sure does a lot of running.*

Confessions wound down till he had no one else standing in wait. He reflected on the murmurs of humans who bared their inner beings. *Who are you God? How do we enlighten the grubby, swampy chunk of our souls?* He sat for a few more minutes, wondering about the cruelty of celibacy. Father Callo startled him when he seemed to appear out of nowhere. The guy always had the habit of popping up, as if out of thin air. "I think that's everybody," he said. "You look finished."

"I think so. Let's say good-bye to Fathers Swinski and Brown, and head to the rectory."

*   *   *

Back in the rectory Father Bob grabbed a gallon of red wine from the cabinet under the sink, unscrewed the top, and filled two glasses on the table. Callo petted Jack while Father Bob retrieved a plate of ham roll-ups from the refrigerator. He placed the treat on the table. "I'm free the rest of the afternoon."

"I'm free too. Want to take in a movie?" Father Callo said. He lit up a cigarette.

"Sure. I've wanted to see *Starman* with Jeff Bridges. Have you seen it?"

"That sounds good." Smoke drifted through Callo's nostrils and mouth. "So, how are you adjusting to life in the hometown?"

He knew that the cagey Callo was fully aware of his disciplinary situation, just like everyone else. "I'm a survivor, sent here to do the work of God. I take my vocation as God gives it to me, but what about you? When are you going to quit those cancer sticks?"

Callo took another puff and blew the smoke towards Father Bob's face. "Remember when it was the only indulgence available to us at the seminary? I'm not ready to kick it just yet. So how's your new assignment?"

Callo always tried to put him on the spot. "I'm still adjusting, but the hometown parish is interesting. There's lots of interaction with people. It's weird seeing old friends and acquaintances, but I seem to have a lot of down time. When I taught high school I didn't have time for anything else. How can you still like to teach after what, seven years?"

"I love it," Callo said. "When I see those boys' eyes light up, I mean, especially after the day following a didactic lessen that they actually put into a spiritual concept, you know, for daily use, it inspires my sacerdotalism."

There he goes with his fancy words. Why doesn't God ever give me those kinds of experiences? He listened to Callo continue. "I heard about all your women in Columbus. You think women chase us, or do we chase them?"

He knew that Callo was pumping him, like a spy sent by the Bishop. "Remember back in the seminary, when Monsignor Conti said that the white collar attracts women?" They both nodded. "You can't tell me that it hasn't happened to you. But yes, celibacy goes against human nature. Why doesn't the Pope realize that this is 1984 and times have changed?"

"Times have changed all right, haven't you heard about that AIDS virus?"

"Of course, we've never had anything that horrible before."

Father Bob refilled both wine glasses.

Callo nodded a silent thank you. "Okay, I've got a story for you." He cleared his throat. "There was a Sister, from the Franciscan Order of Manitoch, who used me as her spiritual adviser. All she talked about was masturbation. Do nuns realize how much that turns us on?"

Father Bob laughed. Perhaps Callo had heard part of the confession with Sister Roxanne. "Is that the sin of the century or what?" he said. "Everybody confesses to masturbating. It's a wonder any work ever gets done with so many people playing with themselves."

They both laughed and Father Bob topped off their glasses again.

"Anyway, this nun, Sister Mary Joe, and I were getting a little too close. People were even beginning to talk. You know, anytime you do some outside activity with a woman, like go to the movies or something, people have to talk. Did you hear anything?"

"No, nothing about you, except that you're getting a Doctorate of Divinity."

"Yes, and that's all fine." Callo looked around the room and then leaned forward, almost whispering. "Sister Mary Joe asked me how wrong it would be if we both masturbated in front of each other, without touching one another. Technically, it wouldn't break the vow of celibacy."

Father Bob tried to contain himself but couldn't. He stood up strutted around the table, howling. "I don't even want that vision in my head!" He knew, though. This story could be made-up just to provoke him into an "I can top your story" kind of thing. He wouldn't fall for it.

"Of course I didn't do it. But I wasn't innocent in the flirtatious aspect of the encounter. I used the opportunity to discuss the loneliness of Catholic priests and nuns. Few people realize what it feels like." Callo stood up and waved his hands around. "Even if we masturbated in front of each other, the need for physical intimacy would still exist. It's hard to experience any form of intimacy when all people talk about to us outside the confessional is news, sports, and weather."

"Yea, yea, yea…divinity verses spirituality and humanity, the age old struggle." He knew that Callo had heard all the details of his getting caught having sex with a parishioner's wife back in his previous assignment. The entire community had heard about it when her husband went public. He shook that memory and remembered the time he had walked into Callo's dorm room at the seminary. Callo's head quickly popped up from the lap of a new seminarian. They had never spoken to each other about it. Now, he had to focus on Callo's hidden agenda, which was probably to see if he was still messing around. "Did you cross the line with the nun?"

For the first time Callo looked sincere. "You must promise to keep it confidential."

He filled Callo's wine glass once again, hoping that drunkenness would open him up. Callo had always been tight lipped about himself. "Of course, I give you my word." He wanted to hear that the "holy Callo" gave in to the same temptations that he himself couldn't resist.

Callo sat down, looked around the room again. This time he whispered, "We hugged each other, lost track of time smelling each other's neck and hair. I didn't want to let her go. The taboo turned us on and we were about to cross the line. Just as we were about to kiss, we both jumped back like struck by an electrical shock. After that we ignored each other, even in the halls of Holy Rosary High. Suddenly she was transferred or reassigned or something, and now she's up in Wisconsin."

What a disappointment. He wanted to hear more than that. Something that would make him feel less terrible about his own indiscretion. Before he could respond, the wall telephone rang. Callo looked flushed. He grabbed the wine bottle and topped off his own glass. Father Bob stretched the curly black cord of the telephone around the other side of the wall.

It was Maria. He could barely understand her and couldn't think about the words. So he flew back into the kitchen and slammed down the receiver. "God help us." He leaned over the sink with both arms outstretched on each side of it. "I have to go. That was Maria Constantini on phone." He stared out the window over the sink.

"What? You mean *your* old Maria? You're kidding. You two are back in touch?"

"Yes, but it's not what you think." He scowled at Callo, was in no mood to hear his high-on-the-horse judgments, after all, he'd just confessed to an indiscretion and now he'd gone back to judging again. "She's in town living with her grandmother, going through a divorce with that Mario guy in Vegas. God be with us. I can't believe it."

Callo stood up and walked over to the sink. He put his hand on the front of Father Bob's shoulder. "What's wrong? You can't believe what?"

"She has a son who was just rushed to the Emergency ward at Holy Cross Hospital. They think it was a suicide attempt. I have to get up there. Murphy has the car and I don't know where he is. Can you drive me?" Callo stroked his beard and Father Bob gave him a look of expectation.

"Of course, let's go. I'll do whatever you need."

Chapter 3

High Mass

Father Callo dropped off Father Bob in front of the Emergency Ward at Holy Cross Hospital. "You sure you don't want me to come in with you?"

He had enough to worry about without Callo's head games. "Yah, no...I mean, thanks."

He gave Callo a quick wave and hurried into the hospital, a familiar setting where he already had administered the Eucharist and hope to the sick. Through the glass doors of the waiting room, he saw Maria pacing as Grandma Amelia sat on a plaid couch holding a rosary in one hand, twisting its beads with the other. He approached Maria, her face flushed from crying.

"How's Boss?" He asked.

She stopped, shrugged her shoulders and crossed her arms. "Monsignor Murphy's back there with him. They pumped his stomach." After a second of sobbing, she sighed, "My poor baby, I didn't know things were so bad."

"Murphy's here already?" He hugged her briefly and felt moisture soak the side of his neck. He straightened up and took a step back. Maria appeared worn, like a worried mother.

She cocked her head at him. "Murphy was here right away. We figured you'd want to know too, since you're the one who talked with Boss this morning." She started pacing again. "He swallowed some valium from one of my old scripts. I don't know how many, but he was unconscious. It's not your fault. Boss is going through rough times, rougher than we thought."

She's blaming me? He walked fast to keep up with Maria's pacing. "Let's pray for him."

She stopped and faced him. "What do you mean, let's pray for him?" Father Bob opened his arms to her, but she smacked his chest with the heels of her palms, pushing him back. "You don't have a clue, do you!"

What is she talking about? He could not understand her reaction and wondered if the spiritual guidance he gave Boss this morning could be to blame. Speechless, he looked at Grandma Amelia, who sat on the couch moving her lips to the twist of a rosary, oblivious to their conversation. Lights flickering from the reflection of the glass rosary beads shot small sparkles on the ceiling and walls.

The sound of the automatic double doors opening diverted everybody's attention. Monsignor Murphy stood in the doorway. He had a serious look on his face, but he usually looked that way when he wore the black biretta.

He cleared his throat. "The doctor said that Boss will be okay, but they need to keep him overnight for observation." He looked at Maria. "She'll want to talk with you soon."

Maria collapsed onto the couch beside Grandma. "Thank you, God, thank you."

Confused by Maria's anger, Father Bob decided to minister to Grandma. He placed his hands on the top of Grandma's frail shoulders and kissed her on the side of her cheek.

"Thanks a million for being here," she told him. "You're like part of our family." Maria looked at them and rolled her eyes.

"We'll do everything we can to help Boss recover from this." He cupped his hands around Grandma's as she raised them to her lips, where she kissed the white ceramic Jesus, swinging on its shiny black cross that dangled from the rosary's silver chain. Although Monsignor Murphy seemed to be the priest in control, Father Bob asserted his spirituality in an attempt to bring peace into the room. "Lord, shower Your healing grace on Boss, and our family, Your servants." He made the sign of the cross over them.

After a brief pause following the prayer, the doors opened again. Dr. Brighton walked into the room. "Mrs. Constantini?" Maria jumped up. Dr. Brighton pulled her off to a side room. Father Bob strained to listen to the conversation between the two women. "You can see your son now, but he's groggy. We'll keep him overnight."

"He's going to be okay?"

"Yes, but his body endured tremendous stress and toxicity. He'll be sore, and right now he's on an IV for nutrition and re-hydration." She smiled. "Can we talk about therapeutic counseling?"

"I want to see my son."

"Yes, of course. We'll talk later."

"Thank you so much, doctor," Maria said and bolted for Boss's bed.

Father Bob walked behind her, with Monsignor Murphy and Grandma Amelia following. Murphy grabbed Father Bob's arm, stopping him. He whispered, "Let Grandma go into the room first before us."

"How did you get up here so fast?"

Murphy pulled out a stained handkerchief and blew his nose. He voice choked, "Stabo had a heart attack. He's being prepped for transport to Pittsburgh for open-heart surgery." Before Father Bob could respond, Murphy walked into Boss's room.

The monitor beeped while Boss lay motionless in bed with an oxygen mask covering his nose and lips. Maria climbed into the bed and lay next to him, on the side void of plastic tubes. The scene reminded Father Bob of an Italian funeral he once presided over, where the mother climbed into the casket to lay with her dead son. Grandma Amelia walked to the other side of Boss's bed, holding her rosary. She bent and kissed the needle's point of entry into the top of Boss's hand.

Father Bob did not know what to do. He said another short prayer over the entire group. Boss widened his eyes, from behind the mask, as if wanting to tell him something. Or perhaps, worse yet, Boss feared him. Maybe Boss got the wrong idea from what he heard this morning. Father Bob regressed to the memory of a summer day when he almost killed himself, and stood on that highway bridge ready to jump. It was the day Maria had eloped with Mario. Monsignor Murphy had given him hope back then, and he longed to administer the same comfort to Boss.

Monsignor Murphy looked at Father Bob and motioned with his head, a gesture meant to meet out in the hallway. The two priests walked outside Boss's room. "I'll stay up here with the Stabo family for a while," he told Father Bob. "You take the car, there's no need for both of us to stay here."

Father Bob envisioned Stabo dropping to the floor from a barstool at the Knights of Columbus hall. He saw the pain in Murphy's eyes, the worn sag in his ashy cheeks, no doubt the effect of worrying about losing his long-time lay friend.

"I don't need to go anywhere. What can I do for you or the families?"

Murphy shook his head. "There's nothing you can do, except say the High Mass for me tomorrow and maybe come to the hospital after that. We'll play it by ear," he said, pausing to take his friend's hand adding, "and please, don't hold yourself responsible for Boss's behavior."

That statement stung. Priests give out advice all the time, mostly good, not always perfect. Murphy should understand. Maria had lashed at him, but she was going through tough times. He felt like he was in the way, ineffective as a priest, in some way responsible for everything wrong. He turned to leave, "Okay, whatever you want." Father Bob took the car keys and then paused. "I'm going to go pray in the Chapel for a while before leaving."

He heard his own footsteps echo in the drab hospital hallway. His eyes fixed on the small, stained-glass window near the top of the tiny chapel's door when opening it, and then he walked past the five rows of pews. The holy room was void of people, and smelled like church incense. Sitting in the front pew, he stared at the sterile altar below a barren cross, which was bolted to the wall. A spotlight illuminated the white cross and a blond oak pulpit faced the congregation's left side. A statue of Our Lady flanked the opposite side, Her hands outstretched above several glass candles, flames flickering with hope for the faithful. His throat dried as he envisioned Boss lying in bed with tubes growing from him.

"Who are you, God?" He prayed out loud. "You guide us. Yet everything went wrong here. Please give me the grace to help people in need, I beg You." He replayed how confessions were disastrous this morning, saying the wrong things to Boss, dashing any hope of moving Maria with his spiritual guidance. A drunken man came to church for a hint of salvation, and after talking with him, the man left in anger. He felt guilt over thinking that it was funny when Boss ran from Roxanne, and for harboring lustful thoughts about the young nun. All of those people had opened their souls to him and maybe he gave them all the wrong advice. *Am I less of a priest since my terrible mistake?*

"Show me how to serve You," he said aloud. His eyes filled with emotion and pain. A tear escaped down his cheek. He looked around the tiny chapel to make sure he was still alone. "Give me a sign," he prayed silently. "Use me as an instrument of Your peace."

As he heard the door squeak open he straightened his hunched shoulders.

"Hey!" Barker's yell echoed in the small room. "What're you doin'?"

His surprise appearance jolted Father Bob into recovering his composure. He looked back. "What are *you* doing here?" Barker was the last person he expected to see.

"I came up to see Stabo," his voice resonated. Father Bob bounced his index finger from his lips a few times as a signal to be quiet. Barker lowered his voice to a whisper. "Stabo had a heart attack. I came to see if they needed anything, but the nurses won't even let me in." He walked through the chapel and sat next to him. "I saw Murphy and Grandma Amelia having coffee with Maria in the cafeteria. I guess that kid of hers almost bit it."

"How'd you find me? Did you come to the chapel to pray?"

Barker snorted. "You kidding? Murphy told me to come and give you a ride home so he can keep the car. You ready?"

He reluctantly succumbed. "I guess so. Let me go give the keys back to Murphy and say goodbye to the family." He figured to leave before he messed up things even more. "Give me five minutes and I'll meet you in the parking lot. Are you on the bike?"

"No." Barker sneered. "Would I be dressed like a citizen if I was on the bike? I'm in the cage, man. This is the first Saturday night I've had off in a month so hurry up. I'll be in the old bomb waiting by the front doors."

Father Bob approached the cafeteria where Maria sat at a table with Grandma and Monsignor Murphy. Maria stared blankly at a cup of coffee. Father Bob was accustomed to shining in hospitals, where he would roam from room to room, bearing gifts of grace like an angel of mercy. But this whole scenario felt awkward upon him, especially with Murphy around. *Why did they even call me if they wanted Murphy to run the show?*

He stood behind Maria and placed one hand upon her shoulder. She stiffened and he whispered. "Let me know if you need anything."

She stared straight ahead and sighed. He removed his hand quickly, as if he should not have touched her. She remained silent.

Monsignor Murphy broke the silence. "Remember that we have a High Mass tomorrow. Get to the sacristy by nine-thirty to meet with Note, the choir director. You take care of things on that end. I may stay here tonight with Stabo's family."

Father Bob nodded in resignation, too disheartened to argue. He handed Murphy the keys and walked towards the exit doors.

Through the glass he saw an old, rusted pickup with a small blue stream of smoke puffing out the end of the exhaust pipe. He did a double take at Barker sitting behind the steering wheel, hair dangling long and unbraided. He opened the squeaky passenger-side door, plopped down onto the worn, springy upholstery, and inhaled the fusty smell of a vintage vehicle and enjoyed the scent of gasoline.

"I hate hospitals," Barker said and slid the shifter into first gear, making a grinding noise. The handle was attached to the steering wheel, three-on-the-tree style. "We got that nasty stank of Lysol bleach or something on our clothes."

Father Bob shook his head, didn't say anything.

"You look like hell. Need a beer? I've got cold ones in the cooler."

"Sometimes I don't know what to do." He sighed, lifting his hands. "And I'm supposed to be a spiritual leader?"

"You just need to blow off a little steam, that's all." The steering wheel made a cracking noise as Barker turned down a steep hill. "Listen, I'm headed down river to Wheeling. Come along for a few. They must allow yunz guys out once in a while. It's Saturday night."

Is this Your sign to me, God? "That's the best offer I've had in a long time." Father Bob wished he hadn't sounded so enthusiastic. "I probably shouldn't, though."

"Bullshit! Murphy told me to take care of you. Imagine that, *me* take care of *you*, a priest? Fuckin' aye!"

He couldn't resist. The timing was perfect. "Okay, I'll have a few, but no 'Wheeling Feeling' stuff." They laughed and Barker put up his hand in the air for a "high-five." Father Bob tapped his hand with a limp touch.

"Remember when we were what, fifteen and went down there?" Barker chuckled. "Pumpkin blew his load while that whore was washing his pecker! He didn't even get laid, but still had to pay ten bucks. I'll bet she'd never seen a big head like his before."

Nobody had talked like that to Father Bob in many years. He slid back into his past life quite naturally. "I almost fell in love with my girl," he recalled. "Then I tried to talk her into quitting, and she looked at me like I was nuts."

"You always were Mr. Romantic. Shit, you used to fall in love all the time, and I guess you know, that'll get you in trouble." Barker pulled onto the highway ramp where the road ran parallel to the river. When he reached across to the cooler on the passenger side floor, he bumped Father Bob's knee into the corner of a cassette player, bolted under the steel dashboard. He pulled out a Pabst Blue Ribbon and popped the top. "You ready for one?"

Father Bob remained silent. *Why would he think I fell in love so much?* He'd never really loved anybody, other than maybe Maria. Barker sipped his beer, and the wind blew strands of his blonde hair into his grizzled beard where it stuck like Velcro. "I'm sorry, Bark, but seeing you drink while driving makes me nervous."

"Ah c'mon, lighten up." Barker chugged down his beer and tossed the can out the window. He looked over and laughed. "I still can't believe you're a priest." He reached back into the cooler, and this time threw a can onto Father Bob's lap. He grabbed one for himself also. He slid in a cassette, and George Thorogood warbled, "Who do you love?"

"Once, me and Pumpkin went down to the Wheeling cat house and saw Pumpkin's dad sitting in there. Man, we ran out of there so fast, I couldn't stop laughing, but Pumpkin didn't think it was so funny."

Father Bob placed his beer onto the floor where it rolled under his seat. He wanted to lighten up, not much else went right today, but the last thing he needed was for somebody to see him in his white collar drinking a beer in an old truck. "Pumpkin's dad was a good looking man," he said. "It's hard to imagine he fathered a child with such a huge head." He He positioned his hands as if holding an invisible beach ball. "Women chased his dad all over town. Why did he need to visit a house of prostitution?"

"Man, that has nothing to do with it. I don't care if he was so good looking he had to bring a banjo with him to take a shit in the outhouse." He waggled his head at Father Bob. "You mean to tell me you never snuck into a whorehouse alone before to get laid without any bullshit afterwards?"

Faking a laugh, he didn't want to bring up anything about sneaking into brothels. "What in the world does that mean? A banjo? Are you talking about *Deliverance*, the movie?"

"I know a place on the Wheeling Island we could go." He tossed another can out the window that clanked down the bank of the Irontown River. "You have to wear that collar?"

"Don't knock it. You'd be surprised how many women chase it." He tugged at the collar.

"Yeah, well women chase me too, usually with a bat in their hand." They laughed. "I'll buy you a shirt, a stupid polo shirt or something so you won't stick out so bad, Sugar Bear. Don't worry, we're just gonna have a few brews, nothing crazy."

He turned onto an old steel bridge that clanked as they drove across the river. Father Bob stared out the window at the muddy current as they approached the island. "Should we really buy me a shirt?"

"Yeah, no problem." He parked next to a meter, along a sidewalk with a row of shops. Father Bob got out of the truck and fumbled around in his pocket looking for loose change. "Don't worry, the meters shut down after six."

They walked into the Weis Men's Clothing Store, where an elderly salesman walked straight up to Father Bob. "Hello, I'm Morris. Looking for a shirt? You look like a large."

Morris didn't act like this was the first priest he'd ever served. Father Bob avoided eye contact and nodded yes. Barker insisted on paying for the red polo shirt. "Tonight's my treat." Father Bob didn't argue. He just wanted to get out of there before Morris might remember him.

Back in the truck he changed shirts behind the passenger side door, and they headed for the Elbow Inn. The red pad wrapped around the "L" shaped bar and made a sharp right turn along the back wall. Crowded with men, Barker found two open seats, next to each other. They plopped down and ordered two large drafts of Iron City beer, and two shots of Jack Daniels. Father Bob started to loosen up after the second round and began preaching to Barker about how humans create their own destiny, and how their thoughts manifest into physical reality. "We are all responsible for what happens in our lives," he said. "God guides us, but we have to make our choices." Barker listened. Then he poked Father Bob hard, in the middle of his chest with his index finger a few times.

"You wear that funny priest costume every day. Makes it a lot easier for you to say that shit." He pointed his thumb at his own chest. "I wear asbestos work clothes and a hard hat and sweat my ass working third-helper in the blast furnace, making pig iron every fuckin' day. You telling me that I create that hell?"

Both buddies paused, became silent, as the buxom, blonde waitress came into focus and served fresh drinks. Barker asked, "So I don't imagine you were able to do any more boxing in this whole priest thing you're in?

"Some older priests used to, but I don't know of any going on these days." He shook his head. "I wasn't very good at that either."

"Quit whinin', man. Create yourself a better mood." They both laughed and toasted drinks to being old friends. "It's really

41

great to see you after all these years," Father Bob was starting to feel much better. "It's just like when we were kids, taking up right where we left off."

Seven beers and shots later, they stumbled out of the Elbow Inn with their arms on each other's shoulders. Barker looked into his wallet. "I'm stoppin' at the Wishing Well for a quickie. You can hear my confession afterwards."

They laughed long and hard. Father Bob slurred his words. "I don't blame you. I wish I could too."

"C'mon, I'll buy. Nobody knows you down here."

He pictured the priest from back in that sex addiction therapy group, who'd admitted to sneaking into brothels. *How pathetic.* Father Bob only stayed in that therapy group to keep his priesthood, that's all. He never needed therapy. Having sex tonight would be the first relapse, though, after being celibate for over six months.

"I'll wait out here."

"Why?"

"Because I'm a priest." After a moment of silence they both started laughing.

"Just come and sit at the bar. They're not allowed to serve alcohol though."

"Why not?"

"It would bring too much heat, man."

Father Bob followed Barker into a well-lit room at the Wishing Well. Women dressed in lingerie filled the place. Two women holding drinks with tiny umbrellas immediately approached Barker.

"Who's your cute friend, Barker?" a petite brunette asked. She slid her arm around Father Bob's waist, grabbed his hand, and placed it upon her breast. He felt her softness and warmed his ribs by squeezing her against him. She looked up. "I have a special deal for you, cutie…twenty bucks for a half and half."

Barker stumbled up the narrow stairwell with his girl, and the other woman pulled Father Bob along. He tripped on the stairs and a voice inside of his head told him to leave before it was too late. *One's too many and a million's not enough. I shouldn't do this.*

In a small bedroom, the petite brunette filled a ceramic basin with water. "Let me see that thing, cutie. Whip it out, then hold this basin under it so I can wash it off, nice and easy, with warm soap and water."

He touched his cold belt buckle and became self-aware, as if watching himself from afar. Christ would decline the prostitute's offer and invite her into the Kingdom of Heaven. Father Bob was too drunk for that, spiritually impotent. He wanted the woman badly, yet he remembered making love to a distraught mother on the floor of the rectory at his previous parish. He felt the shame of the act, the humiliation of getting caught. Suddenly, he was sick to his stomach and muttered, "I can't." He pulled out his wallet and threw twenty bucks towards her, then hurried out the door and slid on his backside down half of the stairwell. Downstairs, he staggered through the room full of women and made it out onto the sidewalk. Once near the truck, he opened the door and the musty old smell pushed his nausea over the edge. He vomited there between the curb and the truck. Lying on the front seat of the truck, although sick, he was relieved that he didn't give in to the prostitute.

The sound of the truck door opening awoke him. He had no idea how late it might be. Barker moved him to where his head now leaned up against the passenger side window and pronounced, "Still a lightweight."

He opened one eye once in a while, focused on the shiny black river, which glistened from the industrial lights that fed from it. Train whistles howled and Barker stuck his head out the window once in a while, wailing along with them. Barker lit a joint, sweetening the air with the scent of marijuana, and turned up the cassette player, Deep Purple, "Smoke on the Water."

Finally, Father Bob sat up. A towering, blue flame that roared from a smokestack lit up the sky like the entrance to hell. "Welcome to Irontown, as Strong as Steel," a sign read. In the main hollow of town, Barker's two-story, brick box house sat next to a row of others much like it, within walking distance of the mill. A stagnant sulfur-laced cloud hovered over the slag dump in the humidity. The clanging of coupling train cars symphonized with shrills from the release of high-pressure steam in the mill. Barker lugged him up a few steps onto the front porch, through the house, and plopped him onto the couch. Father Bob groaned as his head hit a pillow. *He can bring me to the rectory in the morning.*

A few hours later, a telephone rang and woke Father Bob. Barker yelled from the other room, "Don't answer that! It's probably the mill calling me out to work."

He shuffled into Barker's kitchen and made a pot of coffee, head throbbing and stomach needing some food. When he opened the refrigerator door, he decided to pass on the milk and eggs and grabbed a plate of brownies. Barker must have scammed them from the reunion the other day. The brownies felt hard, probably stale, so he dunked them into his coffee.

"Holy shit!" Barker blurted out as he walked into the kitchen. He wore nothing but a pair of stained, once white boxer shorts. His long hair wrapped strands around his face.

"No kidding," Father Bob responded, "Rough night. I made some coffee. You've got to bring me back to the rectory. I have Mass pretty soon and my head's throbbing."

Barker laughed like a devil. "You shouldn't feel any pain pretty soon, bro."

"What do you mean?" Barker's arms, sleeved with blue tattoos, waved around like two snakes.

"I made those brownies with killer bud. They're potent, man. I only eat half at a time!"

"What! These are magic?" He threw a half-eaten brownie across the room. "That was my second one and I have to say Mass today!"

"You'll be one stoned preacher, my friend." Barker shrugged his shoulders. "I didn't tell you to eat them." He picked up the half brownie from the floor and chewed it. "Stick your fingers down your throat and puke them out."

Father Bob ran to the bathroom and retched into the toilet, which was rimmed with dotted splashes of dried brown. Barker's laugh resonated through the house. He wanted to wash, but there was no soap, only leaking water running down a rusty sink. He splashed his face but couldn't find a towel to dry it. He wished he were at the rectory. "You got to get me home!" he shouted.

"You're a pain in the ass, you know that? Give me a few minutes." Finally they climbed into Barker's old truck. He kept glancing at Father Bob. "You feel anything yet?"

"I haven't been stoned in so long, it's hard to say. My headache's going away though." He rubbed his eyes. His heart pounded with paranoia. *How can I say Mass? I might forget the words or start laughing or throw up in front of the entire congregation.*

"You'll be okay," Barker tried not to laugh.

"I suppose this is what I deserve. Today's a High Mass, which means the choir will be singing and the church will be full."

"I'd say it's going to be *high* all right. Your eyes are as red as roadmaps."

He put his face in his hands. "Oh God, what's wrong with me?"

Barker looked hurt. "Don't you remember who you're talking to? We did worse shit than this a hundred times. I can't even remember how many times we dropped acid. Shit, I don't even consider weed a drug."

"Yes, but I wasn't a priest then," he snapped, irritated that Barker didn't understand.

"Oh, I get it." Barker slammed hard through the gears. "All that shit you told me last night about creating a positive life with attitude? That was all bullshit?"

"Yes."

After a long pause, he started laughing. So did Barker. Before long, Barker pulled the truck over because he was laughing too hard to drive. Father Bob couldn't stop either. Tears rolled down his cheeks as the guffaws gained control of his psyche. The more he looked at Barker and the more he cackled, the higher his pitch grew, hopelessly out of control. He desperately opened the truck door, and knew that he had to step back into the priesthood.

"I'm walking the rest of the way up the Hill of Churches. Maybe it'll look like I've been jogging or something. Bark, you're dangerous!" Barker waved him off.

He tried to sneak through the alley between the rectory and the convent. He felt his collar in his pants pocket. *Thank God.* An elderly woman dressed in black approached from further down the alley.

Mrs. Hellinski lifted her veil and tried to straighten her crumpled neck. "Monsignor Murphy called me in to clean up Jack's mess. He had an accident on the living room rug." She shook. "You've got to at least take care of that dog, Father Santoro. Monsignor Murphy's getting dressed for Mass." She stared at his polo shirt, his face. "Good Heaven!" She tried to storm away, as if trying to run, but her worn legs couldn't move that quickly.

"I'm sorry, Mrs. Hellinski, it won't happen again," he said to her back as she stomped off. Getting admonished by her felt like a bad dream. He had no doubt about being stoned, though. He floated, tried to gather his thoughts. He crept into the kitchen, where Jack greeted him with enthusiasm. Monsignor Murphy walked in from the living room and just stood and stared. "You look disgusting."

He hung his head and ran one hand through his hair. "You don't have to dress for my Mass. I'll say it. You don't have to do it."

"I know what that polo shirt means. I wasn't born yesterday, you know." Murphy spoke through closed teeth. "You have vomit all over the bottom of your pants. Don't' let anybody see you."

Father Bob stood up from his chair, trying to look sober. "I'll take a shower and will be okay."

"I forbid you to say Mass in my church! You reek." His face flushed with anger. "I'll deal with you later. After Mass I'm going to the hospital. Don't leave this rectory." Murphy gave him the stare of a challenger. "You'd better listen to me."

The room started spinning. Father Bob sat down. "Maybe you're right, Monsignor." His heart raced. "I'd better go lay down." He stood up again, almost falling this time, and stumbled up the stairs straight to his bedroom. He sat on the edge of his bed, across from his reflection in the mirror, where his eyes looked like red slits, the red polo shirt was wrinkled and stained with vomit, and his black shoes and pants were sprinkled with specks. He peeled off his clothes and lay down in bed, Jack by his side. *I'm pathetic.*

As he lay there, a strange calm came upon him. He hadn't been stoned in a long time. His thoughts streamed. *What's the harm in letting loose once in a while? Eating Barker's brownies was an accident. At least I didn't have sex.* He had conquered the temptation. Passed the test. The image of the petite brunette burned into his memory, frightened him a little at first because of his battle with abstinence, but eventually she stirred the sexual part of his being. He hadn't masturbated in a long time. As the temptation grew, he heard a knock on the door down in the kitchen. Jack barked, jumped off the bed and flew downstairs. Father Bob rolled out of bed and threw on a clean black shirt and priest pants, without the white collar. The knock pounded louder. *Isn't everybody supposed to be at Mass?* He ducked into the bathroom and rubbed some toothpaste onto his teeth with his finger. Then he walked downstairs to answer the door, where he looked through the window and panicked. Is that the petite brunette? *Oh no, Maria.*

CHAPTER 4

THE TEMPTATION

Father Bob peered through laced drapes dressed over the kitchen door's window. A petite brunette stood before him. *Shouldn't she be at Mass?* He opened the door, unsure if Maria came to admonish him, like everybody else had this morning, or if she had news about Boss.

"Hello, come on in." He opened the door and stepped back. "How's Boss? Everything okay?"

"I don't know." She walked into the kitchen and sat down at the table. "I can't face all those people in church." She threw her tiny black-suede purse onto the table and sat with hands cupping her face, speaking through them. "Everybody in town knows about Boss and asks about him. I'm not used to people knowing my business like this anymore…I know that they stare at me, thinking I'm some derelict mother."

Father Bob leaned against the sink and ran a hand through his hair. He hoped that she would not recognize that he was stoned.

She looked up at him with despair, "My whole life's in shambles, and Boss is suffering the most. I'd give my life for him. How did I screw things up so bad?" As if on cue, Jack stood up and placed his front paws on top of her lap. She kissed the top of Jack's head and rubbed the side of his face.

Lord, give me the strength to overcome this buzz and administer to one of Your children. "I'll make us a fresh pot of coffee. But first, tell me, how's Boss?" *Geez, that's the last question she wanted to hear.*

"They should let him come home this afternoon." She looked up at his face and frowned. "You look tired, Bob. You sick or something?"

"I'll be fine." He turned around and looked through the cupboards, trying to find a clean coffee cup, then changed the subject back to Boss. "It's difficult raising children today. Not that I claim to know how to do it, but I've learned a few things, you know." He found two cups and set them on the table.

"Number one–you've got to take care of yourself first. Pray for the strength to love you, instead of beating yourself up. You're no good to Boss or anybody else without being kind to yourself." Sitting at the table across from her now, he locked onto her green eyes, turned his palm upwards and flipped out his pinky and ring finger. "Number two." His mind went blank. Lost his thought and had to make something up. "Don't blame yourself or anybody else. Blame creates a destructive energy, and it only causes resentment."

Maria seemed to pay attention, held in his gaze. He thought about how Maria's mother had abandoned her. She had never met her father, but her grandparents took her in, didn't miss a beat. Through hard work, they were better off than most folks in Irontown. Yet he felt her pain, knowing firsthand how the feeling of hitting bottom equalizes everyone.

"We had to leave Vegas," Maria didn't make eye contact any longer. "Me and Mario were partying every night. First we did coke together and then we started doing it by ourselves, you know, like hiding it from each other. My son ran loose on the streets as a youngster while we worked crazy hours in the casinos." Her green eyes widened like cat's eye marbles, but glazed with a look into the past. "There's no difference between night and day out on the strip. I know now that Boss partied as much as we did, I mean…weed, coke, pharmaceuticals, every-thing was available all the time. My God, I couldn't stop him, because I couldn't stop myself. He started doing drugs way early in life, kind of like you, only he had more around him than you did and I should have done something but didn't know what to do because I was in no shape…" She cocked her head sideways. "Are you sure you're all right?"

"Yes," he groaned. "Don't worry about me. Go on, talk."

"Well, like I told Monsignor Murphy, I had to leave Mario." Maria clenched her teeth and took on a menacing look in her eyes, like an opponent at the opposite corner of a boxing ring. "That bastard abused us, controlled us with money and threats and horrible things so I came back home to Grandma's for a while, you know, to feel safe and loved again and try to straighten our lives out. We're so lucky to have her." She pounded her fist onto the table. "And what happens? Boss OD's! All that crap we went through in Vegas, and he takes too many drugs here in fucking Irontown! I think Boss hates me for making him live with Mario for so long." She looked up and Father Bob wanted to touch her hand. Instead, he got up and grabbed the coffee pot and poured two cups, hands trembling when he poured Maria's.

He heard himself recite, "It's natural for Boss to harbor resentment over the divorce and the move and everything. That's a load of issues to deal with all at once." He placed the pot back on the burner and opened a cabinet, where he pulled out a bag of chocolate chip cookies. *These can't be spiked.* He thinly smiled while ripping open the top of the bag. Then he offered some to Maria after shoving a few into his mouth. She declined, tilted her head slightly sideways as if sensing that something was not quite right with him.

He chewed the cookies with a swig of coffee, like communion wafers with wine. "Sounds to me like you did the right thing, you know, getting out of that environment," he said through a mouthful of cookies, now sitting next to her. *Irontown was full of drugs too, she was just smart enough to not do them back in high school.* "Now you have the opportunity to rebuild. We can turn this trauma around." He clasped one hand over hers, gripped tightly, wanting to heal her. Silently he prayed, *Lord, let your healing grace flow through my hand and into Maria.* Then he spoke, "God is here with us in these difficult times, but we need to take action."

"I don't know what to do." She seemed puzzled and removed her hand from his grasp, then tapped the coffee cup with her long red nails, sounding like a mellow wind chime. "I've talked with Sister Roxanne a few times. She seems like the only woman I know who can think beyond hairdos and pedicures…and food." She snickered, "All everybody ever does around here is plan the grand meal of the day, and talk about work and what to eat tomorrow." They both nodded in agreement with half-smiles. Father Bob ate another cookie, himself wondering what dinner would be today, with Mrs. Hellinski having the day off.

As they drank coffee, Maria talked about some plans to move out west to Phoenix. He studied her lips, noticing how her lower lip curled each time she pronounced the letter "u." A tiny speck of glitter sparkled on the soft skin in her cleavage, between tender rounded mounds dusted in translucent fuzz. He had caressed those a long time ago, and moved his hand inside her bra. He couldn't stop remembering how he had slid his hand down the front of her pants, right on the couch in Grandma's living room. They were both in the eighth grade. Afterwards, he smelled sweet nectar on his fingers as he walked down to the pool hall to work as a rack boy for a quarter a rack for nine-ball games. If it were any other girl than Maria, he would have bragged to his friends about it. But she was special to him.

Maria interrupted his daydreams with a rise in her voice. "Are you listening, Bob?" He sat up in his chair, mumbled something affirmative.

She grimaced. "You aren't even listening to me." Maria stood up and her chair fell over backwards, hitting the floor with a cracking sound. "That's okay. I'm so damn exhausted. Sorry for rambling on and boring you." She walked toward the kitchen door, sounded ready to erupt into tears. "Don't worry. I won't take up any more of your time, Father Bob."

He got up and followed her, grabbing the back of her arm. "No, please, Maria, I'm listening, honestly! I was just remembering that's all. Please don't leave."

Maria tried to wriggle out of his grasp. He let go of her and she turned around, backed up a few steps.

Father Bob lifted his arms, turned both palms out towards her. "Okay, okay, I'm sorry. I didn't mean to upset you." His loins aroused. A part of him wanted to throw her down onto the floor and take her this very moment. She showed that expression of pout, just like when they used to make love to each other in their teens, after a fight or playful wrestling that escalated out of control. "Please," he said again.

Maria relaxed her stiffened shoulders a little.

"Good." He sighed, picking up the chair from the floor and holding it a little ways from the table. "Here, sit down," he said.

Maria stepped in close to him, her face inches from his chest. She looked up into his eyes and he wasn't sure if she was going to smack him or kiss him. So he just stood his ground. "I'm sorry," she said. "I know it's not your fault. I didn't mean to take everything out on you. I'm so tired." She leaned her forehead against his chest.

He stood still for a moment, afraid to grasp her with his arms though he wanted to pull her body tighter against his. Her nearness aroused him even more, and he feared she would feel his growing hardness against her. *I can't make the wrong move here.* The mere accusation of sexual misconduct would be the proverbial "final nail" in his priesthood.

Finally, he wrapped his arms around her, pulled her the rest of the way in, flush against his body. He bent his head down and smelled the luring scent of perfume in her hair. Her warm body pressed against his, promising to fill the void of human touch, inherent in the celibate priesthood. He lightly kissed the top of her head, his lips grazing her dark hair. Maria turned her face up to meet his. Their eyes locked. She looked as vulnerable and innocent as Sister Roxanne. He felt her chest take a breath against him as she sighed. Deliberately drifting his face closer to hers, he waited for a clue, something to tell him whether to proceed or back off. He moved his lips close to hers and then grazed her upper lip with his lower one in one soft stroke. They held tighter and then he kissed her, moving his lips gentle and slow. She tasted like tender delight…and then Jack the dog suddenly barked. It startled them. Maria jumped away, as though stung by something.

Father Bob's heart pounded with panic. *It's Murphy.* He quickly adjusted his groin to try and hide the evidence of his lust. Maria hurried towards the living room, fiddling with her hair as she passed. Jack jumped at the kitchen door, continued his frantic yapping, so Father Bob walked over and pulled the curtain aside. He glimpsed a black cat's tail as it jumped off the porch, then took a deep breath and was no longer aroused. He looked at Maria, who stood in the entry of the living room staring back at him. Speechless, he faked a nervous laugh. Maria smiled.

"Who was it?" She looked terrified.

"He shrugged his shoulders. "Just Jack barking at a cat."

She looked at the floor and shook her head. "Listen, this is the last thing that both of us need. I can't believe it. I'm so sorry, Bob, I should know better. I've got to get up to the hospital." She walked into the kitchen and grabbed a cylinder of lipstick from her purse, opening a small mirror. She applied a fresh coat of lipstick and rubbed her finger and thumb across the corners of her mouth to wipe up the excess. "Sister Roxanne is driving me up there after Mass."

Father Bob exhaled. *How can she bring Roxanne up to see Boss after what happened? Maybe the boy hadn't told her about seeing Roxanne naked.* "Maria, listen, please…just now, that was my fault, not yours." His body drained of energy and filled with exhaustion. "I made the move and honestly, I promise that I won't let it happen again."

Maria looked at him, composed and apparently recovered. "Let's just forget about it. I have more important things to worry about." She grabbed her purse. "Really, I need to go see my son."

51

"Yes, I suppose Mass is almost over." Father Bob took a deep breath. "Maybe I'll try to get up to the hospital to see Boss today, if that's all right." As much as he wanted to ask her if Boss talked about seeing Roxanne naked, he could not. Confession was confidential, despite his not feeling much like a priest.

"Oh, that'd be great." She walked towards the kitchen door and opened it, but stopped for one last look at him. "You know maybe Boss has a hard time relating to men on account of Mario."

Is she inviting me, or warning me? "Okay, well maybe I'll try and talk with him, if he wants to."

Maria walked out without saying goodbye. He watched her through the window, the way she moved swiftly through the alley alongside the convent. She'd always walked fast, way too fast for such short legs. *I can't fall for her again. She'll leave me in her wake.*

He poured himself a glass of water, downed it with one long gulp before pouring another. This glass he carried up the stairs to his bedroom and set it on the stand next to the bed. Jack had jumped onto the bed already, curled into a snug pile of black fur like a discarded shag carpet. Father Bob undressed to nudity, the way he always slept, and sat on the edge of his bed for a moment. He spoke to the crucifix nailed to the wall. "Do you still want me to serve You? What are You trying to tell me?" Confused, he crawled under the stiff white covers and muttered, "Your will be done," before he nodded out.

Father Bob jolted out of a sound sleep when Murphy tugged at his shoulders. Jack jumped off the bed.

"Wake up, son, we have work to do!" Monsignor Murphy shook him again. "C'mon, get up!"

He turned to where Murphy's face came into focus. "What time is it?" He wiped dried slobber that had formed a hard line that ran from the corner of his mouth to his chin, pulled it off his face like a thin piece of plastic.

"It's time to get up. One o'clock and I can't wait any longer," Murphy said impatiently. "I need you to drive me to the hospital. Hurry up and shower. I'll be in the kitchen."

Father Bob coughed and rubbed his face with both hands. The room reeked of alcohol. He wasn't sure if from him or Murphy. Eventually, he shuffled into the shower where the warm water splashed down upon him and cleared his head. He made a deal with himself to never carry on again like last night, or this morning. *Forgive me, Lord.* He thought about being a man first, a priest second. *I cannot let things escalate with Maria. God, grant me the grace and strength to administer to Your flock.* He could feel his spirit start to rise from the canvas, getting ready for the next round. He brushed his teeth, spit out the remaining memories of overindulgence, combed his hair and strapped on the white collar. *What's Murphy's hurry?*

He walked downstairs into the kitchen, went straight for the coffee. Ham roll-ups, arranged in perfect rows on a plate, lay on the middle of the table next to a bottle of scotch. He plopped down in a chair across from Monsignor Murphy.

Murphy picked up the scotch and poured a little into Father Bob's coffee. "This will help you feel better." Father Bob sat quiet and obedient. "I need you to drive me up to the hospital." Murphy looked away. "It's time to give Stabo the 'Rites of the Dying and the Sick.' His heart was too weak for surgery, so they didn't' transport him to Pittsburgh."

Before he could respond, Murphy raised his hand up to quiet him. "Stabo's family is bed side. I want you to bear witness in there with me." Murphy locked his eyes onto his. "Stabo's my best friend on earth. Like an angel sent from God to me, probably made me a better priest. Now, God is taking him back."

Father Bob didn't know what to say. He envisioned Murphy and Stabo driving down to Wheeling, slamming shots, laughing like regular guys like he and Barker did last night. He took a sip of coffee. Murphy continued to stare at him. "I need you to be a priest," he said sternly. "Understand?"

He nodded his head, stood up and placed the plate of ham roll-ups into the refrigerator without eating one. He tugged at the tightness of his collar around his neck before following Murphy out the kitchen door.

CHAPTER 5

EXTREME UNCTION

Father Bob drove the twisty road alongside Deer Creek at the bottom of Coal Run Hollow. The creek's chime echoed off of the few cement walls erected to support small bridges. These bridges arched the running water and led off to rows of houses perched on small flats. Some of the houses were made of sturdy red brick, with porches and meticulous yards where cutouts of wooden children wearing Dutch shoes stood like statues in the grass. A few small decaying shacks sat amidst the better houses, and all properties had gravel driveways that either led to front yard parking or slag parking pads. He could almost see again the deer of November, where the animals would be gutted and hung from trees to bleed and cool, like trophies on display for neighbors to admire.

Monsignor Murphy stared out the passenger window into the wooded hill on the other side. Father Bob tried to engage him in conversation, maybe divert some of the worry he sensed. "Do they still hunt deer and hang them from the trees around here?"

Murphy grabbed hold of his arm, almost pulling it from the steering wheel. "I've never seen him sick, or even weak in the thirty-some years I've known him. You know, son, Stabo tried everything he could to save your father."

Father Bob clenched his teeth and pulled his arm out of Murphy's grasp. *Please don't tell me that story again, where each time you and Stabo become bigger heroes. I'll turn this car right into the creek!*

"You have your father's blue northern-Italian eyes," Murphy nodded, "Always did, even when you were only three-years-old, when I first saw you at his funeral."

"Yes, I know, I've been told that before." He grimaced and tried to change the subject, "I've never had to give the

Anointing of the Sick to a personal friend. How do you manage your emotions?"

Murphy again ignored the question. "I'll never forget the day Stabo called me from the slag dump, right after he called the ambulance. He was the first one to find your dad. He yelled at me over the phone, 'Santo Santoro's squashed in between the coupling of train cars!' I told him I'd be right there."

Father Bob purposely ran over a deep pothole, jolting the two priests in the front seat. Murphy bounced up, almost hitting his head on the Lincoln's ceiling. "Take it easy, son. I just had these wheels aligned!" He cleared his throat. "Anyway, when I got there, Stabo told me there was no way we could get your father out. The trains coupled together were the only things keeping his body together. Stabo stood right next to me while I administered the Anointing of the Sick to your father. He was still alive, your dad, and tried to make the sign of the cross, but couldn't move his hand high enough to touch his forehead. I did it for him." Father Bob ran the car slightly off the road to miss a couple of black turkey vultures feasting on some road kill. One front wheel skidded in the gravel before he regained control.

Murphy, oblivious, continued. "Stabo and I watched your father breathe his last breath."

Father Bob sped up, wanting to get to the hospital. Murphy's voice sounded scratchy, like he needed to clear his throat. "I remember how they uncoupled the train cars and Santo's body twisted one full turn before crumpling to the ground. His blue eyes remained wide open." Murphy choked up. "Stabo hugged me, thanked me, and took care of the crucial business afterwards. I think we've been inseparable ever since."

Father Bob pulled into the parking lot of Trinity Hospital, said nothing, but ached to ask, "Did my father ever mention anything about me as he lay dying or did he only care about the guys at work?" He vaguely remembered his father hugging people and laughing, and wished that he could remember more. He struggled with his seat belt then leaped from the confines of the car, almost like being trapped between two train cars himself. Finally he opened the door, stood, and took a deep breath of air.

He followed Murphy into the hospital and through the corridors to the intensive care ward, where Stabo lay motionless in bed, uncharacteristically vulnerable. His wife Carla sat bedside with her son, Johnny. It was the first time he'd seen Stabo without hearing some insult from his lips. Stabo always greeted people with the wit of a rattling, baritone voice. Father Bob felt nothing but indifference, the opposite of love, for Stabo, one of the last men to see his father alive. *There's the man who harassed me my entire childhood, always said that I'd end up in prison.* Today, as the son of Santo, he found it bitterly ironic to stand alongside Monsignor Murphy watching Stabo die.

Nevertheless, Stabo's gaunt appearance shocked him. Several tubes protruded from his body, most notably the oxygen strap under his nose. His eyelids twitched when Carla tried to stand, a look of terror on her face, as the priests positioned themselves around the bed. They both wore black with white collars, an echo of the roadside vultures. Murphy hurried over and hugged her before she could rise completely. He gently guided her back into the chair. Then Murphy whispered something into her ear and the worn wrinkles in her face shook as she nodded. Murphy adjusted his black biretta and shook the hand of Stabo's son, Johnny, "Little Stabo," the forty-three-year-old steelworker who looked more like Stabo's twin than his son. He was about ten years older than Father Bob and they had never really talked to each other before.

"Thanks for coming," Little Stabo said, sounding just like his father with his rattling voice. He had inherited his father's body type as well, the square face and barrel torso. Little Stabo smiled and nodded in reverent acknowledgement. Father Bob remained standing at the foot of the bed with his hands together in praying position. He returned Little Stabo's nod, and remained quiet. The beeps of monitors and hissing of sucking air gave off the only sounds in the room, Stabo's final industrial noise.

Father Bob couldn't shake the shadow of his father, as he watched Monsignor Murphy now engaging in an older version of the "Rites of the Dying and the Sick." Murphy dipped his thumb into a small bowl of oil, and his hand shook as he gently grazed Stabo's ears, eyelids, nose, and the tip of one hand while chanting, "Through this holy unction and His own most tender mercy may the Lord pardon thee whatever sins or faults thou hast committed, *quidquid deliquisti,* by sight, by hearing, smell, taste, touch, walking, carnal delectation…"

What's he doing now? Murphy added the ancient anointment of the loins, where he lifted up the white sheet and put his hand under, a rite rarely done in the West, and never on women. Father Bob's knee banged on the steel bed frame as he stretched to watch this portion of the ancient ritual, a part of the ceremony eliminated because of disputes over such private exposure. Carla and Little Stabo glanced at him for a moment, before returning their attention to Stabo.

Next, Murphy laid a small, white cloth on a table near the head of the bed as he maneuvered around the tubes and medical monitors. He slid open the boxed "Crucifix-Sick Call Set," provided by Carla. The actual crucifix slid from the top, leaving a hollowed box in the frame of a cross, which stored candles, cotton, a small bottle of holy oil, and a note of instruction. He placed the cross into a slot at the top of the box's base. Then he inserted two small candles into the candleholders. He looked at Little Stabo. "I need a half glass of water and a spoon," he whispered. Though his hands still shook, he had a calm, stoic look on his face. Carla pointed to the table beside her, her mouth quivering, eyes filled with tears. Little Stabo grabbed the glass and spoon, already prepared by Carla, and handed it across Stabo's body to Murphy who unraveled the white communion cloth and twisted off the cap of a small bottle of holy water.

In anticipation of the Sacrament of Extreme Unction, Carla had placed a small plate with salt and some soft cotton onto the table, next to another plate containing crumbs of bread. *Rituals give people something to occupy themselves, a distraction for temporary comfort.* Monsignor Murphy said more prayers, inserted some Latin phrases, and dipped the cotton into the holy water while making small signs of the cross on Stabo's forehead.

Candles flickered while Murphy pressed his wet thumb into the breadcrumbs and barely grazed Stabo's lips with the Oration of the Eucharist. Murphy remained expressionless, focused on his duties. When Father Bob saw Carla trying not to weep, a lump of sorrow suddenly crept into his throat. Struggling to remain detached and professional like Murphy, he turned his gaze from Carla to Little Stabo, who bowed his head and grimaced.

Then he imagined Stabo watching Murphy when he administered the Anointing of the Sick to his own father. As much as he tried to bury the image, he felt for the first time in his life a portion of how Stabo and Murphy must have felt, and most frightening, wondered at what his father felt. He found himself fighting back tears, not so much for Stabo since anger and sorrow bite each other, but tears that rose from the family's grief, the reality of Murphy's mortality, and something else deep inside of his own soul that he couldn't identify.

Monsignor Murphy looked over and noticed his unsettled expression. He whispered, "I'm going to stay with the family. Go make your rounds, administer to the sick. Don't worry about me, I'll find a ride home."

Father Bob couldn't wait to escape. *Why am I so emotional?* He poured the sign of the cross over the entire family. "Lord, bring us to salvation, in the name of the Father, Son, and Holy Spirit, amen." Carla lifted her limp hand towards him, and he leaned over to grab it, lightly kissing the top of it. He patted Little Stabo on the shoulder and departed the intensive care room with hunched shoulders. Trying to look as meek as possible while the emotional toil inside him was growing, he looked straight down the hall towards the bathroom door, yet tears started to come. Inside the bathroom he hid in a stall, where he locked the door shut. Sitting on the toilet lid, sobbing with his head in his hands, he was as alone as Jesus in the Garden of Gethsemane. He mourned for a father he barely remembered and a mother he had never met. He tried to breathe and wondered if Santo thought about him during his final moments. *My dad would never know how I struggled my way through life to become a priest.* Moments later, he pulled himself together and stood up. Then he opened the door to the stall and quietly closed it on his way to the sink, where he washed his face. *Some doors should remain closed.*

His confidence started to build the further away he walked from Stabo's ICU room, pulling strength from the feeling of walking the streets as a kid, ready for anything. He summoned the Holy Spirit, rose from the canvas. *I'll bring salvation to those in need.* He stepped straight towards Boss's room, suddenly aware that he'd been strutting.

In the bright room, Boss raised his eyebrows at him. He sat upright in his bed, eating the hospital version of sliced roast beef on white bread next to a scoop of whipped potatoes, topped with brown gravy.

"Hi, Father." Boss said, dropping his fork onto the tray.

Father Bob felt that spiritual glow emanate from his eyes. He took the food tray and slid it away from the bed before placing his healing hand on Boss's arm. Boss didn't flinch this time. "You are loved, son, by many people. Our Lord is by your side."

Boss looked straight into Father Bob's eyes. "It's not what you think, Father."

"It's okay, son. Sometimes we can find inspiration in tragedy, like falling through a trap door into a better world." He paused, thought of what else to offer, then said, "God gave us life as the greatest gift of all...We lose out when we don't see it."

Boss frowned. "I didn't try to kill myself! I don't care what they say. All I was doing was getting high, that's all." He wrapped his arms across his chest.

"That's okay, Boss. But think...See how you could have died?" He noted the sullen look on Boss's face, saw him withdraw, so he stopped himself. He hated these adult lectures when he was a kid. "The main thing is that you still have the gift of life."

Boss shrugged his shoulders. "Then why's my life so screwed-up? I'm always alone and I have to protect my mom."

Before he could respond, Maria walked into the room, with Sister Roxanne trailing her. Maria gave him a quizzical look, and he smiled long at Sister Roxanne.

She smiled at Boss, "I'm so glad to see you looking better. You scared us!"

Boss looked away at the television set, which was playing a Pirate's baseball game. Maria bent down and hugged Boss for an awkwardly long time. She avoided eye contact with Father Bob. He wondered if she'd heard what Boss had just said. Her dark hair shined in the light. Even in this setting, she stirred something in him. He suddenly wanted to unhook his collar. After a few moments, Maria stood up and composed herself, purposefully falling into her façade of familiarity—the perky, petite brunette bubbling with wit.

"I just visited the Stabo's," Sister Roxanne said to Father Bob, now unfazed from the death scene and strong again. "They're taking Stabo's dying pretty hard." She cocked her head sideways. "How's Monsignor Murphy handling this? I know they're best friends."

He loved the soft tone of Sister Roxanne's voice, and answered, "It's strange. I've never seen him so moved and...tender, I mean, usually he's so stoic. I've always thought of him as solid as a rock." He shook his head. "That man's as strong in his faith as anybody I've ever seen."

"Hmmm," said Sister Roxanne. "I guess I haven't known him as long as you." She smiled. He moved closer to her, about to say something...

Maria bulled in between them. "C'mon you guys, coffee's on me," she interrupted, perhaps wanting to escape the room the way Father Bob wanted to escape Stabo's. She gave him a quick glance from head to toe, but kept a safe distance. He grinned as she smiled with white, straight teeth bordered by red lips. Her penetrating green eyes rarely blinked, even when her black bangs bounced around them. *She's toying with me, yet always acts perky when avoiding things.*

"We'll be right back, honey," Maria said to Boss, who ignored all of them pretending to focus on the baseball game. "Do you want anything from the cafeteria?"

"No," he said, without looking away from the television.

The three of them walked down the hallway towards the cafeteria. Father Bob strode behind and Maria chatted, but not as blithely as usual. Roxanne put her arm around Maria for a moment, and he wondered how they could have bonded so soon. He felt drawn to these lovely women. *Why do I feel this way Lord? Why is it a sin to do what makes us happy?*

Monsignor Murphy came out of the same bathroom where Father Bob had just cried. He saw Murphy fiddle with the inside pocket of his black jacket and figured it with his flask. Murphy walked stiffly towards them in the hallway, trying to move more quickly than his body could handle. He looked at Maria smiling and then at Father Bob and seemed irritated. "Greetings," he said to Sister Roxanne and Maria as he passed them "Excuse me," as he grabbed Father Bob's arm by the bicep and pulled him downward to where their faces came to within inches of each other. "Before you go off on another one of your parties, there's some priest work that needs done." Murphy jerked his head toward Maria, pointedly, and then back at him. *This can't be happening.* Sister Roxanne and Maria paused and turned around to look. Maria's eyes widened momentarily, but Sister Roxanne just looked thoughtful. *She's not one to get caught up in other people's drama.* The two women walked along towards the cafeteria, leaving him behind. Murphy's cheeks shook while he continued through clenched teeth.

"Listen to me now. A young couple are burying their newborn this afternoon. They couldn't afford a funeral and so are down at the county cemetery right now." His face flushed, shook even more. "A damn gravedigger called the hospital asking if somebody could lend them a preacher. They're not Catholic, we don't know what denomination they are, but they're in need, so you take the car and get down there right away!"

Father Bob tried to make sense out of this situation. He wanted to yell back at Murphy, tell him to never reprimand him in public. How was he supposed to know somebody was looking for a minister? He took the keys from Murphy's hand, nodded, then left without a word or eye contact. Maria and Roxanne were long gone. *I need to keep calm—Murphy's hurting but I have to move on.*

In the car driving madly, he muttered, "I hate this bullshit," to the air. The asphalt road along twisting, green hills curled its way down to the county cemetery, home of the poor and forgotten. *What a depressing place. I never had to deal with an impromptu burial before.* He was used to the confines of the church altar and the hospital, those safe havens that brought newness to his day within the routine of familiar surroundings where friends and staff treated him with reverence. The fighter inside him kicked and screamed in rebellion. *I don't want to do this!*

He pulled in along the narrow road, parked alongside a chain-link fence, and turned off the engine, then just sat there for a second. No other cars were around, only a man and woman standing among the tiny blocks of rectangular, gray stones. The headstones were perched about two inches higher than the unkempt grounds, where brown dirt and a few patches of wilted weeds adorned the dead. As he approached the couple, who stood as still as statues and stared at a fresh mound of ground, he could tell they were young, babies themselves. The boy's T-shirt resembled a junkyard worker's, graying white, pocked with small holes, while the girl's oily, long blonde hair hid her face as she hung her head. An occasional tear dripped from her, and she wiped her nose with her pale wrist. *She can't even afford a handkerchief.*

"Hello, I'm here to help," he said and pressed his own handkerchief into her hand. She didn't look up. The boy shook his hand, giving him a look of appreciation mixed with devastation.

They stood a while in silence, gazing at the fresh grave. He would not ask either of them if they belonged to a church. Again confronted with the look and feel of sorrow, he improvised a prayer, "Our Holy Mother mourned the loss of her son, Jesus, but found comfort in the faith of knowing He was in heaven, living the promise of eternal life." The look on the couples' faces did not change. He knew he fell short...so he sprinkled the marker and surrounding ground with a small bottle of holy water and then stood with the couple in silence. *Lord, give me the grace to comfort this young couple.*

They stood motionless, heard a wind whipping through, bringing cool, gray clouds with the start of a light drizzle. He too felt the wind and rain, while time, whether thirty seconds or thirty minutes, passed without meaning. Finally the young mother looked up into his eyes, tears dripping off of her chin, yet appearing for a moment filled with compassion, as if she were his own young mother sensing his confusion. Nothing was spoken as he locked eyes with her and entered into a portion of her remorse. He felt warmth in his chest from her eyes, a young soul transformed in his eyes into the Holy Mother. He wished he could work a miracle for her, raise her infant from the dead, but his knees almost buckled in weakness. As the young mother hugged him, Father Bob sobbed uncontrollably, suddenly afraid to let go of her and face her husband. The young man tugged on his shoulder. "Thank you for coming, Father. We better get going." Father Bob could only nod. The boy put his arm around his wife and they walked towards the gravel road that led out the gate. He wanted to ask if they needed a ride, but couldn't speak.

He stood there in the rain. *I didn't even want to come here, and yet this is my job.* He had no parents to cry for him, and these parents no longer had a child to love. *Have I helped them? What kind of priest am I, Lord? This is the real world, not the academic world of Father Callo's, but a sacred sighting. Here I look into the poorest of the poor and feel the very eyes of the Virgin Mary, and I fall apart...*He sighed, and walked towards the car. He had to pick up Murphy.

When he pulled into the hospital parking lot again he sat in the Lincoln and reflected. *How could I be angry with Murphy?* He was the only person outside of his now deceased aunt who'd ever cared about him. Murphy rescued him from the drugs, alcohol and gambling of Irontown, and gave him a place of solace when he had nobody left. He loaned him his couch to sleep on, taught him how to box and steered him into a vocation, the only family he'd ever found. *I must rise up against the pleasures of the flesh and find humility in my mission.*

He walked into the hospital and down the hall where a slew of workers wearing white smocks scurried about. They were wheeling Stabo's body now shrouded in a sheet on a cart. Murphy stood in the doorway of the room, where the Stabos talked with a hospital official. When he spotted Father Bob, he came out into the hall.

"Did you find the couple at the cemetery?"

He nodded yes. "Monsignor, it was one of the most touching events I've ever witnessed. I felt the light of the Holy Spirit and presence of Mother..."

Murphy interrupted, "Yes, and you're all wet...must be raining. How about driving me back to the rectory? There's nothing more we can do here. Stabo's funeral will be next Saturday, after a three-day viewing."

"Certainly, Monsignor." Once again, his spiritual high smacked the ground. The two men hurried through the rain to get the car. Murphy winced in pain when he plopped into the passenger-side seat. Once they drove out of the parking lot, Murphy reached into his jacket and removed a silver flask, then took a healthy swig. He held the flask out to him, while a dribble of liquid leaked out of the corner of his mouth.

Father Bob figured he could use a drink and took the flask, holding it up in one hand with a flourish. "To Stabo!" He took a swig. "From the Godfather and his son." The toast was superficial, obligatory, but it made Murphy smile and for a moment, Father Bob too. They passed a cop on the road when he turned a corner, the flask still balanced in his hand against the steering wheel. *And I tried to stop Barker from drinking while driving the other night.*

"I miss that old bugger already," Murphy said. "He teased you a lot, but I'm one of the very few people who knew the real Stabo. Trust me. He loved but just didn't know how to express it. He told me many times that your father and mother must be very proud of you, from up in heaven. 'Up in heaven' he always said. I loved to ask him how he knew heaven was up. He'd point to the ground and say, 'cause there's nothing but slag heaps and coal mines down there!'"

Murphy smiled, and looking out the window into the woods, pulled the flask out of Father Bob's hand with his head still turned towards the woods. He took a healthy swallow. "One time, Stabo jumped off the dock, into the half-frozen Irontown River to save a coal handler who fell in during a job. A few weeks later, the coal handler, I forget his name, went to the slag dump to thank Stabo and had to run for his life because Stabo wanted to beat him up! Stabo yelled, 'I almost drowned trying to save your dumb ass!' He sure was one of a kind."

"I wish I could have talked to him about my father, but being around Stabo was always embarrassing for me." He pulled into St. Anne's parking lot.

"I know." Murphy nodded. "I think that in some way Stabo felt responsible for the accident with your father. He acted like everybody's protector, like he was Michael the Archangel." Father Bob winced.

Murphy got out of the car near the rectory's front door while Father Bob drove off to park. Then he strolled towards the alleyway between the rectory and the convent. The rain slowed to a light drizzle through the gray sky. A figure of a woman, in a long black dress with a black scarf over her head, approached him.

"Good evening Mrs. Hellinski. Rather drab weather, don't you think?" Father Bob said.

Crack! She slapped him across the face with a force he hadn't felt since his boxing days. He reeled back, holding his cheek and his temper. "I know what happened in the rectory kitchen this morning. I'm not as stupid as you think!" Spittle shot out with her words, "You're still that hooligan running the streets. I knew you wouldn't change. I never understood what good Monsignor Murphy ever saw in you." He read fire in her eyes. "After all that man has done for you you'd better not even think about bringing scandal to St. Anne's. You'll regret it so help me God! You do no good for anyone in this town." She galumphed away, making unidentifiable squeals.

He stood there in shock and watched her silhouette flee with amazing quickness toward her car in the parking lot. He shouted. "What do these people want from me? I've given my entire life and have no possessions, not even a car! I'm sorry if I'm human!" He slammed the kitchen door in the rectory and stormed up the stairs to his room, past Murphy who already sat at the kitchen table. Murphy ignored him. He was looking at what appeared to be a hand-written note.

Upstairs, he grabbed Jack's leash. Monsignor Murphy tried to show the note to him when he came back down into the kitchen, but he stomped past without looking at him.

"What's the matter with you?"

"I don't know what these people want from me. I'm going downtown to find out!" He strapped the leash onto Jack, who wagged in bliss. "Don't wait up," he said on the way out the door.

Jack trotted ahead of him down the Hill of Churches in the light rain. Father Bob rubbed his stinging cheek as he hoofed towards the steel mill. Smokestacks steamed even more heavily because of the rain. The scene pulled some stress from his chest. The downtown area of Irontown stretched for one long street, part of which served as a gateway for steelworkers to enter the mill. In this mill town, eight bars lined the street, along with three barbershops, two bookie joints, and one pool hall. A laundromat, bank, grocery, drug and hardware store squeezed into the remaining space.

He looked through the open door of a popular bar, "The Argonaut," before entering it. Laughter and loud rumblings from human figures, barely visible through the smoke filled room, brought back feelings of intimidation he'd conquered as a street-running child. He'd beaten those same inferior feelings when he first entered the society of priests as well. A song blared from the jukebox, "Fire," by the Ohio Players. He'd been in town almost two weeks, and this was the first time he'd been down here. *I'm not supposed to go in there.* He walked in with Jack on the leash.

"Son of a bitch!" A large man in a flannel shirt lifted him into a bear hug and turned a small swirl. Jack barked and tried to bite him, but Father Bob pulled back on the leash in the nick of time. "I'm buying you a drink, brother." Pumpkin yelled for everyone to hear, "Hey everybody, it's Father Bob come down to hang with the mill hunkys!"

He hadn't seen Pumpkin since his being drafted into the war with Vietnam. But he'd heard how Pumpkin loved combat, called it the ultimate hunting experience.

All sorts of remarks flew through the air. "Hey Padre!... Father Bob!...Yo Bear, where'd you buy that collar!" He couldn't recognize half of these folks. They had aged hard the past fourteen years. *Well, they sure seem to recognize me.*

Barker bulled his way in front of him. He grabbed "Weed," a thin but wiry steelworker, by the back of the shirt and pulled him clean off the barstool. "Sit down Padre! Good to see you again. Shit, it's been what, almost a whole day?" Barker's drunken laugh stirred the crowd into random laughter. He was shocked by the way Barker manhandled the barstool's occupant. "I'm the thumper around here," explained Barker, eyeing the guy sitting next to Weed. Father Bob recognized Santé Fe, a kid from his youth who shot heroin daily. *Still alive.* Santé Fe quickly got up from his barstool and scurried away without a word. Barker plopped down onto it and yelled at the bartender, "Wolf! Two Blue Ribbons and shots of Jack!"

"So, do I need to ask, what's a thumper?" He had to shout over the music and crowd noise.

"I keep the peace. You know, if these numb nuts start fighting, I end it. Twist heads. It keeps me drinking for free."

Inverted shot glasses piled up in front of him, representing purchased rounds of drinks from excited patrons. He slammed a shot with Pumpkin. *I have to be careful.* The hoopla of his presence in the bar slowly died down. The song, "Roxanne" by the Police now blared. He leaned close to Barker's ear.

"I saw Maria this morning. Does she ever come down here?"

"I seen her in here a couple of times. Why? You lookin' to tap dat ass, *father?*"

"C'mon, Bark. Why do have to talk to me like that?"

"I'm just sayin'. She's pretty hot. Don't pass it."

"That's not what I mean. I just wonder what's going on with her and her son, you know, what are you hearing?"

"Hah! That kid's a loser. So is she. She might even have been a whore up in Vegas."

Father Bob suddenly stood up from his barstool, steaming. "I should have known better than to come down here."

"Settle down man. I heard that Mario guy used to pass her around to pay-off favors. What do you care anyway, ain't you some kind of faggot nowadays? Shit, you ran out of that whorehouse screamin' like a little girl."

Barker leered at him. Rage flushed Father Bob's face with heat and he couldn't take it anymore. The emotional roller coaster of the day erupted into this moment of pure instinct. He twisted on the balls of his feet and turned his hips into a perfect left hook, his fist snapping like the end of a bullwhip, just like Monsignor Murphy taught him many years ago during Golden Glove training. He landed his knuckles smack onto Barker's cheekbone. The cracking sound made the bar patrons take full notice. It fell quiet. Barker buckled backwards, down to the floor. When Barker started to climb up onto his hands and knees, Father Bob pulled him by the back of his shirt and belt. He ran, Jack nipping and barking as if urging him on, sliding Barker along the narrow space before falling through the open door onto the sidewalk. The two men skidded along the sidewalk, slick with wet graphite dust, byproduct of molten steel that filled the air and dusted the windowsills.

Dazed now Father Bob started to stand. *I can't believe this.* Wheels screeched. Then he heard the yelp of a dog. A coal truck slowed, almost stopped, but the driver grinded gears and resumed rolling down the street. He was horrified.

"Jack! Jack, my boy!" He ran into the street, dropped to his knees and picked up his dog. Jack was no longer breathing, but smashed and bleeding. "Oh my God. God in heaven, No!"

Whap! The sound from the heel of Barker's boot striking him on the side of his left eye socket sounded like a shovel smacking mud. He went numb. Then he crumpled onto the street like a pile of rags, next to his dead dog.

He couldn't get up, then heard Barker's panhead chopper fire-up and rumble away. He must have faded in and out of consciousness, because he was vaguely aware of people standing around him mumbling, two of them policemen.

*   *   *

At three o'clock in the morning, Monsignor Murphy drove him back from the ER to the rectory. Father Bob slumped in the passenger seat, ailing. Murphy looked straight ahead at the road and said, "I never thought you'd make it through the seminary. When you proved me wrong, I marveled at God's miracle. Figured He had a higher purpose for you. Now I can't see anything but one big mistake."

Father Bob hung his head in silence. He could feel Murphy turn his head and look at him. "We'll need to see the Bishop for legal consultation and control of media release. You've been cited with misdemeanor charges of assault and disorderly conduct." He looked up, and Murphy glared blankly at him, and then turned his head away. "I had to wake the Bishop."

The rest of the drive home was silent. When they pulled up in front of the rectory, Murphy finally looked at him again. His face was unkind, hard. "You're on your own this time. I'm washing my hands of you."

Chapter 6

Conditional Love

Father Bob's own snoring woke him from a deep sleep. The left side of his head throbbed. He slid his hand above his eye and found lumps. *Oh Lord, what a night.* He wanted to lie there longer, but had to see how his eye looked, so he covered his nakedness with a short robe and shuffled down the hallway towards the bathroom where he inspected the blood-filled eye in the mirror. Although bruised around the edges, he could see just fine. He turned on the tap and splashed his face with water, reciting his morning prayer from a card adhered to the bottom corner of the mirror. *"Good morning, God, and thank you for the glory of the sun, and thank you for the health I have to get my duty done. I know there have been many days that I have whiled away...."* A door slammed downstairs, most likely Monsignor Murphy coming back from saying daily Mass. He tiptoed back to his bedroom, where he stood momentarily, searching the room. Empty. Where's Jack? Then he heard again the squeal of tires and Jack's last yelp. He sat on the edge of the bed staring at the crucifix on the wall. Tears welled. *I lost my best friend.*

The pitch of a woman's voice echoed from down in the kitchen. He could barely hear the conversation coming from downstairs, so he crawled out of the bedroom to the top of the stairwell, where he leaned back onto his haunches with his head close to the floor like a dog stalking its prey. The smell of coffee made his mouth water. *Maybe I'll go down there.* First he would eavesdrop on the conversation. The woman's voice sounded familiar. He listened more closely. *What's Maria doing here?*

"Thank you," Maria was saying. "So he's going to be all right?"

"Yes, he'll be fine." Murphy cleared his throat. "Sometimes I forget how fast news travels around this town. He's a little bruised up, that's all."

"I'm so mad at Barker, and all those downtown guys. I mean, can't they at least take care of one of their own? And that poor dog…are you sure there's nothing I can do to help?"

"Yes…I mean no. There's nothing you can do but pray for him. Pray for us all." Chairs slid across the floor, squealing. "Thanks for your concern, Maria. We'll let you know if we need anything."

"Okay, but please tell him we care and tell him Boss is home from the hospital. And, oh yes, we're not going to do the counseling program."

"I'm sorry to hear that, but thank you, dear. Give my love to Grandma Amelia."

When the door closed, Father Bob crept back into his bedroom and dressed into his black priest garb, except for the white-collar tab, which he couldn't find. His head throbbed and he held onto the railing during his sluggish walk down the stairs and into the kitchen. *Oh no, didn't know Hellinski was here too, should've stayed in the bedroom longer.* They glanced at each other briefly, and then looked away in silence. He stood facing the countertop and poured a cup of coffee.

"Well, if it isn't Rocky Balboa," Murphy said while adjusting his chair. "I think you're too old at thirty-three to make a comeback."

He turned around and sat down with his coffee, across from Murphy. "Don't worry. I'm not very good at it. Just like I'm not very good at being a priest these days."

"Humph," Mrs. Hellinski mumbled. She dropped a plate of scrambled eggs onto the middle of the table and stomped quietly towards the kitchen door, walking out without saying goodbye.

Murphy pulled the eggs towards him and scooped some onto his plate. "Your eye doesn't look too bad. How you feeling?"

He bit his lower lip, shrugged his shoulders. "I don't know." Jack would have been right against his knees. He choked up. "I feel so awful about Jack."

"Yes, but that's the least of your problems," Murphy said in a disgusted tone. He stood up, walked to the cabinet and retrieved his bottle of scotch. He splashed some into his cup of coffee and sat with the bottle on the table. Father Bob slid his cup over for a topping as well. "One thing you have going for you is that the police aren't going to file any charges. They really don't want to bring criminal charges against my priest and nobody from that bar will tell them exactly what happened anyway." He flipped his palm into the air in front of him. "You know your street buddies and their sacred code and all that stuff."

"Well, that helps, I guess." He sipped some coffee, puzzled by how Murphy appeared more aloof than angry. "What about the Bishop? Have you heard from him yet?"

"Of course I did. About three times since three o'clock this morning." Murphy raised his eyebrows. "He wants to sit down with you, soon. What else? You've been down this road with the Bishop before, what, six months ago?"

He knew all too well how Bishop Malone dealt with rogue priests. There's nothing more to it, a fight in a bar, that's all. "Oh, yea, this will be my second sitting before the grand Bishop Malone." He looked for a rise from Murphy, some reaction, but received nothing except the slurping sound of an old man eating scrambled eggs. "I don't know what to say. I'll do whatever he says, go wherever God sends me." Still he got no reaction from Murphy. "Everytime somebody in the vocation goes through crisis, all the Bishop does is reassign them to some other town, or send them to rehab. I was just in rehab and can't see much sense in going back."

Murphy set down his fork and leaned back in the chair. "What are we supposed to do with a priest who gets into a bar fight?" His tone was somber, face expressionless.

"I'm not justifying my behavior, but I was among real human beings last night." He stood and went for another cup of coffee. "Just when I felt myself getting closer to God, the whole world came crashing down upon me, the way it does for those people who work to survive."

Murphy shook his head. "Son, I'm weary of your human pursuit. If getting drunk and into a bar fight is what you call being human, I don't understand. I probably look like a pathetic old drunk too in your eyes. Is that not human enough for you?" He shook his head and slammed his fist onto the table. "Tell you what...save it for Bishop Malone." Murphy looked away, talked towards the door. "We'll have to drive up to the Cathedral on the hill to see him."

"Don't you even want to hear my side?"

"No, I don't." Murphy stood up, gulped the rest of his coffee, walked to the kitchen door and opened it. He paused. "I said Mass for you the last two days. I thought you were supposed to help out around here?" Father Bob remained silent. Murphy continued. "I'm going up to the Knights of Columbus hall for a meeting with the council about Stabo's plaque, his honorary profile. I suggest you stay in and do some soul searching, son."

He stopped himself from getting into an argument with Murphy. *I need to go for a long run. Can't sit in here and stare at the walls.* He went upstairs, removed his priestly clothes and threw on his workout gear. He bounced down the stairs, through the kitchen, and out the door, running through the alleyway where Hellinski slapped him in the face last night. *That nosey old lady spies on me. She needs some compassion in her life.* Jogging down the hill of churches, the further he flew from the rectory the better he felt. Figures of steelworkers wearing orange hard hats mulled around inside the railroad yard, far down the hill. His father used to walk with those guys. He pieced together the events of last night. *I can't believe I punched Barker.* Butterflies revved up in his stomach when he thought of Maria. *Oh, Maria. I can't be in love with you and be a priest.* "And I want to continue being a priest," he mumbled then quickened his pace.

He took a left turn towards the river, rather than run through the one commercial street of Irontown, scene of last night's nightmare. He breathed in the musty fog, heavy this morning with the fumes of scorched coal and spent diesel fuel. The left eye throbbed the more his breathing and heart rate increased. He turned onto a white, smooth gravel path that once served as a road but was since blocked off. The worn road wound around a discarded park, bordering a field of weeds with tall mustard flowers that blew with the wind towards a forested hillside. A cleansing sweat dripped from his forehead and elbows in the humidity.

Butterflies returned to his stomach as he saw a figure run towards him. *Could it be Maria out here?* The woman stopped her jogging several feet in front of him, panting. "Maria, what are you doing out here?"

"You're not the only jogger in town," she raised her eyebrows. "You're definitely the last person I expected to see down here, though!" She stepped closer and embraced him, her body moist too with sweat. He didn't return the hug, so she stepped back. "You must be feeling pretty good to be out running. What in the world were you thinking going down to that snake pit of a bar?"

Is she stalking me? "I'm trying to figure that out myself. I'm trying to figure out a lot of things right now."

"I hear you. Want to sit and talk for a while?" She pointed towards a small stone wall near the field of weeds, about fifteen feet from the crumbled curbside. She cocked her head to the side and put her hands in the air. "No funny stuff this time?"

This probably isn't a good idea, but I need to hear what people are saying. "Okay." He looked around to see if anyone could spot them. They walked to the bench where he wiped some dirt and fallen leaves from the cracked stone. The wall unnoticed amongst wild growth and erosion still provided a view over the railroad tracks, across the river towards the lush green Appalachian foothills of West Virginia.

Maria lightly touched his swollen eye. He froze. Her touch hurt, but the closeness and care she showed felt rare in the priesthood. "I still can't picture you in a bar fight, with that white collar on and all." She laughed. He smiled out of embarrassment. "Lots of people are glad that you flattened Barker. Nobody's ever done that before."

He was fully aware that he sucker-punched Barker before he had a chance to defend himself. "I don't think priests are supposed to act like that. I have to quit drinking."

"Oh, no, don't do that. You're the talk of the town! People are even talking about going to Mass this Sunday, just because of you. You know, you're like some kind of hero or something." She squeezed his knee. "Even Boss can't wait to talk to you, ever since he heard about the fight."

"Oh, great, a priest gets into a bar fight to bring people back to the Church. Maybe I could tell that to the Bishop when he decides to defrock me." Maria stared into is eyes, confused.

"This whole scenario feels so absurd," he said. "Like something out of the 'Twilight Zone.'"

Maria nodded in agreement. "Can you believe us sitting here in the weeds, looking at the river after all these years? Life plays funny tricks on us, huh?" She looked him up and down. "I know I hurt you years ago. I'm sorry about that. I was young and stupid and haven't gotten much smarter. I mean, I'm back in this shit town living with my grandmother again, my kid's on drugs, and I'm flirting with a priest." She looked out over the river. "You know I'm flirting, don't you? So, maybe I'm more like my real mother than I know, just not disowned by the family yet."

She lay her hand on top of his, which was resting on his knee and lightly squeezed his fingers. Nobody touched him like that anymore. The distance priests have to keep between casual and intimate touch spans an eternity of unquenched thirst. He felt her tenderness, pulled his hand away and ran it alongside her hair, as if moving her bangs away from her eye. "You're a wonderful person, Maria. You had nothing to do with the choices your mother made. She's the one who left, not you. Look at how lucky you are to still have Grandma Amelia and Boss, people who love you."

She locked onto his eyes. They moved their lips closer to each other. His heart hammered knowing he shouldn't be seen acting like this with Maria. He retreated. "I can't do this." He turned his gaze to the river, so much cleaner now than when he was a youngster. "I want you so badly, you know that, but I can't."

"We don't have to do anything that makes you uncomfortable." Maria stood up from the bench and walked over a flattened patch of a majestic display of pampas grass. She sat.

He walked over and sat next to her, looked around again for signs of other humans, but saw none. She pushed him, playfully. "Oh, I can't do this either. Not to you, not to me. You're a priest for God's sake. Why do I always go for these doomed relationships?"

"Maybe we always want what we can't have." Father Bob loved her little gestures. The way she could act so vulnerable simply moved him, even though he knew she was far from naïve. "I'm sorry. I should be the one to know better, the 'holy' one. And look at me. I got drunk, got into a bar fight, and here I sit in the woods flirting with a woman of the world. God help me."

She arched her eyebrows. "What exactly do you mean 'a woman of the world'?" Her pitch rose. "You think I'm some kind of slut or something?"

"No, no, it's not you. I mean that I'm a priest falling for you all over again and I can't let that happen." He shifted onto his left hip. "I don't want to hurt you either. I'm not sure what I want, but I'll tell you one thing, this powerful energy between us must mean something."

She fixed her eyes onto his. He wished that he hadn't said that he was falling for her. The distant sound of a retreating train whistle competed with the faint beat of a barge chugging a load of iron ore up the Irontown River. A few birds chirped into a squabble with each other. Then came the sound of pounding footsteps, along with panting.

Two young guys, wearing Irontown High School football jerseys, strode past on the worn river road while Father Bob and

Maria hid from sight, below a patch of wilted weeds with their hearts pounding in excitement. This was like the time when they were kids, kissing under Grandma's porch, listening to Caesar's footsteps creaking on the wooden planks above them.

Finally, the joggers ran out of sight. "We'd better move on. Don't worry about anything, Maria. Let's take this slowly, let it unfold naturally."

Her eyes narrowed. She jumped up. "Woman of the world, huh?" She slapped away some torn leaves from her shorts. "Don't worry, holy one, this worldly woman won't cause you any more trouble." She took off jogging before she stopped a few feet away and turned around. "You know, you've always had a problem with intimacy. I thought you might have changed, but you're worse. All you think about is yourself." She took off towards town.

I didn't call her a slut. He shook his head and watched her jog away, still unable to resist admiring her well-formed calves, hamstrings tight as a trampoline.

He ran in the opposite direction, towards the thicker woods. "If this is what You want for me, God, I'm a *tabula blanca*," he said out loud to nobody. He reflected on what Maria said to him, about being some sort of "tough guy" priest, and for a minute basked in the empowerment. *Shouldn't I feel guilty if I really did something wrong? I don't know what's going on anymore.* "Give me some sign, God!" he yelled. "How can I serve You?" He thought about his favorite part of being a priest–saying Mass for the people. Now, even a Mass might not comfort him. The hypocrisy of it all, how most parishioners lived righteously for only one hour each week at Mass. *I'm not the only priest who has cheated on his chastity vows. Aren't we human too?*

Approaching the dump he used to set on fire as a kid, he took in the first scenery he'd really noticed since he'd left Maria fifteen minutes earlier. Here, he stopped in the middle of the half-paved asphalt road and shadowboxed again, using Barker as an imaginary opponent. Sweat flung from his fists into the air as he tried to move his feet with balance and quickness, but was rusty and awkward. *A man has to start his comeback from somewhere.* He smelled Maria's perfume on his hands when he held his fists against his face. His senses enjoyed her essence. *My old girlfriend, she's just as wacky as I am.*

Eventually, he jogged back towards the rectory, but not without passing Grandma Amelia's house and scanning it out of the corner of his good eye. He reached the alleyway between the convent and the rectory, slowed his pace to a walk near the area where Mrs. Hellinski slapped him. *What is that?* From a distance he saw colorful clutter on the rectory porch, some of it glistening in the sun, shooting flashes of light like sparkling mirrors. The closer he came, the more the bright oranges and blues came into focus, pots of flower arrangements and balloons appeared. *Oh no, did I miss Stabo's funeral or something?* Then, one by one, he held and read the tags on each arrangement. Most of them said something like, "Have a speedy recovery, Father Bob," or, "We pray for you and love you, Father Bob," and "Your dog is safe in heaven."

He shook his head and carried the gifts into the kitchen and read every card, before placing each arrangement on the table, covering the entire top. Then he set the remaining flowers and balloons onto the floor. They filled half the place. Their abundance crowded him with emotion, a sense of appreciation and acceptance for the first time since coming to this church. *I'm reaching these people. They're starting to love me.* He could not wait for Monsignor Murphy or Mrs. Hellinski to witness this outpouring of affection. Certainly, he hadn't felt much of that from inside the rectory lately. In this moment he tasted a glimpse of unconditional love.

His appetite returned and he opened the door to the fridge. Tired of Hellinski's scrambled eggs, he found and devoured a handful of ham rollups straight from the serving plate. Then he ran up the stairs, shed his sweaty workout clothes, and lingered a long time in the warm then cool shower. *Just when I need it, You give me a sign.* He finished his shower with a twist of totally cold water, revived his body and refreshed his mind.

He pulled on his black priest garb, and while adjusting the white collar, Monsignor Murphy yelled from downstairs. "Who died now?" Father Bob recognized Murphy's carefree laugh, the one reserved for when he was totally hammered. "I hope to Jesus it wasn't me, lad!"

He tripped down the stairs in his haste to see Murphy's reaction to all his flowers. Hurrying towards the kitchen he said, "Do you believe this?" Murphy shook his flushed, saggy cheeks, along with a wild expression from reddened, blue eyes. He paused briefly, surprised to see Murphy this far gone so early in the day. *Chalk this one up to Stabo's death.* "I guess some people in this parish are taking a liking to me, even after my sins of last night."

Murphy grabbed a balloon and it popped. "Well, if it takes a hooligan to recognize one, you've been signed." He laughed as he made the sign of the cross. "We're supposed to be going through parish renewal, but there's nothing wrong with re-recognition. What say, son?"

What's he talking about? Parish renewal? "Yes, I'm really touched."

Murphy stumbled over a pot of flowers and Father Bob grabbed him, held him in his arms. Murphy squeezed him into a hard hug. "Yes," he said into his ear, "Me too."

He guided Murphy towards the stairs, one arm around his shoulder, the other across the front of his chest. "We'll get you into bed." The old man's weight dragged Father Bob closer to the ground, but the two priests took the stairs one by one. Christ carrying the cross up Mount Calvary. Father Bob grinned as Murphy kept muttering under his breath and then laughing, as though he was hearing one good joke after another. They huffed heavily and plopped onto the hallway floor at the top of the stairs. A fit of laughter struck both of them, as they lay entangled on the carpet. "I love you like a son," Murphy mumbled. Father Bob stopped laughing, wanted to snuggle his head into Murphy's chest like a child, but quickly stuffed that emotion out of consciousness. *Don't open that door.* Murphy was the closest thing to a father that he could know.

He stood up and pulled Murphy onto his feet. "C'mon old man, we're almost there." *I'm so glad to see him like this. Human, just like me.* He guided the old man into his bedroom, laid him onto the bed, removed his black shoes, and pulled off his black pants. Murphy's legs flung into the air, and then smacked back down onto the mattress, making him laugh. Then he removed Murphy's collar, decided to leave the shirt on him, and tucked him into bed. He stared at Murphy, who already began to snore. *This is the man who was always there for me, not Santo.* "I love you too," he whispered.

He retreated downstairs to his office to get a head start on this coming Sunday's sermon–The Prodigal Son. *The power of forgiveness.* He decided to leave all the flowers and balloons in the kitchen. He thought about spilling some dirt onto the floor for that bitter old Hellinski to clean up tomorrow. *Nah, that's not the message of the Prodigal Son. I'll turn the other cheek like Christ would do.* Before he could get started on writing the sermon, somebody knocked on the kitchen door.

He moved the floral arrangements to widen the pathway through the kitchen to the door. Through the window he saw Boss standing on the porch, still in the same Aerosmith T-shirt he'd been wearing for many days now. He opened the door. "Boss! Hello, come on in. How you feeling?"

"Oh, I feel great. I never really felt bad." He looked around the kitchen. "What's all this?"

He downplayed the flowers in front of Boss, when he saw the smirk his face. "Gifts of love." Boss looked confused. He motioned for Boss to follow him into the office.

Boss sat down in a chair, stared at Father Bob in silence. *He's looking at my eye.* "So, what's going on, big guy?"

Boss continued to examine him, and finally said, "Well, I want to thank you for understanding stuff, I mean, my mom told me that you didn't' think we needed to go to counseling. I really appreciate that."

I didn't say anything like that. "Well, it's always good to talk about things. We can talk through this together if you like."

Boss nodded once, flicked up his head in one quick movement. "So, you going after Barker?"

"What? Going after? No, of course not. I'm a priest, not a street fighter."

"I heard you were a boxer, and that's how you knocked out Barker. He's the baddest dude in town. You can't let him get away with kicking you in the face."

"I'm not a boxer. I mean, I fought Golden Gloves once, but that was a long time ago. I lost at the junior state championships."

Boss looked away, made a sneer. "Listen, I had to kick ass twice in the last few weeks we've been in this town. You can't let Barker get away with that."

He raised his voice. "That's not the way we handle things. If I wanted to be a street fighter I'd have stayed on the streets. I don't' understand what you want?"

Boss stood up. "Teach me how to throw a hook like that. I'll go after him if you won't."

"Sit down." Father Bob said. Then he stood up and noticed Boss clench his fists. He lifted his arms and turned his palms towards Boss, the universal body language of non-resistance. He lowered his tone. "My fight with Barker is over, done. I have more important things to do." He sat back down and Boss remained standing.

"Oh yea, like what? Water your flowers or something?"

He stood back up and walked out of the office towards the kitchen. "Come here for a minute."

Boss slowly followed Father Bob into the kitchen. "You see this, all these flowers? This represents love, the love of Jesus Christ. People show their love like this sometimes. This town is full of loving folks. That's what I try to do, son. I'm sorry about the fight and sorry if you don't approve of me, but I won't street fight anymore."

Boss shook his head, said nothing. He walked towards the door, feet almost sliding across the ground. "I thought maybe you'd teach me a few things, that's all."

Maybe boxing could be a way to reach this boy. "Listen, Boss, I'd be willing to teach you to box someday, but it's a sport. We don't do it just to beat people up."

Boss turned to him, cocked his head like Jack the dog used to do. "Yeah, uh, well, you let me know, Father." He walked across the porch and down into the alley.

Father Bob shut the door, looked at the flowers and no longer reveled in their grace. *That was weird.* He strolled into his office and sat at the desk. *I have no idea how to reach that boy.* He tried to focus on writing the Prodigal Son sermon, but somehow could not concentrate.

CHAPTER 7

PRODIGAL SON

Father Bob sat at his desk, preparing the Prodigal Son sermon to accompany the gospel at Sunday's Mass. He pulled out some old notes from his previous sermons on the subject. *No, I need something more dynamic. I love this parable from St. Luke. It shows the enormous love and forgiveness from God, just for the asking. Maybe I'll ask forgiveness from the entire congregation.* He scribbled down a few notes: "I was lost for a few hours the other night. Similar to the Prodigal Son, I returned to my Father's house. I expected to be punished, but instead received an outpouring of love and forgiveness." *A public penance could demonstrate the lesson of how we all need God's forgiveness and our need to forgive each other in order to grow spiritually.* He realized with a pang that he needed to do some forgiving also, and immediately thought about the folks he'd been perturbed with lately. *I forgive you for your rudeness, Boss. I forgive you for slapping me, Mrs. Hellinski. I shower both of you with love.*

After he scribbled a few more lines, his stomach growled with hunger. He dodged a rogue balloon while walking to the refrigerator, and then read the card dangling from it: "We pray for you and Jack." *Oh, Jack. You were so innocent.* He suddenly found himself sobbing into both hands as he leaned over the sink and splashed his face with cold water. *Please forgive me, Jack, I miss you so.*

He looked around the kitchen, where warmth radiated from kindness, and his spirit started to soar for the first time in a while, as if forgiven by Jack. He fantasized the congregation giving him a standing ovation after his homily this Sunday, lifting his spirits even higher. He marveled at the abundance of love in the universe and how tragedy can turn to triumph. Then he opened the door to the refrigerator. Empty. *Where are the scrambled eggs and ham rollups?* Murphy must have devoured everything, or he threw it in the garbage when he was drunk. *It's hard to forgive Murphy for this, but I will.* No food meant that he would have to drive to the store.

He dreaded running into people. He so needed this chance to be alone, away from the craziness for a few hours where he could reflect on what recent events meant to his spiritual life. Absorbed by the Prodigal Son story, he now envisioned himself as the main character. Perhaps he should be the Father in the story instead of the son. He needs to be in the role of forgiving father, maybe start by greeting Boss with open arms. *Teach him to box the way Murphy taught me.*

Pleased with himself, he walked back to his office and sat behind the desk, readied to focus on polishing the sermon. Forgive and be forgiven. His stomach growled again. He threw down the pen. *The spirit is willing but the flesh is weak.* He grabbed the car keys and hoofed to the Lincoln, started the engine, pushed the button to roll down both front seat windows, and headed toward DiCino's Hilltop grocery store.

He drove through downtown Irontown en route to the store. When passing the Argonaut Bar he rolled up the passenger side window, refusing to look for any relic of Jack's blood on the street. That's when he noticed a boarded-up hardware store a short ways down the road, on the other side of the street. He wondered if Big Chew Louie still owned it. Maybe they could make a gym out of it. Slowing down past the store, he could hear the machine gun sound of boxers hitting speed bags, along with the thumping of heavy bags rattling the rafters and ringing of a three-minute bell. He rolled down the passenger side window again and breathed in the air, fresh today from a cleansing, daylong rain yesterday.

Eventually, atop the hill north of town, he pulled into the grocery store parking lot and saw several parked cars. He paused for a moment, suddenly conscious of his black eye and still embarrassed by last night's drunken brawl. He examined the eye in the rear view mirror, licked his fingers, and wiped some dried blood from a small scab above his eyebrow. *Oh, where are those sunglasses when you need them?* He hoped he wouldn't run into anybody he knew, but that was impossible. The white collar attracted attention like moths to light, especially in this small town. Either way, he knew that people would gawk at any priest with a blackened eye. His heart started to race because he had to go in. He was starving, so he walked into the store, conscious about not strutting, wishing he could be invisible. As soon as he passed through the door, the cashier looked him up and down in curious recognition.

"Father Bob?" she said. "Remember me?"

How he hated that question. He couldn't recognize half of them anymore.

"Let' see. It's been a while." He studied her white, round face and blue eyes and how her blonde hair curled around the corners of her chin. "I'm sorry, I don't, Teresa?" he asked.

"No! I can't believe it. Have I changed that much?" She stretched out her arms. "I'm Sheri, remember?"

Like a rush, he recalled once taking Sheri to the drive-in movie to see "Easy Rider." They made out in the front seat of his rusted Ford Galaxy to the sound of a scratchy metal speaker, while her younger brother slept soundly in the back seat. He could not get it up for sex, had had too many joints and Quaaludes. Sheri tried to help, but it didn't work and she ended up passing out. They woke up to find that they were the only ones left in the drive-in movie lot.

"Oh yes, of course. I remember you." He hoped she wouldn't remember his lack of manliness. *Women never forgot those things.* "I'm sorry, but I've seen so many people this past week. It's been hectic. How's your family?"

She hustled around the counter and gave him a full-bodied hug before taking a step back and sizing him up. "You look great. I heard you've been jogging around these hills."

He glanced at her from head to toe, a subtle habit he'd mastered long ago. "Yes, thank you. You look good too." *She'd put on a few pounds.* He changed the subject, avoided talk about his eye, and brought up her little brother's name, the one who slept in the back seat at the drive-in movie. "How's Kenny?"

"He'll be graduating from Kent State next year." She stared at him for a while, and he knew she was thinking about his eye. He tried to turn slightly sideways, show his good side. "We're really proud of him, the first college graduate in the family."

"That's terrific. Congratulations. It's nice to see you again." He turned away. "Tell Kenny I'm proud of him."

"Great to see you," Sheri said. "It's so weird seeing you as a priest." She giggled. "Maybe I'll see you in church sometime." She walked back behind the counter.

"Perfect, please come down this Sunday." He walked towards the deli and bent over to pick up a pack of hard rolls. Out of the corner of his good eye he noticed Sheri checking out his backside.

He reached the deli at the end of the aisle and ordered a pound of provolone cheese and a stick of pepperoni. A man yelled his name from the end of the aisle, a recognizable voice. *Oh no, here we go.*

"Father Bob!" Pumpkin yelled, half pie-eyed. He hurried his pace towards him, wobbling like a monster in some "B" grade horror flick, his huge body practically filling the entire aisle. A wiry man with a familiar face followed behind him. "How you doin' slugger?" He had a 12-pack of Pabst Blue Ribbon beer in his hand. "I guess I left the bar too early and missed all the action last night. Nice shiner!" He turned to his friend. "Hey, this is my buddy, Muledick. Hey, Muledick, meet Father Bob."

Muledick jabbed Pumpkin in the ribs with his elbow, disgusted. "Hello, Father, I'm Jim Hodgekirk." He held out his hand. "Nice to meet you. Some guys don't know how to keep mill talk in the mill."

"Nice to meet you, Jim. Try to stay out of trouble hanging around with this guy." He looked at Pumpkin. "Do you know if Big Chew Louie still owns that old hardware store?"

Pumpkin nodded, "I think so. That tight-ass holds onto everything, probably still has his first paycheck. Why, you wanna' buy it?"

"No, no, I was just wondering what he's going to do with that building, that's all." He looked at Jim. "Are you Larry Hodgekirk's brother? I used to run around with him a little when we were kids."

"Yes, I remember you." Jim hung his head for a moment. "Larry died about five years ago. Had testicular cancer."

"Oh...I'm sorry to hear that. God rest his soul. We had some good times together." He again remembered when he and Barker were kids and had to run from Larry, who chased them through the water with a hard-on while they were skinny dipping in the creek. They had pretty much avoided Larry after that. And now he was dead. "Well, you guys take care and come see me in church this Sunday."

"If *Jim* stepped into a church it would catch fire," Pumpkin said laughing. Jim shook his head. The three men stood in an awkward silence until the deli attendant asked, "Anything else, Father?" He gladly gave his attention to the deli clerk and waved good-bye to the guys.

During the drive back towards the rectory, he unraveled the pepperoni and cheese. He rehearsed his Prodigal Son sermon for Sunday's Mass—God's forgiveness for sinners. Should be a larger-than-normal congregation, since many people would come to church this Sunday just to see the priest who got into a bar fight. Even some of the barflies may show up. They'd be looking for clues of when to kneel or stand and want to get out quickly. Father Bob preferred the intimacy of the daily Mass, though, where a priest did not need to prepare a sermon, but simply shared the closeness with Christ.

He took a different route to the rectory, down a hill he hadn't seen for years. His thoughts jumped around erratically, and he wondered again about the possibility of a boxing gym. He decided to drive past Big Chew Louie's house and turned down "Hog Hill" onto a half-paved, cobbled brick road. He slowed past Big Chew Louie's house, the brick shaded charcoal gray from years of graphite dust spewing from the steel mill. Big Chew was sitting on the porch, which was tucked in the shade of a steep-pitched roof.

He parked the black barge and approached the porch. "Mr. Dravich? Hello, I'm Father Bob Santoro." He stuck out his hand.

Big Chew squinted his eyes and stood from his chair, looked him up and down. "Yeah, I know you." Father Bob tried not to fidget under his scrutiny. Big Chew stood above him, on the porch, while he stood below with one foot on the bottom step. Big Chew squeezed his hand so hard he could feel his calluses.

He hoped Big Chew wouldn't remember the time he and his friends stole tomatoes from his garden, and worse yet, they did not eat them, but threw them at each other. It reminded him of *Confessions*, by St. Augustine, in which the Saint admitted to stealing pears with his friends, not because he was hungry, but for the sake of gratuitous wickedness. *Old Augustine was always repenting for something.* He turned from that thought by summoning some writings from his favorite saint, Thomas Aquinas, and his concept of "Natural Law," where any choice is a choice of the good, and man was free to direct himself, or not, to his true end. He liked not knowing his true end, open to what came.

He pulled his hand from Big Chew's grip, reminding himself that he was no longer twelve. He could rightfully stand on Big Chew's porch and ask for a favor.

"What chu doin' up here?" Big Chew asked.

Both of Big Chew's cheeks sagged when not filled with a pack of Mail Pouch tobacco. Everybody knew that each morning Big Chew stuffed one side and it puffed out his cheek as if he had had a baseball in there. His lips on that side stretched enough that a few teeth came into view from the corner of his mouth. The chew stayed in throughout meals and beverages. When he removed the tobacco at the end of the workday, around three o'clock, his stretched-out cheeks sagged. And yet, nobody had ever seen him spit.

"Well, Mr. Dravich, I was wondering about what you're doing with that closed-up hardware store. Or, to get straight to the point, I wondered if it would be possible to use it as a small boxing gym." He paused, then added, "That is, if you're not using it."

"A boxing gym?" Big Chew tilted his head sideways like a curious hound. "Seems to me that all you need is a bar to fight in, not a gym." Big Chew laughed, showing his brown-stained teeth. Father Bob knew he would have to take a lot of guff and almost wished he hadn't stopped. He stared up at Big Chew, a short, portly man a few steps above him. When he finally finished laughing, sensing that Father Bob didn't find him funny, he called, "Ahh, c'mon up and have a seat. We'll talk. I'll tell ya, I'm using that place for storage right now, but all them counters and shelves are still in it because I'm trying to sell it. I can't see turning it into a gym." He threw a fake jab to Father Bob's shoulder. "Who's boxing, anyway?" He sat onto a worn recliner, motioned for Father Bob to sit on a green and white lawn chair beside him.

"I'm thinking about training a couple of young boys, you know, amateur. It wouldn't be too serious, just a place to work out and help keep these kids off the streets."

"You mean like you? Oh man, I remember you running the streets around here. Looks like you ended up making something out of yourself." He grinned. "Nice shiner." Big Chew yelled through the screen door for his wife to bring out some iced tea. "I watched you win the first round of Golden Glove tournaments, what, about fifteen-years ago or so?"

Father Bob remembered better than anybody. "That's right. I made it to the semifinals and then lost what I thought was a win." He raised his fists as if to guard his face. "I guess I had a different calling." He laid his hands back onto his lap when Mrs. Dravich came out and handed two large glasses of ice tea to the two men. She wore a red babushka over her hair and dressed in work clothes from the mill.

"Thank you, Mrs. Dravich," Father Bob nodded. "Beautiful day today, huh?"

She nodded. "Too nice to be sittin' on the porch. Why aren't yunz out enjoying the sun?"

"He's talkin' about using the store for a boxing gym," Big Chew chuckled.

She looked puzzled. "Well, I don't know about that. I'm going out back to finish weeding the garden. They're calling for rain tomorrow." She rubbed her hands together. "Well, I'd better get to it. Good to see you, Father."

"You too, Mrs. Dravich."

She disappeared into the house and the screen door slammed shut on its own. A warm breeze rang a few wind chimes hanging from the porch rafters. An occasional clang boomed from the steel mill. From Big Chew's porch, one could see the tops of smokestacks spewing in silence.

"Too bad you didn't have your guard up last night," Big Chew laughed.

How much of this am I going to take? Father Bob shook his head in agreement. "You know, you talk about the kind of kid I was, running the streets and all, but boxing was one of the things that helped me see a different world out there. Monsignor Murphy got me started, and boy, did my life change after he took me in."

"Yes, Murphy's a good man. I don't know, Father. I heard you still have a pretty good left hook." Big Chew laughed again. Father Bob bowed his head and shook it. "Don't worry son, people can't take a crap in this town without somebody talking about it. I was glad to hear that Barker finally got what he's been dishing out all these years."

Father Bob took a deep breath. "Barker is a good person. We grew up together. You know that. If I'd gotten a job in the mill right after high school like he did, obviously my life would be a lot different. Steel working biker and a priest, and you know, none of us are that much different down inside."

Big Chew held out his hands and shrugged his shoulders. "I'll tell you what. I don't know about turning my place into a gym, but we could take a look at the basement. There's lots of junk down there that needs cleaned out. Yunz clean out the basement, and then maybe we'll talk about using it for some training." Big Chew sat back in his recliner. He covered his mouth with one hand and spoke through his fingers. "You know, unless I sell it in the meanwhile or something."

"Thanks. I'll get a hold of you if this thing gets off the ground. God bless you and your family. Please, thank your wife for the tea and tell her I said good-bye." He downed his glass of iced tea and hurried off the front porch to the car.

Big Chew's offer smelled foul. He wasn't going to be used to clean out a basement just to make the old store more sellable.

Back inside the rectory, he gorged on meat and cheese and tried to focus on preparing his sermon, but the day had left him exhausted. After he cracked Murphy's bedroom door open and checked on him, he went to bed early. Murphy was long lost snoring in slumber.

*   *   *

The next morning he woke early and hurried over to the church sacristy, before Murphy and Hellinski would be in the kitchen. He wanted Hellinski to see the flowers, but didn't want her to see his blackened eye. He dressed into green vestments in the sacristy when Anthony the altar boy entered.

"Good morning Father, I'm serving today." Anthony focused on his eye, and then ducked his head and leaned his weight from foot to foot a few times. He looked back up at Father Bob, stared at his eye again. Eventually, Anthony cleared his throat, "Boss said that you were going to teach him how to box. Will you teach me too?" Anthony's big brown eyes glowed with hope.

He used as soft a tone as he could muster. "Anthony, I'm not sure if we can pull this off or not. I'd have to get permission from Monsignor Murphy and the Bishop, and you need to get permission from your parents." Anthony's expression lit up. He didn't want to kill the boy's spirit. "Then, maybe we'd have a chance to fix up a gym somewhere."

"Thank you so much, Father," Anthony said. "My folks already said it would be okay."

He rolled his eyes. "I hope we can work it out, but don't get your hopes up too high. Right now, we have a Mass to do."

He strutted out of the sacristy, caught himself, and slowed, walking normally. He turned solemn from the smell of sweet incense mixed with burning candles, a scent which comforted him and brought him back to the Mass. Saying Mass remained his favorite part of being a priest, whether the Mass were inside a church, outdoors, or in somebody's house. He stood behind the altar and faced the congregation. Anthony took his place off to the side. He scanned the small crowd and said the opening prayers with his hands towards heaven. The ritual of Mass transformed him into a pure spiritual being, especially during the Eucharist, the changing of communion wafers into the body of Jesus Christ, and wine into His blood. Each time he said Mass, he became Christ for a few precious moments. Those huge granite pillars and stained glass windows of St. Anne's have little to do with the presence of Christ. He treated each Mass like it was his last one, because it might be, and he enjoyed the bliss of the present moment. He often counseled married couples to follow that way, to approach each other like it was their first and last time together. For most priests, this state of spirituality filled the void of longing for human intimacy. *I wish I could feel this way all the time.* He knew that the spiritual highs came in spurts, not unlike the bliss sought out by drug and alcohol abusers, but without the physical addiction.

Maria sat in the front row with Sister Roxanne, and Mrs. Hellinski across the aisle with the row of widows; even Boss and a few unknown stragglers scattered about the mostly empty pews. They stared at him as though they wanted him to fill some need in them, the empty hole that children called the monster under the bed. Whatever Mrs. Hellinski would think of the flowers mattered little to him now. Even his blackened eye, which was getting better, didn't matter, in this spiritual state.

After he swallowed the body of Christ, the small congregation scooted through their pews and lined up in the middle aisle to receive communion, staring with eyes full of hope for happiness. He noticed no distinct individual during communion, not even Maria or Boss this time, and focused solely on their eyes, where he tried to connect with the spiritual being inside of them. In the oneness of human spirit, he would be the conduit of light from the Lord, shining in a flow of golden grace. He found peace of mind here. He wanted to share it with everybody, as Jesus did. *This is my calling. I am your servant.*

"We are all God's children. Now go in peace to love and serve the Lord. In the name of the Father, Son and Holy Spirit, Amen."

Back in the sacristy, he pulled off the green vestment and when he lifted his head, he was surprised to see Maria and Boss standing in the doorway. Still riding his spiritual high, their presence made him want to share his love with them. He looked into Maria's green eyes and she glanced away. He looked into Boss's blue eyes, and he turned his head down, towards the floor. Then, he looked back at Maria, gave her a full body glance where her tight, black dress made a flutter in his stomach, and his spiritual high started its descent.

"Good morning. How are you two today?" He sensed that they had never seen him so spiritual before. *Yes, I am a holy man.*

Maria reverted to her wide smile. "We're good, great this morning. Nice Mass…you're eye looks better too." Boss looked at Maria when she said that, then looked away again.

"Thank you. I'm glad that both of you could make it." His spiritual high may have faded, but he was still powerful, dominant, like Big Chew Louie back on the porch when he stood above him. "Is there something I could help you with?"

Maria clasped her hands together, in front of her chest. "Oh, no, I mean Grandma Amelia wanted us to invite you and Monsignor Murphy over the house for dinner, you know, after this Sunday's Mass."

He gave her another quick once-over. He hesitated, "Well, I'd have to check with Murphy. We have a pretty tight schedule this Sunday." Boss stared at his eye.

"Well," Maria sighed. "See what you can do. Grandma said she's making homemades, Murphy's favorite." She backed up to the doorway. "Let us know."

"Thanks a lot," he said. "I hope we can work it out. Sure would hate to miss out on Grandma's cooking."

"Okay, we'll see you later." He watched Maria's legs as she walked away. Boss caught him checking her out, and grinned.

He sat in the chair in the sacristy for a few moments. The ornamental chair had been hand carved many years ago, adorned with angels and sword-bearing spirits defeating snakes, surrounded by crosses and cherubs. The uncomfortable seat was upholstered in red velvet and tacked along the chair's arms. Every time he got close to God, Maria seemed to appear. *What does that mean?*

He locked the sacristy door and walked to the rectory. Monsignor Murphy sipped coffee in the midst of a room that looked like a tropical jungle. Mrs. Hellinski fumbled around with some pans, and Murphy looked hung over. One of the half-deflated balloons barely floated, bobbing Murphy on the side of his head on occasion from a slight breeze that blew from a small fan, but Murphy ignored it. Finally, Mrs. Hellinski removed the intrusive arrangement, humming the hymn, *Amazing Grace*, under her breath. "Where would you like me to put these gifts, Father Santoro, in the office?"

"Sure." He tried to read her reaction. "Please, anywhere you think would be fine. Sorry for the mess." She said nothing, but stared at him for a moment, as if surprised by his politeness. She lifted her arm as if she was going to hug him for an awkward instance, but she simply adjusted her babushka.

He wanted her to love him. He saw her as a lonely widow who lost the ability to smile ever since her husband died. He wanted to reach out to her, but she scared him. Deep down, he knew that she thought him a fraud.

Her face twitched, the lower part of her mouth quivered for a moment. *Is she going to smile at me?* She just turned her head away, continued humming, and carried the arrangements out of the room. He smelled fresh Ivory soap when she walked past. "I'll be back this afternoon to do some more ridding up," she said with a wave.

He refilled Murphy's coffee cup and poured himself one. "How're you feeling, Monsignor? Are you in the mood to talk about a few things?"

Monsignor Murphy burped. He stood up from his chair and limped over to open the wall cabinet high above the refrigerator. He pulled out a fresh bottle of scotch and his hands shook when he tried to pour some into his coffee. "Every time you ask me if I'm in the mood to talk, I must prepare for something bizarre."

Father Bob pulled the bottle of scotch from Monsignor Murphy and poured a healthy belt into his own cup. Then he put the bottle back into the cabinet.

"Remember when I was sixteen-years-old and you put those boxing gloves on me? You held up leather punch mitts and let me pound away at them." He slid his feet into fight stance, raised his fists and tossed a four-punch combination into the air.

Murphy nodded with a smile. "Of course, I remember. You took to boxing like a duck to water." He forced a forkful of scrambled eggs into his mouth. "Apparently, some of the skills stayed with you, judging by all the rumors."

There goes that nervous nausea in his stomach again. "Okay, what are you hearing?"

"People in this town continue to amaze me. Just when I think I know them, what they're thinking, you know, after thirty some years as their priest, they surprise me." He took another drink of coffee and shuffled to the wall cabinet to retrieve the bottle. His hands steadied while he bolstered his coffee with more scotch. "I wanted to sleep in this morning, but got too many damn telephone calls. You've stirred everybody up."

Beads of fear formed on Father Bob's forehead. He sat down and leaned onto the table, sliding his elbows on the tabletop and resting his chin in his hands. "So what is it? What are they saying?"

"What are they saying? What aren't they saying? All these flowers and balloons and the Stabo's sent over a cooked ham. I would never have imagined this. I figured they'd want me to run you out of town on a rail." He took another slug of coffee and stared at a small clump of egg that escaped from the plate onto the table.

"Whaa…" Father Bob tried to contain himself and looked for patience that wasn't there. "So are you going to tell me what people are saying, or do I have to kick your butt too?" They both grinned and Monsignor's laugh turned into a gag, which culminated into his handkerchief.

"Don't think you can take me, son. You may have fought Golden Gloves, but I was State Champion in my day. There's a big difference between just fighting in the championship and winning it." He held up one fist over his head.

"Yea, yea yea…you were the champion. Don't you think I've heard that story before, like about a hundred times? But what are they saying, c'mon."

Murphy was irritated. "I don't know where to start, but at least I'm starting to feel better." He placed the stained handkerchief back into his pocket and motioned for more coffee. "You've become some sort of town hero. People respect what you did to Barker. They're all afraid of him. He's put many a drunken man into the hospital. Nobody stood up to him before *my boy* came to town. Yes, some of them call you 'my boy' now." Murphy paused, stared. He went on. "They're saying, 'how's the champ.' Or 'when's he saying Mass again?' You know, they want to know if we need anything or how they can smooth things over with the Bishop. I'm not sure how to respond."

Father Bob leaned back into his chair and breathed a sigh. "I'm way over my head, Murphy. I didn't expect anything like this. I mean, I was getting ready to ask your permission to start a boxing club, like you did for me years ago. I don't…"

Murphy interrupted, "Yes, Big Chew Louie called me too, wondering if you're legit or not. Nobody's ever asked that about one of my priests before."

He bit his lower lip. "I'm not so sure I trust his motives. I'm not going to clean up that basement of his only for him to sell the joint."

Murphy slammed his fist on the table. "His motives?" he shouted. His face reddened even more than it normally was. "What about your motives? Did you forget you're a priest, at least for now?" Murphy started coughing, stood up, and sat down again. Father Bob was afraid the old man would choke. He started to say something. Murphy interrupted him. "Shut up! For once, shut up and listen!" He pointed his finger at Father Bob's face. "You think I'm a stupid old man, that I don't have a clue, you and that humongous ego of yours. For God's sake, son, I can see right through you! You're stepping way over the line, and if it keeps up I'll throw you out of here myself, save the Bishop a trip."

"What are you talking about?" He expected a pat on the back, a loving arm, but received Murphy's wrath instead.

"You know damn well what I'm talking about!" He'd never seen Murphy so angry.

"This business with Maria must stop. People around here see things. They talk, and don't you think it gets back to me? I need you to be a priest, Bob, remember? A priest can't run around flirting with women, and getting into bar fights this day and age for goodness sake. You imagine the potential lawsuits?"

He hung his head like a dog that'd gotten caught chewing his owner's shoes. He was burning up inside, and wanted to unload on Murphy about how old-fashioned and out of touch he was. Then a wave of fear struck him. *Throw me out of here? Where would I go?*

"I thought a boxing club could be a way to capture some kids, get them off the street." He looked at Murphy with sincerity. "Remember how you helped me with boxing?"

"It's not that simple anymore. The Bishop is coming down here, this Sunday." Murphy calmed down a little. "He's coming to meet with you after Mass. The Bishop rarely comes to St. Anne's. You're in trouble, son, and I can't stick my neck out for you anymore. Not the way you've been acting."

Horrified, his mouth completely dried, and he could barely get the words out. "Bishop Malone is coming here?"

"That's right. He plans to attend your Mass, and then talk with you afterwards." Murphy stood up and headed for the door. "Consider this the fight of your life, your championship round, and there's only a few days to get ready for it."

Father Bob sat in his chair, stunned. *Is the Bishop coming to kick me out of the priesthood?*

Chapter 8

Mount Calvary

Father Bob slept-in and missed breakfast. He paced the rectory's floor late in the morning until stopping to stare out the kitchen window at the darkening clouds. *I'll lose my mind sitting here alone.* He quickly dressed into his workout garb and felt relief the moment he stepped out of the rectory. The entire river valley below clouded in dark purple, threatening rain at any moment. He knew that the familiar smell of sulfur and diesel fuel provided the bread and butter for dinner tables in the community, like manna from molten steel. He decided not to run through the woods near the river, where he might cross paths with Maria, so he turned toward the one long street of commerce downtown. The reality of the Bishop coming down to St Anne's motivated him to sprint across a short straightaway that momentarily chased the butterflies out of his stomach. *Why would the Bishop come here rather than make me travel up to the cathedral on the hill?*

Once he felt his heart pounding in his throat, he slowed the pace. The buildings of downtown Irontown came into focus, combined with the roar and clang of the steel mill, which threw him back into his roots. Slowing his stride even more past the Argonaut Bar, scene of the infamous fight, he peeked through the open door. Cigarette smoke already smoldered from oversized metal ashtrays, in front of a few human silhouettes elbowed against the bar, as if in praying position. He rehearsed the account of events he would give the Bishop—a true blow-by-blow description. *But what about my messing around with Maria? Should I confess?* He slowed even more to look through the picture window of Stephiano's Cigar Store, where a man could place a bet on any game, including high school football parlays. Wagers on the three-digit daily number stayed alive here, despite some states in the country starting their own profitable lottery systems. As usual, a handful of elderly men, wearing fedoras, sat in metal chairs along the wall where they gossiped, gambled, and gossiped more. He knew that their gossip sounded much the same as when he was a kid. Who's sleeping with whom, who lost too much money gambling, and rumors about the mill shutting down or restarting some divisions resulting in either lay-offs or new hires. Suddenly he tripped on the uneven sidewalk, glad to have barely missed running into a parking meter.

He passed the Knights of Pythias building, a square, graphite gray-stained redbrick box structure where years ago he had thrown a rock through the front picture window for no good reason. At the age of ten, he didn't care. The Knights replaced the window, and hung their mission on a white sign with large red letters: FRIENDSHIP, CHARITY & BENEVOLENCE. Today he stopped, leaned against a parking meter, and read the smaller print under the letters: The first fraternal order to be chartered by an act of Congress in 1864, around the end of the Civil War. *Why had I done so many random acts of violence back then?* He chalked it up to just showing off for friends, boys who stole beer and cigarettes and hung out in abandoned shacks in the woods. *Ah those shacks, our clubhouses for the fraternal order of displaced kids, consuming things in life we were too young to taste.* They wore cutoff jeans and white T-shirts for the most part, and listened to the scratchy music from old records, 45's by musical groups such as the Supremes and the Temptations. Motown music ruled, and the discarded 45 records made perfect kamikaze Frisbees. Leaning against a parking meter, he thought about some of the older "cool" guys in town, who called it "nigger" music, but even they listened, sang and danced to it. He never really saw color on people, even as a kid, and inside the steel mill, all laborers turned the same shade of gray, judged solely by how hard they worked. *And then the whistle blows to end the shift.*

As the pubescent boys were growing into men, full of curiosity and hormones, they experimented with masturbation, naked pictures and, once in a while, a real live girl. He tried to erase the vision that flew into his mind about him and his friends masturbating to naked pictures in the shack. Only one, Billy, knew what sex was really like back then. The quest for girls motivated most of their bizarre behaviors.

He performed his crazy acts for Maria, a "goodie girl," meticulously clean and tidy, but mannered and somehow out of reach. He'd heard rumors that she thought he was cute, and desperately played up his bad boy image around her as much as he could. Not long before her grandfather died, he lured her to the shack one summer day, with a few other young couples, where the twelve-year-old boys showed off their cigarettes and beer. He kissed Maria and felt he should try to slide his hand down the front of her cut-offs. He had barely touched a line of silky hair with the back of his fingers when she jumped away frightened, then ran through the woods back to her home. As he watched her fly out of the shack, he felt awful that he upset her. He wanted to chase after her, but the other boys laughed, so he had pretended that it was funny. A few days later in private, he apologized to Maria in the schoolyard where he waited for her to walk past. She turned her head away and tried to walk fast; her grandfather, Caesar, had grounded her after learning of her being in the boy's shanty. She was forbidden to hang around with him. He knew it.

A pang of nostalgia overtook him downtown now, sorrow over the death and awful fate of several shack boys. At the same time, he knew that his past made him the good person he had become. *There's nothing like a tour of your hometown to humble you.* Back then he'd done anything to make people like him, even if it meant breaking windows. Acceptance meant everything. He smiled thinking of how the acceptance of God and Christ eventually filled that need, with a calling to a vocation that he could share with all. *This is why I run...clears my head. This is when God talks to me.*

He resumed his run and reached the end of the street, which connected with the highway that paralleled the river. At this intersection, boys used to hitch rides to the pool halls in Pittsburgh. *People don't hitchhike much anymore. Too many weirdos running loose.* The other option for this running route would bring him up Knott Hill, a mile-long, forty-five degrees hill that nobody ever ran. The road remained the most hazardous street of all during winter when covered in snow and ice, because if you couldn't make the turn at the bottom, the car would run through a brick wall and fall fifty-feet down onto the railroad tracks inside the steel mill. It had been done by Denny, one of the shack boys. Denny died too young. At the age of sixteen he drank too much Wild Irish Rose wine, and so didn't make that awful turn at the end of the hill. His rusted Ford Falcon bashed through the cement wall and was totaled on the railroad tracks below, his body flown through the windshield when the car smashed onto the tracks.

I'm running this hill. His lungs burned and legs fatigued within the first fifty-feet, and yet he had a gargantuan distance to go. His stance widened with choppy steps up the steep slope. *I'll push my body to the limit. My heart might burst, or I could simply collapse.* The sun sneaked through the clouds and doused humidity all over his body, mingling with sweat that dripped onto the ground. He found himself thinking about Christ carrying the cross up Mount Calvary, and he could almost hear the crowds shouting. If he should die, at least he wouldn't have to face the Bishop.

Stepping around the cracks in the cement sidewalk, he moved to the worn asphalt on the edge of the road for a softer surface. He'd never felt his heart pound so hard and fast. Lightheaded and staggering, he might look like a drunken fool to an unknown passerby, but the determination to make it up this hill would not be compromised. *I sacrifice for You, Lord, for my sins.* The rumble of drag pipes, distinctly Harley Davidson, popped up next to him.

Barker weaved on his bike. He was having a difficult time maintaining balance on two wheels at such a slow speed up the steep hill. He pulled up alongside of him.

"Hop on!" He yelled. "You ain't gonna make it."

Breathing hard, Father Bob waved him off, unable to speak.

"You trying to kill yourself?" Barker yelled, above the drag pipes. He pulled in the clutch, revved the motor a couple times, and steered in front of Father Bob, still weaving. "Hop on!"

But Father Bob moved back onto the sidewalk, ignored Barker and tromped laboriously up the steep hill.

Barker gunned the bike up a little ways, came back down and made a U-turn. He rode beside him again. "You're not gonna make it!" he yelled. "C'mon!"

Father Bob continued his crazy pilgrimage, baby stepping and gasping for air up the sharp incline. His face flushed. Sweat and slobber sprayed from him. But he was enamored yet maybe dying, frothing at the mouth.

While Barker shot back up the hill to keep balance on the bike, he turned his head back. "You're gonna kill yourself, man!"

He barely heard anything and couldn't even look in Barker's direction any longer. Lungs bursting and legs stumbling, at this moment nothing else mattered. Almost there, he slipped to the ground in parts, first his knees, and then his hands smacked the pavement. From all fours, he coughed in between heavy breathing and rose from his knees. *Get up. Get up. How did He carry a cross? I'll die before I stop and take a ride.* He envisioned faces yelling at him and heard a crowd and imagined a scene from the Crucifixion, when Christ carried a wooden log across the back of His shoulders, His hands tied to it and when He fell He landed on His face. Onlookers, too afraid to help, were shouting as He stumbled up Mount Calvary.

Father Bob would take this small mountain for Christ. Heavy breathing found a rhythm with a roaring heartbeat. Perhaps a second wind blew into his lungs, bringing with it a renewed strength of conviction. He lurched to the crest, where he fell onto his knees right in front of Barker, who had turned off his bike and sat waiting. He grabbed Barker's jeans, leaned onto the bottom of his leg. Barker tried to shake him off, but he held tight. He moved his head away, coughed, and threw up foamy liquid, watching it ooze over the warm asphalt and under the motorcycle.

"You're one crazy bastard," Barker said. Father Bob stared at the back of his head, how Barker's hair culminated into one long braid that snaked its way out from under a red bandana and wound down the middle of his back. When Barker smacked Father Bob on the shoulder, sweat splashed.

Finally Father Bob struggled to his feet and climbed onto the back of the chopper. "Just don't kill me," he said, still out of breath.

"Jesus, you're soaking wet." Barker didn't kick-start the bike this time, but pushed the electric start button and when he twisted down on the throttle almost flipped Father Bob off the back who had to reach one hand behind his back and gripped the sissy bar as they rolled around the winding roads through the wooded hills of Irontown.

Barker tuned his head and yelled, "You should never ride on a motorcycle in a pair of shorts."

The cool air was now soothing Father Bob's wet body. His conquest of North Hill gave a taste of ecstasy. "You should wear a helmet," Father Bob shouted back, trying to make Barker laugh. Although the humid wind cooled him in his sweaty clothes, the dwindling dark clouds refused to cleanse him with rain.

Barker opened up the throttle and shot down the road's brief straightaway. The bike's drag pipes ricocheted machinegun pops from the sides of the hollow as they sped into the dank, Appalachian foothills. Barker howled and Father Bob ululated like a jackal in return. *This is how we apologize to each other.* Barker gunned the engine again, snapping Father Bob's head back. He peeked around Barker's shoulder to see how fast they were going, but the speedometer was broken. He hadn't been this far out in the area near the woods in a long time.

Finally Barker pulled off the road onto the gravel next to "Second Bridge," which ran over the creek a short ways down from a black train trestle, several miles out of town. The creek under Second Bridge formed a swimming hole, unlike the shallow rapids under First Bridge, a few miles farther back. He shut off the bike. Father Bob squeezed Barker's shoulders as he dismounted the machine.

"Wow!" He took a deep breath. "I haven't been out here since we were kids! Man, is this beautiful or what? Reminds me of Chunk King." He laughed with delight.

"How could I ever forget Chunky?" Barker lit up half a joint. "Don't worry, this is not for you." He waved it in his face. Father Bob ignored the implied offer and walked towards the water.

He climbed about halfway down the bank overtop large boulders that had been smoothened from centuries of running water. There it was, the old rope, hanging from a tree limb. Still had two large knots tied near the end for gripping. Could it be the same rope he'd swung from as a kid? He walked back up the bank and stood on a different boulder, where he stretched the rope to its capacity.

"Go ahead!" Barker shouted. "Maybe it'll take some stank off you."

He had already launched. Swung out over the creek, still wearing his workout clothes, including tennis shoes, and let go of the rope just as it made its descent back to the boulders. He knew exactly where to release, along with a quick memory of Dolph, another deceased shack boy, who once let go of the rope too late and cracked his head open on the rocks. Dolph had lapsed into a coma and took weeks to die.

He plunged into Cross Creek with perfect timing, catching the only deep part of the stream. He quickly emerged from under the water and stood shoulders deep. "Whew." He wiped his face and shivered. "It's cold!" he shouted. Then a familiar stench rose from where his feet had stirred the creek bottom. "Woo, smells musty, just like it always did!"

He heard Barker shout something. Barker had pulled off his boots and bandanna, and stripped down to his stained, used-to-be-white Jockey underwear. He found it amusing, watching tough-guy Barker walk so daintily, like a ballerina dancing in bare feet, overtop the boulders. Barker positioned the rope.

"Wait!" Father Bob started to move out of the way but Barker had already leaped from the rock. He soared directly over him, with his knees tucked into his chest. Barker tried to perform a cannonball but ended up hitting the water more like a baseball player sliding into second base, barely missing Father Bob's head.

Barker's face popped up from the water and he let out another howl. A trickle of blood ran down the side of his face. "I hit bottom!" They laughed.

"It's time I baptize you!" Father Bob grabbed onto Barker's head and tried to dunk it under the water. Barker fought him off and the two men wrestled, like when they were kids. Light brown, flaky balls of mud mixed with something darker brown stirred up from the creek bottom and floated in the copper-colored water.

They climbed up onto the boulders and sat, looking out over the creek. Barker still in his underwear, and Father Bob fully dressed in dripping workout gear. After a while, Barker said, "Yea, this reminds me of Chunk King too." They each recounted parts of the story of Chunk King, the kid who was as round as he was tall: After lunch one afternoon, the entire junior high switched buildings to go to the auditorium for an anti-smoking presentation, which featured "Smoking Sam," the clear plastic dummy with white cotton lungs. Smoking Sam sucked in a cigarette with the use of an air pump and his white lungs turned tarry brown. Year after year Smoking Sam bored the students, especially the shack boys. Father Bob and Barker were ninth-graders back then, and, on a whim they darted behind the crowd of students and ran down the steps that led to downtown Irontown. Chunk King followed them, but wanted to turn back. They egged him on, actually pulled him by his shirt all the way to the railroad tracks just in time to hop an empty, slow-moving freight. If Chunk King went back to school they'd get caught for sure.

The three boys sat with their legs dangling off the side of the empty flatbed, and cupped their hands in order to keep a match lit for the last Marlborough. They shared a smoke until the train reached a trestle next to second bridge. Chunk King didn't want to jump off because the train had gained speed, but Barker pushed him into the weed-covered hillside. Barker and Father Bob had leaped off in unison.

Father Bob and Barker were already skinny dipping in the creek, and then Chunk King swung out overtop them on the same rope, with a wild look, revenge-like in his eyes, as if he were going to bomb them. He let go of the rope too soon, and the momentum flung him onto a small island of mud, where he sank waist deep into a quicksand-like mound. He screamed as if in pain, so they did what friends would do at such a time...they laughed, until they saw Chunk King pull his bloody foot up out of the mud and it had a piece of broken glass, probably from a coke bottle, imbedded into the arch. Then they bolted out to Chunky and lugged him to shore, and at some point the sharp glass fell from his foot and the blood flowed even more. Barker pulled on a pair of underwear and ran for help, a short ways up the hill to old man McKinney's rotted, rag picker shack in the woods.

Old Man McKinney had walked down the hollow with Barker. The boys thought McKinney was ninety-years-old, but was probably only forty. When McKinney looked at Chunky, who was still naked, he let out a yelp, "Whoo wee, look at the tits on that heifer!" Then he coughed, which flung his Pall Mall non-filter from his lips to the ground. Barker picked it up and took a drag. McKinney's gaunt body shook with laughter. Father Bob thought the guy looked a lot like "Smoking Sam," which he told the other boys later for a good laugh of their own. McKinney made Barker give him one of his socks and wrapped Chunk King's foot with it. Then he gave each of the boys a fresh Pall Mall and hauled them in the back of his rusted pick-up to Chunk King's house, where his mother, who looked just like her son, stood horrified at the site of his foot.

"What are you doing hanging around with these hoodlums!" she yelled.

Chunk King wasn't really a shack boy, he was a halfway good kid, and his coal miner dad would certainly whip him with a belt for this. His mother drove him straight to the hospital for stitches, and Chunk King became yet another kid who was not allowed to hang around with the shack boys. When he went back to school the shack boys teased him, sometimes punched him from behind for no other reason other than being too stupid to land in the water.

"Those were fun days," Barker said with sincerity. "Is that why you kept your tennis shoes on?

"What do you think?"

"You know, you tried to dunk me but couldn't do it. If you weren't a priest I'd kick your ass right now."

"You don't see a collar on me, do you?" They laughed again. Barker kept laughing as he watched him get dressed.

Barker kick-started the chopper, "Back to the rat race, Padre."

Oh shit, reality. That nauseous stomach reappeared. He mounted behind Barker on the bike and felt the breeze chill his damp body. As his clothes dried in the wind, the "committee of know-it-alls" snuck back into his head and had convened another meeting. Random thoughts flushed the agenda, with issues such as the Bishop, boxing, making out with Maria, Sister Roxanne naked, Boss, Mrs. Hellinski, too much drinking, fighting, and now, riding on a Harley with Barker squeezed between his legs? He yelled, "I don't have a voice in my head, I have a whole committee. It sounds like the Last Supper!"

Barker turned his head in the wind and let his wet ponytail smack Father Bob across the forehead. "What?" he yelled.

"Nothing!" Then he had an idea. He loved the idea. The idea gave him some relief, a ray of hope. He pulled up on Barker's shoulders and lifted from the seat high enough to yell into his ear, "Promise me you'll come to church this Sunday."

Barker let go of the ape hangers with his left hand and flipped Father Bob the finger. He took that as a "yes." He leaned back against the sissy bar and patted Barker on the back. Wondered what time it was, and figured late afternoon.

They rode up the Hill of Churches. The sky threatened rain again and the sun disappeared. Barker stopped by the alley between the rectory and the convent. Father Bob jumped off the back of the bike and hugged Barker goodbye. Though steel workers and coal miners in Irontown generally didn't hug each other, other than the Italians, the shack boys did.

"See you in church Sunday," he tried to say, but Barker revved the engine, blasting away. He yelled back, "I already went to church once this year."

Barker rumbled away on the bike, probably headed for some bar somewhere. *Wish I could join him.* Worries about the Bishop dogged him once again, and he tried to divert those thoughts. *I should polish up my homily for Sunday.*

As he approached the porch by the rectory's kitchen, somebody was sitting on the gray-painted, metal swing. The closer he came, the more he made out the familiar posture, long beard, and barrel belly. Father Callo, a welcome distraction. He hurried his pace and jumped the steps onto the porch.

"Callo! How you doing old friend?" Father Callo stood up and they hugged. He stepped back and wrinkled his nose.

"You're moist. And what's that smell?" he asked.

Callo looked him up and down, put-off by his workout gear. *I've never seen Callo out of priest garb before. He's so tight I'll bet he even makes the diocese buy his socks.* "It's the smell of confusion," Father Bob laughed, "And a swim in the creek. What're you doing here?"

"I came down to talk to you." He shook his head back and forth with an expression of doom. "Why didn't you call me? I heard you're in a bind with the Bishop again. Maybe I can help you. I can't believe you didn't call me, Bob. Were you just with a biker?"

Even though Callo worked at Dominican University, only twenty or so miles away, Father Bob would never call him. Callo had never just dropped by before. "Call you and say what? That I screwed up?" He opened up the kitchen door to the rectory. "Come on in and sit down. I need to take a shower and get out of these clothes. How long do I get to have with you, professor, or should I call you doctor?"

"Go shower, please." Callo waved his hand across his nose. "Let's have a long glass of wine together." He opened up the cabinet under the sink and grabbed a glass gallon jug of red wine.

Father Bob stared at him for a moment, taken off-guard by Callo acting so familiar. He'd only been to the rectory once before. Callo wrapped his index finger around the thin handle on the jug of wine. He rubbed his protruding belly. "The professor's thirsty. He'll be waiting for you, my son."

During his shower, he watched the water turn brown as the creek on his skin washed down the drain. Callo was not to be trusted, that suck-up who just got a cushy assignment from the Bishop. He figured that the Bishop sent his boy here to get a heads-up on him. He hated being envious of Callo, and patted himself on the back for his tremendous feat today, the workout of all workouts, topped off by a swim in the creek and a ride on a chopper. The exhaustion in his legs converted into soreness. *What a workout.*

He dressed into black priest garb, fitted his collar, and looked in the mirror. *I'll be professional and courteous.* He walked gingerly down the stairs, feeling soreness throb in his calves and thighs. Callo had a full glass of wine waiting for him on the table. Father Bob picked up the glass, "I need to formally toast you on your appointment as full-time Doctor of Theology at Dominican University."

"Here, here," they clanked glasses. "It's a dream come true for me." He smiled smugly and nodded his head towards the doorway to the living room. "What's with all those flowers, funeral leftovers?"

Father Bob knew how to play poker, and not show his hand to Callo. "I'm going to bring them to the county cemetery tomorrow. They just..."

Callo interrupted. "I couldn't believe it when I heard you'd gotten into a fistfight. What in the world were you doing down there in that bar?"

Yes, no doubt, Callo's was the Bishop's spy. He'd play with Callo awhile, see if he could get him to admit that the Bishop sent him here. Father Bob remained standing while Callo sat. "Well, Professor, there's a certain amount of risk involved if you venture into a steel-town bar, you know, where the real people in the community hang out."

Callo gave a curious look. "But what were you trying to accomplish? Did you wear your collar down there?"

He threw the question right back at him, already losing patience with Callo's smug demeanor. "What are *you* trying to accomplish here and now?"

"I thought maybe I could help you. Share some spiritual guidance, whether it be confession or simply two friends discussing issues with each other."

Friends? He wanted to snap at Callo, the man who always acted spiritually superior, worsened now by his new assignment. He kept his cool, the upper hand, knowing that Callo wanted a confession. He paced around the table before standing closer to him. He'll make Callo confess. He's no match for a shack boy who knew how to get under his craw. "When's the last time you ran a parish, or administered to the working-class people in a real life congregation?"

He stared into Callo's eyes. Callo's face turned pink. He pushed out his lower lip with his tongue, broke eye contact. "Well, we each choose our own path, our unique way of serving God," he said finally with a hint of irritation in his voice. "I came down here to help you." He shrugged his shoulders. "Sounds like you have some kind of problem with me?"

He loved watching Callo squirm and fueled that reaction with a little sarcasm. He walked away, talking to Callo without facing him. "Problem with you? The holy one up on the hill? Who could ever doubt your spiritual guidance?"

Callo stood up from his chair, poured more wine, and then raised his voice. "I'm here because I want to be. You're the one who thinks he's Jesus Christ. That's always been your problem."

Father Bob laughed. He turned around and locked onto Callo's eyes. "If I'm Jesus Christ then who are you, Judas?"

Callo sat back into his chair and broke eye contact again. His lips moved like he was starting to speak for a moment, and then he closed them tight as though he decided not to say whatever it was he was going to say. He pondered the question. "I don't follow you. Judas? You think I'm selling you out or something?" His voice didn't sound as authoritative this time.

Father Bob knew he had gained total control. He remembered that same expression on Callo's face, about ten years ago, back when they were roommates in the seminary together. The day he walked into the dorm room and he'd interrupted Callow with his head in the lap of a new seminarian recruit. They ignored the incident, never discussed it.

"Are you going to make me ask, or are you going to tell me the truth about who sent you here?" He kept a calm demeanor.

"Oh c'mon. What's your problem?" Callo stood and paced around the kitchen on one side of the table. "Does it really matter?"

"So, the Bishop sent you here."

Callo's ears turned red. "He called me." His voice elevated. "That's all. He knows we're friends and he cares about you."

He resented the way Callo emphasized the word "cares," as though the Bishop were one of the shack boys.

Callo continued, "I'd have come to see you anyway. We only live twenty miles away from each other now. News travels fast around here."

"I knew it." Father Bob poured more wine, hid his rage by acting cool. "Why'd you make me have to pry it out of you? Is that your way of gaining trust? I may make mistakes once in a while, but I'm not stupid. Not like the scholars with their head in the clouds and their make-believe perfect world."

"So that's what you think of me?" Father Bob was probably the only one who had ever talked to Callo in this manner.

"Head in the clouds? Well, maybe you should try putting your head in the clouds instead of chasing women and getting into bar fights."

Callo's face shook and eyebrows frowned, like back in the seminary when he'd had a rare, inappropriate burst of temper. One time Callo tossed the chess set after the fifth time in row Father Bob checkmated him. He found Callo's anger amusing, almost charming. So he remained calm, resisted the urge to bring up the ambiguous incident with the seminary recruit.

"Oh, good one, Callo. You got me on that one. You can go back and tell the Bishop what a jackass I am, maybe that can help even up the score from the cushy assignment he gave you."

Callo dumped the rest of his wine into the sink. "I'm leaving before I say something in regret." He pointed his finger at Father Bob, who was still sitting. "You've got a problem with anyone being intimate, *Father.*"

"Well I guess that makes two of us." He nodded his head with a sinister laugh. Callo was just about to grab the door handle when a pair of boxing gloves flew into the kitchen from the living room. Black, leather sparring gloves landed onto the table, and freshly greased punch mitts hit the floor. Monsignor Murphy walked in wearing a smile.

Father Bob didn't realize that Murphy was in the rectory. Murphy stared proudly at the old boxing equipment.

"Sounds like you two guys might be able to use these," Murphy said with humor in his tone.

Father Bob grabbed one of the boxing gloves. He smelled the inside, still reeked of dried sweat and mildew. *These are my old gloves.* A boxer just knows. He stood up from the table. "They look brand new."

"Well, they're far from new, but should suit our needs." Murphy put a punch mitt loosely on his left hand and popped Father Bob in the stomach. "Protect the body with the elbows."

Father Bob didn't know what to say, so he just stood there. He looked at Callo, who stood by the kitchen door with an expression of fright. Then Murphy tossed a boxing glove at Callo, who hugged himself and made a slight shriek. The glove bounced off his shoulder and onto the floor. Callo gave Murphy a look of surprise.

Father Bob looked at Murphy also, speechless because Callo sounded so much like a woman. He didn't know what to say. He couldn't figure Murphy out, especially since the man had scolded him just this morning.

Murphy broke the ice. "Do you have time for a drink with us, Father Callo?"

Callo fidgeted. "I'm sorry Monsignor, but I was just leaving. Maybe next time."

Father Bob walked over to Callo and patted him on the shoulder. "Don't worry, we'll figure things out. After all, we're *friends*, right? Maybe I'll teach you how to box sometime."

Callo gathered his cool, tilted his head up, nose in the air. "Call me when you want to have a real discussion." He walked out the door. He bent a little when he stepped down the few porch steps.

Murphy laughed at Father Bob. "Looks like Bishop Malone sent one of his admirers down on a reconnaissance mission."

"Ah, you noticed? I didn't even realize you were home."

"I was upstairs greasing the gloves when I heard you guys come in."

"Yeah, Callo, my buddy from the seminary, was always first in line, maybe first to be in heaven, who knows?" He slid a boxing glove onto each hand and pounded them together.

Murphy opened the top cabinet and reached for his bottle of scotch. "Don't worry too much, son. We know how to throw a punch. They don't."

Chapter 9

Off the Cross

Father Bob trudged his way into the kitchen dressed in his robe. Rain had slapped against the bedroom window most of the night, no need to put on jogging gear. He passed by Monsignor Murphy, sitting in his usual spot hidden behind the Saturday morning newspaper, and he slid open the kitchen window to hear the storm through the screen. Closing his eyes, he hung his head and leaned over the sink, sure that his slight nausea was from distress about the Bishop coming to St. Anne's tomorrow to meet with him. The dreary weather fed the fear in his heart. *How could I face those same counselors if he sends me back to rehab?* His heart pounded faster. *If he fires me, where would I go?*

He poured himself a cup of coffee hoping the caffeine might rev him up. He pined for Jack. *My boy loved me no matter what.* He turned to the fanned-out newspaper hiding Monsignor Murphy. "You can barely see anything but rain out there this morning."

"Nothing like water from heaven to wash away our sins," Murphy said without looking from behind the paper, then added, "You have confessions from nine to eleven o'clock by yourself this morning. I doubt you'll have many takers. Saturdays are slow and even slower when it's raining."

He rubbed his eyelid with one hand, hoping the fading bruise would be gone by tomorrow. "Great, at least I don't have to see anybody in person today. It's a perfect day to sit in a dark box full of eternal sins." He wished that he didn't sound so full of self-pity.

Murphy folded a section of paper he was reading and replaced it with another. The headline predicted Ronald Reagan's re-election. Murphy commented again from behind the paper. "If Reagan gets re-elected that could be the final blow for the steel industry."

Father Bob paced, despite feeling drained. He stared at Murphy's newspaper for a while and felt like he was mimicking Jack, remembering the way Jack used to stare at Mrs. Hellinski when begging for a handout. Murphy kept on reading, oblivious to Father Bob's dire circumstance. *Maybe he's happy to get rid of me. I just can't figure the man, especially when he seemed so supportive around Father Callo yesterday.*

"I need to work on my sermon for tomorrow anyway, so I could use some down time today." He sat on a chair across the table from Murphy, and read the back of his paper. The silence from Murphy made him uneasy, so he stood up again and started to pace. It didn't make him feel better. He spoke loudly, "So, do you think Bishop Malone will attend my Mass tomorrow before he disciplines me?"

Murphy finally laid his paper on the table. His bottom lip stuck out on one side, like he was getting ready to spit a chew. "Probably," Murphy said. "Depends on what time he gets here." He pulled out a stained handkerchief and blew his bulbous nose, sounding a trumpet note, before stuffing it back into his pocket. Then he locked eyes with Father Bob. "I know you're nervous, but don't forget who you're saying Mass for the congregation, not the Bishop." He picked up another section of newspaper. "Pretty ironic that the Gospel reading tomorrow is from St. Luke's 'Prodigal Son,' don't you think?" Murphy studied the newspaper.

Father Bob took a deep breath and scratched his eyebrow. "It's all I can think about, trust me!" He tried to talk with a calmer tone and fidgeted his fingers on the tabletop. He used the side of his thumb to scrape loose granules of sugar into a small, organized pile. "I'm struggling with the sermon, you know, in terms of how much to divulge about my personal life." He paused, waiting in vain for Murphy's response. Rolling his eyes, he spoke on, despite feeling like he was bothering the old man. "On one hand, I'm not bound to reveal anything personal, but on the other, I think I owe the parishioners some degree of acknowledgement about my behavior." Murphy set his paper down and this time removed his eyeglasses, forcing him to give total attention. Father Bob raised one eyebrow and shrugged his shoulders, turning up his palms. "And then I have the Bishop in the audience."

Murphy cocked his head sideways, the way Jack used to do when somebody asked him if he wanted something. He smiled unexpectedly. "I remember back when you were seventeen, and living on our couch here in the rectory." His voice reflected some fondness, which comforted Father Bob a bit. "It was right before high school graduation, after your aunt died, and Maria eloped. I told you the whole spiel about how priests had to renounce all worldly possessions and family. You made that very same gesture, that same shrug, and said to me, 'I'm already there. Don't have nothing left to renounce.'" Murphy smugly chucked through his teeth. "Those words always stuck with me. I even used them in a homily or two throughout the years."

Murphy brought him right back into that wave of insecurity, when he had nowhere to live and slept on the rectory couch as a teenager. The nervous reaction invaded his stomach first, and he suspected it was worse than a simple case of butterflies. Years ago he could relieve those same butterflies after the first punch was thrown in a boxing ring, or on those occasions when he snuck into a married woman's bedroom. Now, as soon as he woke this morning and looked around his barren room, nothing could relieve the anxiety of possibly losing his livelihood. It used to be that saying the Holy Mass shooed away the butterflies, replaced them with the loving spirit of Christ. This morning, anticipating the religious ritual provided no solace. The Bishop would be out in the congregation scrutinizing him, like an invisible opponent throwing punches, with no bell to end the round.

Even Murphy this morning seemed to be mocking him, like he had already written him off. Maybe he knows something he doesn't want to share.

"That was a long time ago, what, '70? I have some serious problems right now and all you can do is laugh about it?" He spilled some coffee when he sprung out of his chair. "I'm going to take a shower and go hear sins. Have a nice day, Monsignor."

Murphy gave him an inquisitive look and shrugged. He jabbed his finger towards the chair. "Sit down." The tone made Father Bob hesitate. He followed Murphy's point to where he slowly sat down. He locked onto Murphy's reddened eyes, leaned his head forward, and readied for a challenge.

"I just bailed you out of trouble six months ago." Murphy's pink cheeks quivered. He slid his newspaper off to the side. "I may have played my last ace. I was afraid you'd revert to your old ways when I pulled strings to get you reassigned here in the first place, remember?" Murphy looked away, seemed to be trying to calm himself down. Then he pushed off the table top with both hands, grunted as he stood up and feebly walked to the cabinet, where he retrieved his bottle of scotch. He poured some into his coffee and set the bottle on the table.

Father Bob clenched his teeth. He remained silent while he tried to process a flood of emotions and thoughts. He couldn't lash out at the old man. He remembered how Murphy saved him when he was a youngster. Fast forward to six months ago, and how Murphy intervened when he was caught having sex with a married woman in the parish–a double whammy, not only did he break the vow of celibacy, but he'd committed adultery while counseling a distraught mother. *Murphy's right. I let him down.*

He hung his head for a moment, and then looked up at Murphy who was staring at him, seemed to be sizing him up. He didn't know what to say. He pursed his lips, relaxed them, and gave Murphy a cowering nod of agreement. He forced himself to ask Murphy an awkward question, one he wasn't sure he wanted an answer to. "So, have you talked with the Bishop about what might happen tomorrow?"

Murphy's expression turned as soft as a father who approved of his son's manner. "Just be yourself, son. Trust in God's will." He mimicked Father Bob's shrug. "What else can you do?" He stifled a laugh.

Before he could respond they heard a giggle from the living room. Mrs. Hellinski stuck her head through the doorway to the kitchen. She wore a crooked smile on her face. "Goodbye Monsignor, I'll see you at Mass tomorrow." Ignoring Father Bob she left through the front living room door rarely used by those familiar with the rectory.

He hadn't realized that Mrs. Hellinski was in the house. He figured that Murphy hadn't either, judging by the way he had looked askance at his bottle of scotch when she stuck her head in the room. He usually never took the bottle out of the cabinet until she left. He scrutinized Murphy's expression looking for a clue. *Maybe Hellinski and Murphy are already making preparations for a different priest to move in.* "I believe that's the first time I've ever heard her laugh."

Murphy didn't answer. He hid behind the paper again. He was through talking. He nodded and Father Bob walked upstairs to the shower, confused and distant, paranoid.

He looked at his face in the mirror while shaving, moving the razor carefully around his meticulously trimmed moustache. *I have no fight left. Throw in the towel. Your Will be done.*

He grabbed his pants and shirt, which were hung up in the bathroom, and returned to the mirror to fit the white collar around his neck. Donning it brought some confidence, similar to the excitement before a boxing match when Murphy would swipe gobs of Vaseline onto his headgear, nose and lips. He talked himself up, the way Murphy used to when he would nudge him into the ring and say, "Go tear'em up, champ." *I'm going through this troubled time for a reason.*

He walked down the stairs, out the kitchen door, and through the covered hallway, which shielded the rain. The storm had now intensified into thunder and lightning and he strolled through the middle of a waterfall, with the water rushing down the eaves on both sides of the narrow roof. *This could be the last time I hear confessions.* He looked at the two-inch tall figurines of various saints, perched equal distances apart on top of the ornate-trimmed baseboard lining the hall. Were they praying for him, as though he were leaving for good? At the threshold of the church, he became aware of his walking with hunched shoulders, without a trace of his cocky strut.

The scent of incense and stale perfume inside the dimly lit church straightened his posture. *I love this smell.* He walked with growing confidence behind the altar, and lit the two candles that stood freely on each side. He genuflected in front of the altar and bent over to kiss the top of it, pressing his lips against the stiff, white linen. His spirit rose, as he prayed for strength and an elusive sense of security. *This is my true home.* The actual name or location of the church doesn't matter. The presence of God and the Holy Spirit called him to the vocation, and God would have the final word, not any man. Not even the Bishop.

He walked down the two steps from the altar and paused at the first pew. A moist breeze blew through a few cracked-open, stained-glass windows, bedewing his nostrils with the cool fragrance of fresh rain. Applause from thick drops pounding down upon a tin roof outside greeted him. Then he sat down in the front pew for a moment to prepare his mind to hear the inner conscience of sinners. He disliked hearing confessions more than any other priestly duty, but was always astounded at how the Sacrament of Penance transformed a person into total honesty. If only Murphy would be honest with him. He stared at the white plaster Jesus, attached to the shiny, black crucifix hanging behind the altar. *What is Your plan for me?* Silence.

Father Bob always found the wooden box confessionals to be too old fashioned, behind the times. How he dreaded sitting in blackness, the middle of the box, while the faithful knelt on kneelers, hidden within dark closets on each side. Most parishioners attended the community confession held on the first Saturday of each month, where the whole crowd experienced group forgiveness followed by benediction and communion. That's more his style of forgiveness, along with the face-to-face confession that often turns into a spiritual guidance session. But some need privacy and anonymity.

Ready to hear sins, he walked towards the back of the church through the middle aisle, noticing three silhouettes kneeling with their heads down. They kept quiet and didn't look up, strategically stationed in pews a great distance from each other as if trying to be invisible. The two wooden confessionals loomed in opposite dark corners near the main entrance of the church. He chose to enter the confessional box to his right, drawn by a few stained glass windows set aglow for a moment by the lightning outside. He entered the middle box and shut the door. When he sat on the wooden stool, a small green light, the size of a toggle switch, lit up indicating that the priest was ready to hear sins. He heard two doors open on each side of him, and when the people knelt, a pinhead-sized green light glowed on the inside of his dark closet, giving the priest the signal he had customers. He slid open the right side panel, revealing a dark screen.

"Bless me Father for I have sinned," a voice whispered from behind the screen. It sounded like a teenage boy because of the nasal, insecure and mumbling tone. "My last confession was three months ago and here are my sins: I cussed at my *mother* five or six times and she told me I needed to go to confession."

The ungrateful manner in which the kid pronounced the word "mother" irritated him. He wished he had a mother to love him, especially now, when he was on the brink of losing his priesthood. *This young man does not recognize how lucky he is to have a mother.* "What made you curse at your mother?"

"Well, she comes into my room and snoops around when I'm at school. She found some naked pictures and a little weed. I was saving that weed for the *Duran Duran* concert, and she flushed it down the toilet."

Duran Duran? With Deep Purple, Santana, and The Who on tour, this kid wants to go see Duran Duran? "Okay, son, is there anything else you would like to confess?"

The young man sighed. "I might as well tell you that I play with myself a lot. I know it's wrong and I swear I'm going to quit after each time, but I never seem to quit." The kid's whisper got lower. "My mom said she knew what I was doing, and then she freaked out and said she was going to tell dad. That's when I cussed at her."

Here we go again, always the masturbation. He allowed a period of silence to dwell in the darkness, but before he could respond the boy spoke.

"My dad said if I keep doing it that my brain would go soft and I'd end up like Wackers."

Father Bob knew Wackers, oh a real character from his shack boy days, though Wackers had been older. Wackers would masturbate in front of people, anybody who'd asked him to, and then they'd laugh at him. Mentally retarded from birth, masturbation had nothing to do with it. Even Wackers had a mother. She probably loved her son no matter what. He wondered if Wackers still had his mother? He'd heard the old myth of masturbation leading to blindness before, but brain softening? He responded in as stoic a voice as he could muster. "Is there anything else you would like to confess?"

"That about covers it. Except for, uh, I did some cocaine with the new kid the other night. I mean, I never did it before, but this kid stole a baggie of it from his mom. It was free and I just did it because my other friend did it. I swear, Father, I'll never do it again. I didn't even like it."

Father Bob's heart dropped. *The new kid? How many new kids have moved into town recently?* His mind starting to race, though he knew he had to say something. The young boy was waiting for absolution. The boy broke the seemingly long silence. "Something the matter?"

Still, he didn't react. He grew angry, picturing Maria with her flippant laugh. How she had pretended to listen to his advice about her son. She had cocaine? Boss just overdosed and she's so careless she let him get into her stash? Now the kid's spreading it to buy friends, probably the only way he can get anybody to like him. He wanted to punch the inside of the confessional, thinking about how Maria was screwing up so bad. Instead, he took deep breaths, forced himself to focus on the present moment, for the soul who knelt before him.

"Father?" the boy asked, this time with fear in his voice.

His stool squeaked when he adjusted his position. "Son, God forgives you if you are truly sorry for your sins. But the love of God sometimes takes an effort on our part." He poured the sign of the cross over the screen, "By the power of The Holy Father, His Son, and The Holy Spirit, your sins are forgiven. For your penance, I want you to sit for about twenty minutes. Just think about all the good things in your life, such as how lucky you are to have a mother who cares about you. When thoughts of guilt come into your head, acknowledge them, let them go, and get back to meditating on the good things God has provided for you. Drugs can destroy the good things in your life. The love of Christ can give you the strength to control your urges before you hurt yourself or your family."

"Should I say an act of contrition too?"

"Of course, go ahead and say an act of contrition and be sure to come to Sunday Mass tomorrow." *This kid does not understand my "delight" penance.*

He heard the boy leave the confessional and he wanted to leave too. Maybe he would march down to Grandma Amelia's and confront Maria and Boss. What kind of mother would still have drugs in the house with a kid like Boss around? *No wonder Mario left her and wants nothing to do with the boy.* But he was stuck in a claustrophobic, dark box and had to take on everybody's problems, and people wanted to crucify him for blowing off some steam once in a while? Another person knelt down, and he already had somebody waiting on the other side. He closed his eyes, breathed slowly and deeply, and did his best to bring himself back into forgiveness mode. Then he spun on his stool and slid open the other black panel.

"Bless me Father for I have sinned," said a loud, middle-aged woman, whose breath reeked of garlic through the screen. "My last confession was about two years ago or so, and I can sum up most of my sins for you."

"Welcome back to God's house. God will listen to whatever you want to say."

"I've been having an affair," she whispered. Her voice had gone high pitched. She sobbed for a few seconds. He had heard this sin many times, and had a rote response prepared. The woman continued, "I've been cheating on my husband for almost two years. I don't know what to do, whether I should tell him or not."

The words flowed through his lips effortlessly, "If you tell your husband about the affair, you'll make him also have to live with the pain and hurt that you now feel. You can spare him the suffering by keeping this to yourself." He wished that he could hide cheating on celibacy from God. "Now if you're truly sorry for your sin, you would end the affair. God forgives you. God loves us and never leaves us. We are the ones who fail to recognize His love, which is…"

"I'm gay." She interrupted him. She must have had her hand covering her mouth. "I can't help it."

She shuffled around in the box and he wondered if she was going to take off. So he raised his voice, "Okay, please listen." yet his voice grew softer. "Really, there is nothing wrong with your being homosexual."

"Shh," she whispered. "I just wonder if God will ever forgive me or if I can still be Catholic, or if I'm just plain evil."

He clenched his teeth. The woman sounded desperate, a feeling he understood in his own life, as he had cheated on his vow as well. *Sex fills a need in us. Why does God give us a body and our religion condemns us for fulfilling our needs?* He leaned close to the dark screen, tried to whisper. He had to bring comfort to a Catholic homosexual woman.

"You are not evil for one second." He paused involuntarily, and tried to shake the image in his mind of the gay teenage boy who committed suicide after the Monsignor at his former parish tried to "heal" him. He should have intervened, but only found out about the episode too late. He had comforted the parents after their boy's death, and presided over the funeral. The Monsignor did not attend the boy's service. While comforting the distraught mother several weeks later, he held her in his arms for a long time. They breathed together and floated in grace while making love on the floor of the rectory's office. If only she hadn't told her husband. If only he hadn't crossed the line.

The woman's stomach growled and brought him back into the moment. *I need to make her feel like she's not alone.* "We're all human. We have needs that cannot be denied. Yes, the Catholic religion fails to comfort homosexuals. But look at us, the clergy, some of whom you must know are gay. Jesus would never turn His back on you or anybody else. We can pray to Him for the strength to control our natural impulses, whatever they may be, but we can't deny who we are." He struggled with his own impulses, and figured he hadn't really cheated fully yet with Maria, but definitely crossed the line. The church could be more generous than a jealous husband, though. The Bishop gave him a second chance, rehab and a re-assignment. This soul that knelt before him probably wouldn't get a second chance. In fact, her husband might beat her before kicking her out.

He chose his words carefully. "Listen, everybody is human with urges and lustful desires, but we try to manage our behavior with the help and love of Jesus, who understands and showers us with love."

The woman sniffled. Through a cracked voice, she whispered, "My lover's a nun."

Father Bob couldn't speak. She continued. "We're not just playing around. We're in love, and the Church strictly forbids it. I feel like a phony when we go to Communion together, yes, the three of us, her, me and sometimes my husband. She's talking about leaving the order and I feel like I, the sacrilegious one, am the cause."

The sin he'd just heard showered him with reassurance. *Finally, somebody else in the clergy around here feels as I do.* He itemized the number of nuns in the convent next door. Most were elderly. Some were there when he was a grammar student. *Sister Roxanne? Gotta be.* He leaned so far forward the tip of his nose scratched against the dark screen. Again, he mustered up the grace of God to help him focus into forgiveness mode and try to lend support the sinner on her knees.

"Sorry. A nun?" He paused for a second. "Yes, that's very powerful. Listen to me." He heard muffled thunder rumbling outside the church. "Your lover is responsible for her own decisions. A vocation is a calling that none of us can explain. If any one of us decides to leave, that's as personal a choice as was our original calling, not the fault of any other person." *Am I consoling myself?* "Remember that we are made in the likeness of God, and He will never turn us away." He poured the sign of the cross over the screen. "All your sins are forgiven by the grace and power of a loving God." She did not respond. "For your penance, just sit in the church and meditate on the crucifix. Not in guilt or unworthiness, but in love, knowing that you are loved. Give thanks for everything in life that delights you. Jesus showers you with love, not blame. And please, come to church tomorrow."

"Thank you, Father. I'd heard that you were a different kind of priest. God bless you." She slipped out of the confessional. He wanted so badly to crack his door and catch a glimpse of her, but even he would never go that far outside the rules. So he sat there, in the darkness, reflecting on how unfair celibacy can be. Homosexuals had it harder than he did. At least Catholic dogma didn't shun him. *Hide everything, hide our desires, hide our bodies and cover up the nuns' heads.*

He sat on the stool in the darkness, leaned his elbows on his knees and cupped his head in his hands, feverish with worry. His cold hands cooled his forehead. *What am I going to do about Maria and Boss?* Jesus once ransacked the temple, throwing vendors' tables against the walls in a rare account of wrath in the New Testament. Maybe he should mimic Jesus and wreak wrath at Grandma Amelia's, throw Maria's purse on the floor and reveal a bag of cocaine and other drugs. The Bishop would definitely fire him for that. A cough interrupted his reveries, where another sinner had been kneeling in wait. He inhaled slowly, once again, and exhaled quietly, hoping this would be the last confession of the day. He swung on his stool and slid open the dark panel.

"Bless me, Father, for I have sinned," It was another teenage boy. "My last confession was three weeks ago, and here are my sins: I've only masturbated twice since my last confession, so I trying to be good, Father."

My altar boy, Anthony. "That's wonderful when you try not to sin, son. Go on."

"Is that you, Father Bob?" Anthony recognized Father Bob's voice also.

"Yes, but please, it doesn't matter who I am while we're in confession." He tried to make this as painless as possible, knowing Anthony felt awkward. "Confess your sins to God."

"Well, I steal a pile of Church bulletins every Sunday." Anthony sniffled, like his nose was stuffed-up. He whispered, "You know, I take them to the store after Mass and hand them out to the kids who skip church. They give me cigarettes and stuff for them. Then they bring the bulletins home and their parents think they went to church."

Father Bob hadn't heard this old trick in a long time. Anthony's honesty made him smile. "Okay, that can be easily rectified." Then the figure of Boss skipping church popped into his head. He knew Anthony hung out with Boss. The thought of Boss buying a bulletin and fobbing it off on Maria made him angry, though he knew Boss had more serious problems. He wanted to pump Anthony for information about cocaine and Boss, but had to focus on the purpose of confession. "God forgives you for your sins. For your penance, tell the church skippers they'll have to get their own bulletins from now on, by coming to church."

"I can do that, Father Bob. Thank you. Should I say an act of contrition?"

"Do you have any other sins you would like to confess?"

"Well, not really. Nothing I can think of right now." Anthony coughed more, into a spell that lasted several seconds. He wanted to ask him about cocaine with Boss, but for the confidentiality of confession. He poured the sign of the cross over the dark screen. "Your sins are forgiven, by the power and grace of The Father, the Son, and the Holy Spirit." He heard Anthony finish whispering the act of contrition and then leave the confessional.

Father Bob remained in the darkness. Even the tiny, dim green lights lost their glow because confessions had ended and he had nobody kneeling at his side. Maybe he'd just stay in there. Even though it must have been around lunchtime, he had no appetite. *Be with me, Jesus.* He reflected in the blackness and heard nothing but the increased growl of thunder from the storm outside. Wind pounded rain against the windows and he figured he should get up and close the ones that were cracked open, but not yet. His hands started to tremble. Outside the door, giant serpents relentlessly gnawed at his soul. *Why does the idea of Boss and Maria doing cocaine bother me so much?* He clasped his head in his hands again, sobbed a couple of times, but could not even muster a tear and lost track of what he was feeling. *Oh my Lord, show me the way. Maybe I'm wrong about it.*

At that, a loud crash blared through the church.

He jumped. It sounded like an explosion, as though a window had blown out or something worse. His body jolted and his heart hammered. *Something terrible has happened.* He was almost paralyzed as if in a dream where you couldn't run even though you tried. He stood up and the adrenaline rush made his hands shake to the point where it was hard to turn the doorknob. Stumbling in his haste to get out of the confession box, he tripped and caught his balance on the end of a pew. He stood up and looked around, fully expecting to catch a glimpse of a culprit fleeing the scene. *That was surely more than a door slamming shut.*

He slowly walked down the right aisle, inspecting the stained glass windows. The wind may have blown one apart. He turned the metal hand crank at the bottom of a few partially opened windows to close them, and almost wished that a lightning bolt would blow him up while his hand touched the steel. Inspecting each window along the entire aisle, all appeared intact, so he walked across the church, checking the statues of saints, Francis, Mary, Joseph, Anthony and Anne, all stood still in the eternal position, some with arms outstretched. He wished they could take him.

He continued to search the source of the explosion and walked more swiftly down the aisle on the other side of the church. Rain splashed his hand as he cranked a few more stained glass windows closed. All the windows looked unmolested. The Stations of the Cross hung between the windows intact. He paused at the fourth station, which read in caps, "Jesus Meets His Mother." Figures of a black silhouette of Jesus stood erect, holding the cross, while he looked at His Mother Mary, her head covered. The prayer for that station grabbed his attention, so he recited it:

"Oh Mother of my Savior, you stand beside your Son. With love beyond all telling, you share His grief as one. How shall I know your sorrow, your tears beyond compare? Deep in my heart stand watching, and call my memory there." He was forsaken in his yearning for a mother's hug. His chest hurt, his heart raced and he could barely gasp for breath. Nausea returned to his stomach. He hung his head and slowly slid his feet across the floor towards the front of the Church. *I want to die and be with my mother.* Only a mother would understand his fear. He would die right in front of the crucifix and Holy Tabernacle. Mother Mary could hold him.

He approached the altar with his head still down. *Am I losing my mind?* Maybe that was the sound of him cracking up. Maybe he'll check into rehab, beat the Bishop to the punch. He wanted to run, sprint through the rainstorm and calm the voices in his head but was lucky to stand erect.

He walked up the two steps and froze in his tracks, hardly able to believe his eyes.

Jesus lay on the floor, shattered in pieces.

He gasped and grabbed his chest with his right hand, horrified.

Christ's head lay face up, decapitated and missing an eye. The other eye seemed to stare at him. He quickly moved his gaze from the eye to inspect the hollowness inside the broken head. Intact, red-stained hands lay on the floor, separated from the crumpled body of Jesus. White powdered mist of pulverized plaster covered the shiny black marble floor around the smashed statue, like the chalk outline of a murder victim on the streets of New York City.

Chapter 10

Invisible Nun

From down on his knees, Father Bob marveled at the broken pieces of Jesus scattered on the marble floor near the altar. His nausea subsided. The pain in his chest dissipated yet he had no feeling in his legs. A welcome calm descended upon him as he tried to pick up a piece of the plaster, but he could not move his hand. His body paralyzed, the dim glow from candles and lights inside of St. Anne's grew clouded and he thought he would pass out.

This is it. Jesus is taking me.

Astounded by his lack of fear, he faced his imminent death. A sensation of floating delighted him. He hovered above the floor and looked down at its shine. *I'm ready to be with You.*

Jesus was taking him home.

I am one with You.

Expecting to see light, or our Lord Himself, suddenly he saw the altar and the barren cross. His body anchored back to the ground, amidst the broken Christ figure. A chill rushed through the top of his head, and shivered down his spine. The faint whistle of a train blew in the distance. His knees ached and he did not want to come back.

Father Bob turned his head to see if anybody else was in the church, but he was alone. Desperate, he leaned and kissed the marble floor, where plaster dust scratched his lips. Straightening his back, he folded his hands in prayer position. *Please take me.*

The lunchtime steam whistle shrilled from the steel mill. Prior to the whistle, he wasn't sure how much time had passed, but now realized that he had not eaten yet and was hungry. *Jesus isn't taking me.* He grabbed a piece of Jesus' broken finger and stared at it. *You are magnificent. I want to serve You but don't know how anymore.* Tears welled in his eyes and he dropped the broken finger. The finger bounced onto the floor, tittered into silence. *I must be losing my mind.*

Suddenly, a woman's screech jolted him.

"Oh God in Heaven!"

Slowly scrambling up and to his feet, he turned to see Mrs. Hellinski standing in front of the first pew. Her mouth hung wide open. Her eyeballs magnified behind large-lens glasses.

Oh no, of all people. He moved toward her, wanting to ask what was the matter.

She made a fast sign of the cross. "Stay away from me!" She grabbed onto the top of the front pew with one hand. "You blasphemous devil!"

He took another step towards her, and then stopped, fascinated at how Mrs. Hellinski's body began to shake. Her wrinkled, long face twisted and trembled.

"I didn't..."

She interrupted him, enraged.

"You devil!" She pointed her shaking finger, spit flying. "Be gone, Satan!"

He shrugged, dumbfounded. She turned down the aisle, giving him one last horrified look, before hurrying out of the church towards the rectory. Frightened moans resounded through the covered hallway.

"I'll clean it up!" he called after her. But she was gone. *She thinks I attacked Jesus.* He looked at the broken pieces of Jesus. Then he laughed loudly, envisioning the mangled look of terror and accusation on Hellinski's face. *Is this my sign?* Nearly hysterical he laughed in a devilish manner, bending over and resting his hands on his knees. He straightened up. *She's running around telling everybody of the anti-Christ priest.* He imagined an angry mob gathering, with burning torches and pitchforks. By this time on Saturday, some of them were probably drunk. *Let them kill me.*

Father Bob walked into the sacristy to grab a broom and plastic garbage bag from the closet. He stopped to pick up a full gallon of sweet altar wine that was sitting on the floor. He unscrewed the top. A large gulp choked him, and he coughed some of the wine onto the ornamental chair in the corner. After wiping the chair, he turned to see if Hellinski was watching. She wasn't, so he screwed the lid back onto the bottle and carried the broom and bag to where Jesus lay in pieces.

He walked up the two steps leading to the altar. "Look at You," he said to the pulverized plaster. "You've fallen to pieces, just like me." He wrapped his fingers around a chunk of blood-painted forehead, which held a partial crown of thorns. A piece broke in half and shattered on the marble floor. *I'm so sorry to have forsaken You.* He made the sign of the cross out of habit.

Slowly, and more carefully, he filled the bag with large chunks of Jesus, first wondering about how real human beings had experienced similar fate on the battlefields of war, the poor souls who had the job of cleaning up such carnage. *I've never really had it so bad.* He swept the remaining small pieces into the bag. *This statue must cost a fortune. Perhaps Sister Roxanne and her students could piece Jesus back together, like a puzzle, but not likely. It's too far-gone.*

"It is finished." He carried the bag into the sacristy and placed it into the closet next to the altar wine. Should he hunt down Murphy and explain the episode? *Nah, let it play out.*

He faked a chuckle and strolled through the covered walkway towards the rectory, his only home. A feeling of doom washed over him, since it was a home he might lose. Scanning the small saints on the baseboard, he asked, "Got any miracles?"

The empty house filled with a rain-chilled breeze that blew through an open screen in the kitchen. Tired of worrying about the Bishop and everybody else's problems, he plopped onto the desk chair in the office. All the flower and balloon arrangements were gone. Murphy must have taken them to the cemetery already, like they always did with leftover funeral arrangements.

He opened the Holy Gospel to Luke 15:11-32 and tried to reread "The Prodigal Son," but could not focus, so he slammed the Gospel shut. In the kitchen, he opened the refrigerator and grabbed a handful of sliced provolone cheese right from the wrapping and shoved it into his mouth. He stuffed too much, and the cheese oozed from the corners of his mouth while he chewed. He was emotionally tapped-out and exhausted, but free.

He swung open the cabinet door above the refrigerator and retrieved a half-full bottle of scotch, taking a chug directly from the bottle. Then he grabbed a glass from the sink, didn't care if it was clean or not, and poured a pure one with no ice. After he drank that glass, he poured one more, which finished off the bottle. He looked at it glumly, then staggered up the stairs and collapsed into bed without drawing the shades.

*   *   *

Father Bob woke at four o'clock the next morning flat on his back, the exact position he'd passed out in. His neck stiffened and an ache pounded behind his right eye, now almost totally healed from the fight the other night. His throat was parched as dry as powdered milk as he shuffled along the second floor hallway into the bathroom, where he peed enough to douse a brush fire. He took his shirt off and washed his face in the sink. Though the door was closed, the snore of Monsignor Murphy resonated over the running water as he washed his hands. He splashed soothing water on his face. The Morning Prayer he recited sounded different. The words of the prayer came alive this morning, unlike the rote memorization of most mornings. He realized that he was still a priest, even if the Bishop planned to change that. *I'll serve You as long as I am able.* He recalled being pounded with punches in the boxing ring and knew he had to quit feeling sorry for himself in a hurry if he was to survive.

Barefoot and shirtless, he headed down the hallway. He had slept in his pants. Normally he'd dress for breakfast, but didn't expect anybody to be in the kitchen this early in the morning. The wood creaked under the carpet as he stepped down the stairs leading to the kitchen. In search of coffee and cool water, he stubbed his toe on the leg of Murphy's blue, vinyl-covered chair. "Ouch!" He grabbed the can of Maxwell House that sat on the counter, flipped open the plastic lid, and dumped the contents into the coffee machine, spilling grounds all over the countertop. Ignoring the mess, he filled a glass with water, and a note on the table caught his attention. He could barely focus enough to read the messy handwriting, which he immediately recognized as Monsignor Murphy's:

"Father Bob, get me up if you wake before me. I need to talk to you before the Bishop comes. It's urgent! I couldn't wake you last night."

Murphy will have to wait. He stood up and poured a cup of coffee while the pot was still brewing. The coffee droplets sizzled on the hotplate. He sat back down and savored how the warm liquid soothed his throat. Coffee provided hope of feeling normal, that this was just an ordinary day. There was no Bishop Malone coming, no Maria tempting him, no bar fights, no broken Jesus, no Boss doing cocaine, and no Mrs. Hellinski screeching. He was grateful that the morning sun didn't shine through the window yet, because he wanted to be gone before Hellinski showed up, her shriek, the way she had accused him.

How could she think that I smashed Jesus? That's the least of my worries. This morning he knew what to say, as if enlightenment entered his mind through his drunken dreams and Morning Prayer. If anybody wanted to make an issue of the broken Jesus, go ahead, he'd like to know what happened as well. Either way, he would remind them it was only a statue, nothing more than pieces of hollow, cold plaster. The greatness it represented was all that mattered.

From where he sat, he could see the Catholic calendar stuck to the side of the refrigerator with a Saint Anthony magnet. Captions under the date wrote: "Sunday, June 15th, 1984…Eleventh Sunday in Ordinary Time…Father's Day."

I don't believe I forgot it was Father's Day. That made the sermon easier. He could just use his homily from last year and focus on the fathers in the crowd, summing things up with the forgiveness that comes from God the Father to everybody. They should forgive him as well. He'd devoted his life to help them. *I am what I am.*

The sound of a flushing toilet upstairs interrupted his daydream. He hurried up to his room to throw on a shirt before Monsignor Murphy could come downstairs.

When Father Bob, properly dressed, walked back into the kitchen, Murphy had his back to him and was occupied twisting the top off a bottle of scotch. He poured a healthy belt into his coffee. Then he banged the bottle onto the countertop and mumbled something.

"Good morning Monsignor," he said, trying to lighten the situation with a show of gratitude. "Thanks for letting me sleep yesterday evening."

Murphy turned around and looked at him like a dad about to dole out a whipping. "I didn't let you sleep," he barked. "I couldn't wake you."

Murphy plopped down and sipped some of his coffee cocktail. "I had to go back out last night to buy another bottle. If you're going to drink all of my scotch, you need to replace it. Never leave me with an empty bottle."

How could he get so peevish over a bottle of scotch? I'm sick of everybody arguing with me. My head hurts.

"Yea, well you just may have to replace *me* after today." He sat down across from Murphy and stared him right in the eyes. "Remember what you said to me a long time ago before the first round of the Golden Gloves tournament? You said, 'There's nothing more dangerous than a fighter who doesn't care,' and I believe I've reached that stage." Murphy replied with an immobile, cold stare. Father Bob shrugged his shoulders and turned his palms toward the ceiling.

Murphy clasped his hands in front of him with his elbows on the table and looked down, as if he were praying. He sat that way for a moment, and then breathed a deep sigh. "I doubt you're going to get off that easy, son." He looked back up. "I talked with Bishop Malone on the phone yesterday. He's coming to Mass today and said that he has something for you. And then, you're going to have dinner with us at Grandma Amelia's afterwards."

Father Bob's injured eye twitched. He shook his head quickly, as though he had taken an uppercut and was trying to regain focus. *Grandma Amelia's dinner?* "I can't play these games anymore," he said. "This whole thing's driving me nuts. Now we got dinner with the whole gang? Fine...whatever. What about Hellinski? Did she hunt you down?"

Murphy laughed. Spittle shot from his mouth onto the tabletop. "She's probably afraid to come too near the rectory." His laugh turned into a cough. "I figured you'd liven this parish up a bit when you first came here, but I don't know if my old heart can take much more of this."

He laughed half-heartedly, only because of Murphy's laughing. Confused, he asked, "She's afraid because of me? What's the Bishop going to give me? What did you do with those boxing gloves and punch mitts?"

"Slow down, son. First, let me tell you, she came right into the Knights of Columbus hall in a tizzy like I've never seen her before. Said you smashed Jesus to pieces." Murphy slapped the table and his saggy cheeks shook. The sudden noise startled Father Bob, who just stared at Murphy's animated face. Murphy went on, "I didn't believe her for one second." Then he held up his index finger. "But, some of the Knights heard the story and wanted to lead a lynch mob of sorts." He took another sip of scotch-laden coffee. "We've needed to reinforce some old bolts on those statues forever, but the budget didn't have room for renovation this year."

"Who? Which Knights wanted to come after me?"

"Take it easy." Monsignor Murphy blew his nose into the same yellow stained handkerchief he had been using for the past week. "Everybody knows Mrs. Hellinski's a little off kilter. It didn't take much to calm them down. But...you won't believe it. Well, I don't know, maybe you already know the whole story."

"What? Know what story?" *He's toying with me.*

"Oh, never mind." He grabbed yesterday's newspaper, which was still lying on the table. Father Bob snatched the paper out of Murphy's hand. Murphy looked at him and said, "I thought you didn't care anyway, right? Isn't that what you just told me?"

He tilted his head sideways at Murphy, still holding the newspaper. "You can be a very cruel man sometimes."

"Okay, okay." Murphy raised his right hand. "You're not going to believe this, though." He cleared his throat.

"Are you going to tell me what happened or what?"

He nodded. "I got a phone call up there from Mother Superior." Murphy slowly shook his head. "She called to inform me that Sister Roxanne had tendered her resignation."

"What! Why?"

"Said she was gay. Yeah, said she was a woman who loved women." Murphy pushed his coffee cup over towards him, as a nonverbal command for a refill.

"Oh, no. Oh, that poor dear…but she can still be a nun." *Was this because of my advice to her lover to end the affair?* Father Bob grew sick to his stomach but tried to keep his composure. More immediate, he had to refill Murphy's coffee if he wanted to hear the rest of the story. After pouring more coffee into both cups on the table, and then hurrying to put the pot back onto the burner, he flipped his hand out in front of him, giving Murphy the clue to continue.

Murphy nodded in approval. "Then, completely out of the blue, Mother Superior said that Roxanne committed a worse act than *my* priest," he pointed his finger at Father Bob. "That she was in love and having an ongoing affair with a married woman, not just a one night fling!" Murphy paused with his mouth partially open, like he was going to sneeze. "I've never heard Mother Superior talk like that in all of my years."

Father Bob's face flushed warm. He bent and laid his cheek on the Formica table, covering the back of his head with his hands. The coolness of the blue tabletop felt refreshing, so he turned his cheeks from side to side to soothe the feverish heat in them.

"What's wrong with you?" asked Murphy.

Knowing where Murphy stood on the gay issue, Father Bob did not want to engage with him. He had to find Sister Roxanne. "Where's Sister Roxanne?"

Murphy shook his head. "I imagine she's packing her bags. Might even be gone by now. The Church won't tolerate an actively gay nun. Everybody knows that. Roxanne made her own bed, so to speak."

Murphy wouldn't know a genuine feeling if it slapped him upside his head. Is this what happens to us later on as priests, we become cerebral administrators?

Murphy stared at him, as if waiting for his response. Father Bob had to choose his words carefully. Grabbing the bottle of scotch, he splashed some into his cup and then into Murphy's.

Finally, he responded. "How many gay priests do you think we have in our diocese? Maybe there are even a few Knights in the Boy's Club who are gay." *I shouldn't have said that.*

Murphy looked sour. He reached for his coffee cup and knocked it off the table, where it bounced off the floor. The ceramic cup cracked into pieces. Liquid flowed overtop the linoleum floor.

Father Bob jumped out of his chair and grabbed a broom from the closet, sorry that he had challenged Murphy because he already knew where Murphy stood on the issue. He swept the ceramic and liquid into a pile, while Murphy stood, wiping his pants. He looked irritated. "I'm just saying that the Church ignores gay priests, you know, 'don't ask, and don't tell' right?"

Murphy interrupted with a shout. "Don't tell me what our doctrine teaches!" He remained standing, held himself up with one hand on the table, and wagged his other hand in front of Father Bob's face. "I've lived by the doctrine my entire life, unlike you!" Anger sprayed from Murphy's mouth. "Being homosexual is one thing, but *acting* on it is different and cause for dismissal and no, that's not going to change, nor should it. Everybody knows the rules coming in. Our Church has withstood and outlived every fad there ever was for over two thousand years. Roxanne makes her own choices, just like you do."

It was clear that the church was not very forgiving. He needed Murphy on his side, though, so he pretended to agree and acted humble. As much as Murphy seemed insensitive to Sister Roxanne's plight, Father Bob could not. She was a person with whom he felt a connection. He swept the broken cup into a dustpan and dumped the trash into the garbage. Then he wiped the floor with a dishtowel. He looked up and asked Murphy one more question. "Where will Roxanne go?"

Murphy sat back down in his chair. He seemed a little calmer after Father Bob cleaned up his mess. "Her family lives in Wisconsin. I imagine she'll go back there." He fanned out the newspaper and disappeared behind it.

Go back home? Families often disown gay children. Leaving the convent would make it even worse. He stopped wiping the floor, looked up at the back of the newspaper, and told himself over and over to keep his cool. He wanted to yell at Murphy for being so insensitive. Tried as he could to control his emotion, he had to say something. "Her family may not want her, you know." Murphy didn't respond.

"I'm going over to the convent to see if she's still here, at least to say goodbye."

"Don't be too long, Father, you have a big day ahead of you. You can throw stones later if you want," Murphy said from behind the paper.

Father Bob walked through the alley separating the convent from the church. Rain puddles on the cement road shined like black oil slicks in the darkness. He recalled how a few of the gay seminarians used to look down on him for being too honest about his heterosexual desires. They acted superior, more advanced spiritually because they didn't lust after women. He admired Roxanne's courage to come out of the closet, though, and liked the way that some of the Knights may have been shocked when Murphy undoubtedly shared the news. Then he thought about getting exposed for having sex with that mother in Columbus, whom he had counseled after her gay son had committed suicide. The Monsignor at that parish had tried to heal her son, like homosexuality was some sort of disease. He knew, though, that if he had publicly gotten caught having sex with a man, he would have been ousted. At least he didn't have the complication of a closet to come out of.

His mind still swam in rambling thoughts as he climbed the steps onto the convent's porch. When he pushed the doorbell, the button stuck to the oval frame, immobile from years of dried, gray paint. Waiting there, he resisted the temptation to look through the front room window. *What will I say to her?* She had confessed to him about masturbating, and they'd shared feelings about the isolation of celibacy. He should have realized that she was not as innocent as he had thought. She was more like he.

He knocked on the door this time and finally the porch light came on. The door cracked open several inches. Mother Superior, dressed in full Dominican garb, stuck her head out and asked if she could help him.

"Excuse me, Mother Superior, sorry for the early hour, but I came to check on Sister Roxanne."

"Oh, Father Bob," she peered more closely at him, looking inquisitive. "I thought for a moment that you might be the taxi driver." She opened the door with a blank expression on her face. "You can wait in the living room, Father. I'll go tell her that you're here."

He sat on a worn couch next to a hard-sided, powder blue suitcase sitting upright on the wooden floor. Besides the presence of a coffee table, the room was barren and smelled of Clorox bleach. *What a different world.* He twanged with guilt comparing the nuns' lack of possessions with the comforts of the rectory, a place that had cleaning ladies and leather furniture and stately offices and never-ending bottles of scotch.

The wooden stairs creaked when Roxanne walked down. This would probably be the last time he'd ever see her. She wore a Pittsburgh Steelers T-shirt, her hair tied in a brown ponytail, and her eyes held a radiant glow. He wondered if she was going to leave without talking to him, as though blowing him out like a candle.

"I'm so happy to say good-bye to you in person," Roxanne said. "You brought a smidgeon of fun to the parish, as brief as it was, and some understanding." She laughed nervously.

He stood up and hugged her with a full body twist, from one side to the other, almost lifted her off her feet. The top of her head smelled like roses. Here was this beautiful woman he was embracing and yet his urges were to hold and comfort her. "I can't believe you're going," he said.

She gently moved him back with her palms against his chest. "Let's sit for a minute." She positioned herself in the middle of the couch. "I've already called a taxi. I'm ready to go and have been pacing around. You didn't have to come over. I'm sure Monsignor Murphy told you all about it…I planned to write you a letter."

"You must be devastated. It breaks my heart." He sat next to her on the couch and his knee touched the side of her thigh. He felt her tenderness on his knee, so he moved it away. He wanted to comfort her, but was not sure how.

"I just couldn't play the game anymore." She locked eyes with him. "I feel like a weight with sharp spikes has been lifted from my back. Just a few hours ago, I tendered my resignation into laicization." She paused, looked towards the suitcase. "Funny words, huh?"

Those words cut. She was really leaving, and probably didn't sleep at all last night. The thought of possibly losing his holy orders frightened him, but Roxanne seemed to be fully grounded. "Terrible words, terrible," he said. "We'll miss you so much around here."

"You'll be just fine, Bobby." She smiled and showed her perfect teeth. Her parents must have been fairly well off to afford orthodontics. "I think you have a gift, I mean it, Bob. People are warming to you. God knows the Catholics in this town need somebody *real* to talk with."

"Well, you're the same way. The teaching, the kinship with the community, what will you do out there in the real world?"

She raised her eyebrows. "I'm looking forward to it. I mean, with seven years of teaching experience, I could get a job as a teacher anywhere, and maybe even get paid for it. Imagine that, a real paycheck!"

"No, a paycheck is hard to imagine, after the small stipend we're used to." He hadn't thought that far ahead, despite the possibility that he could be ousted as soon as today. "Honestly I hadn't realized that you were gay."

Roxanne grabbed the top of his hand and squeezed it. "It's not like I chose it. Obviously, it complicates things."

He clasped his hands together and knew he was blushing. "You can be gay and still be a nun. Why leave?"

"I couldn't stay here and live a lie any longer, unlike…" She bowed her head and shook it. "I'd better be quiet."

"Roxanne, look at me. Talk to me. I want to know what you're thinking."

"Well, okay. You received a second chance, and I'm sure that your previous indiscretion torments you…and then there's Maria." She paused. "Are you sure you want me to go on?"

He was speechless, yet tried to decipher what she had just said. Everybody knew about his second chance, but Maria? Then he realized that Roxanne was speaking with her heart, that truth gave her strength. He will help her, by allowing her to help him. "Roxanne, I have nothing but respect for you. I am honored by your honesty…please, continue."

"Okay, if you want me to." She cleared her throat. "I think that you're living a lie as well. I mean, it's obvious to me that you love Maria. Even if you didn't, you still lust for women. Trust me, I feel the same attractions to women that you do. Both of us have even acted on it. How can we be devoted to God at the same time?"

Butterflies ran rampant in Father Bob's stomach, but for once he did not automatically counterpunch. Trying to hold

Roxanne's gaze, tears welled, so he hung his head, looking at the meticulously clean wooden floor, pondering her question. At last he took a deep breath and made eye contact again. "I don't know." Shook his head and said, "All I know is that I haven't felt effective as a priest ever since my incident, even after spending three months in residential rehab."

"I'm sorry to hit you with this," Roxanne responded calmly. "But you asked. And yes, I know all about the collar. I've seen how people look at priests. When I walk, dressed in my habit, people look the other way like I'm invisible. Even priests look past me, but you never did. That's one reason why I feel that I can talk with you." Her eyes emanated warmth. "I know how much the truth hurts, but priests aren't invisible like nuns."

He didn't know what to say, so just he sat there. *Invisible?*

Roxanne spoke. "I don't think that you and I are that much different. I mean, maybe we're drawn to relationships we cannot have. And I'm not talking about sex, that's the easy part, what we seek is something much more meaningful and how can we find it without first being honest with ourselves?"

He looked past Roxanne, and fixated his eyes on the floor by the radiator. "I don't know…I've said that already, didn't I?" He looked up and placed his hand on top of hers. "You are a special woman, I *do* know that. I'm still trying to sort things out and God's plan for me will unfold. You, on the other hand, will find what you're searching for much sooner than I will."

"That doesn't matter." A horn blew from the taxicab that pulled up outside. She whispered, "My ex-girlfriend will pay for the statue that she broke, but please keep it quiet." She choked up. "Obviously, I'm leaving her too." She smiled thinly. "You're 'delight' penance doesn't seem to work for *everybody.*"

Father Bob was stunned, not just from hearing about a woman breaking Jesus, but Roxanne's words slowly swept into his conscious like all the broken plaster into a garbage bag, a dark place where he did not have the option to fight back. Lights out.

Mother Superior walked past the living room. "Taxi's here." She continued to the front door and opened it.

They stood up from the couch at the same time and studied each other's face for a few moments. He wanted to talk with her for so much longer, and hoped that she wanted to do the same. *Maybe one day.* Although stunned, he hoped that Mother Superior was not eavesdropping. Roxanne stepped closer to him. He rested his hands on top of her shoulders,

"May God watch over you." He made the sign of the cross over her, thanked her. "Please stay in touch."

"Good luck with the Bishop today," she said.

He reached for her suitcase but she grabbed it before he could. The outdated, blue box held her only possessions. She walked out the door towards the taxi without a word to Mother Superior, who stood there quietly.

Father Bob followed her out onto the porch. Roxanne threw her suitcase into the back seat of the taxi, got in and then waved to him. The taxi spun off. He watched it drive away, with Roxanne in the back seat, until it went out of view. No fanfare.

The convent door shut and he turned toward the alley, unsettled. *Why am I here?* An image sprang into his mind, Maria years ago getting into Mario's Cadillac and driving away. He envisioned walking to the highway bridge back then, and could even hear the sounds of cars whistling past as he climbed over the guardrail and stood there in the wind, close to jumping off when he heard that mysterious whisper to "Come follow me."

So much had happened, so much yet to be done. He headed back to the rectory.

CHAPTER 11

LAUGHING ALTAR BOYS

Father Bob stood in the sacristy, wearing green vestments trimmed in white. He breathed in deep and exhaled slowly a few times to calm his nerves while waiting for the altar boys to return from lighting the candles surrounding the altar. *Forget about the Bishop being in the congregation.* He put some final touches on his garb when the boys rushed back into the sacristy. Both were wide-eyed and had their mouths open. The new altar boy, Aldo, looked pale.

"It's packed like Midnight Mass on Christmas Eve!" Anthony said. "The Bishop's out there!"

Father Bob's mouth dried. "It's just another Mass. We do everything the same way, whether there are ten, or fifty bishops in the pews." He wished he believed his own words.

As soon as the church bells stopped ringing, he heard the soothing sounds of a congregation ready for Mass...the flurry of footsteps, pounding of kneelers, and cries of babies. These familiar noises calmed him. Father Bob readied himself to take center stage and lead the ritual that honors Christ. Anthony lined up first, carrying the cross, followed by Aldo, whose hands quivered holding aloft the word of God. Father Bob stood last in the small procession, anticipating the entrance hymn. St. Anne's choir crooned from the balcony, *"Lord, grant us salva-ation..."*

"Let's go." Both boys turned to him. He nodded his head for them to proceed.

Anthony led the procession down the side aisle, between the row of arches and the wall where Stations of the Cross hung between the stained glass windows. Father Bob trailed behind, celebrating in song with the congregation and briefly scanning the parishioners crammed into every pew. He didn't want to appear to be looking for the Bishop, and so did not return the few waves and smiles directed towards him, trying to stare straight ahead as much as possible until the procession turned around to the back of the church towards the middle aisle. There he glanced at a few standing Knights. *Wonder why they never invited me to join?* A few members of the Catholic men's organization served as ushers, which allowed them to walk around during the Mass, collect monetary offerings, and stood in the back of the church while everyone else squeezed into pews.

The trio turned the corner and move slowly up the middle aisle. Most of the congregation sang along, some undoubtedly lip-synced, their voices overpowered by the electrically amplified choir. The eyes of the congregation fell upon him, and he experienced their reverence. His eyes filled with the light of the Lord, absorbing the energy of the crowd. They had come to support their priest. This was not just another Mass.

He stood behind the altar and faced the congregation, the altar boys flanked on each side. When the hymn ended, the silence of the assembled crowd offered him total control. He paused for a few moments to establish his authority and breathe in the sweet air of belonging. This could be his final Mass. He outstretched his hands to the collective congregation, "The Lord be with you."

"And also with you," they responded.

"Let us pray."

The humidity thickened with silence, with the exception of the sound of creaking wood and a mother muffling the whine of a child. From afar an occasional clank of coupling trains could be heard, reminding the faithful about the life waiting for most of them outside of the church. He bowed his head and felt a rush of grace warm his body, satisfying a craving deep within. *I'm still a priest.* The arguments with Murphy, Sister Roxanne calling him out, nothing could interrupt his peaceful state of grace. He lifted his head up to scan the crowd. His eyes burned bright into the gathered eye returning his gaze. He locked vision with Maria for a moment, almost glued to her glowing green eyes before breaking the stare. He looked again for Bishop Malone, whose height would tower over most of the crowd.

He siphoned strength from the congregation and returned it, creating flow like a conduit delivering electrical grace. The ritualistic words rolled from his lips. After cantering the prayer of the Gloria, he genuflected and kissed the top of the altar.

He performed traditional gestures gently, made all feel welcome in God's house, the only place where humans loved each other openly. After one of the elders read the Epistle, Father Bob sauntered to the pulpit and the crowd stood. When he finished reading the Gospel, he paused, watching the crowd sit in preparation for his homily.

"We honor our fathers today, those with fathers still with them and those without." He locked eyes with Maria again and this time lost his focus. "My own father died when I was very young." He raised his palms. "But God took care of me, like He does all of us. He is our true heavenly father." Maria smiled, and his mind went blank. He looked down at the pulpit and fumbled his hands as if he had notes. *Play me like an instrument of peace, Lord.*

And then he walked down, deliberately leaving his microphone behind on the pulpit, and faced the congregation. Heads in the crowd turned to him and some folks in the back stood up in order to see. On impulse, he turned his hand to the empty cross, the one where Jesus had fallen and cracked into pieces. "We don't need a plaster statue to confirm our faith," he shouted. "We don't worship statues like the pagans." He knew how unusual it was for the priest to come down from the pulpit. He fixed his stare towards Mrs. Hellinski. She removed her eyeglasses and wiped them with a cloth. Father Bob placed his right hand over his heart. "Christ is in here, in our hearts, and in our souls. All we need to do is call on Him to comfort us. Just like the Father in the Prodigal Son."

He walked down the middle aisle, and stopped in the center of the church. *This could be my last sermon.* He slowly turned from side to side. "All of you didn't come to church to hear *my* prayer. This is *your* prayer, *your* church." He outstretched his hands over the congregation. The laity stirred. Some of them sat with their mouths slightly opened, others jockeyed for a better view.

"I'm sorry to tell you that you did not choose me. God did. And I don't know why. I do know that Jesus didn't come down to earth for the righteous, he came to give hope to the thieves and prostitutes, and I'm not talking about midnight shift at the steel mill!"

The crowd laughed, and most them in the back of the church were standing, some children even stood on the pew seats to see. Almost an evangelical event, not one person in the crowd yawned. "If Jesus walked on earth right now, he would not have ended up in a gin brawl down at the Argonaut."

At that, the congregation howled. Mrs. Hellinski made the sign of the cross. Pumpkin raised one fist into the air and shouted something that sounded like, "Right-on!" Maria clapped. Boss stood in a blank stare as usual, and others he did not recognize laughed at each other with surprise on their faces.

The crowd would egg him on. He would perform for them like no other priest ever had. He tugged at his collar. It popped and slid off of his neck, into his hand. He looked at the collar dumbly. Sweat beaded on his forehead.

The church fell silent. The congregation remained locked onto him. He knew that if he looked up at their faces he would see shock. He held up the collar to inspect it more closely. It curled in his hand and inspired him. Surely this was God's will. He turned it in his hand and then lifted the collar higher towards the heavens as if handing it to God. The congregation sat, mouths agape. "This collar proves nothing! It's just a sign that speaks about a greatness way beyond me, way beyond any man of the clergy, even the Bishop!"

The crowd went totally silent. He wished he could take back the words about the Bishop, but it was too late.

"Why I was called to do Christ's work? I don't know. Perhaps because I was forgiven, forgiven for not caring about my life at the time." He turned his palms upwards, shrugged his shoulders, and walked back towards the altar. The look of fright on the face of his altar boys gave him power. He winked at them. He knew these people, his congregation. *I'm one of them.*

He turned around on top of the steps before he reached the altar and faced the stunned parishioners. The white collar was still in his hand, and he wanted to fling it into the crowd, towards the area where Maria and Boss were seated. But he couldn't part with it. He tried to fit it into his shirt collar, like a clip-on tie, but needed a mirror that was not there, so he slipped the collar into his pocket.

"That collar is just a piece of plastic, like the Christ that used to hang on our cross was plaster. What counts most is what we carry inside our hearts." He hung his head, paused and lifted his face to the congregation. "I'm human. Just like you, I'm naked human." He lifted up his green vestments, showing his black pants and shirt. "See, I wear pants. We're all the same. Let us share the love of Christ from our hearts."

He figured that after practically flashing the crowd, he was fired for sure. He turned and walked to the altar, where Anthony and Aldo covered their mouths, trying to hide their laughter. He laughed along with them. Then...he heard applause, loud applause. He turned back around and the entire congregation stood on their feet, clapping. Some whistled. Again he tried to put his collar on, but it just wouldn't stay, so he slipped his hand under the vestments and slid the collar back into his pocket for good. The clapping slowed, as he stood and scanned his congregation. *Did the Bishop walk out? So what if he did.* His eyes welled with joy, and he forgot about his troubles. He had no idea what to do, so he took a bow. That was a first. He held up his hands, palms facing the parishioners.

His genuine charisma could not be shattered, even with the possibility of this being his last Mass. He wanted to stay in this moment. Alas, he had to get back to the actual Mass, the real reason people gathered in the first place. Back into priest character, he said, "Okay." He smiled and nodded. "Now, let's celebrate with Christ. This is His party!"

After the Profession of Faith prayer, a young family carried the offering of bread and wine to the altar. Father Bob stood strong as Anthony, the lead altar boy, poured water over his hands. He dried them with a white cloth and looked forward to the best part of the Mass, his favorite priestly duty.

The transformation of the Eucharist, the consecration, turning bread into the body of Christ, and wine into His blood, made his soul float above the ground once again. The grace magnified tenfold today in the standing room only church. He transformed the physical into the spiritual, signifying the hope that was hidden in every heart. Closing his eyes, he glimpsed at himself from the vantage point of the ceiling of the church for a brief moment, as though his spirit had slipped free from his body and looked down upon the altar. Just like yesterday, when he wanted to die with Jesus. *How could I live without this?*

The giggle of altar boys brought his feet back onto the ground, where he opened his eyes. He savored the symphony of their stifled laughs, remembering how he used to get the giggles at inappropriate times during Mass as an altar boy. Back then, the priest would reprimand altar boys in the sacristy after Mass, and the nuns would sometimes slap them later that day. Those were different times, but some things never changed, like the giggle of altar boys. He grinned and gave them an approving nod.

He walked to the middle aisle with chalice in hand, to administer the Body of Christ to His followers. Although lay Eucharistic ministers handed out communion from the side aisles, on this day, almost the entire congregation formed into two lines in front of him. He was Christ, handing out faith and hope onto the tongues and into the hands of the wretched. Some of them limped in pain, some showed unexplained sores on their face, yet others appeared healthy with youth and light. *I love all of them.*

When Maria approached she slowly slid her tongue out from between moist, red covered lips. He wanted to share his spiritual state with her and placed the Body of Christ upon her tongue with divine authority, able to transcend the physical and he emphasized the words, "The Body of Christ." Boss approached after Maria, and tilted his head sideways as he took the body of Christ into his palm. Boss simply nodded, without saying "Amen."

When Barker stood before him, a few stifled shrieks flew from the crowd, most likely from women. He wasn't sure if the reaction was from Barker simply being in church or from the public display of friendship after a fight. He managed to keep his spiritual aura, even as Barker winked at him. He added the sign of the cross on Barker's forehead. Then Barker tapped the top of his hand, as if to say, "Good job."

Monsignor Murphy and the Bishop must have received the Body of Christ from one of the Eucharistic Ministers, if they were still in the church. He wanted to hand them the Body of Christ, but still could not spot them. Maybe they left in disgust after his sermon, or because of his administering the Body of Christ without wearing the collar.

After the last of the faithful finished the Eucharist and had returned to their pews, he placed the rest of the consecrated, thin wafers into the tabernacle, and sat on an ornate bench a few steps higher than the altar. The end of Mass would begin as soon as he stood. He would bless everybody, and the choir would sing the final hymn, and he would spiral back into reality and life's problems. He surveyed the congregation in silence, and glimpsed the silhouette of a tall man wearing a biretta, who stood in the back of the church, like a vulture ready to swoop down upon his prey with razor sharp talons.

Father Bob's spiritual high slipped away. Maybe he'd stay on the bench, like a child holding onto his father's pant leg as he left to go work in the steel mill for midnight shift. He needed to shift his position as his buttocks numbed. His physical body dominated its presence, won the struggle with the spirit. If he remained on this bench, how long would it be before somebody made the first move? Already some of the congregation began to look around. All it would take is one person out there to get up and leave, then the rest would follow like a flock of sheep. They wanted to get home. Some needed to get to work, others wanted to eat and get drunk, and others wanted to take a Sunday drive, have fun. But he had to stand out front, say "hello" and "goodbye" in one sentence, hug the big ladies whose soft breasts felt more pleasurable than they were supposed to, and then face Bishop Malone. *Ah, that pang of anxiety.* Bishop Malone, the holy grace, was the man who could send him out, away with Sister Roxanne.

He inhaled, breathed out, and finally stood up to face reality. The congregation quickly stood in response and he made the sign of the cross over them. "Go in Peace to Love and Serve the Lord."

The final hymn played and the congregation started milling about, leaving. Father Bob absorbed the church atmosphere one last time, and then followed Anthony and Aldo straight back into the sacristy through the door near the altar. Normally he would sing along with the hymn, but today was different, as he'd broken with tradition and said a Mass without wearing the collar.

Once in back, the altar boys playfully punched each other. Father Bob noticed Anthony's natural balance, as he fluidly ducked Aldo's wild swings. He wished he could be one of them, young and in the midst of losing innocence, consumed only with entertainment. Boxers who fought in the ring during a match never worried about God or spirituality, unless they got knocked to the canvas, or maybe later on in their career when their perfect bodies gave out.

The boys noticed him watching and stopped playing around. "Are you going to teach us how to box, Father Bob?" Anthony blurted out.

"Looks like you've already started."

Abashed, they turned to the closet and began pulling off their white robes. Father Bob doubted he would even have a vocation in a few minutes, let alone be able to start a boxing club. But he saw the desire and hope in the boys' expressions and didn't want to drag them down. He said, "I don't know yet, Anthony, but you'll be one of the first to know."

Anthony punched Aldo. "See! I told you."

Aldo looked at Father Bob. "I'm allowed to box too, when you guys do it."

"Okay boys, I know." He pulled his green vestments off. "I need to greet the parishioners. Please snuff out the candles. Thanks for serving today. You both did a great job. Aldo, you looked like an old pro."

He walked down the same aisle as he did during the procession a little while earlier, but this time the church echoed only his lone footsteps. Butterflies of anxiety replaced the spiritual flutter he had accomplished earlier.

He walked through two sets of doors and appeared on top of the church steps. "Helluva sermon Father Bob!" yelled Ronny Milovick. Bea, his wife, ran up a couple of steps and hugged him. She spoke loudly enough for anyone within earshot to hear, "We're so proud of our hometown priest!" Father Bob felt awkward as she pressed against him for too long. He shook the calloused, strong hands of steelworkers like Dave Karazascik, who breathed hard simply from climbing three steps, and Chucky Slaywart, whose fresh snuff formed a dark pebble in the corner of his mouth.

He made his way towards the Bishop, to get it over with, when someone grabbed him out of nowhere and twirled him around. Pumpkin. His routine always made the crowd chuckle, no matter how many times they'd seen it. "Hey," he heard Pumpkin trying to whisper, which he found laughable, since Pumpkin's deep voice made whispering a challenge. "I've grabbed a couple of painting side jobs. If you ever need some work, just let me know."

Side jobs? He pretended to be grateful for Pumpkin's offer. Before he could even respond, Barker bulled his way to face him and whispered into his ear, "Don't worry about Bishop Baloney, man. I'll take care of him." He watched in fright as Barker busted through the crowd and stood straight in front of Bishop Malone, interrupting the conversation he was having with the Johns family. He heard Barker tell the Bishop, "You can't get rid of Father Bob. He's the only one who'd ever got me to go to church. Besides, he has the best left hook of any priest you got!"

The Bishop laughed and shook hands with Barker. He shot Father Bob a curious look. Seeing the two extremes of his world collide with each other, Barker standing next to the Bishop, brought sweat droplets to his forehead. Then Barker said something that he couldn't hear, before leaving the steps and hopping onto his chopper. How he'd love to hop onto the back of Barker's bike and ride away right now.

In the midst of the social hoopla, invitations, and blessings, he inched his way closer to Bishop Malone. A few folks approached the Bishop, timidly, but they shook his hand and thanked him for sending the young priest back to their parish. He caught another glance from the Bishop, and interpreted it as a scowl. He looked away, and shook the hand of another well-wisher. Then he saw Monsignor Murphy out of the corner of his eye, talking nearby. He was laughing, totally comfortable in this element, like he was sitting at the Knights of Columbus Hall. He acted as sociable as he did after the fight way long ago, when Father Bob had lost the Golden Glove Tournament as a teenager. He shifted from foot to foot, not really listening to what was being said to him by the parishioners, focusing on trying not to be too nervous. His hands sweated and he grew angry for feeling so afraid of the Bishop. After about twenty minutes, the final car doors slammed shut, and the three holy men stood on the steps, forced to face each other.

Sweating in the humid air, Father Bob wondered why the parishioners rallied around him. All he did in the month or so in this parish assignment was get drunk, get into a bar fight, and mess around with Maria. Maybe the congregation was being so supportive because they were afraid of being left without a priest, since Murphy was clearly growing old, and Sister Roxanne had just abruptly left everybody. Perhaps they would follow anyone, rather than be closed down like so many other small parishes and be forced to make the far drive to the Cathedral up on the hill.

"Father Bob, are you with us?" Bishop Malone asked.

Just as the Bishop spoke, Maria drove past the church and Father Bob's eyes locked onto her. Her windows were down. Grandma Amelia sat in the front seat and Boss in the back. She waved at him. Then she stuck her finger in her mouth and sucked on it for a moment.

He reluctantly returned her wave, and had to struggle to look at the Bishop, who grinned at him. "A friend of yours?"

He fidgeted like a nervous altar boy, hoped the bishop did not see Maria's finger gesture. "Yes, well, I knew her and her family while growing up. As a matter of fact, that's where we're going to dinner today, you know, at the Barrones."

Bishop Malone raised his bushy eyebrows. "Oh, okay, I didn't recognize them."

He hesitated, and then masked his discomfort with silence, suddenly realizing that the possibility of being in love with Maria scared him more than the Bishop.

Bishop Malone put his arm around Father Bob, locking his armpit overtop of his shoulder. He instinctively placed his arm around the small of the Bishop's back. He looked up and noticed protruding nose hairs pouring from his nostrils, surprised a man of bishop stature would permit such neglectful grooming.

"Walk with me to my car," Bishop Malone said.

Bishop Malone kept his arm around him as they walked down the stone church steps, onto the asphalt parking with its whiff of fresh tar. *What's going on? Is he going to beat me up in the alley?* He'd rather stoop between the ropes and enter a boxing ring where at least the opponent was visible. He loosened his grip around the Bishop and dangled his arm in between their two bodies, not quite sure where to put it. He glanced back at Monsignor Murphy, trying to get a read on the situation, but Murphy trudged along with indifference and didn't meet his gaze. He pictured the strange sight of three men dressed in black, two with white collars and sporting black birettas, their shoes making a unison clopping sound as they headed towards the Bishop's black Coupe de Ville. He was in a Mobster movie where he would feel the barrel of a gun press against the back of his head at any moment.

Bishop Malone playfully shoved Father Bob towards the back of the car, throwing him the keys. "Open the trunk." He smiled from the side of his mouth.

He caught the keys with one hand, and stared at the massive trunk. Four bodies could fit in there. Could there be a new cast of Christ inside? No, maybe it had his traveling bag? Mrs. Hellinski could have packed it this morning. That would not make sense either. He looked at the set of keys in his hand, and grasped his fingers around the medallion of St. Christopher. Then he looked back up at the Bishop, who simply smirked at him and nodded his nose upwards to egg him on. He glanced over at Monsignor Murphy who had turned his body, and all he could see was his back. *Is somebody going to jump out of the trunk?*

He did not want to be anybody's fool, so he tried his best to act cool. He dug down into his frazzled thoughts to find the confidence of a skilled fighter, but found nothing but confusion. His hand shook as he fitted the key into the lock. The first key didn't fit. Neither did the second, but the lock clicked on the third try. The trunk squeaked as it slowly opened without his help.

His eyes focused on a long cylinder wrapped in cloths. He bent down to get a better look, and thought about how vulnerable he was positioned. The Bishop could close the trunk lid and trap half of his body inside. He quickly straightened up. He looked at Bishop Malone again, shrugged, and received another nose nod urging him to continue.

He unraveled the cloth and identified the object…a black, leather heavy punching bag. He glanced at the Bishop again, and then unraveled the rest of the rags around the bag. He petted the heavy bag as if it were a dog, and smelled the leather. Then he heard laughter and straightened up to watch Bishop Malone and Monsignor Murphy cracking up like altar boys.

Are they sending me away to train boxers or something? He figured they were laughing at his lack of understanding, or maybe he had a confused look on his face. He looked back at the heavy bag and shot a combination down into it, first a left jab followed by a power right. He backed up, shuffled on his feet, and heard the memory of a bell ringing to start the first round of the Golden Glove Tournament. He could not even hear the crowd noise once the fight started, but briefly saw the image of a mute Murphy yelling from his corner.

He stood in fight stance, faced off with the two priests who were still laughing at him. "You guys want some of this?" He shadowboxed playfully for a few seconds, before he also laughed at the absurdity of those two, old men in a fight with him. He knew he was laughing for a different reason than they. He dropped his hands. "Okay, okay. I give up. I don't know what to say. What do you want from me?"

"Don't say anything," Bishop Malone responded, his laughter now dying down. Monsignor Murphy walked towards the rectory, leaving Father Bob alone with the Bishop.

He still did not have a clue. So he looked back at the heavy bag, caressed the smooth black leather with one hand, and lifted the top end by the chains with his other hand.

"This must be a one-hundred and fifty pounder."

The Bishop raised his fists in jest. "You want to fight, let's put your skills to good use." He walked towards him almost chest to chin. "I was out of options with you, you know, until Murphy and I talked about boxing."

He wanted to back up from the Bishop, didn't appreciate the large man getting so close, dominating him. But he held his ground, looked straight up into the Bishop's eyes. He smelled cigarettes on the Bishop's breath, mixed with the foul odor of a mouth that had gone without food for too long.

The Bishop poked his finger repeatedly into his chest. "Listen, you start a boy's club. You teach Catholic boys how to follow rules." He bored his finger harder into the middle of his chest now with a massive frown. "This is your last pass, son. No more after this. Got it?"

Father Bob's body tensed and he clenched his fists, out of habit. He realized, though, he was out of the woods, saved once again. He still had his vocation. Numbed, exhausted, he'd gone from expecting to be excommunicated to given a project to work on. So he nodded in agreement like a tortured prisoner.

"You can count on me, your Grace."

"I'd better."

Murphy pulled up in his Lincoln and jockeyed the car's trunk close to the Bishop's car. He stepped out, still laughing. The Bishop joined him. "Let's load this thing and head to dinner at Grandma Amelia's," Murphy said in between chuckles.

Father Bob summoned all of his self-control to remain silent. He could feel the heat in his blood as his anger burned inside. Murphy had let him agonize over this for days, and he knew all about it. *And I told him I loved him like a father the other day.* The last thing he wanted to do was spend time with these two men, in a small kitchen at Grandma Amelia's, with Maria at the table.

"Come on, sport," Murphy said, sensing his irritation. "Let's load this bag into my car."

He walked to the bag without looking at Murphy, and grabbed one end. They plopped the heavy bag into Murphy's Lincoln and Father Bob slammed the trunk shut.

"You should be happy," Murphy said. "You've just got everything you wanted." He still could not look at Murphy. "We found a spot for a gym, in the maintenance garage behind the Knight of Columbus hall. You'll have to clean it out, though."

He remained silent, afraid of what he might say.

Bishop Malone pointed towards the rectory. "I need to make a phone call before we go to dinner." Bishop Malone walked toward the rectory alongside Monsignor Murphy. Both men laughed again.

He played with the collar in his pocket and wondered if he was worthy to represent the glory for which it stood. He decided not to put it back around his neck. Neither the Bishop nor Murphy had mentioned anything about the collar.

CHAPTER 12

THE LAST SUPPER

Monsignor Murphy and Bishop Malone stood in the parking lot of St. Anne's, watching Father Bob as he bent over to reattach his collar. Using the side view mirror of the Bishop's Cadillac he slid the collar tab into his priest shirt when he noticed a sharp crease in the middle. He pinched the crease in an effort to straighten it, and the collar snapped in half, rendering it useless. Bishop Malone and Monsignor Murphy smirked when Father Bob stood up, holding a piece of his collar tab in each hand.

He started towards the rectory, awkward. "I'll go get another one."

"Hold on," Bishop Malone said. He walked over and opened the passenger side door. "Pretty dynamic sermon today, I must say." After fumbling around in the glove box, he handed Father Bob a fresh collar. "I always keep a spare or two, just in case I feel like ripping mine off my neck."

Murphy laughed along with the Bishop. Father Bob nodded politely. "Thank you." He fitted the collar tab using his reflection in the car window, which made his face look unusually wide. "No, what did you think of my sermon, really?" He addressed the Bishop as if Murphy did not exist. He still fumed at Murphy for not telling him of the Bishop's disciplinary plan.

"Different. I've never seen a priest do that before, but somehow, my son, you aroused the congregation with a meaningful message." The Bishop tilted his head sideways towards him. "I hope you don't get into the habit of lifting up your vestments and showing your pants, though."

Again, Murphy and the Bishop laughed. Father Bob figured he was in for a long afternoon of ribbing, part of his penance. He would take the teasing in return for the joy of retaining his priesthood, yet wanted to change the subject. "We walking or riding to Grandma Amelia's?"

"It's a good day for a short walk," said the Bishop, pointing to the bottom of the slightly sloped street. "That's her house down there, isn't it?" He didn't wait for an answer, just started walking. Father Bob caught up with him quickly, and heard Murphy huffing and wheezing behind them.

He looked across the asphalt playground that surrounded memories inside of St. Anne's Parochial School. Graphite dust from the steel mill had faded the orange bricks to a darker shade. The row of classroom windows on the bottom floor looked smaller than he remembered as a child. Once he drew sharp fangs on the end of a diagramed sentence, making it look like a lizard on the chalkboard. Sister St. Paul Mary pulled his hair and slapped his face in the front of the class. Maria had laughed, though, so it was worth the humiliation. A pang of nostalgia stung him when he remembered how he would drop his pen onto the floor, on purpose, just to bend down and try to catch a glimpse up Maria's school dress.

Grandma's Victorian house grew larger as they approached, lending Father Bob a sense of security, despite his being unwelcome there by Grandpa Ceasar. In his past he usually snuck into Grandma's house. The first time Maria brought him here for lunch from school, they were in the second grade. He had never been inside such an immaculately clean and fully furnished house before. His aunt's house was clean, with only two bedrooms, his window a rock's throw from the railroad tracks. He could sneak out of this window anytime though, especially when a train rumbled past to obscure the sound.

Back then, he and Maria sat at the blue-topped kitchen table while Grandma sliced homemade bread for baloney sandwiches. She'd put several slices of baloney on one sandwich, the thickest he'd ever seen. He was used to one, thin slice per sandwich and here he felt important, like a movie star. Then Caesar came home from the family's beverage distribution business. Caesar looked at him and his face darkened. The old man became furious, yelling at him with insanely widened blue eyes. He called him a thieving street urchin and told him never to set foot around Maria again. He ran from the house, and couldn't wait to return to the safety of the classroom. When Maria finally came back to class, she handed him the rest of his baloney sandwich wrapped in wax paper, and shyly smiled at him.

Maybe that's what drew them together, what would keep them apart. She always bounced between ignoring and caring for him. Eventually, in the sixth grade, they had kissed under Grandma's back porch, the first place that she let him unbutton her blouse. The outside of her bra felt spongy. She let him continue, so he slid his fingers down inside, expecting her to jump up and run away at any moment. Her tender skin aroused him, but her allowing him to enter that special place drew him further and made him fall in love. He had stopped suddenly, and froze in fear when he heard footsteps clomping on the porch above. Ceasar coughed. They both smelled Caesar's cigarette, and before long their fears transformed into stifled laughs.

Today, he squinted when the sun reflected off of Grandma's gutter and glistened into his eyes. This ten-minute walk was traveling through a porthole of the past. Once he saw the pitched porch roof of the house, he relived his favorite memory. Back when he was seventeen, he'd climb the porch trellis, and crawl up the pitch to Maria's bedroom window. He would rap on the window lightly, mimicking the seven-note musical couplet, "Shave and a Haircut...Two Bits." Maria would move the drapes aside nervously. The first time she had slid the window open, just wide enough for him to sneak through was only a few days after his aunt had died. Although Maria had already had a boyfriend, Mario, from Pittsburgh, whose family was in business with hers, yet she let him crawl inside. Mario was allowed to walk in through the front door, since Grandma approved of him then. Mario had a nice car, an important business family, and the arrogance to accompany his good fortune.

Had she ever loved me, or just felt sorry for me? They had slipped under the covers together and held each other tight. He may have heard her cry. Barely teenagers, they kissed vigorously like seventeen-year-olds. This time she didn't stop his advances. He slid off her white panties and made love to her there.

As far as he knew, neither Maria's boyfriend, nor Grandma had ever suspected. He'd snuck through that window several times and always made a quick getaway, oftentimes jumping to the yard once he climbed halfway down the trellis.

Suddenly the Bishop interrupted his daydream when he stopped walking and stood still, a few feet from Grandma's front gate. He turned his head, obviously checking on Murphy, who called, "Have you ever eaten Grandma Amelia's homemade spaghetti before, Bishop?"

"No, but the legend of her cooking precedes her." He checked his watch. "I've visited the house once, though, back during her husband's funeral." He looked at Father Bob, "Do you remember when some families used to show the body inside the household?"

Father Bob realized that the Bishop didn't remember him being at the funeral. "Yes, and I'm glad they don't do it that way anymore," he said, remembering how Caesar's body had spooked him, as it lie in the coffin in front of a never used fireplace. His face was flat and motionless, but could jump up at any moment and kick him out of the house.

Even though Maria was his age, twelve, at the funeral she looked smaller than usual. He envisioned her sunken into a large chair with a blank look of despair. He had poked her while she was sitting in that chair, and she had looked at him for a moment before following him out onto the back porch. He had stolen some cigarette butts from the ashtrays in the house, and offered the best to her, but she shook her head with a grimace that he still remembered. He smoked the cigarette butts himself, under the stairs of the back porch, their secret hideaway. Though Maria didn't smoke, she smiled when he flipped a cigarette butt upside down with his lips, left the lit part inside his mouth, closed his lips around it and blew smoke out the filter. She laughed a little, quickly kissed him on the cheek, and ran away from him too soon. He sat there under the porch, alone, for a long time wondering if he'd lost her for good. But somehow they seemed closer after that day. The smile he put on her face won her. She even brought him to Grandma's for lunch more often, since Caesar wasn't around anymore and Grandma loved to serve him, perhaps because he was so grateful.

He and Maria shared something. He never talked about his deceased parents. Maria never talked about her lost mother, unknown father, or her dead Grandfather. Unspoken pain somehow made them close.

Murphy caught up to the priests, sweating and breathing heavy. He stopped in front of Grandma's gate. "You men running some kind of race or something?"

Father Bob ignored him, opened the gate and walked up the sidewalk leading to the porch steps. He heard Murphy and the Bishop talking, but couldn't make out what was said, so just paused by the front door.

"What are you waiting for?" Bishop Malone asked. He stood close enough to touch Father Bob. He looked up at the

Bishop, and glanced over at Murphy, surprised to sense that they both expected him to take the lead. The mingled scents of boiling pasta, baked bread and tomato sauce, drifted through the screen door. The huge wooden front door, with stained glass imbedded in the middle, was wide open. Through the screen he heard the unmistakable sound of teenage boys bickering.

Just as he raised his hand to knock on the screen door, Anthony pushed it open and tripped through the doorjamb. Father Bob moved off to the side, bouncing off of Murphy, who stepped onto the Bishop's foot, almost falling. The Bishop grabbed onto Murphy's arm until he regained balance. "Take it easy!" Father Bob yelled. Boss stood behind the screen, in the house, with a scowl on his face and a brown paper bag in his hands.

"Sorry, Father Bob. We got to go deliver bread," Anthony said. He stood with his head down, as if waiting to be disciplined. Murphy rubbed Anthony's head. Anthony trotted away down the porch steps onto the sidewalk where he stopped, waiting for Boss.

Boss avoided eye contact as he walked through the doorway, his face paled with dark circles pooled under his eyes. *This boy looks like he had a rough night.*

Father Bob shrugged and led the priests through the door. They stood in the living room for a second, next to a telephone bench crowded with Cabbage Patch dolls. Murphy picked one up and examined it. "What an ugly baby."

Father Bob looked around the room, surprised that nothing had changed. He hadn't been inside this house for fourteen years. The familiar smell of Italian cooking, the clean rug and polished banisters of the stairwell, even the loud tick of the same grandfather clock catapulted him into the past. Although he was mentally and physically exhausted, he finally allowed himself to feel something like happiness.

"You boys better get moving, the priests will be here any minute!" Maria yelled through the half-opened kitchen door. She walked into the room surprised to see the three priests. "Oh, Fathers, I'm sorry. I thought you were the boys."

"We haven't been boys in a long time," Bishop Malone made everyone laugh. "Sorry that we barged in on you." He frowned at Father Bob.

"Oh, no problem. We've been waiting on you," she said, slightly laughing at Father Bob.

Murphy tossed the cabbage patch doll down onto the telephone bench, and it bounced off onto the carpet. Maria bent over and picked up the doll, carefully placing it back onto the bench.

"These are Grandma's. Sometimes I think she talks to them, and they answer her. Like her saints do." She laughed. Father Bob thought that she appeared nervous, but looked nothing short of gorgeous and smelled like flowers when she walked passed him. He scanned her legs and hips in her tight-fitting jeans. A quick flutter of those butterflies in his stomach arose from the excitement of just being near her.

"Come in, come in," she pointed towards the kitchen. "Grandma's in there." The Bishop led the way into the kitchen. Maria raised her eyebrows at Father Bob and gave him an inquisitive thumb up. He nodded, smiled, and returned her thumbs up quickly.

In the kitchen, he saw the same white-countered cabinets, the same blue vinyl table, and that large, metal pot boiling with pasta on the stove. Caesar had soaked his feet in that pot before. Only now it was dented, but obviously still functional. Grandma appeared startled to see the priests. She set her wooden stirring spoon next to another metal pot, full of simmering tomato sauce with meatballs and sausage bobbing around in small pools of oil on top. She looked past the Bishop and Murphy and walked straight towards Father Bob.

"Well it's about time!" Grandma opened her arms and hugged him. "You've been home almost a month and haven't come visit me yet," she scolded in her loving way.

He bent to hug her and kissed her on the cheek. "I know, I'm sorry Grandma," he stayed embraced with her. She felt soft but sturdy, and smelled like fresh bread dough, just like when he was a kid. Better yet, she made him feel special, loved, and gave him the first greeting, bypassing the Bishop and Murphy. He straightened up and looked into her face, with his hands on top of her bony shoulders. The house may have stayed the same, but Grandma had changed. He studied her cloudy eyes, and how one of her eyelids twitched in an effort to stay open. Her wrinkled face shook with a friendly smile. He figured he must have been too distracted at the family reunions a while back to notice how much Grandma had aged. Maybe Maria and Boss were wearing her out. "You look beautiful, Grandma."

"Oh, I'm getting so old I'm starting to bend over like a chicken." Everybody laughed. She locked into his eyes. "You used to come over all the time when you were little. I miss you."

He wasn't sure if she had a tear in her eye, or was just having eye problems. He wanted to stay embraced with her, continue to feel loved, but she moved towards the Bishop, who bowed his head to her.

"Thanks a million for coming to my house for dinner today." She stuck out her hand for a shake and the Bishop wrapped his large hand around her small one, bent down and gently kissed the top of it.

"It's my pleasure, Mrs. Barrone. You honor me with your gracious invitation." He straightened back up and towered over her. "I think the last time I was in your beautiful home was at your husband, Caesar's funeral. What, twenty years ago?"

She made the sign of the cross. "It will be exactly twenty-one years in August. But call me Grandma, like everybody else does."

"Okay, Grandma."

Father Bob raised his eyebrows at Maria while Grandma and Murphy hugged each other. Then Grandma latched onto Maria's forearm and lifted it up. "This is my only daughter, Maria. Isn't she beautiful?" Grandma smiled a smile that made everybody smile. Maria blushed and put her hand up in an attempt to cover her face.

Father Bob wished that the aunt who raised him had introduced him as her son, just once, in the same way that Grandma Amelia considered Maria to be her daughter. His mother died giving birth to him.

"Yes. She is beautiful." Bishop Malone grabbed Maria's hand and kissed the top of it also, along with a bow. "It's truly my pleasure."

Father Bob noticed that his kiss lingered overly long on Maria's hand and he seemed to hold her gaze, like a snake hypnotizing its prey. Maria rolled her eyes in a flash of a moment. She pointed towards a swinging door that led into the dining room. "We set the table in there, so please, take any seat you wish."

"The pasta is boiling over!" Grandma interrupted. Maria hurried over to shut off the gas burner with Grandma following her.

Father Bob was surprised at the way Bishop Malone turned almost giddy around Maria; he even briefly fixed his hair with his fingers in a cabinet window reflection. Maria's sexy aura had that effect on most men. He led the priests through the door into the dining room where the table was set next to a massive dresser supporting a gray grotto of the Virgin Mary. The face on the statue of that Virgin Mary vaguely resembled Maria's.

Maria held the door open. "Sit anywhere you like. I'll pour you some wine while you're waiting for the food." She disappeared into the sanctuary of the kitchen. The three priests looked around the oblong table for strategic sitting, with the Bishop's chair obvious, the only one with arms at the head of the table. Murphy and Father Bob flanked the Bishop on each side. He still avoided eye contact when Murphy looked at him, despite their sitting across from each other.

"It smells so wonderful in here, Mrs. Barrone," the Bishop yelled through the partially closed, swinging door into the kitchen.

"Grandma! Call me Grandma!" she shouted from the other side.

Maria kicked the swinging door open with her foot and walked through holding a glass gallon of red wine with both hands. She clunked the bottle on the table and unscrewed the top. "Homemade Dago Red." She winked at Father Bob. "Uncle Frank made it from the grapes of last fall. All the Old Italian winemakers rave about that batch of grapes, and make a sort of pilgrimage up to Canella's Produce every year. But they all agreed that last year's vintage was the best." She smiled. "Uncle Frank might show up for dinner today, and he could tell you all about how to make it."

He stood to help her, but she shooed him off as she grabbed that big gallon of wine and poured the Bishop a glass. "Be careful gentlemen, this is pretty strong stuff." She filled the glass in front of Murphy and then walked around to fill Father Bob's, who enjoyed the pleasure of feeling her hip brush against his arm. She filled herself a glass, then sat across from Father Bob, and patted Murphy on the shoulder.

Maria looked straight at Father Bob, raised her glass in toast, and said, "Happy Father's Day! Great sermon, too." A smirk played across her face. "You found another collar, I see?"

He wasn't sure if the comment was sarcastic or just playful. So he reverted to humor, his old reliable. "Well, Bishop Malone dug out one of his throwaways for me." He tugged it with one hand. "I think he tightened this one up a bit more than the last one."

Maria interrupted the priests' laughter. "Well, maybe he should put a leash on it."

Murphy roared at that, as did the Bishop, who flung out his index finger and thumb, like a fake gun, to insinuate that Maria had hit the mark. Father Bob couldn't help but laugh too.

"A leash is like getting reassigned to university research," he joked then waited for a laugh that did not happen. They looked at him flatly. *That was not a smart thing to say.*

Maria gave him a puzzled look before breaking the awkward silence. "I'd better go help Grandma." She stood up. "I'll be back." He watched her sweet form disappear through the swinging door, and then looked at Murphy who was glaring at him.

"Is everything okay, Monsignor? You look like you want to say something," he said with a challenging glare.

"Of course, lad, everything is hunky dory." He moved his attention to the Bishop. "This wine's pretty tasty, nice and dry." He licked his lips.

The Bishop smirked, "Have you ever met a wine you didn't like?"

Suddenly Anthony and Boss stomped through the swinging door, out of breath. "We raced all the way back and I won," Anthony said in between gasps. Boss pushed him off balance and Anthony scowled. Father Bob examined the boys closely, looking for signs of jittery, cocaine-like behavior. He figured if Boss looked energetic all of a sudden, then he would know for sure that he was abusing drugs, and probably corrupting his best altar boy. Anthony scanned the priests, while Boss made no eye contact. "How come you priests always wear black?"

Murphy spoke up, "So that we don't have to think about what to wear every day."

"Plus," the Bishop added, "Black hides all the stains."

The Bishop and Murphy laughed, but the boys appeared to take them seriously. Father Bob noticed the boys' eyes looked bloodshot. *Those bread deliveries away from adult may provide several sources of entertainment.* Boss didn't appear to be "wired," which relieved him. *I guess smoking weed is better than doing coke.* Still, he wondered how he might reach Boss's anger and sadness. *Why does this boy get under my skin?*

Maria walked through the swinging door and called to Boss to go into the kitchen and help Grandma. She apologized to the priests for the rowdy boys and then sat down. Murphy topped off her glass of wine. Father Bob felt uneasy by the silence at the table, so he stood up. "I'm going to go see if Grandma needs more help." He walked through the swinging door to find Grandma cleaning a pot in the sink and Boss hunched over the counter, grating cheese onto a piece of wax paper.

"Let me do something to help, Grandma."

Boss looked up at him. "We don't need your help," he said with a sour tone that embarrassed Father Bob. He stood there looking at Boss, who had buried his head in the task at hand. He wondered what to say to the huffy young man. *Why the hostility?* He looked over at Grandma, who had a horrified expression on her face.

"Bring that cheese and plate of bread out to the table, Boss," Grandma ordered. He walked back through the door, ignoring Father Bob's watching him. She grabbed Father Bob by the arm and pulled him down to where she could whisper into his ear. "I always tried to protect Maria, she's like my own daughter, but I'm so worried about Boss."

"Yes, I understand." Father Bob nodded. "The boy's going through a tough time right now. He doesn't realize how lucky he is to have you and Maria in his life." Grandma gave him a look of need, like she was accepting communion. "He'll get through this, Grandma, after all, he's got Barrone blood, the 'will en Dia.'"

Grandma's cloudy eyes sparkled. "You know the Italian "'Will of God!'" She tightened her grip. He wanted to straighten up his posture, but she held him down with surprising strength.

"Maria is smart, Grandma, just like you. We pray for her to make her way out of this and take good care of Boss, too."

She smiled up at him, "I liked your sermon today. You turned out to be such a nice man." She pulled him even closer to her and whispered. "You're not like that damned Mario who robbed our business blind. Boss needs a father who is a good man like you."

Surprised at that statement, Father Bob straightened his posture, overpowering Grandma's grip. He looked her in the eyes. "Grandma, I wouldn't know the first thing about how to be a father to any child. Where…"

Maria came busting through the swinging door. "Are we ready to serve?" She picked up the bowl of salad. "Here, Bob, carry this out." He took up the bowl and headed through the swinging door while Grandma and Maria talked so fast he could not make out what was being said. He set the bowl on the table and started to go back through the door, almost slamming into Maria, who was coming through the other side.

She carried a massive bowl of homemade pasta, smothered in tomato sauce, and topped with meatballs and sausage dusted in grated cheese. Steam rose like smoke from the bowl, and the corners of the windows in the dining room fogged.

She laid the masterpiece on the center of the table, next to an equally huge green salad. A few "oohs and aahs" arose. She shot Boss a stern eye signal, and he went into the kitchen with Anthony. Father Bob started to follow, but she told him, "Please sit down."

Boss carried in a platter of roast beef, pulled from the bone, with Anthony following and holding yet another platter, covered in cut-up, cooked chicken. Grandma carried some extra tomato sauce. She finally sat down, despite three empty chairs with place settings still at the table. Maria filled all wine glasses again.

"Now this is what the kingdom of heaven must look like," Bishop Malone said, "A true work of art." He gestured to the three empty seats. "Are you expecting more guests?"

"No, it's just Sunday at Grandma's," Maria blurted out. "But Uncle Frank and his wife, Denise, might show up right around dinnertime on any Sunday." She looked down at the table, turned her head towards Grandma, and said with a slight choke in her voice. "Grandma always places a setting for Grandpa Caesar." She wiped her mouth with a white napkin, for no apparent reason.

Caesar's empty seat reminded Father Bob of mortality, and how Murphy was aging as fast as Grandma. He looked over at Murphy, who was staring at the bowls of food with an intense expression, as simple as a dog waiting for a handout. *I can't stay mad at him.*

Grandma asked the Bishop to say grace. During the prayer, Boss grabbed a hunk of bread and stuffed a piece into his mouth. Maria shot Boss a look of wrath. Boss cowered, actually slumped over at Maria's will. Boss caught Father Bob staring at him. He opened his mouth, stuck out his tongue, and waggled his eyebrows. Father Bob had no idea how to interpret the gesture. *Is he playful or messing with me?*

After the prayer, Maria filled all the wine glasses again, signaling the time to eat. "Hand your plates down the line," she said. Large white plates with blue etchings of farm scenes moved from hand to hand. Maria habitually held each plate under Grandma, who overfilled them with spaghetti, meatballs and sausage, before it was sent down the line like an efficient production line, Italian-style. Dishes clanked amongst a few Murphy slurps. Father Bob noticed Murphy, *Oh, he cuts his spaghetti with a fork, just like when we're in the rectory.*

"Does anybody want an extra plate for their salad?" Maria asked the group. They either responded with a "no" or shook their head. The Barrone style of eating allowed the oil and vinegar to seep into the rest of the meal, melding flavors together.

"Give the priests some more wine," Grandma ordered.

Father Bob took quick glances at Maria, trying not to appear obvious, while she walked around the table filling glasses of wine. She surprised him though when she filled the glasses in front of Anthony and Boss. Anthony looked at his glass and then at Boss, who immediately downed his. Anthony followed Boss's lead, and downed the entire glass, perhaps before somebody took it away. *She gets too loose sometimes. These boys sneak plenty of alcohol on their own, without being encouraged.*

Maria stopped Boss from grabbing for the jug. "No! One glass, that's all you boys get."

Boss shook his head and made the unmistakable impression of a teenager disgusted with his mother. He locked eyes with Father Bob and they stared at each other for a few moments. Father Bob lifted his wine glass, took a sip, said "Ahh," before placing it back down onto the table with the sanctimonious grace of a chalice. All the while, he maintained the stare down with Boss. *I have to see if he looks away. What is it he wants?*

Boss broke the stare. He looked over at the Bishop. "Mr. Bishop is Father Bob in trouble for getting drunk and beat up in a bar?"

The clanking and small talk at the table ceased. A shot of adrenaline tightened Father Bob's arm muscles. His face grew warm.

"Boss!" Maria yelled with food in her mouth. "That's none of your business!" She wiped her mouth with a cloth napkin and shook her head at the Bishop. "I'm so sorry. I don't know where my son gets his manners." She looked at Boss with her eyes widened as she lifted her palms.

"No, no, it's all right." Bishop Malone looked straight at Boss. "That's a legitimate, honest question, young man. I appreciate your concern about our priest. You're not the only one who's asked me, either. I've been flooded with phone calls and letters of support for Father Bob." He raised his hands and spread them above his shoulders, like a fisherman bragging about a big catch. "It's hard to believe he's only been here about, what, a month or so?" He paused. "No, son, Father Bob's not in any trouble at all right now. As a matter of fact, he's going to start a boxing club for me. Would you be interested in something like that?"

Boss darted a look at Father Bob. "Oh man, would I." He nodded, talking straight to Father Bob. "Sounds like the best idea I heard around here."

Father Bob got a grip on his anger, just like a boxer needs to do in the ring, in order to engage the fundamentals of skill. *I'll let things play out.*

Anthony jumped up from his seat, shot his hand into the air for the "high five." Boss ignored him, left him hanging, and continued sizing-up Father Bob.

The Bishop broke the ice. "You know, Monsignor Murphy was the one who trained Father Bob to box. He even fought Sugar Ray Robinson back in the day."

That statement surprised Father Bob, who roused. "What? Do you mean *the* Sugar Ray Robinson?"

"You didn't know that?" The Bishop addressed Father Bob. "Tell the story, Murphy."

Murphy looked up from his plate, wiped his mouth, and set the napkin on the tabletop next to his half-full plate of food. "Well, it wasn't actually much of a fight."

Father Bob interrupted. "Wait a minute. You fought Sugar Ray Robinson? *You?*" He figured this must another practical joke between Murphy and the Bishop to be played on him, so he tried to calm down.

"Do you want to hear the story or not?" Murphy asked.

He shrugged. "Yes, of course."

"I was in the Air Force back then, stationed at the base in Tennessee." He looked at Father Bob, "You know that I was the Golden Gloves Champion for the middleweight division back in 1951. That's around the year you two were born." He pointed at Father Bob and Maria. Murphy patted his belly, "Yes, middleweight was indeed a long time ago." Everybody laughed.

"Sugar Ray Robinson, *the* Sugar Ray Robinson, became the middleweight Champion of the World that year. He came down to visit us on base, with the USO. We had what they called a 'Smoker,' with a few preliminary warm-up fights, and then the main event, with me and Sugar Ray. So I stepped into the ring, since I was the Golden Glove Champ, to fight an exhibition with Sugar Ray, the pro champ." Murphy knocked over his wine glass, and luckily it was empty. Maria filled it for him again. "So, when the bell rang, I attacked. Went all out, punching with all I had, but Sugar Ray blocked everything I threw. Except, near the end of the round, I connected with my best punch, my left hook squared onto Sugar Ray's jaw. Sugar Ray even staggered for a step." Murphy stared blankly overtop the guests at the table.

Father Bob looked at the Bishop, scanning him for a clue, expecting the punch line at any minute. The Bishop nodded in agreement. Murphy continued.

"I was pretty tanked from going all out in the first round, and when I went out to answer the bell for the second, Sugar Ray looked mad. I mean, he smelled blood, because we were supposed to be playing, not really fighting. You see, I didn't understand exactly what an exhibition fight really meant. It was supposed to be a friendly show, but I just hammered a professional fighter with a lucky punch." He laughed and took a sip of wine. "Long story short, Sugar Ray hit me with something I didn't even see coming, but it felt like a sledgehammer. The next thing I remember was sniffing smelling salts, lying on the canvas."

He raised his glass in toast, "Here's to having the distinction of being knocked out by one of the greatest champions ever, Mr. Sugar Ray Robinson!"

Everybody at the table raised their glass. The story sounded true, but Father Bob had never heard it before. He and Murphy knew everything about each other. Despite not wanting to look like a fool again today, he had to know more. "Okay, okay Murphy, I'll bite." He looked down, then back up at Murphy. "How come you never told me this before? I mean, you trained me for Golden Glove Tournaments for over a year. I've known you most of my life. This story never came up?"

Murphy stared Father Bob in the eyes, as if he were sober. "Let me tell you something, young priest, you know how it is in the confessional? When you hear everybody's sins?" Murphy's pitch raised and his voice rumbled as if he were giving a sermon. "Nobody ever asks about you, now do they? It's not that different with boxing. If you want to train kids how to box, do you think they care anything about your life?"

A warm flush invaded Father Bob's face. *What's he talking about?* The table went silent, so Murphy continued, talking straight to him.

"In the helping profession, we help others and a person in need rarely can see outside of themselves. They don't ask whoever's helping them how they're doing. I chalk it up to the basic human condition, to get so wrapped up in your own problems that you can't see what's in front of you."

Those words stung Father Bob like a left hook to the jaw. *He's talking about me.* He didn't have a comeback line. Murphy had pummeled him. *He probably has many more secrets he's keeping from me.*

"See! That's what happens to boxers," Maria said. Even though she looked pale, Father Bob appreciated that she was trying to come to his rescue, honored that she had made an effort to cover his back. "I don't know about this boxing thing, Boss."

Boss straightened up in his chair, nodding his head with half a smirk. Father Bob figured Boss would want to box simply because his mother didn't want him to. Also, he distinctly remembered when Boss confessed to him about winning street fights twice since he moved back to Irontown. Father Bob sensed that Boss thought he could beat him up too, so he decided that he would teach Boss a hard lesson first, whap his head a bit, old-school style, and then take him under his wing. He'd teach him about boxing etiquette, which might improve his manners in life and perhaps calm Maria's fears about boxing.

"Maria and Grandma, I assure you we'll be safe. It's not like we're going to beat each other up." They looked at him confused, like they needed more explanation. "We train in techniques like balance, and learn how to stand and breathe properly before we even throw a punch at a bag. If we spar with each other, we'll go slow-speed, in a controlled manner." They looked confused, with wrinkled brows. "Listen, you've got to trust me on this one. I promise nobody will get beaten up or knocked-out." He looked at the Bishop for approval, but the Bishop was glancing at his watch. He scanned Murphy, who nodded, finishing the final morsels on his plate.

Then he looked at Boss, who returned his gaze. Boss punched the inside of his hand and nodded, with a sly grin. Boss looked at his mom, "Are we going to be in town long enough to do this?"

Maria turned her palms up, lifted them near her shoulders. "It depends." She fidgeted loosely and spoke with an increasing slur. "We'll head out west as soon as I hear from the real estate certification in Phoenix."

"Phoenix?" Father Bob knew he sounded shrill and regretted it. She had just hit him with a left hook. He had considered that she would leave, but not so soon. He didn't plan on getting so entangled with her emotionally. He didn't want her around, and then again, he did. He tried to conceal his concern as much as possible, but his stomach churned with a feeling of devastation. He could not even finish the spaghetti that lay on the plate in front of him. He had to get a hold of his emotions, find a wall to spring up, or a door to close, anything to help him eat. Not eating Grandma's spaghetti would be the ultimate insult. He groped for something to say. He twirled around the spaghetti with his fork and notice Grandma watching him. "It's awfully hot out there this time of year. I read in the newspaper about one-hundred-ten-degree temperatures."

"Vegas is hot too, trust me," Maria responded. "The real estate market is booming in Arizona. It's booming in Vegas, but we're definitely not going back there. I don't know, we'll see, but I need to get a job pretty soon." She looked down and shook her head. "My ex, Mario, gambled away our business profits." She looked back up at the Bishop. "Excuse my anger, but he took over Grandpa's business. We had no idea he was gambling away the money until one of my checks bounced. That was the final straw. We left. Why stay with an abusive man who couldn't even support us?"

Then she pointed at Father Bob and Monsignor Murphy, and talked straight to the Bishop. "These two have been so helpful and supportive. That's one thing about this small town, the sense of community, people truly caring about you. We never had that in Vegas."

Boss dropped his fork onto his plate. "This town sucks. I hate it."

"Boss!" Maria yelled. "We don't talk like that around guests!" She put her elbows on the table and buried her face in her hands for a moment before looking up. "I'm so sorry, but we've been going through a tough time."

"It's tough to go through life without a father," Bishop Malone said to Boss, wanting, for some reason Father Bob couldn't discern, to return to the theme of the day. "But people do it all the time. Look at Father Bob, for instance."

Boss said sarcastically, "Yeah, just look at him."

Murphy looked up. "Father Bob made lemonade from lemons, but it wasn't easy."

Oh, what profound words. He didn't appreciate the Bishop or Murphy putting him on the spot like that. He forced a spool of spaghetti into his mouth. He swallowed without fully chewing, got ready to say something, when Murphy tossed a piece of bread at him that lightly bounced off of his forehead.

"You're going to need some help hanging that heavy bag tomorrow morning. Maybe Boss could help you."

Father Bob tried very hard not to show anger. He couldn't believe that Murphy would push Boss on him like this. *Tomorrow? Finally I get a day off, and Murphy has to ruin it?* He wanted to go for a long jog and not have to worry about anything for a change. Before he could think of an excuse of why tomorrow would not work, Maria jumped at the opportunity.

"That would be great," she said. She looked at Boss. "Would you rather do that or go uptown to the library with me?" She looked at Grandma, who slightly shrugged approval. "What do you think, Boss?"

Boss bit the inside of his lower lip, as if pondering the thought. He locked eyes with Father Bob. "What time?"

"Me too!" Anthony chimed in.

Maria gave Father Bob her innocent, seductive eyes. "If you do this I'll buy you lunch. Or maybe Grandma will make us baloney sandwiches." She laughed. "Remember those?"

Father Bob knew that he wanted to hold her in his arms right then and there. He would do almost anything to make her happy, even if it meant spending an entire morning with that surly kid of hers.

"Okay, I'll tell you what. Boss, you come over to the rectory around nine o'clock in the morning." He broke eye contact with Boss and looked at Anthony. "You wait until we get the bags hung. Once we get everything ready, then you'll be in on the first round of lessons, okay?"

Anthony was disappointed. "Yeah, I guess so. But I'm not doing anything tomorrow either."

"Trust me, Anthony. If I'm going to teach you guys how to box, then get used to me calling the shots." He shot Murphy a serious stare.

Again, he saw the Bishop look at his watch. "I'm sorry folks, but I have to get back to the Cathedral." He looked at Boss. "I wish you luck, young man. I think you will enjoy boxing with Father Bob." He looked at Anthony. "You'll get your chance too, son."

"At least stay for dessert," Maria said to Bishop Malone. "Grandma made a…" Before she could finish her sentence, the kitchen door swung open. There in the doorway stood a short, stocky man in a dark gray suit and black Tee shirt. The room fell silent. Maria's face drained from flush to pale. Boss nudged up closer to her, with a similar look of fright. The man in the doorway reminded Father Bob of a casino boss, straight from a gangster movie.

"Mario!"

CHAPTER 13

THE SHEPHERD

Father Bob sat on the edge of his chair with his eyes glued on Mario. His heart pounded hard, vibrating his vocal cords. Mario's sport jacket noticeably bulged under his right armpit as he stood in front of the swinging door, scanning everybody at the table. He held a large manila envelope in one hand. A lit cigarette dangled from his lips.

Father Bob quickly glanced around the table, first at Maria, expecting her to respond with some kind of greeting, but she only pursed her lips and shook her head. Her shoulders tensed as she put her arm around Boss, who sank lower into his chair. Grandma's expression changed also and her left eye twitched. Bishop Malone and Monsignor Murphy sat frozen, their mouths closed as tight as the life-sized statues inside of St. Anne's. Mario smirked, slowly nodding his head.

As he stepped further inside the room, a light reflected off of his watchband. Father Bob's mouth dried and he tapped his thumb on the tabletop, until he became aware of it and stopped. He cleared his throat. Mario lifted his hand to take a drag from his cigarette.

Maria whispered, "Oh my God." Father Bob counted the people at the table...seven, including him. *Six bullets in what probably was a .38 caliber handgun.* He flashed back to when he and Barker and Pumpkin used to park their cars in front of the city dump during the night. They would sit on the hood of the car, and as soon as one of them turned on the headlights, they'd shoot at scampering rats.

Father Bob's chest started to pant, and he grew angry for being scared, then his instincts kicked-in. He had survived on the street, trained as a boxer. He returned Mario's stare. Under the table he curled onto the balls of his feet, and slid one foot behind the other for balance and leverage. He wanted to be ready to spring up and onto Mario if necessary. He relaxed his shoulders and arms, like a boxer anticipating the first bell. He took a deep, quiet breath, slowly in and out though his nose as he watched for a clue from Mario, before standing up and addressing him. Dishes rattled when he bumped the table.

"Hello, I'm Father Bob." His voice quivered a little. Everyone at the table looked up at him for a moment, and then turned back to Mario.

Mario nodded twice, rapid and deliberate, then looked over at Grandma. "I could smell your meatballs all the way from Vegas, Grandma." He laughed. Everyone at the table remained silent.

Father Bob glanced again at Maria. She stared straight ahead now, and kept her arms wrapped around Boss's shoulder. He imagined the horror of seeing Maria getting shot.

"Well, boy, aren't you going to hug your dad on Father's Day?" Mario glared at Boss.

Boss's face flushed, scared, while a somber Maria gently shook her son and nodded. Boss shuffled his lanky body over to Mario and ducked under his outstretched arms, one holding the lit cigarette and the other the envelope. After a two-second hug Boss stepped away. Father Bob wondered what might be inside of that envelope. Boss scampered back to his chair. The little tough guy looked like a frightened child, even though he was taller than Mario. It was the first time he'd ever seen Boss appear helpless. When Father Bob glanced at Anthony, whose eyes could not get any wider; he grew more annoyed at the situation. Still standing, he got a grip on his own fear. *What would Jesus do? He'd protect his flock.*

He decided to remain standing, not knowing what to say, yet still stood, stuck in an awkward position. Out of the corner of his eye he knew the Bishop was watching him, probably wondering what he was doing. The Bishop would be worthless if the fight started, but Murphy might grab Maria and Boss and hit the floor with them, if Mario went for that gun.

Mario tossed the manila envelope onto the table. It landed near the place setting next to Father Bob. Then he walked over to Grandma, bent over, and kissed her on the cheek. Much like Maria and Boss she simply stared straight ahead. Father Bob noted with satisfaction that it was the only time she didn't smile at a guest all day.

"Sit down," she said to Mario. "Have a plate." But Mario ignored Grandma's request and stood straight up, behind her while staring at Father Bob with eyes like black stones. He sucked a long drag from his cigarette, blew the smoke above the table, and roamed his eyes across the three priests, sizing them up. Finally, he addressed him.

"The infamous Father Bob. We've heard a lot about you through the years."

What might he have heard? Perhaps it was something about the trouble at his previous parish. He extended his hand across the table to Mario, who continued to stare and did not offer his hand. Father Bob turned up both of his palms and shrugged. Getting snubbed made him a little angry, yet he was beginning to feel more confident.

"Nice to meet you too," he said with sarcasm. Mario looked puny and a little effeminate and had revealed his gun purposely, to terrorize everybody. Father Bob knew how the simple act of envisioning a plan of attack, or escape, could calm a person down when facing a crisis. He'd make Bishop Malone and Murphy grateful for having him for a change.

Maria whispered something into Boss's ear. Boss motioned with his head to Anthony that the boys would make their escape.

Boss stood up and Anthony followed his lead. When Boss walked sheepishly past Mario, he flinched as Mario threw a playful left/right combination punch, a poor mimic of a boxer. Father Bob noticed the manner in which Boss winced, almost covering his head with his arm, just as he did a few days ago when he had attempted to hug him. Mario must have beaten him before. He also sized-up the amateur manner in which Mario threw a combination punch. *He doesn't know how to fight.* He watched as Boss and Anthony walked out, then looked up to find Mario staring at him.

"Is something wrong?" Father Bob finally asked.

"Oh no, heavens no. What could possibly be wrong?" Mario leaned over to shake hands with the Bishop and Murphy, who reluctantly offered their hands to him, both of them slightly rising from their chairs for a moment. The Bishop's hand trembled. Murphy's remained steady. Father Bob kept his focus on Mario though, especially when Mario walked around the table straight towards him. He nonchalantly placed his feet in a balanced position, kept his hands above his waist in the event Mario would make a threatening move; he would be ready.

Mario next sat down in the chair beside Father Bob, at the place setting reserved for Caesar. He reeked of too much cologne. Father Bob felt pressured to sit down, knowing how strange it would look for him not to. Mario reached his fork over the table to the platter of spaghetti, then using the fork like a shovel, he piled two small loads of pasta onto his plate. Maria and Grandma both sat as stiff and somber as the two other priests.

Mario talked at Maria. "Don't worry your pretty little head. You know how much I hate it when you act weak." He sneered. "I'm just blowing through town to take care of some papers for my sister, Carmela. You know the one in the nursing home up in the Burgh? Sometimes she thinks she's on a cruise ship with people waiting on her." He laughed again but no one joined him. Then he leaned over the table, and snuffed out his cigarette on Maria's plate. The lit end singed into a small swirl of tomato sauce. Maria flinched.

Her appearance reminded Father Bob of how Maria looked at her grandfather's funeral, with sunken cheeks and a look of dread across her face. He fumed at Mario snuffing out his smoke on her plate, in front of everybody, yet knew that he had to keep his composure. *Okay, it's just a cigarette, didn't hurt anybody.* The more Maria cowered, though, the more he became frustrated. *There must be a horrible history between those two.* He imagined Mario smacking her across the face, her screaming, and Boss crying, covering up his head with his arms, sprawled on the floor while Mario kicked at him. *Oh, how I'd like taking Mario down and resolving things on the street.* He called on Jesus. *What would You do Lord?*

He'd never seen Maria so fearful before, as she usually turned ferocious when provoked. She didn't think anything of chucking plates or glasses of beer at people. He'd been on the receiving end of her wrath before. Now she just sat there, helpless as a lamb. She avoided his eye contact when he tried to catch her gaze.

Mario leaned forward on his chair and with his right hand, wrapped some spaghetti around his fork, spinning it into perfect symmetry like a toy top. After a bite, he said, "Delicious, Grandma, as usual." He addressed the priests, holding up his fork. "Grandma's spaghetti was the best part of my marriage."

Then he took a sip of wine from Father Bob's glass, again nodding at him. Father Bob looked at the glass, then at Mario, unsure of the meaning of Mario's gesture. *He's trying to provoke me? I'll chop my hand across his windpipe and knock him back-*

wards in his chair to the floor where I can rip that gun from his chest. Forget what Jesus would do. He knew how many times he had begged in vain for an answer from the Lord. That only added to his anger, as now he saw Mario as some sort of devil. Father Bob's old street survival tendencies kicked-in. He saw how little and delicate Mario's hands were, and his face had no scars on it. *He's a phony, short man complex guy with connections. Not a natural tough guy, Mario had lived a life of leisure, born into a successful business family. He never had to learn street skills. Why was I afraid of this guy when I was seventeen? He's underestimating me. That's good.*

Mario picked up the manila envelope in one hand. He addressed Maria again. "Here's all the legal bullshit, you know, copies of the divorce decree and all, plus a big check. Everybody gets what they want. Everybody's happy. Now you can sit on your ass all day and watch soap operas. So, nothing's changed." He tossed the envelope across the table where it landed partially on top of Maria's empty plate.

Maria bit her lower lip. She looked at the envelope and rolled her eyes. She didn't open it.

"Gentlemen," Mario continued. "I guess we could consider this the 'Last Supper,' sort of." He pointed to the priests. "All we need now is Jesus Christ himself!" He laughed. The table remained silent. He looked irritated. "How come I'm the only one talking here?"

Bishop Malone stood up. He towered over everybody and looked at his watch. "I'm sorry, everyone, but I needed to be at the Cathedral up on the hill ten minutes ago."

What a coward. Father Bob saw a man of stature abandoning his sheep. He hadn't even blessed Grandma's house yet. All Bishops blessed the houses into which they had been invited, a long held tradition. And here, this man of tradition was running from danger to save himself. Maybe the gun frightened him. Murphy started to stand also, ready to escape on the coattails of Bishop Malone.

Father Bob had already decided to stay in the room as long as Mario remained in the house, threatening Grandma and Maria.

"No, no!" Mario raised his voice. Then he toned down. "I have to get going anyway. Don't want to bother you and your little family dinner anymore." He stood and looked up at the Bishop. "Sit down, please." He pointed to the Bishop's chair.

Much to Father Bob's surprise, the Bishop sat down immediately. He'd never seen anybody order Bishop Malone around like that before. Suddenly, he wanted to protect the Bishop too. On the other hand, his anger at Mario was building into a rage. He clenched his teeth, wanted to take Mario down and saw an opportunity as Mario stood next to him. He was seated with Mario's gun at eye level, within arm's reach. He placed his elbows on top of the table, and freed his hands. He felt the adrenaline rush through his body. He learned long ago how to turn that human feeling of fear into action. Just like before a boxing match, or before a street fight outside the pool hall, he would use that extra energy, that super power to attack. He'd beaten tougher guys than Mario. He waited for Mario to make his move. Mario turned his attention from the Bishop towards Maria.

"Oh yea, I almost forgot," Mario said. "I've got something else for you." Father Bob twisted his body towards Mario and again perched onto the balls of his feet. Mario paused. Then he reached his right hand into his jacket. Father Bob readied himself to jump. He kept his eyes on the gun. He watched as Mario's hand did not go near the holster, which was still snapped shut. Everyone at the table flinched when Mario pulled out yet another envelope, this one smaller than the last.

"Chill out everybody," he laughed. What, you think I'd shoot a bunch of priests?" He tapped the outside of his suit jacket. "This piece is for my protection, that's all." He flung the envelope across the table and it would have hit Maria in the face if she hadn't caught it. "That's the under-the-table cash we agreed on, you money-grabbing bitch!"

Tears filled Maria's eyes. Father Bob's stomach and arms tingled. He had had all the bullying he could stand. Nobody would disgrace Maria, nobody. *That's it!* He started to spring up, when he felt the powerful hand of Bishop Malone squeeze his bicep anchoring him to the chair. He tried to pull out of the Bishop's grip, but Bishop Malone held tight and nodded his head. His silent lip movement said, "I know, hold on." He would have grabbed the Bishop's hand to pull out of his hold, but felt tenderness from the Bishop's expression. The first time ever that he'd received any hint of fatherly protection from Bishop Malone. He took a deep breath, and nodded. The Bishop let go of his arm.

Mario looked at Father Bob with raised eyebrows. "What do we have here? Feeling froggy, Padre?" He backed up a few steps, turned his palms up and motioned with his fingers for Father Bob to come towards him. "C'mon, leap little frog." Again the Bishop grabbed Father Bob's arm and said out loud this time, "Please, Father. That's not how we handle things."

"Stop it!" Maria finally yelled. She pushed-off of the table with both hands and sprung out of her chair, shooting her arm towards Mario. "Leave this house!" she screamed. "You shame us!" Her eyes glowed fierce behind a face of stone. Her tone shocked the entire group.

Father Bob's body rushed with fresh blood. He jumped up, twisting the Bishop's thumb backwards with one quick movement to slip out of his grip. He started towards Mario.

"Sit down, Father!" Maria shouted. "Sit!" Now her face shook and spittle shot from her lips. He was shocked at how fast Maria had moved, as she suddenly appeared in between him and Mario. She placed her hand up against his chest. He felt her try to push him back, but he held his ground. No way would he sit or take his eyes off of Mario.

"I'm fine, Maria, I'm fine," Father Bob panted.

"We don't fight in Grandma's house," Maria gasped.

Mario cocked his head sideways at Grandma, who was sitting more calmly than anybody in the room, returning his gaze. He paused for a few seconds and then nodded. "Okay, Grandma. You're the only one I respect around here. You always were." He looked at Maria. "We'll finish up our business later, bitch." Then he looked at Father Bob with a scowl. "She's all yours, pal. And you and I have unfinished business. Bet on it." He turned and walked through the swinging doors.

Father Bob started to follow Mario, to make sure he left the house. "Leave him alone!" Maria screamed at him. "That son of a bitch!" she yelled, now in tears. "I'll go lock that damn door."

"Watch your tongue!" Grandma said sternly. "Sit down. We don't talk like animals! I will get the door later, he's gone now."

"That's right," Murphy said. "He's not coming back here."

Father Bob looked at Murphy and dropped his mouth open. He wanted to say, *"Oh, you're here too? You can speak?"* But he bit his tongue. He was fatigued. The adrenaline dump had worn him out. So he sat down with his thoughts returning to the vision of Mario.

"What was he talking about?" he asked Maria. "What did he mean, 'she's all yours'?"

Maria sat down, said nothing and mopped her forehead with a dishtowel. Grandma addressed Bishop Malone, "I'm so sorry you and Monsignor Murphy had to see that. We didn't think he would ever come here."

Nobody seemed to pay any attention to Father Bob's question. He looked around the table, though, and could sense a relief. Everyone's expression relaxed, still shell-shocked maybe, but relieved. Bishop Malone looked tired, and Murphy was returning to his normal, oblivious expression, like when he read the morning newspaper.

Maria opened the small envelope and counted the cash, without taking it out. "I knew he wouldn't give the whole amount. He wants to make me fight for it." She rested her head into her hands on the table.

Bishop Malone stood up and walked over to Grandma. He bent over, "You don't have to apologize about anything, Mrs. Barrone. Thank you for the delicious meal." He placed one hand on top of her shoulder. "I'd like to bless your house before I leave, if you would allow me."

Grandma's eyes sparkled and she smiled. She rose from her chair, using the table as a crutch. "I would love for you to bless my house."

Bishop Malone reached inside his black jacket and pulled out a hand-held, sprinkler of holy water. He flung sprays of the blessed water around the dining room, muttering prayers. Grandma made the sign of the cross and followed him through the swinging doors, along with Murphy. They would bless the rest of the house.

Father Bob sat across the table from Maria. He looked at her for several seconds before she finally made eye contact with him. "Are you going to be okay?" he asked.

She nodded.

He stood up and started gathering dishes.

"What do you think you're doing?" She rose and grabbed a small pile of plates from his hand. "Guests in this house don't do dishes. Just go ahead home, okay? We'll talk later."

"I know you're upset. I just want to help out. What can I do?"

"You've done more than you'll ever know. Thanks for standing up for us." She turned her head away. "But I'm just so upset...leave me alone now, please?"

He heard the Bishop and company murmuring near the front door. "Okay," he responded calmly, sliding back into priest mode. "I understand, but Mario's gone now, so you'll be all right." He walked through the swinging doors. "Call on me if you need anything." He heard her mumble, recognized only some partial obscenities, and walked through the kitchen to the front door.

Near the front door he kissed and hugged Grandma. She held him tight and said, "Thanks a million. We got rid of that stink. God bless you." When he walked out the door, he found Murphy and the Bishop waiting for him on the sidewalk. Murphy looked at him quizzically. "Is everything okay in there?"

He put on a false smile. "Now it seems to be. What a bizarre ending to a great dinner." He expected a response, wanted something from the two priests, at least an acknowledgement. Monsignor Murphy and Bishop Malone turned and walked up the sloped, cement road as if nothing had happened. He barely heard them talking parochial business. His thoughts raced with concerns for Maria, those strange signals from Mario, and how Boss appeared so disturbed. *How can these guys write this off so easily?*

Bishop Malone shook Father Bob's hand when he reached his car. "Let me know how things turn out, Father." He hesitated, and then whispered, "Murphy doesn't look well. Maybe you could make him see a doctor."

He thought about how Murphy wheezed during their walk to Grandma's and realized that his face appeared ashy today. "Sure, Bishop, I'll see what I can do. And thanks for visiting…and for the opportunity you've given me."

Bishop Malone opened the car door and plopped behind the wheel. Father Bob stood by, waiting for a word of encouragement. The Bishop started his car, winked, and drove off, just as Murphy's Lincoln turned up the Hill of Churches. *The old man is headed to his boy's club bar, had a tough day I suppose. He'll probably tell the boys what a hero he was today.* He chuckled, reliving a vision of the look of fright on the faces of his superiors.

He breathed a deep breath and sang a long sigh of relief. He still had a job, was finally alone, and did not want any more drama. He walked into the clean, quiet rectory kitchen and went straight for the cabinet, happy to find a full bottle of scotch. He filled up a glass, threw in some ice, and sat at the table with the bottle. The first sensation of that burning, cool alcohol soothed his lips, before slowly blazing down his throat to ignite a brief fire inside of his stomach. "Ahh…Thank you, God." He raised his glass in toast. "Thank you, oh invisible Father."

Although drained and exhausted, he was bored after finishing his first drink. He got up and poured another, and sat back down again. *What now?* Then he reflected on the most active day he'd ever had—Sister Roxanne leaving the vocation before sunrise this morning, followed by a High Mass where he performed to a standing ovation. *They clapped for me…seems like it happened three weeks ago.* Then the dinner and Mario.

Why had Maria got so withdrawn after Mario left. At least the day is finished, and nobody got hurt.

He counted up his drinks, flicking out his little finger first, then the ring finger, and counted three glasses of wine at dinner. Now he was halfway through his second glass of scotch. He looked down the couch and missed Jack, who would be curled up like a lamb, sleeping with his head propped on the armrest. Tears welled up in his eyes, so he stood and paced around the rectory. *I miss my dog.* He noticed his reflection in the picture window of the front room, set down his scotch and shadowboxed, ducking, bobbing, and throwing combination punches to an imaginary Mario. Jesus would not act this way. He was glad that the Bishop held him down, not once, but twice. *Thank you Lord, for letting me remain a priest. I will act more like one.*

Still, he could not rid his thoughts of Maria...dressed in those tight jeans, that warm look on her face. *She must have gone through hell with that guy. Maybe she told Mario about how I used to sneak into her bedroom and make love to her. That's why Mario acted so surly, so mean. He didn't act that way towards the other priests. Maria married so young. No wonder Boss is troubled.*

He walked back into the kitchen and poured his third glass of scotch. Took a good guzzle and headed for the living room. He set down his glass, removed the collar that the Bishop gave to him, took off his priest shirt and plopped onto the couch. Maria had him totally confused. Despite her crazy life, he wanted to be with her. *Do I love her?* He'd just ducked another bullet, got a second chance at remaining a priest. Part of him wanted her to leave...wash his hands of her like Pontius Pilate did to Jesus.

He untied his shoes and rested his feet on top of the coffee table. Once he leaned back and closed his eyes he finally relaxed. He heard the singular sound of the clock ticking, which lulled him into an alpha state of sleepy consciousness.

A faint thud disturbed him. Either it was the kitchen door, or maybe just a dream. He opened his eyes and listened, but heard nothing but the clock ticking. As soon as he closed his eyes again, a knock on the kitchen door interrupted his peace. He must have dozed off, because his mouth felt dry and tasted musty. The knock continued, louder this time, yanking him back into duty. He threw on his shirt without the white collar, couldn't find it. Then he hid his half-glass of scotch behind a lamp in the living room, and walked towards the kitchen in his black socks. He tried to wake himself up, since he drank a lot and was muddled. Like an actor getting into character, he created his priestly consciousness during the walk through the kitchen towards the door. Any visitors who knocked on this door, the kitchen door across the alley from the convent, were always known acquaintances. Strangers knocked on the front door, next to the picture window, where he had recently shadow boxed.

He pulled the curtains on the door back just a little. When he peered into the darkness he saw a petite figure standing there. Her hair was bathed in the light from the porch, her features shadowed. He'd know her anywhere. Maria.

What in the world? Maria had practically thrown him out of her house, only a few hours ago. He wanted a break from her and all her drama. He wished that it would be anybody else knocking at his door, even Mrs. Hellinski. He stood there, knew he had to open it. Finally he put his hand on the doorknob. As he opened the door, he had no plan. *Why are You doing this to me Lord?*

Chapter 14

Priestly Intentions

Father Bob wanted to be left alone, yet there he was with his hand on the doorknob, twisting it, opening it. He summoned the best of his priestly intentions. Before he could say anything or even step aside, Maria rushed through the doorway, bumping him as she passed. She wore huge yellow sunglasses despite the descending darkness of evening.

She stood with her back to him, leaned over and rested both hands on the kitchen table, her jeans skin-tight against the back of her legs. Father Bob found himself with the doorknob still in his hand, admiring her sculpted thighs.

"Shut the door!" Maria's voice sounded frantic. "Would you please pour me a drink?"

He'd forgotten to hide the bottle of scotch, which sat on the table, next to those wilted ham roll-ups. He guessed there would be no harm in pouring her a drink, though he really wanted to know what was troubling her. "Sure, I'll pour you one. But what's going on?"

She snapped around to face him, still wearing those sunglasses, and then just sat down on a kitchen chair. He opened the freezer, grabbed some ice, and felt her watching him as he threw ice into a glass and poured some scotch. He walked towards her with the drink, and gasped.

"Oh my." He placed the drink onto the table in front of her. The skin over her left eye was swollen and purple. Maria didn't respond, just sat there, so he sat in a chair next to her and placed his hand upon her knee.

"Hold still, let me have a look." He started to reach for the sunglasses and she jerked her head backwards a few inches. "It's okay. You're okay," he assured her, as he continued to reach towards the frames and smelled her light perfume. He wanted to be gentle, trying not to jostle her. He removed the glasses. She stayed still and stared into space. He sat back and inspected her eye. She returned his gaze, and he knew that she was waiting for some reaction. He forced a faint smile, despite feeling sick to his stomach. He wanted to say that the eye wasn't so bad. On the other hand, he didn't want to lie to her. The swelling formed a dark ring that circled her puffed-up eye socket. Tiny, randomly situated slits pooled with blood had started scabbing near the edges of each wound.

"You've got yourself a doozy here, that's for sure."

His heart pumped fast and he fought off feeling angry. He had seen this sort of damage before and knew what kind of force it took to purple an eye like that. It wouldn't take much to blacken a woman's eye. *Did Boss hit his mother? No, must have been Mario.* He pictured Mario smirking after cracking Maria across the eye with a right roundhouse.

Father Bob took a deep breath and gently dabbed some of the swelling above her eye with his finger, examining it, almost cursing Mario as a coward out loud. Then he grew irritated with Maria. *Why would she let that man back into Grandma's house?* Maria winced as he pushed onto her swollen eye socket too hard. He quickly pulled back his hand. "I'm sorry." He knew he had to get a grip on his anger. She was distressed enough, and right now she needed some loving care, unconditional, the way Jesus Christ would give. "Sit right here. I'll make an ice pack for you." He spoke in an even, friendly tone.

She nodded, remained silent. He paused, waiting for her to make eye contact but she just stared at her untouched glass of scotch. A tear dripped from her good eye and dangled from the tip of her chin. She didn't sob, or even move. How he wanted to hug her, let her cry in his arms, but he wasn't sure how she would respond. She seemed so fragile.

He sighed, rose and grabbed a white washcloth from the sink. He put some ice in the middle and wrapped the cloth, tying two ends together. He held the bundle under some tap water to soften it, and sat back down next to Maria. "Let's try this." He slightly grazed the top of her eye with the ice pack. She watched him, stuck out her lower lip like a child about to cry. He didn't want to force her to talk, so he dabbed some more, around the entire eye, savoring the closeness, the sharing of intimacy. At this moment she looked like a wounded angel. His desire stirred. *Oh, woman we are entangled in a powerful and painful love.* He wanted to kiss her wounds, but not like a father, more like a lover. Looking at her lips made him long to press his against them. He craved her, and started to envision making love but shook that fantasy from his thoughts.

She moved her chair back several inches, which made a high pitched squeal, like the wheels of a train skidding to a stop on wet rails. He would not allow his desire for her to block his duty. She acted helpless, like at dinner when Mario appeared. For the first time, Maria was exposing her vulnerable side, where he could tunnel in and find out who she really was, what here secrets were. Maybe, just maybe, he could dare to share his secrets with her, too.

"Does this feel good?"

Maria placed her hand over his, pressed a little harder onto her eye. "Yes." He basked in the warm touch of her hand. When the bottom of his palm started to freeze from the ice, he slowly pulled the ice pack away from her eye.

"We need to let the swelling breathe once in a while. Don't want to frost your skin."

She kept her hand on top of his for a second, and then let go. "I figured you knew about this kind of stuff from your boxing days."

He tried to come off as light as possible. "I've seen much worse than this, but never on a woman." He smiled. "So, is that why you came over? You want me to be your cut man?"

She looked at him, perplexed. "What's a cut man?"

"You know, he's the old guy in a boxer's corner, usually with cauliflower ears. He closes up the wounds, stops the bleeding in between rounds."

She curled her lip. "And you want my son to box? I thought you said boxing was safe?"

He was glad that she finally started to talk. "Oh, it's safe. I mean, I'll teach Boss the basics. Nothing like you might see in boxing matches on television. That's the pros. This will be more of a workout than anything else." He picked up the ice pack and moved his chair closer to her. "Let's give it some more ice. The swelling's going down some."

He placed the cold pack over her entire eye this time. "I'm not hurting you, am I?"

"No, that's good." She placed her hand over top of his as he was hoping she would. "I can hold it myself," she said. "Just tell me how long to keep it on." She reached for her glass of scotch with her other hand and took a swig, then looked into his eyes. "I'm sorry for being so crabby at you after dinner. I was just out of my mind."

He gently pulled his hand out from under hers, and placed his arm around her shoulder. He moved his face close to her hair and she smelled so clean, felt so fragile that he wanted to linger there.

"Listen, you can yell at me anytime you want. I know you're going through a tough time."

She didn't look at him. "You don't know the half of it."

He leaned back into his chair. He wanted to know the whole story about what had happened, and why she really came to see him. He tried to be sensitive as well. "Do you feel like talking about it?"

"I suppose you've figured it out. Mario came back. We argued as usual, and I ended up on the floor, as usual." She drank from her glass again. "I'm just glad Boss or Grandma weren't home. Things could've been much worse."

He shook his head. Bit his tongue. *How could she be so stupid to let Mario back into the house?* His right hand started to tremble and he clenched it into a fist. He almost banged the tabletop, but tried hard not to show his anger.

He stood up. "I'll be back in a second." He walked into the living room and almost punched the wall. *Keep your cool. Christ help me. No judgments, no arguing, no sex, no nothing except to be a friend.* He sat on the couch and put on his shoes. He couldn't find his collar, and didn't have time to look for it, so just retrieved his old glass of scotch from behind the lamp. The ice had melted and the glass was full of cool liquid. He chugged it and walked back into the kitchen. The alcohol made his stomach feel a little better. He poured himself a fresh one and this time, sat across the table from Maria. She held the white ice-rag against her face. "Did you call the police?" His voice cracked, from trying so hard to sound gentle.

She laid the ice pack onto the table, downed the rest of her drink, and pushed the glass forward as a sign for more. He stared at her. *She's not going to answer me?* He topped some ice with scotch. He'll sit and wait for her to talk, when she's ready. Maria took another sip of scotch, and her hand shook. She cleared her throat. "That's exactly what Mario wants."

Now, Father Bob was perplexed. A battered woman sat in front of him, practically half of her face bruised, and her ex-husband wanted her to call the police? "I don't understand," he said. "Mario wants you to call the police?"

She took another sip, dropped the ice rag onto the table-top, and rolled the side of the ice-filled glass against the top of her eye. "He said it's illegal for me to take Boss out of the state of Nevada without his consent. You know, court visitation rights and all."

He leaned back in his chair, almost in a state of disbelief. He should know about those things.

"I thought he didn't want anything to do with Boss?"

Father Bob regretted saying that, adding fuel to the feud between those two. He grabbed the ice rag and tossed it into the sink, without standing up. Maria sat with a blank look on her face.

"I can't let anybody around here see me like this. My life's a total mess." She stared off to the side, head tilted down a little, towards the table. "I feel numb."

Father Bob's legs and arms tingled, along with butterflies in his stomach. He wanted to track Mario down more than anything, stop Mario from messing with her. "What else did Mario say to you?" He strained to speak calmly.

Her lips trembled. "First, he called me a whore. Then he started screaming something about how many different guys could be Boss's real father." She continued to look down onto the table. "He knows that Boss means the whole world to me." She locked eyes with him. "No, you're right, he doesn't really want Boss…just wants to make my life miserable. I put up with his shit for fifteen years." She sighed. "If Boss really had a different father, Mario wouldn't have any right to try and steal him from me." She continued to stare into his eyes.

How many men has she slept with? Father Bob got stuck on that phrase and didn't hear much of what else she was saying. His mind wandered to the night at the bar, where Barker called Maria a Vegas whore. It suddenly occurred to him that Boss looked nothing like Mario. He was taller, lanky, and neither Maria nor Mario had that body type. *No, she couldn't be a prostitute.* He remembered how shy and inexperienced she acted when they made love back in high school. He was accustomed to having sex with older, mostly married women back then. They'd pick him up down by the pool hall where he would stand outside and lean against the windowpane under the green awning. The first woman who stopped her car in the street, rolled down the passenger side window, and asked him if he wanted to drink some wine. He was 14 and jumped right in, and they drank "Red Ripple" right out of the bottle. She parked near the city dump, and took off her jeans. He stuck it to her in her Chevrolet Impala while her husband was working in the steel mill. Lucy had taught him about how to use his tongue, what goes where, and why. The musty smell of the dump and the remains of cigarette smoke in the upholstery had combined to make him feel like an adult. Juicy Lucy, he had called her. She had reddish hair and was a little overweight, but she was nice to him. When she told some of her girlfriends about how she had turned the well-endowed boy into a good lover, they hunted him down and lured him with their own bottles of cheap wine.

Maria was a different story. He was shy when it came down to approaching her. He respected her as a good girl, lucky that she would even talk to him. She had no idea how much he really loved her, wanted her all to himself, needed her love. He would have given up anything to have her, though he really didn't have anything. Something inside him said that she was too good for him. He believed it. Despite having the upper hand in teaching her how to have sex, he still felt inferior. She laid still the first time that they had sex, and brought him, the experienced one, to orgasm quickly. Maybe it was from the excitement of taboo, the sneaking through the window. He loved her so much that he couldn't brag to his street friends about having sex with her. Sometimes at night he would sit at St. Anne's playground and stare at her house hoping to catch a glimpse of her walking past a window, so he could sleep better that night.

As he sat there in the kitchen across from her, she spoke but her words did not register. She had kept him a secret back when he had slept with her. *How many other men did she sleep with?* He thought he had worked through all those issues through his vocation, but sometimes closed doors swung back open, uninvited.

"Jesus, Bob, you listening to me?" Maria yanked him back into the moment. She raised her eyebrows, the one overtop her battered eye barely moved because of the swelling. "You look like you're a thousand miles away. What do you think?" She cocked her head.

Startled, he fumbled for words. "Oh, I was wondering why in the world you let Mario back into the house in the first place." He raised his hands in a gesture to stop her from responding. "He might have some rights to Boss, but he doesn't have any right to hit you! You've got to be smart about it. It may sound stupid, but fill out a form with the police. They could arrest him for assault."

She lifted her arms towards the ceiling. "Wow, whoopee, yeah boy, that sure would fix everything!" She glared at him with the fire of anger. "What the hell? You sit over there, all cozy in your safe little world. You have no clue, do you?"

"C'mon Maria, I'm trying to help you. I'm on your side, remember?" She looked at him as if he was the one who had hit her instead of Mario. He could not understand why she acted so hurt. "Hey, I'm sorry, is that what you want to hear, an apology? Okay, you got it. I didn't mean to upset you." He glanced over at their glasses. Father Bob had entered into "no man's land," a place where no matter what a man says, or doesn't say to a woman, it would be wrong. Still, he knew he had to talk. "I just think it's ridiculous to make it easy for Mario. Why let him torture you like that? He assaulted you! What are you going to do if he comes back, something stupid like let him in again?"

Maria's mouth dropped open. Father Bob knew that he'd said something terrible, just didn't understand exactly what.

Maria popped up from her chair and flung the inside of her glass at him. The drink and ice splashed his face.

"Oh, go to Hell!" She fired the empty glass towards the kitchen door, barely missing the window, where it exploded into shards. "I should never have come here! That's what was stupid!" She stomped towards the door, crunching broken glass under her high-heeled boots.

Father Bob stood up. The cold scotch dripped down his face and rescued him from this tangled banter going sour. He couldn't let Maria leave in such a huff. That would be the second fight they had had today. So he ran around the table and grabbed the back of her arm just as she tried to reach for the door. She spun around, swung at his face. He ducked the first swing, but she connected with a slap across his ear as he stood straight again. The force of her strike surprised him, sent a shooting pain through his own healing eye. He shook it off.

"I didn't call you stupid!" He had automatically moved into fight stance, lifted his hands near his face for self-defense. Maria swung at him again, but this time he saw it coming. He stepped in close to her, and her swing turned into a violent hug. Wrapping his hands around the tops of her shoulders he stopped her momentum. She tried to punch him but couldn't move her arms.

"Let go of me!" she screamed. Then she started kicking at him, tried to knee him. "Let go of me! Let go!"

Father Bob released his grip on her and backed up a few steps. "Please, please calm down. I would never hurt you!" he said in between pants.

Maria glared at him with wild eyes. After several long moments, her breathing started to calm. She placed her hand over her mouth to stifle a smile, and then began laughing. Father Bob laughed along, not sure what was so funny, just catching her contagious fit as scotch dripped from his chin. She snorted, and in a high pitch said, "Oh, God, we look so ridiculous!"

He shook his head, eyes locked to hers. The purple swelling framed one of her eyes, intensifying its mesmerizing glow. Without thinking he stepped closer to her and the chaos silenced. Maria stopped smiling and returned his gaze and he knew what she felt.

"I love you," came from him without effort.

She sighed and lifted her lips to meet his. She slid into his arms and they held each other tight. He softly stroked her ear with the tip of his tongue. Then he kissed the side of her neck, barely brushing her warmth with his lips. Her body went limp.

"Oh, Bob, we can't do this," she said. Then she lifted her head again and he floated his lips onto hers, moist with lipstick, so tender. Warmth flowed from every inch of her as he absorbed her scent of makeup and hair spray and perfume and he heard subtle sounds from her core. The void in his soul, inherent in the celibate priesthood, now filled with the touch of a woman and made him long for more. His spirit demanded flesh. He knew that hers did too.

They pressed their bodies together and turned towards the table. As he pressed her against the table, he moved one hand down to unbutton her blouse, shooting a few buttons off and onto the floor. With one sweep he lifted her bra, and her perfect breasts slipped out and into his palm. He moved his face into the separation between her breasts, that "nun zone" never exposed in any paintings or statues of female saints.

As he nuzzled her there, she rubbed her fingers through his curly black, thinning hair. He looked up and saw her eyes fall glossy, succumbing to the spell of seduction. He paused, rose to study her expression for a clue, and it told him to take her.

"Bob, you have to know something," she said in a melodic tone. "It's about Boss…"

He stopped her words with a passionate kiss. Then he looked into her eyes again. "I want you more than anything," he whispered.

She lay back onto the tabletop and pulled him to her. He unsnapped the buckle on her jeans, reached down and slid off her boots. He then pulled off her pants, threw them to the side. He saw a slit of moisture in the middle of her beige panties, and kissed it. Maria moaned and slowly moved her head from side to side. He maneuvered his tongue just as the cheating wives taught him and he buried his face in her silk, lingering, breathing in the scent of rapture.

When he unzipped his pants and positioned himself between her legs, she did not stop him. *I shouldn't do this...*He slipped inside of her with one thrust. She barely moved moaning sweetly. He wanted this feeling to last forever, but like his spiritual highs, knew the descent would come too soon.

Maria lay still, while Father Bob remained motionless holding her. The woman who had always slipped away from him now was entangled with his body. When she finally did look at him, she made a faint smile that strangely reminded him of the statue of Mother Mary. She began to move under him, and they shared orgasm together.

A feeling of dread now descended upon him. *Oh God in heaven, forgive me. Was Maria my Eve, come to destroy me again?* Maria wouldn't look at him. When he focused on her bruised eye, a strange sensation overtook him. Some blood trickled from a freshly opened wound. He softly kissed it. A rush trembled from the top of his head down through his body. His legs went rubbery, and he floated for a brief moment. Then he pulled out.

A lump in his throat formed when Maria silently slid from under him and retrieved her pants from the floor, without a word. The high he felt earlier had plummeted smack onto the kitchen floor amongst the broken glass. He became aware of his nudity and pulled up his pants, buckled his belt, and watched for a sign from Maria.

She gathered the rest of her clothes and walked to the living room. "Why are the bathrooms in these old houses always upstairs?"

He did not know what to say as he heard her going up the stairs. *Oh God, what did I do?* Puzzled, he cleaned-up the broken glass and scotch that was on the floor, cutting his hand. He sat at the table, waiting for Maria. *This wasn't right.* She came down the stairs and walked into the kitchen.

"I'm so sorry, Maria. This was not your fault. It's mine."

She burst out a hysterical laugh, but only for a moment. Then she glared at him. "You think I had nothing to do with this?"

"I'm just saying, I don't know…are you okay?" He remembered the words from Sister Roxanne that morning, about the way he wanted women that he could not have, about the insinuation of love.

"C'mon, Bob. We're adults here." Then she sat down across from him. "So, what now?"

"Good question." *I wish I could leave, but I'm already home.* His heart raced, pain and tightness gripped his chest, and his forehead beaded with new sweat. His throat felt as if it were closing. He wanted Maria to leave now, give him space. He had never lingered around with a woman after sex.

"Are *you* okay?" Maria appeared strong, almost angelic as if she knew exactly what to do. "You're sweating."

His thoughts scrambled. "I'm sorry." He hung his head, brushed some stains from his black pants. "I said that already. Please forgive me…I won't blame you if you can't."

"Will you stop with that guilt stuff already? What am I supposed to forgive you for, loving me?" She looked away, and then back. "You used to be a much gentler person, you know, not so wrapped-up in yourself. Don't worry, though, I've come to a decision and now I know what to do. I thank you for that." She smiled a smile that resembled disappointment. "No more playing around."

Her words, "You used to be a much gentler person," shot through him like a jagged knife. Somehow he felt nostalgic and searched for some innocent memories to fall back upon, something to remind him of how gentle he could be. The only thoughts he could drum up centered on fighting or sex, or the small sticky stains on the tabletop in front of him. *I mess up everything.* Suddenly he feared that somebody would see them through the window. Monsignor Murphy could return at any time, since it was approaching eight o'clock.

"What do you mean, Maria?" She looked disappointed.

"Nothing, never mind, I should have left this town earlier. I've got to get out of here." She stood up and grabbed her purse.

He didn't want to stop her. He watched her walk towards the door without saying anything.

She turned to face him with her hand on the doorknob. "Don't worry, Bob, nobody will ever find out about this." She put her yellow sunglasses back on.

Father Bob remained silent. He pulled back the curtains and watched her stroll away in those high-heeled boots, down the alley until out of sight. He used Maria's rag from the icepack to wipe away at the tabletop. *I'm losing my mind. Can't do anything right.* His eyes welled up with tears. He spoke. "I hurt Maria. What is wrong with me? How can I be a priest?"

He filled a glass of scotch at the kitchen counter and swallowed half of it. Then he prayed out loud, "God, in Heaven, what kind of priest am I?" He downed the rest of the scotch and couldn't even think of a prayer. When the room started to spin, he decided he'd better sleep it off. Get to bed before Murphy came home.

He stumbled towards the stairs and saw his white collar, curled up around the leg of the coffee table in the living room. When he bent down to pick it up, he lost balance and fell face first onto the carpet. He grabbed the collar, forced his body up onto all fours, and the room spun more pronounced. He crawled his way up the stairs, practically pulling himself up with his hands on each step, and finally climbed into bed. He prayed out loud, "Dear God, I am not worthy to serve You." The last thing he saw was the white-collar fall from his bloodied palm, as it disappeared over the edge of the bed.

CHAPTER 15

THE DAY AFTER FATHER'S DAY

Father Bob woke up when Monsignor Murphy's morning gag turned into a fully-fledged cough outside of his bedroom door. He sat onto the side of his bed, rubbed his face with both hands. Still wearing last night's clothing, he could feel the tightness of his shoes around his feet. An image of Maria popped into his thoughts. *I can't believe it.* He had made love to her on the kitchen table. How she fought at first, and then how they kissed. He could still smell her. He smacked his hands together into the sound of a single clap, remembering Maria's saying that nobody would ever find out about what they did. *Aren't we entitled to a pleasure once in a while?* He grabbed his workout clothes and headed for the bathroom. Glad to have a day off, he said his morning prayers during his shower. The warm water washed away his old skin, and poured yesterday's worries down the drain. He would not harbor guilt. *Jesus had died for our sins.* In the shower Father Bob absolved himself of all wrongdoing.

Standing under cleansing water, he wondered where Sister Roxanne might be this very moment. He felt a new kinship with her and wished she had seen his impromptu sermon at Mass that wooed the crowd to a standing ovation. When he thought about dinner at Grandma Amelia's, Maria sauntered back into his thoughts. He drifted into an absurd daydream where he secured her a job at the rectory, replacing Mrs. Hellinski. She could stay in Irontown and not have to move out west. He smiled as he envisioned Maria on her hands and knees, scrubbing the kitchen floor, his sneaking up behind her to smack her backside and make her giggle. Murphy would be retired. Father Bob would be running the parish his way. Then there was Boss and the promise to box today, if only he didn't have to spend his day off with the boy.

183

He had expected the Bishop to come down and fire him. But no, he ended up with a pat on the back, plus a boxing club. He had finally caught a break? To top off the night, he had had sex with a woman he actually loved. Again the admission of love startled him, but he thought it through. *Why can't I love Maria?* He wanted to find the gentleness in his soul that Maria had accused him of lacking. The gentleness he could not grasp last night. He wished he could talk to her. He stepped out of the shower and talked to his reflection in the mirror. "You are a special priest. God has a prophetic plan for you."

He jumped into his workout clothes and trotted down the stairs. Rejuvenated, he knew that he could love more than one person at any given time. He felt like calling Maria on the telephone, forgive her sins too, and make sure that she was happy. Those awkward feelings they had shared last night were just plain Old Catholic guilt. He wished that the Church did not condone guilt. Guilt prevents people from enjoying God's abundant universe. *Priests used to have multiple wives, until the year 1010.* Although he could not marry Maria, he wanted to see and be with her, and he grew as excited as a schoolchild hearing the recess bell.

While trotting down the steps, he fought off a brief pang of his own guilt...not for his sins, but for being so happy to have a day off. He always enjoyed days off, unlike most priests who rarely took them. So what if he had to spend the morning teaching Boss how to box. Maybe he'd teach the kid a little respect. Then he could spend the rest of the afternoon any way he wanted. Maybe he'd see if Barker was around. Or maybe he'd just drive around, past some of his old digs.

He sprang into the kitchen. The reflection from Murphy's thick eyeglasses sparkled into Father Bob's eyes, as Murphy lifted his head from his newspaper.

"Good morning, your holiness," he said with a mocking bow. "May I join you for a cup o' jo?" He didn't wait for an answer, just poured a coffee. He topped off Murphy's cup and realized that Murphy was studying the smear on the floor, where Maria had thrown her glass last night.

Murphy set down his paper and removed his glasses. "What did you do, break a glass in here? I see fragments everywhere and the table and floor are all sticky."

"I threw a party. How come you didn't come?" He grabbed the bottle of scotch in front of Murphy and splashed some into his coffee. He looked forward to a taste of alcohol that would soothe his slight headache.

"Some party. I heard you sawing logs through your door around nine o'clock." Murphy paused. Father Bob could tell that he wanted more explanation. "I'm glad I didn't come down here in my bare feet. So, did you have visitors?"

"What do you care?" He shrugged. "Aren't I allowed to entertain guests?" He couldn't tell him about Maria coming over, but maybe Murphy already knew. Small towns have few secrets.

Murphy looked right through him.

"Well, you could probably figure it out. I mean, after that strange Mario character we met at dinner yesterday."

Murphy straightened up in his chair. Father Bob enjoyed his grave expression. "Did Mario come here?"

He paused, tried to look serious. "Yes, he did." He fought hard to stop from laughing when Murphy's eyes almost popped out of his head. "Don't worry. I knocked him out with one punch, just like Sugar Ray KO'd you." He couldn't stifle his laugh any longer.

Murphy slumped back into his chair, rolled his eyes. "Feel like playing this morning? Why don't you go say Mass for me if you have so much energy? You owe me a couple."

"Okay, okay, actually, this isn't funny at all. Maria came over." He paused, and tried to not appear nervous when Murphy leaned forward in his chair. "She had a huge mouse-eye. That Mario thinks he's a tough guy, you know, slugging a woman." He clenched his lips together, thinking about Maria's swollen eye. "It's a good thing Mario didn't come over here, believe me."

"Why'd she come here? Was she looking for me?" Murphy seemed agitated.

"What?" Father Bob raised his voice. "You think that people can't come to me for help? I'm a priest too, you know. You're not the only man of God around here." He recalled Boss once saying to him, something like, "My mom said she can't believe you're a priest." He tried his best to feel like a priest, but something was changed.

"I was just wondering why she'd come here instead of going straight to the police or the hospital. You advised her to contact the police, didn't you?"

"Of course I did. We went through all that, believe me." He shook his head from side to side, didn't really want to get into a long discussion with Murphy about the whole episode and regretted telling Murphy she was there, but knew he'd probably find out anyway. "She got mad at me for suggesting that. Threw her drink in my face and flung the glass at the door." He lifted his palms towards the ceiling and shrugged. "She didn't want to hear it." He could sense that Murphy did not approve. He knew the look, the cocked head and raised brow.

"You were in here drinking with Maria last night? Just the two of you!" He cleared his throat. "You like playing with fire, don't you? I sure hope you remembered your role as a representative of the church."

He jumped up out of his chair. Wanted to bang his fist on the table, but stopped. "Why do you have to talk to me like I'm some kind of child? I know you stuck your neck out for me. Trust me when I say that you've reminded me a million times. I also know how to console people." He raised his tone. "It's what I do for a living." He became aware of his clenched fists and slowly uncurled them. He wished he hadn't gone off. He felt sick to his stomach about lying to Murphy.

"Sit down." Murphy said in a calm tone. "I just worry about you, that's all. I know you...remember? Get us a little more coffee. I only have a few minutes before Mass."

He succumbed to Murphy's tone, remembering what Bishop Malone told him yesterday about getting Murphy to see the doctor for a checkup. Murphy looked more than just old. His face showed that ashy tint again, and he kept clearing his throat as if he had trouble breathing. All of a sudden, he wanted to hug the old priest, but grabbed the coffee instead. He filled both cups, leaving a little space for some scotch.

Murphy interrupted his thoughts. "Hey, sit."

He sat and stared into Murphy's blue eyes, rimmed with squiggly red veins. The bags under them resembled red grapes. Murphy slurped some coffee cocktail and Father Bob savored these moments with the man whom he viewed as a father. *I'll miss these coffees and morning arguments one day when they disappear forever, just like everything else.*

Murphy nodded his head. "I'm sure that you did the right thing. All we can do is pray for that family, and be there for them through the tough times." He looked down. "Speaking of tough times, Stabo's funeral has been put-off until Wednesday. The family needs more time." His face suddenly showed a hint of enthusiasm. "Take the car all day, after you give that boy a boxing lesson."

Father Bob raised his hands into the air. "Boss doesn't seem to like me very much. Didn't you pick up on any of that yesterday?"

Murphy stood up to leave. "He's a fourteen-year-old. Need I say more?" He turned and walked towards the door with a slight limp.

"Say a prayer for me, too."

Murphy lifted his hand, while keeping his back to Father Bob as he headed to the church.

He wanted to escape the rectory and pick up Boss before Mrs. Hellinski arrived after Mass. As he walked towards the door, the bottom of his shoes peeled from the sticky part on the floor. *Mrs. Hellinski will clean it up. That's as close to sex as she'll ever get.*

He drove down to Grandma Amelia's, rather than wait around for Boss who might not show up. He parked the Lincoln alongside the curb in front of the house. His heart rate increased when he saw somebody move the curtains on the front door. Maria? He grew excited and couldn't wait to see her. He might even get a chance to examine her eye in front of Boss and Grandma. Realistically, he figured that Maria would probably try to ignore him as much as possible.

Grandma Amelia opened the front door just as he stepped up onto the porch. "I almost didn't recognize you, Father. I've never seen a priest in a pair of shorts before." She looked him up and down. "Uh Dia! You have hairy legs just like my Caesar!" She laughed and motioned for him to enter.

He laughed also. "Yes, Grandma. God has a sense of humor, putting all this hair on my body and slowly taking it off my head." He walked into the house and locked eyes with Boss, who stood by the telephone bench. Boss bit down on his lower lip and exposed a few front teeth. His face looked puffy around his eyes, as if he had been crying. Boss just stood there, saying nothing.

Getting some enthusiasm out of this kid is going to be like shoveling coal. "Are you ready to rumble, Boss?" He saw the unevenness of his blue-jean cut-offs, as well as his hairy legs. *Like mine at fourteen.*

Boss shrugged one shoulder. "I guess so. Do I need to bring anything?"

"No, I think we have everything we need." He looked around the room, paused for a few awkward moments, hoping to catch a glance of Maria. "So, your mom is okay with this?" He would not mention the black eye or the fight with Mario, unless somebody else brought it up.

"Uh huh," Boss rolled his eyes.

Boss was forced to do this. He knew that the kid didn't like him, yet other fourteen-year-olds liked him plenty. Boss held some sort of grudge, perhaps because the kid's life was going through such disruption. He had worked with all kinds of delinquents before, and could not reach this one, who got under his skin.

"Don't worry, Grandma, I'll bring him back in one piece."

Grandma made the sign of the cross. "You already promised me."

Boss kissed Grandma on the way out the door.

When they approached the car, Boss waved goodbye at the upstairs window, Maria's room, above the front porch. Maybe he had pegged Boss all wrong.

"Is that your mom?"

Boss ignored him and jumped into the passenger seat. They drove past St. Anne's Parochial Elementary School. "That's where me and your mom went to school together for eight years."

"Yeah, no shit, Sherlock. I've seen all of those stupid pictures of you guys in them yearbooks." Boss looked out the passenger side window.

Father Bob stopped himself from snapping. He turned his head to look at him, but Boss continued his stare out the side window. *Where's he get off talking to me like that?* He tried to lighten-up the conversation. "Did you register for school yet?"

"Hell no." Boss shifted in his seat. "We're moving out of here. This town sucks bad, dude." Boss pressed the button to automatically roll up his window. "It always smells like rotten eggs or burning coal or something."

"What?" Despite the insolent remarks from Boss, he didn't want to face the possibility of Maria leaving town. He'd hoped she would change her mind, especially after last night. Now that they had crossed the barrier, he was excited and afraid at the same time. "Where you moving to?" he asked.

"My mom has a job waiting for her in Phoenix, in real estate." Boss finally looked at him. "I don't know why we wasted our time coming to this shithole of a town anyway."

"I don't appreciate your language, son. What's bothering you today?" Instantly, he regretted reprimanding him.

"Whatever." Boss stared straight out the windshield. The silence inside the car made them both feel uncomfortable. He pulled onto the asphalt parking lot at the Knights of Columbus hall and drove behind the main pole building. *Finally, we get relief from this awful conversation.* Changing the subject to boxing came at the perfect time. "Have you ever boxed before?"

"Not really. But I've been in a lot of fights." Boss punched his fist into his hand. "I've had to kick the shit out of two guys since I moved here. This place is tough, but I showed them…and they quit messing with me."

Father Bob looked forward to wearing the kid out. He slid the shifter into park, in front of a rusted metal shed with a large garage door. The back of the structure butted up against a wooded hillside. "Well, here we are tough guy. Let's go in and see how much cleaning-up we'll have to do."

He watched Boss get out of the car. *I'll push and see what he's really made of.* That's the way Murphy had trained him, by holding punch mitts and let him exhaust himself.

He stepped out of the Lincoln and walked back to unlock the trunk. He stared in disbelief at the empty space. "Oh no!" he blurted out. "The heavy bag's gone? I know I put it in here yesterday." He mentally cursed Murphy. He looked up, but didn't see Boss anywhere for a second, then saw him strut from behind the rusted garage.

"I had to take a piss," Boss smiled.

"I doubt there's a bathroom in there. Let's take a look inside."

The key would not unlock the main entry doorway to a small office, so Father Bob walked over to the garage door. "This might be a fiasco." He bent down and pushed the key into the bottom handle. "What do you know, we've got ignition, Houston."

The metal door squealed for oil as he raised it, and then stuck halfway up. "Hey, give me a hand here, will you?"

He flipped the light switch. Surprised that the lights turned on, a grand feeling of shock shot through his stomach. "Look at this place!"

Boss looked at him and said, "What?"

He remembered the garage always packed with tools and lawnmowers. It used to smell of gasoline, and puddles of oil dotted the floor. He walked now along the freshly cleaned cement floor and watched his reflection from two, mirror covered walls. "There used to be greasy workbenches right here, where these mirrors are." He grinned and shook his head. "Murphy and the Knights must have cleaned this up last night. They even hung that heavy bag. Holy shit, Murphy did this!"

Boss snapped his gaze towards him when he heard that remark. He smiled genuinely for the first time that day. "Hell, yes!" Boss shouted, punching a fist up over his head. Then he ran over to the heavy bag and started whaling on it, with bare fists. He screamed, out of control, "You bastard!" He yelled at the bag and began to swing as hard as he could.

"Whoa!" Father Bob yelled. He walked towards the bag. Boss stopped punching, quickly fatigued and out of breath. "Look at your knuckles!" he yelled. "Skinned already." He tried to get a grip. "I'm the one that Grandma and your mother are going to yell at." He calmed a little, once he saw a surprised expression on Boss's face. "What are you so mad about, Boss?"

"I want to beat the shit out of Mario, that's what!" He licked some of the blood from his knuckles. "He's lucky I wasn't home last night or I would have killed that son of a bitch."

"I understand how you feel, son. But, he's your father. You…" he stopped in mid-sentence when he saw Boss turn white. Boss snarled with an open mouth, bearing his teeth and a ferocious expression in his eyes. *What's wrong with this kid?*

"Hey, Mario's not my real dad!" Boss yelled. Then he punched the heavy bag with wild haymakers, bloody knuckles and all.

Father Bob's adrenaline pumped up, tightening his chest. "Stop it!" He grabbed the heavy bag with both hands and held it up at an angle, away from Boss. The chains connecting the bag to the beam on the ceiling jingled. The sound distracted Boss for a second, who was out of breath and looked up at them with clenched, bloodied fists. Then he stared at Father Bob.

The words about Mario ran through his head, but he couldn't process it. He had to get the boy calmed down and didn't want him to break his wrists or hands. He returned Boss's stare, but not in a threatening way, more like a loving father trying to understand his son. He waited until Boss unclenched his fists to let go and the bag bounced up and down a few times, before it hung motionless in midair. He'd introduce Boss to his first boxing lesson. He walked towards him with intentions of closing in, within a couple of inches. Boss flinched and quickly lifted his fists to protect himself.

"Chill out, Boss. I'm not going to hit you." He stood, blue eye to blue eye with Boss, close to his face. "Lesson number one…you never walk into anybody's gym and hit their bags with your bare fists. It's gauche, and that kind of behavior gives you away as a raw amateur." He gave Boss a hard stare. "You understand me?"

Boss returned the stare, but backed down with a nod of agreement. Then Father Bob suddenly pushed Boss in the chest.

He watched him fall to the ground and enjoyed the boy's expression of shock. Boss quickly jumped up, ready to fight.

Father Bob raised both of his hands. "Hold on!" he barked. "That's lesson number two...never, ever stand directly in front of an opponent. Stand at a forty-five degree angle. That way you don't give the other guy a full-frontal target." He demonstrated. "Always stand in a balanced position. See how easy you fell to the ground? That's because you were standing with both of your feet straight across from each other. Try standing like this." He demonstrated. "Stagger your right foot behind your left, and keep both feet about shoulder width apart. You need balance."

Boss took the position. "That's it, perfect! Now, point your toes at forty-five degree angles, towards the corner of the room, and unlock your knees. Soften your knees. Never lock them out. Bend them, just a little."

He pushed Boss, and Boss held his ground this time. "See how much stronger you are when you stand with balance?"

Boss looked up and slightly nodded.

"I can teach you a few things if you let me."

Boss grunted.

"You can stand like that on the street, in a pool hall, bar, wherever a fight might break out. Nobody would even notice." He loved the way Boss gave him his full attention, knew the fight talk would grab his interest. "Now, another thing, always keep your hands above your waist." He demonstrated. "That way you can block, or throw a punch a little faster. We're always looking for whatever edge we can get over the other guy. Don't let them catch you with your hands in your pockets."

He walked over to the wall mirror and stood in front of it. "Stand next to me and watch our reflections." He positioned himself into fight stance. "See how my fists are at eye level and my body is balanced with soft knees?" Boss smirked. "Now, you do it. Get into fight stance, just like me." He smiled as Boss tried to mimic him, though Boss looked as gawky as he had as a kid.

He reached out to adjust Boss's arms but the kid flinched again. "Do you want me to do this or not?" Boss looked at him with defiance in his eyes, a Maria-like expression, but gave in with a head nod. He pushed Boss's elbows closer together, and lifted his fists to where his thumbs brushed the sides of his temples. "Don't make an 'A-Frame' with your elbows. Keep them closer together, parallel to each other."

"Perfect, Boss." They both looked at their reflections. "Watch how I move. Notice that my feet never leave the ground. I slide them, always getting back to that balanced position after a movement." He demonstrated some decent footwork, danced around with less rust than he had expected. Boss followed, with Father Bob keeping an eye on him. *Uncoordinated but okay for any first timer.* Sweat rolled down their faces. Father Bob turned on a floor fan.

Father Bob wondered if he was as surly as Boss long ago. Murphy must have had lots of patience. They sparred together most every day, in the old garage down by the river bottom, now rotted and crumbling to the ground. Murphy was old school like, "get in there and fight and we'll sort everything else out later."

Father Bob enjoyed the respect that boxing gave him back then, had even used his street name of "Sugar Bear." Despite losing the tournament, a degree of respect came not just from his street friends, but lots of town folks.

He saw Boss's reflection throw two roundhouses, and then look to him for approval.

"Okay. Now let's learn how to throw a punch with power." He stopped dancing around. "The force doesn't come from your fist, or your arm. The real strength lies in your Chi." He placed his hand a few inches below his belly button. "Right here is where all of our power comes from." He grabbed Boss's hand and pulled it towards his belly button. Boss yanked it away.

Father Bob laughed. "C'mon Boss, don't get the wrong idea here!" He laughed again, but Boss looked wary. "I'm just trying to show you my center of balance." Boss shook his head. "Fine, do it on yourself. Place your hand a couple inches below your belly button. Go on." Boss reluctantly placed one hand there. "Yes, right there. Envision your entire body swinging into a punch, not just your arms, but also your center of balance. That's what makes you powerful."

Boss looked more and more uninterested, but Father Bob continued. "Look in the mirror and watch me throw combinations." He demonstrated in slow motion. "Envision the punches erupting from your legs, up through your stomach. Twist your hips with each throw and swivel on the balls of your feet, like this. We throw whole body punches, not just arm punches. The fist is just a messenger, and like the end of a whip it gets power from the body." He stood behind Boss. "Now you try, while I watch."

He noticed that Boss raised his right foot off the ground when he threw his right hand. He wanted Boss to twist on the ball of his foot, planted on the ground. "Swing your hips into the punch." He moved closer behind Boss. In an effort to exaggerate the swinging motion, he reached for Boss's hips. As soon as he grabbed him, Boss swung around. "No!" Boss yelled.

Father Bob backed up. Boss looked crazy. He thought that the boy might attack him. He raised his hands. Then he turned his palms towards Boss, remembering the universal body language that means, "No threat." He heard a barely audible growl from Boss, still he thought that the boy might try to jump him.

"Are you okay, Boss?"

Boss ignored the question. He resumed his shadow boxing as if nothing had happened. The look in his eye, the expression on his face was all wrong. He watched Boss spar with his reflection. *What had just happened?* Each time he tried to touch Boss, he reacted defensively. *The boy must have been abused, maybe even sexually molested.* He knew that Boss would never open up to him about such a horror. This was not the time to pry anyway.

"This feels weird," Boss said, back with his surly tone.

"You're trying to do everything at once, that's all." He tried to sound as comforting as possible. "It's a lot of learning to process in one day. We're relearning how to throw a punch." He decided to show off, let the kid see that he was still skillful. "With practice, you'll look as smooth as me one day. Watch." He demonstrated some lightning fast combinations, moved around the gym bobbing and weaving, ducking, dancing and changing directions, all the while throwing punches.

Boss looked puzzled. "What's that goofy noise you're making?"

He stopped. "Oh, I forgot one of the most important things. Thanks for asking," pleased to grab Boss's attention again. "I'm exhaling from my nose. Breathing out. Each time we throw a punch, we exhale. It gives us more power and tightens up our core. Plus, our body can take a punch better during an exhale, than if it's full of air. Most people get so full of adrenaline during a fight that they forget to breathe. They hold their breath, and tire out in ten seconds." He pointed to the heavy bag. "That's why you tanked out so fast when you whaled on that heavy bag."

"I'm not tired at all. You tired?"

"Okay, let's take a break. It's hotter than hell in here." He sat on the cement floor in front of the fan and Boss followed. "Can I have a look at your hands?"

Boss was leaning back on his hands. "My hands are fine." He scooted forward, lifted his arms, and waved his hands in front of his face. "Yep, they look okay to me." He leaned back again. "What about *your* hands? They okay?"

Boss was giving him no respect at all. He had given up his day off, and the boy hated him. Murphy always stuck to the boxing lesson. So would Father Bob. It was time to fight, he figured, old school.

Father Bob stood up from the floor, walked over to a wooden box and opened it. Pulled some rolled-up hand wraps from it. "I'll wrap your hands for you today, if you let me, but pay attention, because you'll have to wrap your own from here on out."

"Why do you have to talk to me like I'm some little kid?"

Boss stood with his hands on his hips, still talking through a mean stare. "I've been in a lot more fights than you ever have. I've asked around town about you. Heard how you used to do drugs and drink and chase girls. Why didn't' you go back and kick Barker's ass for kicking you in the head if you're supposed to be so tough?"

What does this kid want from me? He blew out a big sigh of frustration. "What did I do to you, Boss? Why are you so mad at me?" He started pacing around the gym, ready to tell the young man how much he had given up just to be with him today.

Boss was on a roll. "I'll tell you then…you let Mario take my mom away to Vegas, didn't you? He just took her and you didn't do nothing about it, just like you did nothing about Barker, or Mario yesterday. A real man wouldn't act like that." Boss turned his palms and shrugged his shoulders, then moved square in front of Father Bob, stared into his eyes like he was ready to fight. He forgot to stand balanced, like he'd just been taught.

Why would Maria tell him all that? His body tightened, but knew he had to control his rage at Boss. He wanted to tell Boss how much he loved Maria. She must not have mentioned to him how he begged her to stay and not leave with Mario, how she broke his heart.

"Boss, you don't understand." He tried to sound calm but was churning inside. They stood eye to eye. "Your mom left with Mario by her own choice. She wanted to. Maria's the one who left me behind. You have no clue what I went through over that." His mind wandered back to the scene, where Irontown was more bustling than today. He had peeked around the corner of St. Anne's and watched Maria throw her suitcases in the trunk of Mario's Cadillac. He felt nauseous when she jumped into the passenger seat, and wanted to cry and puke at the same time. He was afraid to be seen by Mario, who was from a different world. How many times he'd wished that he had confronted Mario. He was a boxer and could have beaten Mario easily. He was ashamed, running to the rectory, and when Murphy opened the door, he fell and hugged Murphy's knees, sobbing. Murphy had let him sleep on the couch. This kid didn't know any of this.

"Whatever you might think about me, Boss, please know that I didn't just let your mom leave town. I couldn't stop her."

"Well, you could've come to Vegas and got us. I hate that bastard Mario so bad. You don't even know the kind of shit he did to us." Boss clenched his teeth. He stood his ground directly in front of Father Bob. "Just show me how to kick some ass, big priest." They stood staring in silence for a few moments.

Father Bob had no idea what to say. Boss got to him, under his skin. He could not let this fourteen-year-old sucker punch him in the heart like this. He backed down, away from Boss's challenging stare. Turned his back to him and walked towards the box of gear. He grabbed the hand wraps, and started wrapping his hands. He turned to Boss, who still stood in the same spot in the middle of the garage. "Okay, let's wrap-up and do some controlled sparring. Maybe that'll make us both feel better."

He unraveled a rolled-up strip of black cloth and wrapped his hands, paying special attention to his knuckles, twisting the wrap around them six times. Boss watched him, in silence. When he finished, about five minutes later, he held up his hands. The wrappings stopped at his wrists, like black, plaster casts perfectly wrapped around broken hands.

"You going to let me wrap yours, or do you want to do it yourself?"

Boss hesitated before he held his hands out in front of him. Father Bob grabbed one hand, inspected the skinned, bloody knuckles and reached for a jar of Vaseline. He tried not to smile when he saw Boss looking at him strangely. He dabbed some Vaseline onto Boss's knuckles. "This stuff will keep your knuckles from scabbing to the wraps. We'll be smearing this on our gloves and head gear too."

He felt calluses around Boss's knuckles. "How'd your knuckles get so hardened?"

"I punch gravel."

"You punch gravel?"

"Yeah, you know, to build up your knuckles for when you fight. It makes them tough." They both looked over at the heavy bag, then at each other.

"Hmm...I've never thought of that." He wrapped Boss hands and saw several scars, short white slits that formed random patterns on both forearms, like the trails of tiny knives. He asked about the small burn scars on the side of his arms.

"From playing chicken." Boss laughed in a sinister manner when Father Bob made a peculiar face. "You know, two guys put their arms together and drop a lit cigarette between them. The first guy to pull away loses." Boss smirked. "I never lost, ever."

"Well, remind me not to play that game with you." He waited for a laugh from Boss, anything to break the desperate feelings between them. All Boss did was stare. He finished wrapping his hand, and Boss held up his other for Father Bob to wrap. That small gesture surprised him. Suddenly, Boss appeared as a vulnerable, little kid in his eyes, if only for a moment.

"These wraps are fifteen feet long." He could sense that Boss found this wrapping interesting. Maybe nobody ever hugs him. Maria wasn't exactly the tender type. She was too often prickly, hardened, and preoccupied with drama in her life. The boy must have suffered from lack of intimate touch, not unlike a priest. If only he could kiss the top of Boss's hand, a gesture Jesus might perform. But Boss would take it the wrong way.

"Now, let me dress you up." He slid sixteen-ounce, black sparring gloves onto Boss's hands, and then squeezed a head guard overtop his head. "You've got a big head, just like me," he tried to joke.

"Yeah, we have a lot in common," Boss sounded sarcastic.

Back to this. Father Bob shoved a moldy mouthpiece in between Boss's lips. *That'll shut him up for a second.* He pushed the mouthpiece in, roughly. Then he dressed into his own head gear and slid on his sparring gloves while Boss stood there, pounding his gloves together.

"Talking through a mouthpiece is like trying to talk to the dentist when his hands are in your mouth."

"What?" Boss replied.

Father Bob clicked on the three-minute timer. "Throw some left jabs at me, real slow. Try to connect with my face and I'll block them. Understand?"

He nodded. Then he threw a slew of left jabs, as fast and hard as he could. Each time, Father Bob either blocked or ducked the punches, and Boss kept coming out with more until the punches felt like feathers. Boss tanked-out quickly.

Father Bob backed up and shuffled to the side to avoid Boss's barrage. "Slow down!" he yelled. "Quit trying to take my head off. We're not here to hurt each other. We're here to learn. Got it?"

Boss smirked and launched another torrent of slugs, swung with both hands. Father Bob blocked most of the out-of-control swings. But Boss's intensity continued. *What's wrong with this kid?* He had to keep Boss off of him, so he snapped out a sharp right that connected smack onto his nose.

Boss stumbled backwards, dropped to one knee. He quickly popped up and looked stunned, with wide eyes. A trickle of blood dripped from one nostril, which he rubbed at with his glove. He looked at Father Bob with fight in his face.

Father Bob danced back from the boy, assessing the damage. He did not seem too hurt, but Father Bob felt bad when he saw the expression of shock on Boss's face. He waved both gloves in the air. "I'm sorry, Boss, but I had to do that to back you up. Quit trying to take my head off!" He figured the time was right for another boxing lesson. He spit out his mouthpiece and caught it in the palm of his glove. "I was able to hit you so easily because you didn't keep your hands up." He dropped his own to his side. "Listen to me. Every time we throw a punch, we leave ourselves open somewhere." He demonstrated in slow motion, holding his left arm straight out. "See how the whole side of my body is unguarded right now?"

Boss wound up, and before Father Bob could cover himself, Boss swung with a leap. The boy connected with a wild right onto the open side of Father Bob's ribs, who winced and covered his body with his elbows, too late. The blow winded him. A barrage of haymakers shocked both sides of his head. His headgear twisted to one side, blinding him. *He's kicking my ass!* Gasping for air, his survival instincts tuned into full gear. He ducked. Then he slid to his right side. From there, he shot a flurry of left/right combination punches like a jackhammer. He fought for his life. He aimed for Boss's head and upper body area, and a few punches connected.

He turned his headgear around as best he could, hard to do while wearing those sixteen-ounce sparring gloves. Boss sprawled out on the floor. Then, he yelled at him.

"What in the world is the matter with you?" He breathed heavy and his ribs ached. Boss came more into focus. He saw

Boss's mouthpiece lying on the floor and realized that he must have clocked him pretty good. "This isn't a fight! We're just sparring. Man, you've got to learn the *difference*. You don't want to fight me, boy. I'll kick the shit out of you!" He was furious. "I'm not Mario! Get it?" He almost called Boss a degrading name, but started to regain his composure.

Boss stood up. He faced away from Father Bob. It sounded like he was crying, whimpering. He took deep, jagged breaths.

"Oh no!" He realized that he was dealing with an immature boy, but he had to hit him to protect himself. *My ribs might be cracked.* "Are you okay?"

Boss snapped his head around. He shot him a wild Maria look. The defiant glare, yes, the expression of his mother. *Oh God, I promised Maria and Grandma that nobody would get hurt. Told them boxing was safe.* He'd better mend Boss's wounds.

"I'll get your mouthpiece." He bent down to pick it up. He pinched it between his boxing gloves to retrieve it from the floor. While he straightened-up, what felt like a log whapped the side of his knee. It was from Boss, a sidekick of surprising force. Father Bob buckled.

Boss walloped into him with more wild punches. The first punch clipped the side of Father Bob's head, sent him straight to the cement as he was already partially bent over. Boss jumped on him, pummeled his face with punches. Father Bob lay on his back and covered his face with his gloves, but the force of the blows shocked him, bounced his head repeatedly on the cement. "Stop! What's wrong with you?" he screamed.

Still throwing thunderous blows, Boss cried out through tears, "Damn it! You're my father, get it? You're my flesh and blood, dumbass!" Snot flowed down his face.

Stunned, things appeared to happen in slow motion. *Did I just hear that?* The blows from Boss kept coming. Boss was wheezing now. Father Bob tried to lift his head a few inches from the ground. He tucked his chin into his chest to stop his head from bouncing off the cement. *I'm his father?* Boss's blows kept pounding him, so for the moment, he had to try and simply survive. *I'm his father and he's trying to kill me!* He kept covered with his gloves.

Father Bob drifted in and out of what was happening, as though he was having a dream. Finally, the blows stopped. Boss leaned forward, and pressed down hard, upon his shoulders. "You're the only one who doesn't know about it, you dumb bastard!"

Father Bob noticed, dimly, that the boy was slobbering and gasping. He felt spray splatter onto his face, from Boss spewing blood, sweat, and tears. He coughed and struggled for air. His head throbbed. Pain shot through his lungs. He groaned, figured his ribs may be broken. He didn't know what to focus on, the pain or the shock. *Did he just call me his father?* That rattled him more than a knockout punch. He thrust his hips straight up, catapulted Boss off of him, flung him past his face, overtop his head. Boss swore. Father Bob rolled over. He rose up onto his knees. His head swam. *Oh my God in Heaven.*

Father Bob was strangely clear headed for a guy who had just gotten pummeled. Events started making sense to him, like the snide remarks from Boss, and Maria wanting to tell him something about Boss last night. Then there was Grandma Amelia, who had told him in the kitchen at dinner yesterday that Boss needed a nice man like him for a father. Could this really be happening?

A movement caught his eye. Through his twisted headgear, he saw Boss step onto his gloves, and pull his hands free from them.

I'm the only one who doesn't know about it? He had to figure out what was going on, had to hear the truth.

"Listen. What are you talking about, Boss?" Boss didn't answer. Father Bob couldn't summon enough strength to get up. He slumped back onto his haunches. Hung his head, and didn't care if Boss came back to beat him some more or not. He might throw up. He gagged a dry heave.

"Say that again, Boss."

He looked up, beseechingly, and saw the back of Boss right as he was sprinting out of the open garage door. The boy hadn't even bothered to take off his hand wraps. After Boss disappeared, the doorframe transformed into a painting of landscape, still and lifeless.

Alone once again, he yelled, "Wait! Boss, wait!"

Boss said something incoherent, from faint and far away.

He wanted to run after him. His knee buckled when he stood. After pulling his hands out from the gloves, he threw off the head guard and hobbled out the garage door. His knee throbbed, and his ribs hurt as he limped towards the woods behind the garage, hoping to find the boy standing there, maybe taking another a piss. He scanned the woods, noting some distressed weeds and broken branches that formed a distorted path up the embankment. Boss was long gone.

He bent down, hands on his knees. Sweat and blood dripped onto ants in the dirt below. The ants scurried around and he wondered what had just happened, how everything important could change from one moment to the next. The ants had more purpose than he.

"My son." he said out loud. "I have a son?"

He needed to talk to Boss. He stood up and limped back into the garage. His reflection quadrupled in the mirrors on opposing walls and had nowhere to hide, so he examined a few bruises and cuts on his face. *The boy looks like me.* Those nervous butterflies returned back to his stomach. He wiped off some blood with a discarded cleaning rag that reeked of ammonia, which burned the wounds. "I can't believe this," he said to his reflection. "Boss, my son? I don't even know his real name." He looked towards the ceiling and lifted his hands.

"This is what You give me Lord? After a life of devotion, this is it? A son that kicks my ass?" Boss's words played over again in his mind, "You're my flesh and blood, dumbass!"

With great effort, he forced himself to put the gear away. He couldn't make anything right with Boss, but he could at least not leave the garage in a mess. He held Boss's head guard in his hand, stared at it for several minutes. He rubbed the sweat ring, around the front of it, with the tips of a few fingers, and envisioned Boss's face in it. Gone was the feeling of disgust towards Boss, replaced with warmth. Even the way Boss had irritated him, now seemed respectable, almost amusing to him.

A tiny sparrow landed with a chirp, about three feet into the open garage. When he looked at the bird, it flew away. He heard the wings flap. He saw the stick-like outline of the bird's feet. He watched the sparrow spread its gray wings and take off, tripling in size during the ascent. Father Bob had never experienced such a slow, clear world. He even appreciated how soggy, but rigid, the head guard felt. Still, it looked strange to him, as if he had never seen one before. He wasn't sure where to put it.

He looked around the inside of the garage, slowly turning his head, and noticed a brighter glow in everything he saw. Even the heavy bag seemed to shine. The gloves strewn about the floor, a fly straddling a moist mouthpiece, and droplets of drying sweat on the cement, all transformed into a clear focus. He saw everything as if he were seeing it for the first time.

He unraveled his hand wraps, and the scent of the sweaty cloth strangely comforted him. *Jesus being wrapped in cloth after his crucifixion. On the third day he rose again. Jesus rose from the dead.* He was the same age as Father Bob, thirty-three. He looked up and said it aloud, "I can't be a priest."

Jesus never had a son.

Father Bob kicked the box that held the equipment.

He envisioned the rage in Boss's expression. How Boss had pounded his face. He started to feel different, puzzled, but somehow he knew his life was changing. He looked outside the garage, at the asphalt parking lot, and the trees lining the hills around the road. He saw the outline of the leaves on the trees, the dark grooves in the bark. He hoped to see a curly black head of afro hair bobbing through the woods.

He must hunt for Boss, not just to talk to him but to protect him. *The frantic boy might do something extreme.* He hoped that Boss would calm his frenzied mind. He wasn't sure how the boy would react alone in the wild or in town.

Yes, I'll go find him. I have a son who needs me.

Chapter 16

His Only Son

Father Bob winced when he climbed into the Lincoln. His sweaty legs slid across the leather seat. A sharp pain shot through the left side of his ribs. Breathing slowly as that familiar tightness wrapped around his chest, he felt his heart race and his throat start to close. *Please don't let me die. I have a son.* His hands quivered as he pushed the key into the ignition, then slammed the Lincoln into drive and peeled away from the garage.

"Lord, let's find Boss."

What if Boss has killed himself? He couldn't stop the morbid fantasy as it played horrific on the faces of Maria and Grandma Amelia when they would learn of Boss's death. Would he preside over the funeral of his own son?

He was driving too fast, bouncing over top the potholes that pocked the twisted roads around the hills of Irontown. Upon approaching the cemetery, he lightened his foot from the gas pedal and slowed. The distant sound of faded mill sirens blended with the crunching of gravel beneath the tires of the slow rolling Lincoln. The tightness in his chest had lifted. He scanned the wooded terrain, looking for that telltale, lanky figure, topped with a ball of bouncing Afro. The scent of sulfur..."It always smells like rotten eggs or something..." Boss had said.

Despite having not eaten anything all day, Father Bob had no appetite. Too jittery for food, he opened the glove box seeking out the flask of scotch. It was empty so he tossed it back in. *Where would Boss go?* He imagined the worse. The highway bridge—Boss, like him years ago, standing outside the guardrail and hanging onto it, looking down at the slag road below while wind blew dust in his eyes from cars whizzing past.

Father Bob always imagined that a whisper to join the vocation of the priesthood saved him from jumping. *No, I'd been with Lucy that night, as soon as her husband left to work the mid-night shift.* That's one reason he did not jump. Not like Frankie Clampo, a shack boy who jumped off and died instantly. But, Augie "Doggy" Angusto, jumping a few months later, wasn't so lucky. The jump paralyzed him for life. *I was too scared to jump.* When Father Bob slipped during the slide back to solid ground, and almost fell off, he vomited...off the bridge. The shack boys would have made fun of him.

Would Boss think of doing such a thing? He had better go check it out, so he slammed on the brakes near the baseball field parking lot. Then he made a U-turn to head back down through the hills towards downtown Irontown. He stomped onto the gas pedal. The ten-minute drive brought him to the highway bridge where he parked directly under the bridge on the slag road, where Clampo's brains were once splattered amongst the slag. The shack boys had collected twelve of the bloodstained rocks and enshrined them in the main shack in the woods.

Father Bob's knee and ribs ached as he twisted his body to step out of the car. He stood and leaned against the driver's side door. From there, he followed the cement slope with his eyes, up under the bridge's belly. The ledge under the bridge pro-vided a haven for young boys, a sacred lab for adolescent ex-periments, sometimes with girls. *My knee hurts too much to climb up there.* He did not see a person up there anyway, probably just some pornographic litter, empty wine bottles, and maybe a filthy blanket. From this ledge, a person could climb up and over, onto the guardrail of the highway. Then, they could inch their way to the middle, where the bridge straddled the road below...the best place to jump.

He walked a short distance out the gravel road and looked straight up. "Boss! Hey Boss!" He heard nothing but his lone echo. He fantasized about seeing Boss leaning from that guard-rail. Maybe he would climb up and join him. Jump off with him. With his luck, he might end up paralyzed, have someone like Mrs. Hellinski feed him for the rest of his life.

There was no running to Murphy now. He needed to find Boss. He ducked back into the car and drove on. As he passed the highway ramp, fleetingly he was tempted to enter the free-way and leave Irontown forever. *I can't be a priest anymore, not with a son.* Maybe he could head out west, to Phoenix, and get there before Maria and Boss, then join them. He could drain his meager bank account for gas money, ditch the Lincoln in the desert, use a fake name and get a job washing dishes, or selling used cars in a bad part of town. That would be easier than showing his face around Irontown after this freakish morning.

What's the right thing to do? He knew. He'd marry Maria, live up to the obligations of a father with a family. Get a legitimate job, help raise Boss, harness Boss's energy and teach him to box. Got to try and save his son, born in his likeness.

He tooled around the twisty roads of Irontown for another two more hours, until the futility of the search became evident upon his third backtrack. It was time for a drink. So he pulled into the grocery store parking lot with intentions of buying a pint of scotch. Maybe he could force down a bag of peanuts just for the sake of putting something solid in his stomach. He examined his face in the rearview mirror. The bruises looked more like rug burns now. He picked up one of Murphy's discarded, stained handkerchiefs that were wedged in between the elbow rest and front seat. He unraveled it, wiped his face, then tossed the rag onto the passenger seat. Blood formed a light outline of his face onto the handkerchief.

As he sat there in the car, Bea "Honey Bee" Milovick walked past. She stopped her stride and waved at him. He returned her wave, halfheartedly. She hesitated for a few seconds, waiting for him to get out. Eventually, she turned and walked into the store. He didn't want to face anybody. He drove off.

He turned a corner and coasted down Hog Hill, with its wooden houses barely hanging onto the hillside. Passing Big Chew Louie's house, he again recalled stealing Big Chew's tomatoes as a young teen. As he slowly passed Sauna's Sausage Shop, he scanned the neighborhood searching for a glimpse of Boss's head between the parked cars lining the narrow walkway. Still, no sign. Having a son sank in more with each passing minute. *A real father can't be a priest.* His chest throbbed in pain again and he clutched it with his right arm. Hyperventilating made his ribs ache even more. *Oh, God, the pain. If You want to take me, God, do it now.*

He coasted down the hill, but refused the safe haven of the rectory. Murphy might be there, and he didn't want to drop dead in front of him. He slammed the steering wheel with his hands. "Maria knew this the whole time? How could she not tell me? I can't die yet."

He drove on, keeping an eye out for Boss. *And what would I do if I found him?* He passed Barker's place and impulsively pulled into the gravel driveway where he parked the car. He got out and limped up to the covered front porch, hidden in the shade by a red brick wall. Barker was probably at work in the mill. He could die on this porch and Barker would find him after the day shift ended. His body would already be stiff.

Father Bob sat on a frayed, plaid lawn chair, with his elbows on his knees and head between his hands. He heard the cars drive past and tried to calm himself. *"I can't believe it. My Lord, what have I done?"* He cradled his head in his hands again and grieved for his mother. She never got to see him grow up and become a priest. Even she would be ashamed of him now.

How he wished that Barker were home, he seemed the only person who'd ever talked straight to him. Actually, Boss talked pretty straight this morning. Barker might say something like, "Tell'em to kiss your ass. Let'em go to Arizona. What the hell you gonna do with a family?" Then he'd slap him on the back, and offer a beer or a joint. He would let out a loud belch to try and make him laugh. Father Bob smiled at this imagined thought of Barker's comforting him. He wiped his forehead on an old, stiffened T-shirt that was hanging on the brick wall.

Sister Roxanne talked straight with him also. *Am I a shallow soul? Sister Roxanne must have known about Boss being my son. Oh, how the boy looks like me. Everybody in town must know, just like Boss said.*

Should he break into Barker's house to get a beer? He got up and shook the door, but it was locked—Barker's hiding of a stash of drugs or guns. Then he noticed a small, Styrofoam cooler next to the door. He flipped off the lid—*Ah, three cans of Pabst Blue Ribbon floating in some cool water. There's the Holy Trinity–P, B and R.* He cracked open the flip-top can, toasted Barker, then guzzled over half of the can in one gulp. The foamy nectar quenched a thirst that he wasn't aware of.

For a half-hour, he sat there mourning his demise. During the second beer, he replayed how Boss tore into him with such ferocity. The boy showed heart, like the first time his dog, Jack, had gotten into a fight. He was proud of Jack, and saw him differently after that, not a spoiled couch dog. "My son." He repeated the phrase. "My son whaled on my ass." Good thing that they wore sixteen-ounce gloves. Bare fists would have been really bloody. *Could the kid really hate me that much? He doesn't know me. And I don't know him. He must have been releasing some inner turmoil or something.* Father Bob needed to know about those things. He wanted to know Boss's life. *I should have been there for him.*

As he sat there, finishing the second can of beer, he saw a dirty bumper sticker lying on the porch floor that said, "Go For It." He read it again and smiled. He would drive straight to Grandma Amelia's house. It was the one place he hadn't looked yet. *Maybe Boss made it home safely.* Boss now mattered more than his life, his vocation. He tossed the empty beer can into Barker's patchy yard, then stood up from the lawn chair, a bit dizzy, but full of newfound courage. *Go for it* rang in his head like a mantra.

He drove up the Hill of Churches towards Grandma Amelia's house. The lunchtime whistle blew from the steel mill, and still he had not eaten. Jesus went for three days without food or water before his death, purifying His soul before going to Heaven. *I'll purify mine, even if I'm going straight to Hell.* He approached the house with the intention of straightening out all things. Walking towards this big wooden door had always been a battle to conquer, a fear to overcome. The curtains moved in the upstairs window above the porch, and he caught a glimpse of Maria's dark hair before the curtains closed.

He knocked on the door. No response. He waited a few long seconds, and pounded harder. Nothing. Then he tried to open the door, rattled it a bit and stuck his face close to the stained glass in search of somebody. Nobody. "Maria!" he yelled. "Open up!"

"Go away!" he heard her faint voice.

"Let me in! We have to talk." He paused for a second, searching for the words that might gain him access. Finally, he confessed, "I lost Boss!"

"He's here! Now go away, you fool."

Baffled by her response, he stood on the porch. *I can't leave without talking with the mother of my child.* He knew her well enough to realize that she wasn't coming down. She was stubborn.

He looked at the trellis at the end of the porch. About fourteen years ago the trellis looked brand new with white painted, sturdy 2x2s supporting a bushy green vine full of tiny pink flowers. He used to climb it like a ladder, sneak into Maria's bedroom. He'd tap on the window, she'd pull back the curtain, and he'd smile as wide as he could. She'd giggle and open the window where he'd climb into her bed, slip under the covers and into her heart. Now, the trellis rotted with grayed wood, split in places, reduced to barely supporting a thin, dying vine that exposed nothing except dried thorns.

He decided not to miss out this time. He walked across the porch, grabbed the rotted trellis and shook it. The wood snapped and a few dead leaves fell from it. He would climb that rickety old thing anyway. His knee ached, and a piercing pain from his cracked ribs shot through him. With each step, each time the sodden wood snapped under his feet. A small rusty nail sliced a cut from his elbow to his hand, but he kept on climbing. Finally his hands clinched onto the rooftop as the trellis collapsed. With superhuman strength, he pulled himself onto the shingles, scraping his knees and shins until he stood upright and out of breath on the incline of the porch roof.

Father Bob hesitated a moment, surveying the ground. He could not get off the porch roof now without going through the house. Trapped, he limped up the slope of the rooftop, his knee still aching and fresh blood oozing down his arms and legs. He stood outside Maria's window for a moment and enjoyed the conquest. He turned around and absorbed the view from up there, the roof of St. Anne's Parochial School, the rectory. He gazed out at the steel mill, where steam, smoke, and the heavy sounds of steel production forever rose.

He stood a few moments, collecting himself, and then tapped on Maria's window. The curtain moved and his stomach fluttered. He smiled his old exaggerated smile. Maria looked angry. He knew she would be surprised, but hoped she'd feel a little nostalgic. He wasn't expecting total disgust from her.

"Jesus Christ!" he heard her swear through the window. She struggled to open it, pounding with her fist on each side of the panes to loosen up the layers of accumulated paint. Finally, she pushed upwards and the window moved with a screech. She stuck her head out the half-opened window and glowered at him. "Get in here. The whole God dammed town's going to see you."

He grinned, stuck one leg through the small opening and squeezed through. When his knee gave out, he tumbled to the floor. He lay on his back, grabbed his sore ribs with one hand, and hid his pain.

"I'm getting too old for this," he smiled up at Maria.

She stood next to her bed with her hands on her hips. He wanted to hug her. She scowled, "What don't you understand about 'go away'?"

He stood up and sat on her bed. "What's a matter with you?" He expected something more from her, after climbing the trellis, this time to check on his son, the one conceived back when she used to lift the covers for him.

"You gave my son a bloody nose! Why'd you beat him up?"

At that, he steamed. "Your son? Your son? What about my son?"

Her mouth dropped open. She sighed, as though she had just lost something precious. She sat down on the bed. "Oh, Jesus." She shook her head, waved at a couple of suitcases in the corner of the room. "We almost made it out of this town. I can't believe it, one more day, one more damn day."

He walked over and lifted up one of the suitcases. It was empty, echoing when he dropped it back onto the floor. "You were going to leave and not tell me!" He stalked back and plopped on the bed next to her. "You never met your real father, and want to raise Boss without him meeting his?"

She tried to slap him, but he blocked her. They'd been through this before and she had a habit of telegraphing her punches. Boss certainly didn't get his boxing skills from her. He pushed her arm back onto the bed and pinned her onto her back. Her legs dangled over the side and when she started kicking them, he flashed back to the sex they'd had in the rectory last night. He surrendered, letting her go and sat back up.

She sat up also, not the time for a fight. Or sex. They sat there in confused silence.

"Maria, why didn't you tell me?" he begged.

She refused to meet his eyes. "I tried, believe me. I didn't know if it was the right thing to do or not. Murphy and Grandma both advised me not to say anything."

"What?" He stopped himself from punching the wall. "Murphy knew! Everybody knew but me? Do you have any idea how that makes me feel? How could you do this to me?"

Maria glared. "It's all about you, isn't it? All the time, it's always about you."

She looked worn. Neither one of them were kids anymore. "Even now," she said with frustration, "you don't even ask about Boss. You beat the shit out of him and don't even wonder how he is!"

He gritted his teeth. *This isn't fair.* "Wait a minute, wait one minute. What do you think I've been doing the last two hours? I've been out looking for Boss all morning." He looked for some response, but Maria just continued to look scowl. "Look at my face. Tell me who beat who today?"

She shook her head. "Listen. We're leaving town tonight. Heading to Phoenix, because it's where I have a job. You don't need to worry about us. We're getting out of your hair. You can still be a priest, *Father*," she said with a smirk. "These small townies can wonder about all the rumors forever, but nobody needs to know anything for sure."

I could still remain a priest? A clean getaway? He took a deep breath. A sharp pain shot through his ribs. He couldn't fake it anymore. He had to get a hold on himself, despite how Maria could push his buttons like nobody else.

"So you're going to run away, just like you did when we were in love, and unbeknownst to me, pregnant with my child. You ran out on me back then, and now you're going to do it again." He cleared his throat. "Is that how you build relationships, just keeping running away?"

He could tell by the way her eyes widened that he had hit home. "You bastard and fool! What do you want me to do? Stay here and screw you on the side while I work at the ice cream parlor?" She put her hand on her forehead. "You can't have me and God at the same time, like you try to do. Hell, you can't seem to stay faithful to either one of us" She sneered at him.

That stung. She was right. He gripped the bedspread in his hands. If he walked out, he would not turn back. She was much better at pushing his buttons than he at pushing hers. Could he go to the rectory and act like nothing happened, happy to watch Maria load her car and drive away this time? But no, he couldn't ignore the truth. He had cheated on his vow. Even if folks did not know for sure, he would...God would. He couldn't stay celibate. He was a father. Things had changed.

He could not fight anymore. He was exhausted and realized that his lifelong struggle with the priesthood was coming to a head. Unafraid now, this wave of freedom and relief puzzled him.

"You're right, Maria. I do try to have it both ways. Sister Roxanne even said that in so many words. I'm not fit to be a priest anymore, with or without you. But I'm willing to try and do the right thing."

She just stared at him.

He swallowed hard. "You know, I want to marry you, and become a father to Boss. Would you give me that chance?" He expected her to be delighted.

"Give me a break." Her laughter felt cruel and mocking. "You're way not ready for a family, Bob." She uncrossed her arms in front of her like a baseball umpire making a "safe" call. "You know, I stayed in Irontown longer when I heard you were coming here. I had to check you out, thinking for a minute that we could work something out." She sounded more confident. "I realized a few things about myself. I don't want to be your wife. You helped me to realize that I am not jumpin' smack into another bad relationship, and I should thank you for that."

He gazed out the window in a strange numbness. She had rejected him. His righteous offer not only fell flat, but she scoffed at it. How could his new world unravel so fast? He wanted to leave the priesthood and marry her. He had nowhere else to go.

"Why did you leave me? I loved you."

She rolled her eyes. "Oh yes, you loved me. Right here on this bed." She patted the drum-tight cover. "But you snuck into other bedrooms too, let's see, how many married women can we count—Mrs. Marini, Mrs. Thompson, Mrs. Lucy or whatever? Should I go on?"

How'd she find out about all those women? He wanted to explain that he hadn't loved those women, just lusted after them. He had only loved her. He needed her to understand his heart.

"Okay, okay." He didn't want to hear any more about his seventy-seven antics, there was no way to win this battle with her. He had to try harder to convince her that he'd changed. He moved his face close to hers and held her gaze with his.

"Now, right now, my life has changed. I feel different, I am different. I have a son for God's sake. I need to know him. I'm concerned that something bad must have happened to him. Tell me about Boss's life." He shrugged. "I don't even know his real name. Please, Maria, don't you at least owe me that?"

She jumped up from the bed. "Owe you? I owe you? Where were you the last fourteen years? I don't owe you anything." She pointed towards her bedroom door. "Please just get the hell out of here." She was fighting back tears. "Let's make a clean break. We'll all live happily ever after."

That strange calmness enveloped him again. His world slowed down as it did that morning, when he was in the empty garage. "Sit down," he said softly, and patted the bed. "I don't mean any harm." Maria looked puzzled, remained standing. She rubbed her chin, as if contemplating whether to sit or not.

"I'm sorry for not being there for you and Boss. But, I didn't know. I've never stopped loving you. And just like you, I had to get on with my life after you left." He would not mention that he almost jumped off a bridge.

Her face began to soften and she sat next to him on the bed. She looked at him with an expression of sorrow, which threw him off guard a little. Then she looked straight ahead and said gently, "Gerard. Boss's real name is Gerard." She smiled halfheartedly. "I suppose that's why we nicknamed him 'Boss.'"

He loved sharing this tender moment with her. "He does seem more like a 'Boss' than the patron saint of pregnant women." He made her smile, was making some headway, getting closer to her; then, she stood back away from the bed.

"I told you what life was like for Boss and me last night." She stomped her foot hard onto the floor. "Then you threw me on the table and screwed me. Remember?" Her pitch rose. "You remember that part I'll bet, but you didn't hear a word I said." She bit her lower lip and stared eye to eye.

He really did not listen to her last night, except to know that their life with Mario was horrible, full of abuse. Maria was right. Last night, all he wanted was sex. He felt his life twirling away, like water going down a drain. *She doesn't love me like I love her.*

He took her hand. "Listen, Maria. If you really want it, I promise not to bother either one of you if that's what you want. But I need to know what happened to that boy, my son. He acts like he was abused. You have to tell me. Then you can go, do whatever you think is right. I love you, but I will leave you alone, I promise. Please?"

He had no intentions of leaving either one of them alone.

She sighed and sat down next to him. He closed his eyes and breathed in her sweet scent. When he opened his eyes, she looked frail, small, like when she sunk into the chair during her Grandfather's funeral. Her left knee poked out through a hole in her jeans. He reached out tentatively and rubbed the skin there, so soft and warm. He wanted to kiss it. His heart broke for her. Something about her vulnerability at this moment made him want her, not sexually, but emotionally, forever. He wanted to kiss her, but then a dark cloud arose as he thought of Boss, how terrible his life must have been.

"Okay, one day I walked in on them." Maria gasped, yet looked deadpan. Her voice was flat, emotionless. "Mario was on top of Boss." Her tone cracked and this time a tear dripped down her chin. "Boss's face was stuffed into a pillow. I tried to kill that son-of-a-bitch with a pair of scissors, but he ended up beating the crap out of both of us again. Really bad that time."

211

Father Bob knew something like that had happened, but hearing the tragic tale left him speechless. He just sat there.

"You happy now?" She jumped up off the bed and opened a dresser drawer. "Please just go. I need to finish packing."

He had to say something. "Did you call the police or anybody?"

She turned around and threw a handful of panties she had picked from the drawer. "Don't start that police shit again! It's all in the past now." She stomped across the room and flipped open a suitcase. "You have no clue how the real world works. Mario said that if I promised not to call the police or anything, he would let us go. Let us leave him. For me that was our best deal out of there, away from that devil."

Father Bob took a deep breath and flinched from a sharp pain in his ribs. "Well, he should be prosecuted for that," he finally said. "That animal should get sent to prison where somebody might do the same thing to him."

This time she tried to throw the suitcase at him, but she wasn't strong enough. The small piece of luggage bounced on the floor at his feet. "No! And don't you ever talk about this." She looked ferocious. "We're out of it now. If Mario's mafia friends ever found out about it, he'd come after us. He knows how to find people." She locked eyes with him. "You don't' know about these things. Stay out of this and don't say anything more about it. I'll kill you if you do, I swear."

Before he could speak, the door slammed shut downstairs. "Hello," they heard Grandma Amelia call. She certainly would have noticed the priests' car.

He stood up and grabbed her arm. They both froze. He hoped that deep down inside maybe she wanted to be with him. He wanted another chance, though now wasn't the time. He had to talk with her again, make sure that she didn't leave without him.

"Okay, I'll promise, only if you promise me something in return." He put his lips to her ear and whispered. "Don't leave tonight. Come to Mass tomorrow morning, and let's talk afterwards. We'll talk in the privacy of the rectory. You promise me?"

She nodded. "Yeah, okay, okay, now please just go."

He placed his hands on top of her shoulders and gazed into her eyes. He wanted to kiss her, have a family with her. Finally he knew what he must do. He would leave the priesthood and become a father to Boss. She would change her mind later. He hugged Maria and did not want to let her go. She did not hug him back. He kissed the top of her head, and then her cheek, the moisture on her cheek a tear, a hope for one more chance.

He snuck downstairs and hurried out of the house before running into Grandma Amelia. She yelled for him on his way out the door, but he was too upset and embarrassed. Afraid of what he might say to her, he ignored her calls. He made it to the sidewalk and opened the car door before Grandma yelled from the porch.

"How'd it go today?"

He didn't' turn around. He held up his hand and said, "Okay."

"Where are you going so fast? Come on in, please, I'll make you some lunch."

"I have to go, Grandma, I'm late again...for everything. Thanks."

He sped the Lincoln towards the rectory. He hoped that he would never have to see Murphy again, but that would be impossible. If he pretended that nothing had happened, maybe he could make a quiet escape, tomorrow.

He drove the car, but this time, not aimlessly.

Chapter 17

The Final Calling

Father Bob sped towards the rectory, livid at the betrayal of Monsignor Murphy. *How could he have kept this incredible secret from me?* He braked and sat in the car, outside the parsonage. He stared at the house for a few minutes. The last thing he wanted to do was to sit in that kitchen, alone. On the other hand, he didn't want to explain anything to Murphy. He wished that he could sneak into the rectory without seeing anybody, then slip away tomorrow morning leaving nothing but a note.

A red gauge on the dashboard, next to the speedometer, indicated that the engine was overheating. Got to shut the car down, or get moving. A drive could help him sort things out, since he was too injured to jog. *Being on the move helps me think.*

He peeled away, aimlessly, until he neared the highway bridge. He skidded to a stop on the gravel road underneath, and sat with the car running, where he closed his eyes and took a deep breath to let the dust settle.

It's time to leave this town and the priesthood.

Weird feeling, this fright and excitement together, not unlike when the first woman had unzipped his pants in the front seat of her car. *If I owned a car, I could take off right away, wouldn't have to ask Maria for a ride to Phoenix. Maybe I'll steal Murphy's car as payment for fourteen-years of devotion.*

How he longed for a break, some time off where he didn't have to report to anybody. As a priest he was constantly on call, somebody always in turmoil, around the clock. The thought of having no phone calls, no one looking for him, sounded impossible. Becoming anonymous sounded good. He lay his head back, closed his eyes, imagined a long, relaxing drive across the southern route meandering his way to Nashville, visit Graceland, then detour on down to New Orleans and let loose on Bourbon

Street, where women danced around dressed in black-laced teddies. *But no, I can't leave until seeing Maria tomorrow morning, make our connection.*

The red gauge on the Lincoln's dashboard caught his attention again. A noise startled him from his daydream and his body jolted as he looked around. The sound of popping, like slow gunshots, grew louder as if closing in. Then he recognized the indistinguishable rumbling from the drag pipes of a panhead. Barker pulled up to the driver side window.

"Hey!" Barker yelled over the loud pipes. "Were you just at my house?"

"Yes!" he yelled back.

"Meet me back over." Barker looked at him strangely and gunned the bike away.

Thank you, God, for Barker. He tried to follow him, but Barker was long gone. He winded familiar roads again and when he pulled up at the house, Barker was sitting on the porch sipping a can of Pabst. He pulled the Lincoln into the gravel driveway again and limped up the steps. His knee ached profoundly.

"What the hell happened to you?" Barker grinned. "You been in another fight?"

"It's a long story, man." Father Bob eased himself down and pulled a can of beer from a freshly stocked cooler. He popped the top and shook his head. "I suppose you could call it a fight, alright." He took a long swig. "How'd you know I was at your house?"

"Pumphandle saw you. He flagged me down and told me."

"Does everybody know everything about me in this town?" The frustration of hearing yet another nickname that he didn't recognize also bothered him. "C'mon Bark, I'm not in the mood for this. Who's Pumphandle?"

"Denny Dixon's dad, you know." Barker held his hands out in front of him, a few feet apart. "He's got the biggest cock in the steel mill."

He sighed. "Aren't you supposed to be in the mill?"

"That mill can kiss my ass!" Barker made a furious expression. "They tried to force me to work another double shift today. Eight in a row. I walked out. I suppose they'll give me a few days off without pay for that." He threw an empty can of beer into his yard. They both watched it bounce, and heard it clank down the part gravel, part grass driveway. Then he grabbed a new one. "Right now our union is worthless. All they do is collect dues from our paychecks."

215

Barker took another swig and shifted in his rickety chair. He leveled his gaze at Father Bob, as if waiting for him to say something. "So you gonna tell me what you were doing on Grandma Amelia's roof?"

His face flushed. "What? How'd you know that?"

"I tooled past the rectory after I heard you were on my porch. I saw you from up on the hill, climbing into Maria's window." He laughed again. "I don't know too many priests who do that in broad daylight."

Father Bob hung his head and shook it. "What am I going to do?" He meant that rhetorically, but Barker took him literal.

"Relax, man. Have another beer." Barker lit up a joint. He lifted it in front of him and raised his eyebrows.

Father Bob ignored the lit joint, still peeved that so many people already knew of his whereabouts. "So, I'm almost afraid to ask. Do you know about Boss, too?"

He could tell from Barker's smirk that he was holding back.

God help me. Barker's silence gave him the answer. His heart dropped. But again, that strange calmness followed his feeling of dread. His world slowed down. He could hear the birds chirping and smelled the freshness of the musty hollow. He looked at Barker, noticing the laugh wrinkles forming around his eyes, and shook his head.

"Look, man," Barker's voice sounded soothing, almost gentle. "Ever since that Mass yesterday, when you gave Boss communion, all everybody could talk about was how much that boy looks just like you." He moved his chair closer. "The kid's been asking around about you ever since they came back to town." He took another drag of the joint and handed it to Father Bob.

"No, thanks Barker, but no, I'm freaked out enough as it is." He guzzled down his can of beer and grabbed another. "My whole world is falling apart. Coming back here was a bizarre thing."

Barker shrugged and took another toke. "I heard that Maria and that kid are leaving town. So what you so worried about? You're free and clear."

"Free and clear?" He stood up and dropped the beer on the porch, where the spill formed a sizzling puddle of foam. "You have no idea what I'm going through." He picked up the half empty can of beer and tried to throw it into the driveway, but it smashed against the front of the house, and bounced back onto the porch.

Barker jumped out of his chair and held up his hands. "Chill out, man. I'm just trying to help." He picked up the beer can and guzzled the rest of it, foam and all.

"You bastard, how can you know all this and I just find out today? What's going on? It's like I'm in a *Star Trek* episode or something."

Barker laughed again, but could tell he chaffed his friend. He sat down and pointed to the other, empty chair. "Take it easy, Captain Kirk. Sit down." He again motioned for Father Bob to sit, and he did, reluctantly. "People don't have anything else to do but get into everybody's business around here," he nodded, "and you sure give 'em lots to talk about."

"Sheez." He started to grab for the joint, but stopped. "Nah, I've got too much to think about."

Barker raised his eyebrows. "So, did that kid beat the shit out of you? Is that why you came to my porch? To hide?"

He smiled, knew Barker was messing with him. He rubbed his hand over his left eye, and felt a bump of a bruise. "The boy does have a decent hook."

Barker stood up and howled, before bending over and laughing.

Father Bob laughed too. He felt a shooting pain and grabbed the left side of his ribs. "I didn't even see the little shit coming." He leaned back in his chair and popped the top off another Pabst. "This town sucks." He quoted his son.

"Tell me about it. It's like I live in that God damned mill." Barker turned up his palms. "Then I come out here in this hole and there's nothing to do, except more work on the house, the yard, the bike—it's always just work, work, and work all the time." He mimicked Father Bob's whiny tone of voice, "You have no idea what I'm going through."

"Okay, okay, you got anything to munch on?"

Barker went into the house and quickly retrieved a bag of potato chips and a white plastic container of French onion dip. He set the container on the cooler and ripped the big bag of chips open from the top, releasing that alluring aroma.

"You're lucky. I mean, really you are, if you look at it." He pulled out a handful of chips and then handed the bag to Father Bob. "You have an education, and could get the hell out of here. You know, become a probation officer or social worker or something like Pumphandle's son did. But not me, I'm stuck. Where else can I make this kind of money with no education?"

Father Bob swiped a handful of potato chips across the onion dip and stuffed the bouquet into his mouth. His days of being in the club of "polite society" were long gone.

"I have no money, no car, no contacts, and nowhere to go. I'm stuck too." He shrugged. "I might have to move in with you."

"No, no, no!" Barker shook his head and they both laughed.

Out of nowhere, he confessed. "Listen, Bark, I'm leaving the priesthood."

Pronouncing those words out loud to his friend shook him yet showered him with confidence. He was defiant when they were going to kick him out of the priesthood, but leaving on his own was a different story. His choice made a difference. He looked at Barker, expecting some sort of a response, but Barker just returned his stare, so he prodded him, wanting some reaction from him. "Yeah, sometimes you just know when it's time to go."

Barker paused, as if in deep thought, cocked his head at Father Bob, then he stood up. "You know, I was thinking." He pointed to the side of his yard, "See that rusty old truck we drove to Wheeling? It's a '62 Ford with three on the tree."

"Yeah," said Father Bob, puzzled that he'd just bared his soul to Barker, who seemed to ignore his words.

"I'll tell you what. You can have that old thing if you want to take off. Just pay me back when you get on your feet somewhere."

Father Bob paused, caught off guard. He stretched his neck to look at the truck. A newer model, rusted car was parked next to it, alongside a small, aluminum fishing boat on a trailer with peeling paint. He knew that other guys in the steel mill made good money, and squandered the cash on new cars, boats, and houses they couldn't really afford. Barker kept it simple and cheap. *Should I take him up on this?*

"You'd do that for me?"

"Sure. Shit, I walk to work most of the time, and I've got the bike and that Pontiac. The truck's a bomb. I mean it runs, but breaks down once in a while. There's a set of jumper cables under the seat. I'd lock a bicycle in the bed, just in case you need it, and don't forget that it runs on regular."

Father Bob pondered all this, walking down the driveway towards the truck, growing more excited the closer he came to it. He imagined driving off, alone, with total freedom. He could almost feel the wind blowing through the front wing window. He could head out west. Rediscover himself. Hook up with

Maria and Boss in Phoenix after everybody had some time to think. He stood by the driver's side door, stared inside.

"Open the door," Barker's words jolted him. He didn't realize that he was standing behind him.

The door squeaked when he opened it, and dust rose from the distressed fabric on the front bench seat when he sat behind the wheel. He breathed in the scent of must, oil, and gasoline. "Man, I love the smell of this old thing."

"The key's in the ash tray," Barker said. "Fire it up."

Father Bob twisted the key in the ignition and the old truck started up on the third try. He revved the engine a couple times.

"That's a rebuilt V-8. Me and Cowpie put that in about a year ago. It should run okay, but the brakes suck and the steering is real tight."

He didn't care. The idea of leaving town the next day in the truck had taken over. He turned off the engine and just sat there, still unsure if he should accept the offer. *Accepting a gift when your self-confidence is unsteady can be bad.*

Barker leaned his head into the driver side window and pointed to the floor. "There's a two-inch hole under that mat. It's not rusted out or anything. Nobody can figure out why it's there, but comes in handy if you have to get rid of your stash while on the road."

He turned towards Barker. Their faces were close together and he felt like kissing the gruff biker on the cheek. But knew he wouldn't appreciate it.

"Are you sure?"

"Fuckin' aye. You pay me back when you strike it rich."

"Strike it rich, yeah, head out West in search of gold." He got out of the truck and stood, looking at it. Barker had already turned away and was walking into the backyard.

Barker turned around and said, "I'll fire up the grill. We'll get hammered and eat hot dogs, you know, like a going away party for a couple of old rednecks." He motioned with his head. "Go bring that cooler back here."

"How much do you want for this thing?"

"I don't know. Don't worry about it, we'll see what happens."

Father Bob walked up to the front porch. The vision of Sister Roxanne played in his head, how he watched her ride off in the back of a taxi. She wasn't sure what she was going to do either. He wished that he could talk with her now. He daydreamed about running into her, maybe in some blues bar on Bourbon Street. How cool that would be? He picked up the cooler from the front porch and heard water, ice and cans of beer slosh around the inside while he walked down the few steps. The pain in his knee and ribs did not matter. He was becoming a regular person again, a regular guy. Then he imagined the whispers of his colleagues after his quitting the priesthood. The Bishop, Callo, Murphy, all of them would agree that they knew all along he wasn't going to make it as a priest. *That's okay. Whatever they think doesn't matter now.*

He laid the cooler down in the grass next to Barker, who sat on an inverted bucket, in front of a flame that was burning way too high for the small, Hibachi grill.

"It's about time." Barker grabbed a can of Pabst and threw one to Father Bob.

He sat on a stump next to Barker. "I don't know how to thank you."

Barker stood up. "Okay, just shut up. I'm gonna get the hot dogs."

Father Bob stared into the fire. *Just shut up, he says.* He and Barker were very much alike—alone, unhappy with their jobs, and the same age. They drank, loved women, got stoned and deep down inside loved people. *What will Maria think about this?* He fantasized her sparkling face. She would hug him.

Barker came back outside and threw an entire package of hot dogs onto the grill, then the flame dimmed to glowing embers. He grabbed another beer, and they clanked a toast. "I like my dogs burnt to a crisp."

"Me, too."

"You should probably get another key made. That's the only one."

"No problem."

Soon they were wolfing down hot dogs. Two last beers floated in the cooler water. Evening closed in, and the two friends had run out of conversation. Father Bob knew that the time had come to get back to the rectory. He had to pack his meager possessions and try to avoid Murphy, though he knew he had to speak with him.

Barker slapped him on the back. "I'll be at work tomorrow. The truck will be right here if you want it. Good luck, you lucky bastard."

Father Bob choked up. He gave Barker a brief man hug and headed for the Lincoln. He looked back at Barker sitting on the same bucket, staring at the remaining coals. A slight wind blew Barker's blonde hair up into the air on each side, like wings.

*   *   *

Father Bob tried to sneak into the rectory. He opened the kitchen door and tip toed across the worn linoleum floor. He saw no signs of life, only a dim light above the oven hood. The counters were clean and the table still had the daily newspaper folded neatly sitting on it. No hint of Murphy, whom he figured must be up at the Knights of Columbus. The beige rooms in the big box of a house filled him with emptiness. Maybe it was the stale walls, sanitized smell and lack of sound, except for the clock always ticking in the kitchen. He was always alone here, especially when he thought about celibacy. Now he was a stranger intruding into somebody else's house, Murphy's house, God's house. He warmed to the idea of newfound freedom, homelessness. *Who knows where I'll sleep tomorrow?* He could always sleep in the truck. *Wonder what probation officers do?*

He headed upstairs for the shower where he rinsed dried blood from the cuts on his legs and bruises on his face. He'd say his last Mass tomorrow morning, without a hint to Monsignor Murphy. He went out with a hurrah at Mass yesterday, breaking off his collar off in front of the congregation and getting a standing ovation. *Tomorrow morning's Mass, the Tuesday daily one, would be dead, and go unnoticed.*

Glad that he wouldn't have to bother Maria for a ride, he could see the look of approval on her face when she learned of his independence. They would take some time to think about things and then deal with the relationship. The thought of driving alone, across country in an old truck, appealed to him. *Jack would be in the passenger seat, head out the window.* His eyes welled. *I miss you so much, Jack. Wish you could come with me. Now I have a son to get to know.*

After drying off, he went to his room and slipped into a pair of boxers, and then he retrieved an old, hard, brown leather suitcase from his closet, a hand-me-down from his aunt. He doubted she ever went anywhere with it. Nobody ever left Irontown back then. He laid out what he would wear tomorrow, a pair of jeans, tennis shoes, and a beige T-shirt with a pocket on the front. Other than a few pair of underwear, a collarless shirt with a few buttons down the top, and one more pair of jeans, all he owned were some workout clothes. The rest of his clothing belonged to the Church.

When he opened his top drawer, he pulled out an old manila envelope, and stared at it for a while. He didn't open it, but knew exactly what it held…diplomas, a certificate of ordination, a photo of his graduating class from the seminary, a wallet-sized copy of Maria's graduation photo, and a few black and white photos of his mother and father. He threw the envelope into the suitcase, didn't want to see his parents right now. Those photos always stirred up a longing within him that he could never satisfy.

The only items left in the drawer were three white collars, and Jack's black collar from when he was a puppy. He would take Jack's old collar with him and leave the rest behind. He recited a quote he had memorized from St. John Chrysostom, "I know my own soul, how feeble and puny it is; I know the magnitude of this ministry, and the great difficulty of the work; for the more stormy billows vex the soul of the priest than the gales which disturb the sea."

He looked at the golden chalice, which sat on top of his dresser, and decided to take it. The chalice belonged to the church, but it was the first one that he had used for the Eucharistic Rite, the one he had lifted to heaven to turn table wine into the blood of Christ, during his first Mass as a priest. He carefully wrapped the chalice in an extra pair of boxers, and placed it into the suitcase. He searched the drawer for any leftover possessions, and noticed a small package in the corner of the drawer, a condom, still in the wrapper. That condom had been with him for a long time, "just in case." *It must be dry rotted by now.* He tossed the condom into the suitcase.

"I quit." He smiled. Murphy won't even be surprised. The old man would want him to go through the laicization process. *Forget laicization, a stupid ceremony, turning a priest back into a lay person.* He'd never heard of anybody changing the blood of Christ back into table wine.

He lay across the bed and steamed a little about how Murphy knew about Boss. *He kept a lot of things from me, probably just trying to protect me from the perils of the world, never trusting my judgment. Still, though, the man cared about me like a father. I vow to forgive all, just like Jesus. I want to be kind and gentle to others.*

Walking away tomorrow, he would stroll on down the Hill of Churches to the 1st National Bank to drain all twelve hundred dollars of his savings. That night he tossed and turned in excitement, pretending to be asleep when he heard Monsignor Murphy come home.

The next morning he woke up early and showered again, rubbing off the remaining scabs. After one last gander around the massive, blue bathroom, he dressed for the final time in priestly black. Murphy made noises downstairs. He looked into the mirror while straightening his collar. "You did it. Became a priest and maybe saved a few souls. Now it's time to go. It is time to save your own soul."

He hurried through the kitchen behind Murphy's chair to pour a quick cup of coffee. Murphy laid down his paper and called, "You're late this morning. Is everything all right? How'd the boxing with Boss go yesterday?"

Father Bob stopped from saying, "…like you don't already know?" If Barker knew about it, Murphy, his spiritual savior, had to know. He and Grandma Amelia had probably already discussed it. *How stupid does he think I am?*

"I'll tell you all about it after Mass. I'm really running late." He gulped down hot coffee, which burned his throat. "Gotta go."

He hurried to the church. His mind was working on Maria, the truck, the suitcase he had hidden under the bed and the stop at the bank…nothing to do with daily Mass.

As he pulled the green vestment over his head in the sacristy, he noticed that he had no altar boy. Already ten minutes late, he strutted straight out to the altar. The same strut he tried to lose because of its unpriestly implication. He dipped his shoulder discreetly lower than usual, in the rediscovery of his real soul, the true Bob. His knee hardly ached at all. He stood straight up behind the altar, lifted his hands, and for the final time said, "Good Morning, may the Lord be with you."

"And also with you."

He scanned the twenty or so parishioners in the congregation attending the quick morning Mass. Maria was not there. He followed the swift routine of priestly gestures until Mrs. Hellinski read the Epistle. They had ignored each other quite naturally this morning. During the reading, Father Bob sat while his eyes canvassed the entire church in search of Maria, willing her to appear, as though he could conjure her up like Jesus summoning his Apostles. He hoped to hear the huge church doors bang open at any moment. He walked to the pulpit to read the Gospel, said no sermon, and tripped on his way back to the altar. Maria's absence sunk his strut.

It was while consecrating the bread and wine into the body and blood of Christ, the he knew he was a phony. He no longer hovered as an evolved spirit. He forced himself through the consecration, his favorite part of the priesthood, the plateau from whence the Holy Spirit swept his soul into the divine. Yet his spirit was slag on the road, once molten, now crumbled, dried and cold. This holy ritual could not end fast enough for him. He chose to not consume the Body of Christ, unheard of for a priest. He doubted that anyone would notice anyway. "I am not worthy to receive You," he whispered and walked to the center of the church, where he handed the communion wafers to the faithful, an imposter passing counterfeits. His dread of not seeing Maria made his hands heavy, as if moving through sludge.

Though it was his last Mass, he noticed more clearly the individual characteristics of the parishioners who received communion. Without the spiritual high he could hear the sighs and grunts of twelve elderly women, ten of them dressed in widow's black, and Mother Superior dressed in black nun. Mrs. Milovick dressed in modest blue. The humble side of Mrs. Hellinski endeared him, as she accepted the wafer with shaky palms. Grandma Amelia approached and he raised his eyebrows in a gesture of inquiry. Grandma closed her eyes, and he sensed the worse, that Maria had already left. He hoped he was wrong. Grandma stuck out her tongue. His heart went out to Grandma Amelia. *Such sorrow in life, yet she stands as the pillar of a worn family. She had disowned her only daughter, Maria's mother, and that had to be eternally painful. She acted out of love, nothing else.*

Father Bob tucked away the remaining hosts before he sat on the bench where he had once reflected upon his spirituality. Now his heart pounded fast. *What if I never see Maria again?* She probably left town already. He realized that he was drawn to the priesthood largely because of her breaking his heart. Though the small congregation stirred, he did not want to get up from the bench. He scanned what was his personal sanctuary for almost half a lifetime. But this really was his last Mass. He had chosen his path this time.

He could work in the helping profession as a counselor, probation officer or something. The faces of the congregation looked impassive, as expressionless as the statues of saints. *If everybody had known about my situation, then they would know that this was my last Mass and come to fill up the church to say goodbye.* But they stayed away, like the Apostles avoided Christ the day before his death.

He stood. "Go in Peace to Love and Serve the Lord."

He turned from the congregation and walked into the sacristy to disrobe from the green vestment. While he hung it back up in the closet, Grandma Amelia slowly walked in through the other door. He knew it was her. She stopped a few feet away.

"Good morning, Father," she made the sign of the cross.

Father Bob tried to hide his expression of doom when he turned around and looked at Grandma. He knew that she had never come into the sacristy before. It must be bad news. He nodded. "Good morning, Grandma."

Grandma looked up directly into Father Bob's eyes. "Maria and Boss left late last night." She cleared her throat. "She wanted me to tell you good-bye." She extended her hand, in a gesture of peace.

The numbness in Father Bob's throat almost choked him. He grabbed Grandma's cold hand, kissed the top of it and said, "Thank you, Grandma. I know you love her." He knew about the shame Grandma would have to endure if Maria ran off with a priest, especially the father of her child.

"I love you too, Bobby." He turned away so Grandma wouldn't see his tears. "I'll see you at Mass tomorrow morning," she sighed.

He heard her walk away, just as he collapsed onto the ornate sacristy chair, with its lush padding and glittery gems fit for a king. He took a deep breath and stared, thought about the irony of Maria leaving him once again. Tears rolled and he sobbed. He tried to put things away as his emotion had transformed into numbness. He had lost his passion for the vocation, regardless of Maria and Boss. He prayed for the strength of Sister Roxanne. Slowly and softly, he vowed to live a life of Christ by loving all people outside the formality of the Church. In the silence, he lost track of time. Eventually, he heard the church doors open. His heart pounded and broke his numbness with a glitter of hope. Maria?

Monsignor Murphy walked into the sacristy. His eyes moistened yet he fought off the longing when he saw Murphy's grimace. *Murphy knows all.* Murphy held out his hand. "Come with me, son, to the rectory."

Father Bob stood up and Murphy walked with his arm around his shoulder. They strolled through the hallway leading to the rectory. The two priests entered the kitchen and sat down at the table. Murphy filled coffee cups in front of their chairs. He grabbed the bottle of scotch, topped off his cup. Father Bob put his hand over his as a gesture of refusal.

"I'm so sorry, Bob." Murphy took a sip. Father Bob said nothing, drank nothing, and just stared at the floor.

"It's very strange. I remember you sitting here fourteen years ago. Remember? Back when your girlfriend left you?"

Father Bob didn't know what to say. He had nothing running through his entire body. But then Murphy's words rang in his head, *my girlfriend? All he can call her is my girlfriend?*

"I owe you some explanation." Murphy started to say more.

Father Bob slammed his hand onto the tabletop. "I don't want your explanation. You have no idea what it's like to be in love." He stood up and sat back down. "What? What kind of explanation can you give me?"

Murphy cleared his throat. His cheeks shook. Age seemed to be running rampant on his face. Suddenly Father Bob wasn't angry. A strange calm claimed him once again.

Murphy looked him in the eyes. "I love you like a son. Maybe keeping things secret wasn't the right thing to do." Murphy pointed to an empty kitchen chair. "You're right. I've been celibate my entire life. I don't know what you're going through." He pointed to the chair a second time. "Sit down, please."

"Listen. I quit. I'm done here."

"Please! Sit down with me, one last time," Murphy pleaded for the third time. "I have something for you."

Father Bob sat. He rested his elbows on the table, cradled his chin in his hands. Murphy hobbled over to the cabinets and opened a drawer. *Here we go again, a fresh bottle of scotch.* Not this time. Murphy pulled out a photo album buried beneath several ragged edged telephone books. He lay the album on top of the table in front of Father Bob. "There's only a handful of photos in there, some black and whites of your mom and dad."

Under Murphy's watchful eye, Father Bob tentatively opened the album. The corners had yellowed and come unglued. The black pages smelled of musty perfume, as if somebody had splashed it throughout the years. Smeared blue ink from a fountain pen formed a once formal letter on the inside, but now the words were blurred, indecipherable. A few black and white photos slid from crackled, white-laced corners. Father Bob held one of them in his hand, gingerly, as it felt brittle. Santo Santoro, his father, stood with his arm around Restituta, his mother. Santo dressed in a dark suit and posed stoic, with his thick black mustache, and one long curl of hair over his forehead, while Restituta looked serious in her dark, long dress. She was much shorter than Santo and wore a hat. In another photo, Santo pressed wine grapes in the basement. Bob stared for a long time at the photo of Santo in the steel mill, standing on the train trestle, wearing his hardhat sideways in jest, with his arm around Stabo, his best friend. *How these men could look happy in such a rough setting...gray background of train tracks and piles of iron ore resembled a war zone.*

"Open the envelope." Murphy pointed to a pouch inside the front cover of the album. "Your parents made me executor of their modest estate. It's worth about twelve thousand dollars by now."

Father Bob wondered if he had heard Murphy's words right, twelve thousand dollars? He looked at Murphy, who grew impatient. "Didn't you ever wonder who paid for the seminary? I never expected you to graduate, to be honest. Anyway, the money's all yours to keep."

Father Bob looked at the legal papers. He folded them back up, put them into the envelope and tucked it into the album.

"You don't seem surprised. It's like you saw this coming. Were you keeping this money for my day of departure?"

"You have a spiritual soul, son, and you love people. I know you want to help them." Murphy poured a little more scotch into his coffee, shook his head slowly. "But down inside, my intuition told me you didn't fit into the priesthood." Murphy gazed towards the tabletop. He pulled out that yellow-stained handkerchief and blew his nose. His face was flushed. Father Bob saw a tear drop escape from the old man's reddened eye. He didn't want to cause Murphy or anyone more pain.

"You did what you thought was right. That's all anybody can do. You gave me more than one chance." He walked around the table and hugged the top of Murphy's head. He felt like crying, but he placed his lips onto Murphy's thinning, slicked down hair and smelled barbershop hair tonic. "I'll always be grateful to you. I can't blame you for anything. Thanks for being there for me."

Murphy lifted his face and hugged Father Bob's. He kissed him on the lips. Tears ran down Murphy's cheeks. "I don't know. I just wanted to fix everything for you, son."

Both men abruptly loosened their lock on each other. He knew he had to leave now. He also knew that Murphy was not going to try and talk him into staying. "Well, I'm going to change into some blue jeans and hit the road."

"I know. It's okay, I knew you wouldn't go through any rights," Murphy wiped his face with that old handkerchief and blew his nose again. "You know where I'll be if you ever need anything. Stay in touch. I want to know how you are and what you end up doing."

Father Bob went upstairs, changed his clothes, and as he looked around his small room, took down the small crucifix hanging on the wall and placed it into his suitcase. When he walked downstairs again, he paused and looked in the kitchen. Murphy said, "Do you need a ride to the bus stop?"

"No thanks, I'm good."

Murphy nodded and they hugged one last time. There was not much else to say. Father Bob walked out of the rectory, carrying the absurd, brown leather suitcase with one hand. He had not wanted to tell Murphy about Barker's truck. He was on his own now.

While crossing from the alleyway to the parking lot, he heard a yell from an older woman. At first he thought it could be Grandma Amelia, dressed in black widow, and his heart fluttered for a minute. But as the figure approached, he recognized Mrs. Hellinski.

Out of breath, she said, "Here, take this. It's for you. Good luck, Father Bob." She handed him a folded piece of white paper and walked away. He stood shocked. *That's the first time she's ever called me Father Bob.* He unfolded the paper. It read:

Maria Constantini
Centurion Realty
812 Why Worry Lane
Phoenix, AZ 81242
Office (602) 916-2469

Smiling as though the sun had just risen, he placed the card in his pocket and strutted down the Hill of Churches, his aunt's suitcase swaying from one arm, looking forward to jumping into that old truck. He was sixteen years old again, and he could hear Murphy say, "Throw your hips into the punch, we throw whole body blows!"

He thought about Boss and Maria. Yes, he would find them, but only after he figured out what this new freedom really meant. Excitement combined with relief. His eyes shined with a new light and he could focus clearly on his surroundings...Mrs. Sheline's laundry hanging on a line, the deep smell of the mill, the faces of kids running on the playground, and the black terrier in a fenced yard snapping at flies. *If only my dog, Jack could ride with me. He'd be a great travel companion.*

He walked into the bank, glad to be the only customer. He withdrew three thousand dollars and verified the remaining nine thousand in a different account. Then he walked up the hollow to Barker's.

When he reached the truck, he opened the door and saw an atlas on the front seat, with two joints resting on top of it, along with a cassette tape of "Skeletons from the Closet," by The Grateful Dead. He laughed, and then hid the joints under the seat. Before driving off, Bob slipped one thousand dollars under Barker's front door. He would drive straight through Wheeling, and head south, down state route 77. He would twist through the hills of Kentucky and Tennessee, head all the way to the Gulf of Mexico to see the palm trees blow in the wind. That sounded like a good place to rest for a few days. No rush to meet up with Maria and Boss, they all needed time to sort things out.

The old truck fired up on the first try. He turned out of Barker's driveway for one last cruise through old Irontown. Then he shot onto the highway ramp, and this time drove straight across the highway bridge.

Ron Mitchell grew up in a steel mill village along the Ohio River in the Appalachian foothills. His wide-ranging life experiences have provided him with material for *Broken Collar*, his first novel. Ron's fiction presents painfully real people in honest settings. He draws from work as a young man in a steel mill and decades as a supervisor of adult probation officers in the Arizona criminal justice system. He also drawn from his prior service as a Eucharist minister for the Catholic Church and his experience training boxers and peace officers. His journeys, from riding thousands of miles on his Harley-Davidson to traveling untold miles to the far reaches of the world, contributed even more to his understanding of man's struggle for redemption. His travel articles, profiles, and essays have been published in numerous magazines and newspapers. He has degrees from Kent State University and the University of Dayton. The author lives with his wife Marilynn in Phoenix, AZ when they are not traveling the world.

OTHER BOOKS BY
BIRD DOG PUBLISHING

A Poetic Journey, Poems by Robert A. Reynolds
86 pgs. $16
Dogs and Other Poems by Paul Piper
80 pgs. $15
The Mermaid Translation by Allen Frost
140 pgs. $15
Heart Murmurs: Poems by John Vanek
120 pgs. $15
Home Recordings: Tales and Poems by Allen Frost
$14
A Life in Poems by William C. Wright
$10
Faces and Voices: Tales by Larry Smith
136 pgs. $14
Second Story Woman: A Memoir of Second Chances
by Carole Calladine, 226 pgs. $15
256 Zones of Gray: Poems by Rob Smith
80 pgs. $14
Another Life: Collected Poems by Allen Frost
176 pgs. $14
Winter Apples: Poems by Paul S. Piper
88 pgs. $14
Lake Effect: Poems by Laura Treacy Bentley
108 pgs. $14
Depression Days on an Appalachian Farm: Poems
by Robert L. Tener, 80 pgs. $14
120 Charles Street, The Village: Journals & Other Writings 1949-1950
by Holly Beye, 240 pgs. $15

BIRD DOG PUBLISHING
A division of Bottom Dog Press, Inc.
Order Online at:
http://smithdocs.net/BirdDogy/BirdDogPage.html

CPSIA information can be obtained at www.ICGtesting.com
Printed in the USA
BVOW030839270412

288839BV00001B/1/P

9 781933 964560